AMAZO

FIRST DO NO HARM
BY A. TURK

This was one of my top picks. I was spellbound and couldn't put it down. *First Do No Harm* was Grishamesque. Loved it.

A. Turk's first novel is a legal thriller that is both a fun read and an interesting one as well. The characters in the story are well developed and rich in personality.

As a practicing attorney in Nashville for nearly 36 years, I have recommended this book to clients to read so that they can get a clear understanding of the legal process. . . . Whether you are a Plaintiff or Defendant in any piece of litigation, this book is a MUST READ!!!. A. Turk's three decade career as a litigator is shown in his attention to detail, and the reader becomes a part of the litigation. And if you love the city of Nashville as I do, this thriller is a guided tour of Music City USA. It is an enjoyable journey to Nashville, Middle Tennessee, and its judicial system.

"First Do No Harm" accurately captures and conveys the excitement of a real blood and guts lawsuit. The stakes are high for all concerned, and the suspense is compelling. We get to see inside the mind of a dedicated litigator, and we are privy not only to what he does, but why he does it. The portrayal of the legal system is the most accurate I have read in any book of fiction.

A thoroughly enjoyable read. I hope we see more of A. Turk and his protagonist, Ben Davis.

Attorney Ben Davis takes on the case of the estate of Rosie Malone (amongst others), who died as the result of the incompetence of two doctors who together are complicit in performing unnecessary expensive tests and surgeries. The author A. Turk is a born storyteller and brings to life a difficult court case all the while explaining the intricacies of the legal procedures to the reader.

AMAZON REVIEWS OF *SECOND DEGREE* BY A. TURK

This second installation of the Benjamin Davis series was better than the first. I found this work more thrilling than the first and appreciated the nods to the first book. Kudos to Turk for stepping up his game and making me want more from good old Davis.

A great legal thriller with sex, politics, medical "practice" and a lot of greed. Davis and associates fight to the finish for justice to be served.

Alan does a really good job with legal stories. I can't believe anyone could make depositions interesting, but he did. Looking forward to his next book.

Great storytelling. The plot is very good and the protagonists are in great form. The outcome is somber but sets the stage for more action.

So happy to find this author. He explains so much about the law and procedure wrapped up in a great story. He gives insights into why juries often surprise us with their verdicts.

AMAZON REVIEWS OF *THIRD COAST* BY A. TURK

Who is Morty Steine and why is he so beloved as a lawyer, mentor, confidante, and friend? In Third Coast, A. Turk tells Morty's story while remaining true to the series theme of legal thriller involving Attorney Benjamin Davis. This is the third book that reveals more about Morty and Benjamin. Each novel can stand alone as a read, but together, the entire Benjamin Davis series is a testament that our legal system is a crucible where justice prevails. Third Coast is the best A. Turk book to date, mainly because Morty is so endearing as a character and person. This is a definite must read.

So I've now read Turk's third book. Hard to put down. At first, I thought that perhaps he'd gone just a little overboard with all the legal terminology. And after the first third of the book, though, it seemed to smooth out and was a nice read. Learned a LOT about the complexities of a civil trial . . . very enjoyable.

REVIEWS OF
FOURTH OF JULY
BY A. TURK

"A. Turk retired Nashville attorney in his latest book in the Benjamin Book Series provides the reader with insight into the daily operations of a law office. Rather than focus on one case as his earlier books this book weaves multiple cases together providing the reader with a very enjoyable read."

"A, Turk does it again, another riveting legal thriller. This book has the Davis team return to help find a missing wife and mother. Davis turns over every rock in the city to find her and is rewarded for his effort. The book tells multiple stories, which only enhance the main storyline."

"If could give six stars I would, I think this the best book in the series."

"I'm in love with Ben Davis. He's smart, resourceful and he always tries to do the right thing. That's commendable."

Great read, with twists and turns. I like Turk's use on an epilogue to add that final twist at the end."

CAST OF MAIN CHARACTERS

is' Team

ımin Abraham Davis– attorney/protagonist

Steine– attorney/mentor

ıie Adele Davis– paralegal/attorney/niece of Davis

Rosario– secretary/office manager

e Hopper– investigator

Stone– court reporter

anner– ex-FBI agent/polygraph taker

ıldwell Davis– wife of Davis

e Davis– daughter of Davis

Jake" Davis– son of Davis

n Caldwell– father-in-law of Davis

aldwell– mother-in-law of Davis

avis– father of Davis

"Nana" Davis– mother of Davis

Davis– brother of Davis

& Costello– Davis' pugs

ımes– injured student/bartender

ames– mother of Randy James

Max– surgeon of Randy James

berts– insurance agent of Davis

ger– Channel 5 newscaster

Carmicheal's Team

Roscoe Carmichael III– antagonist
Vincent Gray– attorney/Covington & Burling
Richard "Dick" Tate– attorney/Covington & Burling
Sara Browne– investigator/Covington & Burling
Anthony "June bug" Estes– traitor/informant
Mr. Mike– Carmichael's grandfather
Maggie Kennedy– sixteen-year-old strip poker player

Oz's Team

Phillip Oz "James Smith"– antagonist/cameraman
Amy Pierce– attorney
Susan Oz– wife of Oz

Videoed Women

Elizabeth Swann
Mary Doe
David Fields– husband of Mary Doe
Jane Doe
Dominique Watson
Sydney Ingram
Carol Strong
Pamela Leonard– woman #7

Other Defendants

Gerry Neenan– chief of police
Robert Sanders– detective
Jay Turner– detective
Keith Rogers– detective
Michael Sanchez– police officer
Arnold Pyle– agent-in-charge
Robert Tuke– TBI agent
Carlos Ramos– TBI agent
Evan Tuke– TBI agent

Karl Moore– TBI agent
Johnson Tory– district attorney

Lee's Team

Bucky Lee– Roscoe Carmichael's former attorney
Jack Barnes– Bucky Lee's attorney
Mindy Hart– Equity Insurance Company/malpractice insurance attorney
Gregory Daniels– Dean of Nashville School of Law

A-1 Fireworks Company

Tom Miller– grandfather of Pinky
Steven "Pinky" Miller– juvenile delinquent
Darrell Miller (deceased)– father of Pinky
Derek Miller– uncle of Pinky
David Edison– attorney for Aetna Insurance Company, A-1's carrier

Hillwood Country Club

Karl Goodwin– manager of Hillwood Country Club
Hope Cash– attorney of Hillwood Country Club
Gary Peller– president of Hillwood Country Club

American Insurance Company

John Whitefield– attorney
Burton Cox– in-house-counsel
Robert Patterson– insurance executive

Experts

Dr. Andrew Resnick– psychiatrist for defense
Dr. Adam Little– psychiatrist for the plaintiffs
Beverly Newman– therapist for the plaintiffs

Courts

Honorable Barry Howard– judge for privacy actions/townhouse search warrants (Davidson Co.)

Honorable James Wyatt – issued the farmhouse warrant (Cheatham County)

Honorable Joseph Peck– judge for Carmichael's criminal case (Davidson County)

Honorable Thomas Wise– federal judge in Carmichael/Oz vs. American Insurance Company

Honorable Randolph "Sandy" Sanford III– retired judge/mediator

Arthur– Judge Sanford's servant

Dan Weaver– sheriff of Cheatham County

A Legal Glossary has been included in the back of the book to assist the reader with legal terms.

Dedication

During the course of one's life, one comes in contact with many people. Most make no impact on you and remain mere blips on your radar as you learn from life's experiences. Few either negatively or positively have a lasting impact. You try to forget the jerks, who made your life just a little bit more difficult. Never forget those positive forces, your good friends, especially the ones who taught you important life lessons. Winnie Bray, aka Bella Rosario, was someone who helped me become a better lawyer and a better person. She will be missed by her family and friends, but she will forever live in the Benjamin Davis book series.

A.Turk

CHAPTER ONE

A LONG-AWAITED BUST

Wednesday, October 16, 1996

(THIRD PERSON)

The retrofitted Cessna 421 landed in a tree lined field on the outskirts of Cheatham County near Highway 49. Tiki-like torches illuminated the runway of the newly paved airfield. Roscoe Carmichael III and his cohorts had spent several days getting the airstrip operational and the asphalt only just hardened, allowing landing. The crew didn't have time before the delivery to install the permanent lighting in time for the shipment. The stripping equipment sat on the side of the runway ready to finish the job. There was an overpowering smell of tar lingering in the air.

The airstrip was nestled in the midst of a heavily treed area of the two hundred acre parcel recently purchased by Carmichael, adjacent to the family farm. He'd purchased several neighboring properties in the last few years.

With the construction of the new airfield Carmichael anticipated increasing his distribution network. This would require an increase in capital investment and expenses, but it also meant greater profits. Carmichael felt a sense of pride as he saw the plane approach.

What Carmichael didn't know, despite having his tentacles in local law enforcement and with the means of acquiring information, was that the Tennessee Bureau of Investigation ("TBI") had managed to infiltrate his organization. Surveillance of Carmichael by the Nashville office of the TBI began almost five years earlier, and the frustration of agent-in-charge Arnold Pyle grew as he watched his nemesis become the largest distributor of cocaine in Cheatham County and a prominent supplier in neighboring Nashville.

At the same time Carmichael ran many successful legitimate businesses, which laundered his illegal gains. Out of necessity, part of Carmichael's drug money found its way into the pockets of local politicians, sheriff's deputies, court clerks and others, which permitted him to operate.

Pyle suspected that the County Sheriff's department was compromised, so he insisted that Sheriff Dan Weaver himself secretly walk the search warrant of the Carmichael family farm over to the county judge only an hour before he planned to execute the raid. Pyle's search warrant was issued based upon the sworn affidavit of an informant who'd flipped because of an unrelated arrest; the witness revealed the date and time of the rendezvous. Pyle was ready with an army of TBI agents and a few well-chosen local sheriff's deputies, who the Sherriff insisted were beyond reproach.

This evening the pilot hadn't filed a flight plan with any governmental authority, a clear violation of FAA regulations. The plane was flown at the lowest possible altitude to avoid radar. An airport tower along the route occasionally picked up the aircraft; but the skilled pilot managed to fall off the screen just before any traffic controller could get a verifiable fix. He'd made this run from Cuba to middle Tennessee without incident many times before. The flight was just less than 950 miles; the aircraft's range meant it did not require refueling.

A dark green Jeep Cherokee slowly approached the aircraft and using the pre-arranged signal, flashed its lights four times. The plane appropriately responded with the lowering of its flaps twice; contact was made. Two men exited the Cherokee and approached the plane.

A long-standing business relationship existed between these men who were now shaking hands. They'd conducted more than twenty transactions, and a certain degree of trust had developed.

The exchange was recorded by the TBI for posterity and for a future trial if one became necessary. Sheriff's deputies and agents were waiting crouched or lying on the ground in the woods for Pyle's signal to bounce. Sheriff Weaver sat next to Pyle and commented, "That little rich shit, I can't tell you how many times he slipped through my fingers either because of bad intelligence, or earlier because his granddaddy, who owned one-third of the county, bought his way out of trouble."

Carmichael's history with Pyle didn't span the almost thirty years of frustration that Weaver had. Pyle's introduction to Roscoe Carmichael first came in a 1989 drug bust that went sour. Looking for drugs, he found Carmichael playing strip poker with a sixteen-year-old girl. Only a small amount of cocaine was confiscated and the focus of the case quickly shifted from drugs to underage sex. Bucky Lee, Esq., a Nashville attorney, zealously represented him in the case before a Davidson County jury and all felony charges were dismissed. Carmichael respected and revered Lee's ability as a lawyer for those not guilty verdicts. At the time of the verdict, Carmichael gave a sigh of relief and commented under his breath, "I was really caught with my pants down."

After a short side trip to the penitentiary for eleven months and twenty-nine days for two misdemeanors convictions, Roscoe Carmichael III was back on the street professing to be a talent agent on Music Row, using his merchandise to infiltrate an already corrupted and drug-infested record industry to promote his semi-talented clientele. It was amazing how money and drugs advanced their careers. The female singers could probably carry a tune, but more critical to their success was the product that Carmichael either sold or gave away to the record producers and executives as part of his deals.

Carmichael hugged the pilot and after a short exchange, two duffel bags with cash totaling $500,000.00 for the drugs were exchanged. The product would find its way through Carmichael's network, much of it sent to Music Row.

Tony "June Bug" Estes, took charge of the product. Carmichael tried his best to convince Raul, the pilot, to come back to the house to party and spend the night, but his business partner wanted no part of it. He wanted to fly back to his island and deliver the money to his bosses. They were expecting him, and they were not men to be kept waiting. They wouldn't understand if he was a day late because he decided to get stoned and laid by the Americanos.

"I need a clear head to get this baby back without being detected," he gestured to the two duffel bags of cash. "I'll have to pass."

The Cuban was all business. He started filling up with petrol, which Carmichael made available in twenty-gallon cans. It took longer than expected to refuel and the plane sat on the runway while the Jeep took off back to the farmhouse. After the Jeep was out of sight, the TBI, relying on the search warrant issued by the local judge, the Honorable James Wyatt, moved in silently and arrested the pilot and other men helping with the refueling, seized the aircraft and confiscated the two duffel bags of cash without a struggle.

The airstrip was secured and agent-in-charge Pyle over the radio ordered his second in command,

"Andy, once they open the front door and the drugs enter the threshold of the farmhouse move in for the arrests."

Under Pyle's plan everything in the farmhouse would be considered part of an ongoing conspiracy and would be subject to being confiscated, whether purchased legally or illegally. Pyle confidently claimed,

"We'll be able to hold as evidence all his personal property and itemize them on the evidence list. That will really piss him off. Hit them when the doors open and execute on the warrant."

Pyle had organized his team into three distinct groups. The first was to confiscate the plane and the money; the second was to seize the drugs and inventory in the farmhouse, and the third was to implement and execute on a second search warrant, fifteen miles away at the Carmichael's townhouse/office in Davidson County on Music Row.

Because of detailed information provided by the informant, in anticipation of the delivery of the shipment, Pyle had secured two separate search warrants. The first for Carmichael's farmhouse in Cheatham County by Judge James Wyatt, and the second by Judge Barry Howard of Davidson County for Carmichael's residence/office on Music Row. Both orders gave the TBI and the Cheatham County Sheriff's office the right to search the farmhouse and the office/residence, "to enter the premise to find illegal drugs and related matters, including but not limited to currency, false identification, or any other matter evidencing a criminal activity."

After Estes and Carmichael had unloaded about half the cargo out of the Jeep onto the porch of the farmhouse, two deputies jumped the gun and moved in too early, followed by twenty TBI agents. "Damn it," Pyle, who was still at the airstrip, yelled into the radio, "Damn" cursing the premature action by the local boys.

"Don't move a fucking muscle," Agent Andrews, who the other agents called "Andy" declared. "Hands up!"

Carmichael, ever the smart-ass, said defiantly, "I can't do both. Either I don't move a muscle or my hands go up. Make up your mind!"

Andrews repeated, "Hands up, and then don't move a muscle, asshole."

Simultaneously, two agents forced the arrestee's hands behind them and secured their wrists with cuffs. The move had been practiced by the team on a regular basis, and they'd become quite good at the process.

Agent Pyle arrived on the scene, did the honors and read them their Miranda rights, "You have the right to remain silent..."

Carmichael didn't let Pyle finish his sentence.

"We're taking the Fifth. We don't have to say shit. I know my rights. I want to see my lawyer, Bucky Lee" insisted Carmichael. Pyle reacted almost violently.

"Shut up! Let me finish telling you your rights, all of them, and when I'm done, I'm happy to hear whatever bullshit you want to tell me because, it will be held against you."

After Pyle finished his Miranda warning, Carmichael volunteered again, "I'm taking the Fifth. Call my lawyer, Bucky Lee. He does the talking for me. Otherwise, I'm taking the Fifth."

In Cheatham County almost two-dozen men and one woman, TBI and locals, went through all of Carmichael's belongings. They were making quite a mess. They were looking for anything remotely related to drugs. At his bedside nightstand they found various oils and sexual devices. Each item was bagged, tagged, and cataloged. In the house they found three handguns, two rifles, and a shotgun. Items of interest were added to the master evidence sheet, which was becoming extensive.

In Nashville, in Davidson County, a second team of ten men went through Carmichael's townhouse/office at Epic Talent on Music Row as per the search warrant issued by Judge Barry Howard.

Pyle walked up to Estes and released him from his cuffs.

"What the hell?" Carmichael exclaimed and Pyle shot back,

"Shut up! You're taking the Fifth, so shut the hell up! Let me introduce you to my number one witness. I believe you've met before, he's your loyal friend Anthony 'June Bug' Estes."

Carmichael momentarily looked shocked. He didn't expect betrayal by his childhood friend. With his hands cuffed behind him, he lunged at Estes. He was yanked back by one of the agents. *Damn that hurt.*

Arnie Pyle smiled at Carmichael and then quickly turned to June Bug.,"Good job, have a nice life in witness protection."

Carmichael swallowed hard and shouted, "You son of a bitch, Benedict Arnold."

Pyle, who'd waited a long time to maneuver into this position loved needling his prisoner, "I thought you were taking the Fifth?" Pyle stuck the knife an inch deeper. That shut Carmichael up fast.

"Get him out of here," Pyle ordered, gesturing to Estes, and two agents ushered him away.

"Looks like it's just the two of us and these twenty other officers of the law. Anything you want to tell me in confidence?" Pyle continued to dig.

These men had a long and stormy history, neither of them satisfied by its outcome. Pyle was frustrated and angry that Carmichael was selling product right under his nose. Over the years, frustration turned to anger.

Just then, Sheriff Weaver walked over and asked, "Has our boy said anything?" He'd watched Carmichael grow up from a rich kid punk to the county kingpin. He turned to Carmichael and said, "Not the big football star, anymore, are you, son? I suspect Mr. Mike would be pretty disappointed in you right now."

"Go to hell, you fat old bastard."

Like Pyle, Weaver was really relishing this moment as he replied, "I may be old, I may be fat, but I'm not going to prison for a long time. You were lucky as hell that Mr. Mike took you in. Unfortunately, he couldn't teach you right from wrong. You were just a bad apple."

Pyle signaled to three agents to take custody of the prisoner and transport him to headquarters.

Once Carmichael was gone, Pyle addressed Weaver, "We've got him this time. He's not slipping away. The warrant at the office may provide us with additional proof. We've even got authority to open his safe there. Who knows what that might yield?"

Weaver wished Pyle "good hunting".

Pyle decided he'd leave the farm, return to Nashville, and see how the search of the Music Row office was going. He jumped in his black on black Fiat Spider and drove the twenty-five minutes from Carmichael's farm in Ashland City to Epic Talent Agency located at 223 16th Avenue South in the heart of Music Row.

The Row was a three-block area near Vanderbilt University and Peabody College. At one end was the Spence Manor, a high-end hotel, with its legendary guitar-shaped swimming pool, and at the other end was the campus of Belmont University.

Metro police had cordoned off half the length of 16th South, and Pyle had to show his ID twice. When he got to the doorway, Tuke, one of his agents, announced, "We found about 28 grams of cocaine and we're still looking. But you won't believe what we did find!"

Pyle followed Tuke into the house, where the other agents were on the first-floor cataloging evidence.

Tuke turned to Pyle,

"I stopped the search of the upstairs until you could see what we found. No one has been in the exercise room except me. Three of us have been in the bathroom but I don't think we disturbed anything."

Tuke wasn't making a lot of sense, so Pyle continued to follow him upstairs to a bedroom and an exercise room with an adjoining bathroom between them. One wall of each room consisted of a ten-foot high, ten-foot wide mirror. Pyle and Tuke moved from room to room, and Pyle finally asked, "I don't get it. What's the big surprise?"

Tuke smirked and insisted; "Look carefully at the mirror in the exercise room.

Pyle ran his hand over the glass. "So, what?"

Tuke took him into the bathroom and directed him to a hidden small grate between the toilet and shower. Tuke removed the grate, revealing a hole of eighteen inches by a foot and directed his boss to wiggle one shoulder and then the other into the small space and carefully crawl through. The two men walked into a ten-foot by three-foot space between the exercise room and the bedroom.

"Holy shit," Pyle responded. In the space was a professional-looking movie camera on a heavy metal tripod, a stool, and a bookcase of videotapes. What was shocking was that the mirrors that ran the length of each room from floor to ceiling were two-way, and the men could see clearly into the bedroom and the exercise room. Pyle soon realized that the bathroom mirror was also two-way. It made the space between the rooms feel like you were in one big room. Pyle reached into his pocket and put on a pair of gloves. Without touching the bookcase or its contents, he started looking at the labels on the videos; no words, only dates.

"I think we have an undercover movie producer under arrest." Pyle called District Attorney Johnson Tory, "Johnson, that little birdie was right. We're going to need Judge Howard to issue a second warrant for the office to remove camera equipment and view these videotapes. I'll bring the popcorn."

CHAPTER TWO

JAIL BIRD

Thursday, October 17, 1996

(ROSCOE CARMICHAEL'S VOICE)

I'd promised myself on the soul of my dear departed granddaddy, Mr. Mike, that I'd never be arrested again or see the inside of jail cell, and here I was in the Davidson County holding tank. Next to the drunk tank, the holding cell was the place you were deposited after booking, before you got arraigned. Other than repeating my chant that I was taking the Fifth, I'd not said a word except to demand my right to call my lawyer, Bucky Lee. After repeated demands, I was given an opportunity to call Bucky, but I got his answering machine. I couldn't leave a message because there was no one to accept the charges. *Where the hell was his secretary*? We'd not spoken in more than a year, and I now regretted that we'd left things on such bad terms, but he was my lawyer. He'd been my lawyer since I was fifteen years old. Fight or no fight, he'd accept my phone call in my time of need. I told my guard, "I'll have to try my lawyer later. He's not answering."

"This isn't the telephone company. You have three shots a day to get through. That's the policy, and then you get assigned a public defender. I'd suggest that you wait at least ninety minutes before you try again, but that's your decision."

They'd taken my watch so I didn't know what time it was. Alone in my cell, I tried to recount my arrest. That son of a bitch June Bug had betrayed me. I'd get even with that bastard. He led the TBI right to the pick-up. I figured that I was out the product and the cash, but would still have to make good with my Cuban partners. My immediate problem was connecting with Bucky and getting the hell out of jail on bond. I was going to have to dip into savings. Bucky wasn't going to be cheap, and I was going to need to put up a bond.

I waited for what I thought was another hour and a half and then impatiently yelled through the bars, "I need to call my lawyer. I need to make a phone call."

A few minutes later, a tired-looking guard walked by. He'd probably been napping. "Shut the hell up. It's 1:00 a.m. Your lawyer's sleeping. You'll get your phone call after eight tomorrow. Go back to sleep."

I must have passed out from exhaustion or fear and woke up confused. At least I knew the time. I tried to do as I was told, but I couldn't sleep. They'd caught me red-handed. I was looking at some serious jail time. I needed Bucky to do his magic and find some legal loophole to get me out of this mess. I'm sure he's still mad, but he'll have to get over it. I'll apologize. That should set things straight. More importantly, he'll be paid a big fee, that should go a long way in smoothing things out.

At 8:15 a.m., a guard took me to a pay phone. I had no money, so the call had to be collected. The recording announced, "This is a call from Roscoe Carmichael in the Davidson County jail. Press one if you will accept the charges for the call."

No answer. I got his machine, but because of the circumstances, I couldn't leave a message. *Where the hell is he? I need him to get me out of here.*

At 10:15 a.m. my jailer let me try Bucky again. Frustrated, I dialed the number. I was relieved when Bucky pushed one and we were connected.

"I heard about your arrest. Before you say anything, I hope you realize this conversation is being recorded. This is an open line, and there's no protection of the attorney/client privilege. Don't make a rookie mistake and start blabbering to anyone in your cell. Treat everyone as if they're a snitch looking to trade you for a better deal. Keep your bragging to yourself."

"I need you to get me out of here, preferably right now."

"Have you been questioned by the TBI?"

"They hammered me for about three hours, but I said nothing, other than that I was taking the Fifth and I wanted to see my lawyer, Bucky Lee. I tried you three times yesterday and once this morning. Where the hell were you?"

"That's none of your business. You seem to have forgotten, I'm not your lawyer, and I won't be helping you get out of jail. I can recommend some good criminal defense lawyers, but that's the extent of my willingness to get involved. We need to end this conversation right now. Remember everything we say is being taped. The cops don't need to know our differences, so let's move on and not get bogged down."

"What the hell do you mean, you're not my lawyer? If I hire you, pay you a retainer, then you're my lawyer."

There was a long pause on the line and then Bucky Lee, my former lawyer, chose his words carefully and loudly, "Let's not do this right now. You're tired and you have more important concerns than why our attorney/client relationship has terminated."

I cut him off, "Things may have been said and done in the heat of the moment..."

"I'm calling bullshit, Roscoe," Bucky screamed into the receiver. "I fired your ass as a client, and then you brought disciplinary charges against me before the Board of Professional Responsibility on some nonsense charge. You're a real bastard and I'm not your lawyer. We haven't spoken in over a year, except for a brief drunken exchange at Sperry's. I'll give you a recommendation for your new counsel and that's it. Take it or leave it."

I knew Bucky was mad about how our last business deal ended and it didn't help that I filed those charges, but it never dawned on me that he'd refuse to help me when I needed him the most, in a time of crisis. He'd been my lawyer from the beginning, even for my juvenile stuff that Mr. Mike got me out of. The old man hired the best professionals, paid them accordingly, I learned that lesson and always tried to do the same.

In a too desperate tone,

"I'll make it worth your time and effort. How about a fifty-grand retainer?"

"Roscoe, you couldn't pay me enough to take this case, and besides, I retired last year from private practice. I'm teaching at Nashville School of Law. So, even if we'd not gone our separate ways, I still wouldn't represent you."

Before I could react, the recording stated, "This call will terminate in three minutes."

"Do you want that recommendation or not? If not, then have a good life and good luck with your current problems."

I was about to blast him, but I needed that recommendation. "Who would you recommend?"

"I'd hire Vincent Gray of Covington & Burling. The Washington based firm bought Gray's firm out last year and it's now an international firm, the biggest in Nashville. They've got the resources, and Gray's tried plenty of criminal cases. I'll call him when we hang up, so he'll know to accept your call from jail. He wouldn't just accept anyone's call out of the blue."

"Can't you just get me out of here? I'll call Gray when I'm on the street."

"I'm not getting involved. You're lucky I'm calling Gray and alerting him so he'll accept your call. Gray can hold your hand at the arraignment and get your bond set."

"How much do you think the bond will be?"

"I'm not your attorney or a clairvoyant. Your bond will be whatever the judge sets it at."

The call terminated without warning.

I had to wait until 11:45 before I could access the phone again. After suffering through a disgusting lunch, some brown meat, I called Vincent Gray. "This is a call from the Davidson County jail from Roscoe Carmichael. Push one to accept the call."

Gray pressed one. He knew he had a paying client on the line. Bucky mentioned that I was looking for first-rate representation, and that I had the ability to pay.

"Mr. Carmichael, Vincent Gray. This is an open line. Let's keep our conversation brief. The police are listening to every word we're saying. I can be at the jail in less than an hour, and we can discuss your situation in private under the protection of the attorney/client privilege."

"That would be great. I'll be waiting. I've got nowhere to go."

"See you soon," and Gray hung up. True to his word, in thirty minutes, Vincent Gray of the law offices of Covington & Burling, was sitting in front of me when I entered the conference room. He wasn't physically impressive, a short, bald man in his mid-fifties with horn-rimmed glasses. He went right into his sales pitch. The firm was based out of Washington DC., and Gray presented a 143-page impressive color brochure, which displayed its offices in sixteen sister cities, including London, Paris, Barcelona, Prague, Madrid, Moscow, Berlin, Geneva, New York, Chicago, Los Angeles, San Francisco, New Orleans, Miami, Atlanta, and Nashville, Tennessee. The firm employed and pictured more than eight hundred partners and associates with brief bios on each. The section on Nashville proudly identified Vincent Gray as the Managing Partner, three other partners, ten associates and their accolades. The brochure emphasized that the full weight and resources of the firm were behind its clients in every case. On one-page Covington & Burling was depicted as a two-thousand-pound gorilla tearing the arms off the other lawyer with his briefcase still in hand, the judge with his hands on his head yelling, "I haven't even called court into session!". The caption announced proudly, "Wouldn't you at least want Covington & Burling on your side?"

I handed the brochure back to Gray. "Nice calling card, very impressive. It must have cost a fortune. If I return it, do I get a discounted price?"

I thought some humor in the conversation might be worth trying to save a few bucks, but Gray wasn't interested in joking around. He jumped right in and took control.

"We can talk freely in here. The police aren't allowed to eavesdrop on our conversation- attorney/client privilege. Let me ask questions rather than you giving me a narrative. There may be certain questions I don't want to ask you and things I don't want to know. What have you said to the police and the TBI? I need to know exactly what you've told them."

"I haven't told them shit. All I've said since they read me those rights was that 'I take the Fifth' and 'I want to call my lawyer, Bucky Lee'. Nothing else. I just kept repeating those words over and over again. You'd have been proud of me, and you don't even know me.

"Did you say anything before they read you your rights?"

"I called that son of a bitch June Bug Estes a son of a bitch. He's the bastard who turned me in and set me up."

"This was in front of the agents and the cops?"

"They held me back, or I would have killed him. I have to admit I have a temper when provoked, and Agent Pyle was trying to push my buttons when he let Estes go right in front of me. He knew what reaction he'd get."

"I wish you hadn't done that. The state will argue that your gut reaction was an admission against interest, whoever heard you can testify as to your words and demeanor. Anything you might have uttered can be used to prove your guilt. Well, we can't put the chicken back in the egg. Let's set some reasonable goals. We need to get you before a magistrate and have an arraignment. Do you know what an arraignment is?"

"Too well. This isn't my first rodeo. I spent time at Riverbend Maximum Security."

"How many convictions do you have?"

"Three or four juvenile matters. Mostly pot related, but they don't count, right? They're sealed, right? I also have two misdemeanor convictions and served eleven months for contributing to the delinquency of a minor."

"Correct. Those juvenile records are either sealed or expunged, whatever the order provides. At least you don't have any felony convictions."

I decided to ask a pretty important question, "What's it going to cost to get me out of here?"

"That's not an easy question to answer, depends on who's the judge...what was the market value of the product they confiscated at the farm?"

I minimized by stating my cost, not market value.

"About $500,000."

"What about at the townhouse?"

"Less than an ounce."

Gray looked like he was deep in thought and then said, "The bond will be higher than that. I'd count on the judge setting bond at twice the value of the product, so at least $1,000,000. That would sound about right. You can get a bondsman, and you'll have to pay his fee. That's negotiable, but that will cost you at least ten percent or $100,000. Or you can put up property or cash valued at $1,000,000 without using a bondsman and carry the risk yourself, in case you don't show for every hearing. If you put up real property, you must prove to the court's satisfaction fair market value and good title, with no mortgage. Cash gets a little tricky. If you have $1,000,000, then the court will want to know the origin of the funds, and the burden is on you to show that the funds are not part of a criminal enterprise. Can you make the bond, or should I contact a few bondsmen?"

"Let's see what the judge says. I think I can cover the bond."

Gray paused and opened his briefcase. "I have an employment contract for you to review and sign before I proceed on your behalf."

I started reading the two-page document and then reread it. "They say don't sign a legal document at times of stress. I guess this is one of the $50,000 exceptions."

Gray smiled. It was the first time he'd done that since the meeting began. I guess it was because we were talking about his favorite subject, his fee.

"If I understand this correctly, it says I deposit $50,000 in your firm's escrow account, and each month you withdraw your fee based upon the hourly rates for you and your staff and then each month on the 1st I bring the retainer back up to the $50,000. Your hourly rate is $400, and you're the most expensive."

"That's correct, but before my firm can accept any money, you'll need to disclose to the court the source of your payment. We can't accept drug money."

I almost laughed out loud at his hypocrisy.

"I've got twelve hundred acres on Highway 49 in Cheatham County. That should cover the bond, and I'll borrow against it to pay your fee. I figure at $3000 an acre, I could post a $2,000,000 bond if I have to. I've got a line of credit at the Ashland City Bank to pay your fee."

Gray seemed satisfied. "Well, it will all have to be approved by the judge."

I inquired, "Which judge?"

"It depends who's sitting on the criminal docket, the judges rotate."

I suggested, maybe a little to forcefully, "Try to get me before Judge Alford."

"How do you know Judge Alford? He may have to recuse himself if he has a conflict?"

"He won't recuse himself. We have an understanding. Just try to get him to set my bond, but most importantly get me the hell out of here today!"

I signed the contract. We visited a few moments longer, but Gray had what he wanted. He was off to try to see who was presiding over the criminal docket, to find out if Alford was available, and if all else failed, to get me on some judge's calendar.

I went back to my cell. As I walked down the long corridor, the stench of someone's backed-up toilet nauseated me, and I gaged. I could feel the breeze of the closing door behind me. *I've got to get out of here.*

CHAPTER THREE

THE ARRAIGNMENT

Friday, October 18, 1996

(ROSCOE CARMICHAEL'S VOICE)

The thought of spending the weekend in jail depressed me. Gray hoped he could get me in front of a judge today, but he braced me for the possibility of Monday. I told him if he didn't get me out before sundown, we were going to have a talk about reducing his fee. I explained that securing an arraignment was a test that he was in fact a first-rate lawyer worth a $50,000 retainer. I knew that would motivate him, the greedy bastard.

My ploy worked. Gray sent word through the grapevine that I would be arraigned before Judge Joseph Peck at 3:00 p.m. I was disappointed he couldn't corral Judge Alford; he was in my pocket and I knew he wouldn't recuse himself and would be very reasonable in setting bail.

At 2:30 p.m., my jailer handcuffed me and transported me to the First Circuit Criminal Court of Davidson County. I was held in a waiting room until it was my turn to appear before the judge. At 3:00 p.m., I was escorted into the courtroom.

Gray was already seated at the defense table. DA Johnson Tory, with whom I had previous dealings, and two unidentified assistant DAs were seated at the other.

The clerk made an announcement, "The matter of the state of Tennessee vs. Roscoe Carmichael III, docket # 96-23472, the Honorable Joseph Peck presiding. Stand and you will be heard. God save these United States of America and the great state of Tennessee."

The assistant district attorney announced, "The state is ready, Your Honor."

Gray indicated he was prepared to proceed.

Judge Peck gave me a hard stare. It was clear that First Circuit Criminal Court would not be a warm and embracing environment for an accused drug dealer. I'd have to figure out a way to change that.

The white-haired judge with a white goatee, almost eighty, in his black robe, looked down from the bench and opened, "The defendant is charged with a Class B felony, the distribution of a Schedule II drug, cocaine. The police have confiscated the drugs, and the state alleges that it has videos of the exchange. How does the defendant plead?"

Gray stood, adjusted his glasses, and answered on my behalf, "Vincent Gray for the defendant, not guilty!"

Tory stood and was recognized.

"General Tory, you have something to add to the charges?"

"Yes, Your Honor, as stated in the incident report of the defendant's arrest, a second search warrant issued by the Honorable Barry Howard of the Third Circuit Criminal Court for the defendant's office resulted in the police confiscating videotapes of the defendant engaged in various sex acts with several women. A second person hidden in a secret room operated the camera. The police are investigating these facts. Several assistant DAs, detectives, and federal agents have been working through the tapes as per Judge Howard's search warrant. They are trying to locate the women, and my office is reserving the right to charge the defendant with other crimes, depending upon that investigation."

Tory produced a list of the nine police detectives, assistant DAs, and federal agents who'd watched any portion of the tapes.

Gray jumped to his feet,

"I object to the confiscation of these tapes, they're private property and their seizure is outside the scope of Judge Howard's search warrant. These law enforcement agents are invading my client's privacy by watching the videos".

Gray demanded that the court direct the police to return my personal property. Gray pointed out that where the tapes were found, at the Music Row townhouse, only a small number of drugs were found and that the videos weren't related to the drugs or within the scope of the search warrant.

I was impressed by Gray's little speech. I hoped the judge was too. Peck paused for a moment contemplating Gray's demand, then said, "Let's address the drug charge. I'm going to let some other judge address these additional charges relating to the videotapes after the state has completed its preliminary investigation and the DA's office is prepared to present such charges. Mr. Gray, do you have a motion?"

"Your Honor, I make a motion for the court to set bail. The defendant is prepared to post bond."

Peck asked, "Is there a bondsman involved?"

"The defendant has a farm in Cheatham County that has been in his family for over fifty years. The defendant inherited it in 1986. It is owned at this moment without any liens, but we request that the court approve a line of credit. I can state as an officer of the court that the proposed asset could not be the fruit of any illegal activity. The defendant proposes posting the property for his bond. If approved, my firm's retainer of $50,000 will be paid from that line of credit with Ashland City Bank. My firm will then bill hourly and be paid monthly for our services preserving the retainer in our escrow account. I've spoken to the president of the Bank of Ashland City, and the bank is willing to take a position behind the court's bond if the court approves the line of credit."

The judge asked, "What is the amount of the line of credit?"

Gray whispered in my ear. He knew the answer, but I guess he was being theatrical. I whispered back, hoping I wouldn't have to speak.

He turned back to the judge and stated, "$500,000. Mr. Carmichael has been doing business with the bank for many years. He operates several businesses, which maintain an on-going relationship with the bank. I'm sure there were many intangible factors that went into the bank officer setting the dollar amount of the line of credit. We asked for $500,000 and he agreed to that amount. I suspect if we asked for more, based on our conversation, he'd have agreed to the higher amount."

Gray presented an affidavit signed by Donald Murray, President of Ashland City Bank.

Peck asked a few more questions, and he appeared to be satisfied that the asset was clean, not tainted by drug money.

"How much is the farm worth, Mr. Carmichael?"

Gray had warned me the court might take this track and get me to participate in the hearing. Gray had suggested that I appraise low.

"It's worth at least $2,400,000 or $2,000 an acre. It has twelve hundred acres."

Both facts were true. It was worth closer to $3,000 an acre.

The next question surprised my attorney and me.

"Your legal residence is Nashville, not Cheatham County?"

"Yes sir, a few years ago I changed my residency to the townhouse on Music Row, it functions as an office and I live on the second and third floors."

"How much equity is in the townhouse?"

The question was directed to me, so I answered, "The building is paid for and is worth what someone will pay for it, sir. I have no mortgage. I bought it for $240,000 five years ago. The house has appreciated at least $60,000, so I'd say it's worth at least $300,000."

It was closer to $500,000.

"Do you own any other real property?"

"I own several additional adjacent parcels to the family farm in Cheatham County, and partial ownership in two strip centers in Davidson County. I wouldn't want to involve the other limited partners in those ventures with my legal troubles."

"Mr. Tory, what say you?"

"I move for this court to try the defendant here in Davidson County, the county of his residence rather than Cheatham County where more drugs were confiscated. The two raids were coordinated and should be tried together. This court has venue over these charges and should hear the case."

Peck turned to Gray and asked, "Will the defendant acknowledge the jurisdiction of this court?"

"I had intended to file a motion for change of venue with a supporting brief citing controlling authority. But, we challenge the jurisdiction of this court as to the drugs seized at the farm. These charges should be brought separately as Cheatham County Criminal court should hear that matter."

Peck retorted, "Does your client deny the county of his residence?"

"No sir, but the alleged crime occurred at the farmhouse in Cheatham County."

"Drugs were found at both locations. It was a joint task force lead by the TBI and the search warrants were issued as part of one conspiracy to distribute narcotics."

"But those drugs were discovered under a separate search warrant issued by Judge Wyatt of Cheatham County."

Peck was ready to rule, "It was a single action and arrest by the TBI. I order that this court does have venue over this proceeding."

Shit, my contacts are far more reaching in Cheatham County. I have a way into the county judicial system. More importantly, I know the people and would have access to a jury. I guess I'm going to have to make new friends in Davidson County.

"Mr. Gray do you have a motion on behalf your client?"

"I move for the court to set bail."

"General, what is the state's recommendation as to the dollar amount of the bond? I remind you that bond amount is determined by the likelihood of the defendant to appear in court and for depositions when directed to do so."

"Your Honor, with the court's permission, the state wants to present testimony."

I was deflated when Peck directed Tory to proceed.

"The state would like to call agent-in-charge Arnold Pyle."

Pyle testified to the fact that I maintained a private airstrip and had access to airplanes, to my arrest and confrontation with Anthony Estes and the screaming match that ensued. He correctly testified that after I was Mirandized, I kept taking the Fifth and asking for my lawyer. Pyle testified that I was a flight risk and that I had the ability to disappear. He pointed out that one of my co-conspirators was a Cuban and I had associates in a country that wasn't friendly to our country and that didn't maintain an extradition treaty.

Gray objected, "What does this testimony have to do with whether my client will appear when directed?"

Peck sustained the objection on the grounds of relevancy as to the confrontation with Estes, but not as to the airfield or to my association with individuals from Cuba.

Tory called Sheriff Weaver of Cheatham County. The sheriff testified that he'd known me for my entire life and that I'd been in trouble with the law since age ten. He described how me and my fellow football players terrorized the high school.

"Carmichael has been involved with drugs since he was sixteen."

Gray objected, pointing out that juvenile records were sealed and not relevant, that the issue was whether I'd appear.

"The issue of the dollar amount of the bond, is the risk of flight."

Judge Peck sustained the objection.

Sheriff Weaver testified that I had two convictions for nondrug-related charges and that I'd served time from 1990 to 1991.

"We've been watching him. I had an inside man who led us to the bust. This man has money and an airfield. He's the definition of a flight risk. He can go anywhere in the world before we would ever know he was gone. He planned on distributing kilos of cocaine that would have ruined the lives of hundreds of people."

That old bastard was going out of his way to get me. I was waiting for my lawyer to interrupt and stop the momentum.

Gray elected not to question the sheriff. The video and testimony went to my guilt, so he took a different approach with the court, "Roscoe Carmichael has lived in Cheatham County, and now Davidson County, his entire life. He has informed me that he doesn't have a passport and has left Middle Tennessee only on a few occasions to attend functions in New York and Los Angeles. He's a Middle Tennessee boy. He's operated a family business on the Cheatham County Town Square since the death of his grandfather and maintains an interest in several others in that county, employing dozens of persons. He has ties to this community as well. He has a townhouse on Music Row, and he's a respected member of the Nashville music industry. He's not a flight risk. He'll appear when directed to do so."

I nervously watched the judge deliberate. He held absolute discretion as to the dollar amount of the bond. It would be a very bad sign if the first pleading in the case was an appeal of the dollar amount of the bond.

"Bond is set at $1,500,000. The farm and office building will act as collateral for the bond. Mr. Carmichael will be permitted to borrow $500,000 from a bank for the express purpose of paying Mr. Gray's firm's retainer, continuing legal fees and for living and legal expenses. All other accounts are frozen until further order of the court. The farm, but not the office building shall secure the bank loan, but the bank's security interest of $500,000 shall be behind the court's security interest for the $1,500,000 bond. In other words, Mr. Carmichael, if it becomes necessary to sell the farm and the office building, the first $1,500,000 goes to the court to satisfy the bond and the bank is secondary to the court. I will prepare an order and file it with the Registrars for Cheatham and Davidson Counties, imposing the bond in the chain of title. Mr. Carmichael, the office posted as collateral is a private home and office, correct?"

"Yes, sir."

"I understand you have no passport?"

"No, sir."

"I order that you be confined to your office located at 223 16th

Avenue South, until further orders of this court. You shall be required to wear an ankle bracelet restricting you to the curtilage of the property, that would include the full extent of the property, the front and back yard. Your lawyer shall be given unlimited access to the property, but all other guests shall be approved on a visit-by-visit basis through the Davidson County sheriff's office. Permission for you to leave the property shall be subject to court order. I warn you that permission to leave the county will be denied. Any medical needs can be addressed in Nashville. Do you accept these terms of bond?"

I conferred with Gray for a moment,

"You never said anything about an ankle bracelet, or being confined to..."

Gray cut me off, "That will be a fight for another day. Let's get you out of jail now".

I wanted out of jail so badly I agreed, I felt compelled to speak.

"That's acceptable, sir. Can I post bond now and leave with my lawyer?"

I wondered whether Peck would send me back to my cell and have me spend the weekend in jail.

After a minute, which seemed like an hour, he said, "Let's adjourn. The defendant shall remain in custody. I'll go back to chambers and draft an order. If approved by all parties, it can be executed, and the defendant will be free to go back to the office building where a sheriff's deputy will attach the bracelet".

No one objected, so Peck left the bench to complete the task.

Gray turned to me, "You got your money's worth. I got you out of jail."

"Bullshit, you never told me I'd be confined to a small house on Music Row."

"From what you've told me, the jewelry store and your other

legitimate businesses operate on autopilot. You're confined to your place of business in Nashville, and with permission, you can meet clients. You also have unrestricted use of your telephone. I'd be thinking about how much worse it would have been if he kept you locked up."

Gray had a point. I could make the best of a bad situation. I was just getting used to being confined when Gray added to my burden, "You know they're trying to figure out what additional charges could be brought against you because of those tapes. The drug charges are very serious. A Class B felony carries a sentence as long as thirty years."

I was aware I was in trouble.

"You should also be concerned about possible civil suits by these unidentified women. When they're identified, I'd expect trouble. We should probably get you independent counsel if you have to defend civil suits. I'm a criminal defense lawyer. I've tried just a few civil suits. You'll need another lawyer to defend any actions filed by these women. You're lucky that my firm has sixteen offices with lawyers of every specialty. I'm going to start looking over my firm's roster to see who we'll need to add to our team to defend possible civil suits from these videoed women."

More goddamn lawyers. As I waited for the paperwork to be approved and signed, I hatched a plan to avoid civil lawsuits. *I wish Bucky was here.*

CHAPTER FOUR

A NEW CLIENT

Wednesday, October 23, 1996

(ELIZABETH SWANN'S VOICE)

I arrived at the law firm of Steine & Davis right on time, 3:00 p.m. Petrified, I rode the elevator up to their office on the eighth floor of the old Steine's Department Store. I entered through the rear. The building's back door opened onto Printer's Alley in downtown Nashville. Honky tanks, bars, and strip joints replaced the once respectable places of business, such as book publishers and artists. This transformation took place over decades, but had been one of moral decadence and decline.

Although I was nervous, I also felt a sense of confidence because I'd done my homework in preparation for this meeting. I'd never needed an attorney before so I'd asked around and done my research about the firm of Steine & Davis. I'd read a few articles about the firm. Morty Steine, age seventy-six, a legendary trial lawyer, earned his stripes during the civil rights movement of the 1950s and 1960s. I'd discovered that in the 1970s and1980s he represented many country music stars. He'd fought for songwriters against the big record companies. He'd helped several of them make the jump from Nashville to Hollywood, including Dolly Parton and Johnny Cash. He'd also helped the Outlaws; Johnny, Willie, Waylon, Kris, and others, out of several drug-related and other self-created jams. Morty Steine tried murder cases and won large civil judgments over a forty-year span, and legal scholars throughout the country respected his legal opinion.

Benjamin Davis, age forty-two, had been with the firm for almost twenty years and had rung up an impressive list of wins on his own. As Steine's protégé, he'd worked closely with his mentor to earn a national reputation. He was aggressive in a courtroom, often testing the limits of the judge. I was informed he could be charming, yet he could turn and attack unmercifully. Comparing two pictures taken ten years apart I could tell that his boyish good looks were fading. One of my sources insisted he now relied more on the skills he'd acquired. He advised me that Davis's foes referred to him as "tenacious".

The firm was small: only two lawyers and two support persons. Despite its size, three sources assured me that Steine & Davis was the firm I should retain. The recommendations were stellar, "These guys are not only exceptional, they're personal. Clients can trust and open up to them. Morty Steine is like a Dutch uncle, and when he talks, everyone in the room pays attention, more importantly, juries and judges listen. Davis is like a junkyard dog after a bone. He's aggressive, and with that Yankee accent and a deep radio-type voice, he commands a room. He impresses juries and judges, managing to get them to do what he asks."

I got off the elevator at eight and walked to the door marked with a bronze plaque, Steine & Davis. I noticed the ten-inch-high mirrors along the wall. I later learned that the eighth floor had once been the shoe department of Steine's Department Store. Without knocking, I entered, and an older woman behind the reception desk said, "I'm Bella Rosario. You must be our three o'clock. Ms. Swann, can I offer you a cup of coffee and one of my husband's delicious pastries?"

The woman's motherly voice had a calming effect. She reminded me of Martha, my mother's sister.

I smiled and said, "That would be lovely." I immediately felt more relaxed.

My brief trance was disrupted when a much younger woman, smartly dressed in a black jumpsuit, entered the room. What I first noticed were her deep steel blue eyes. They were piercing, yet there was a sense of warmth. Her long blonde ponytail hung down to the middle of her back. She was quite striking, tall, more than six feet in heels, with an exceptional figure.

"Ms. Swann, I'm Sammie Davis, Mr. Davis's niece and paralegal. He'll see you in our conference room. Please follow me."

Bella interjected, "I'll bring your coffee and pastry to you, dear. How do you take it?"

"Black, please."

I followed the young woman down the hallway into a large room that had a long mahogany table with twelve navy blue leather chairs. There were three walls with floor-to-ceiling bookshelves filled with dusty books. There was a wooden ladder on wheels to allowed a researcher to reach the highest of shelves. The fourth wall was all glass, and you could look out and see the Cumberland River and one of the city's bridges that crossed it. I was placed at one end of the table just as my coffee and a hot apple strudel arrived. I blew on the strudel and took a bite. I could feel the hot apples go down my throat, and I washed them down with a gulp of coffee. I was nervous again. The secretary's charm only lasted so long. A moment later, a tall man and Sammie joined me.

"Ms. Swann, I'm Ben Davis, and my niece Sammie is a law student and paralegal at the firm. She'll be sitting in on our meetings, and if we take your case, she'll be working closely with us."

Those deep steel blue eyes were obviously inherited by the niece from her uncle's side of the family. Davis' longish sandy hair with signs of gray around the temples was thinning a little on top. A large man, both in height and weight, he smiled, and I relaxed a little bit in return. "We work as a team. You can expect a call back within twenty-four hours from one of us. Despite our small size, we pride ourselves on our responsiveness to our clients and we always try to do the right thing."

The man made an immediate strong, positive impression. His deep voice and how he carried and projected himself, I could tell he was a man of substance. Then I remembered the other lawyer's name, the first in the firm's name, and asked, "What about Mr. Steine? Isn't he going to sit in on this meeting?"

"Mr. Steine's semi-retired, and he picks and chooses the cases he wants to work on. I can't promise he'll work on your case, but he's a valuable resource in our firm. He's always available for consult since he lives on the sixth floor of this building."

"I live on the ninth floor," Sammie volunteered.

"That must be convenient."

Davis added, "I don't live in the building, I live with my family, but sometimes it feels like I live here."

He laughed, I liked his laugh.

Despite our light moment, I was a little disappointed that Mr.

Steine might not be involved in my lawsuit, and it must have shown on my face.

Mr. Davis reassured me, "You seem a little nervous, relax. This is a safe place. Everything you say here is confidential. It's in the vault. Everything you say is protected by attorney/client privilege."

"That won't help me. My problem is already out in the open. In fact, that's my problem, I'm about to be publicly humiliated, and I don't know what to do. I'm desperate and frightened, and I need someone who can tell me what my options are, if I have any."

"Ms. Swann, or may I call you Lizzy?"

I jumped at the opportunity to get familiar, "Please do."

"Look, you're our last appointment of the day. Kick back, and take your shoes off."

Davis did just that with his loafers. Referencing my high heels, he added, "They look mighty uncomfortable. Let's get to know each other. I'll go first."

The man told me how twenty years ago, as a New Yorker he came to Nashville to Vanderbilt University Law School and graduate business school. Within a week he met and began working for Morty Steine.

"His wife, Goldie, found out I was new to town, and she invited me to Sabbath dinner. Something happened that night. Despite the fact that both of my parents are alive, I was adopted by the Steines, and I've worked for him ever since."

He explained how the woman at the front desk, Bella Rosario, Mr. Steine's secretary taught him the inner workings of a law office, while Mr. Steine taught him the important aspects of law and legal ethics. Davis described how he met and fell in love with his wife, Liza, a Vanderbilt nursing student and that they eventually had two children: a girl, Caroline, and a boy, Jake. He paused waiting for me to say something. Nothing came out. I wasn't sure where to begin.

"Now it's your turn."

The man had opened up to me and left me no alternative but to do the same. So, I did, "I'm thirty-three years young and unmarried. I grew up in Evansville, Indiana on a dairy farm. In high school I starred in every school play and held the lead role in every musical. Everyone I ever knew at home told me I had talent, and I believed them. I believed in me. So, after high school it was off to New York University and for five years I enrolled in acting, singing, and dancing classes. During that time, I supported myself as a waitress by day and took classes at night. Every penny I made went to improve my craft. I had very few auditions and no parts. At twenty-three, I was discouraged and washed up. I left New York University and came to Nashville. As a waitress I put myself through real estate classes and after a few years became a reasonably successful real estate agent. As I was about to turn thirty, I longed for my old profession. I began by singing in karaoke bars, then open mic talent nights. It was on one of those nights that my real problems began. I'm not sure how to tell the rest of my story."

"Just start at the beginning, and we'll see where that takes us. As Mary Poppins would say, "It's a very good place to start."

I liked him, a little corny, but funny.

He unwrapped a Tootsie Pop and used it to signal me to go on.

"Four years ago, in the fall of 1992, despite my real estate career I felt dejected and at a low point in my life, just off a bad break-up, when I met this guy at Robert's on Broadway. I'd just finished singing two Patsy Cline songs. The audience actually brought me back for a second number. I was feeling pretty good and a little full of myself. I'd had a lack of confidence since my fiancée had broken my heart. The bastard found someone else and without warning gave me my walking papers."

I paused and asked, "This is confidential, right?"

"Absolutely!"

"After I sang my song I wandered over to the bar where I met this guy who bought me another drink. I was in a frisky mood and we switched to doing shots. I got tipsy really quickly. He then invited me into the men's room and we snorted cocaine. I lost perspective and dropped my guard. He claimed to be a big shot music agent with offices on Music Row. I'd regularly smoked pot, but I'd only done cocaine a few times, years ago when I was living in New York. I remembered how the game was played, I was trying to fit in, hoping to keep his interest and advance my career. I guess I reacted badly to the drugs, or to the combination of that and the bourbon. I kind of lost control. As I remember that evening, I'm now embarrassed."

He read me like a book. "Ms. Swann, for this to work, you must be completely honest with us. I don't care what you did. Sammie and I aren't here to judge you, just to help you. Hell, everybody does silly things when they're young. That's part of being young. You make mistakes. I know I made plenty of them, still do, just not as many, and I don't make the same one twice."

Wow, that's pretty insightful. I really like this guy.

I felt much better, so I continued, "He told me because of the way I sang and looked, he was ready to sign me up. He asked me if I could go straight to his office to review a contract. It was almost midnight. I should have known better, but I wasn't thinking. I left my car downtown, and I rode with him to his office to 'talk about my career.' He asked me whether I wanted to 'audition' for him again in his office. He told me that a big screen TV and a karaoke machine were upstairs. We went up to his exercise room. He had one of those weight machines, free weights, a 'stripper pole', and a large blue mat. That's when things got out of hand. I did another bump of cocaine and sang karaoke. I picked out another Patsy Cline song, "I Fall to Pieces." He told me, I had 'what it takes,' and he wanted to represent me. I sang a few more songs with his continued encouragement. Between his compliments and the drugs, my head was spinning. I felt like my life was finally moving in the right direction."

I stopped for a minute and asked, "Can I have a drink of water?"

Sammie retrieved a glass from a pitcher on the credenza on the far side of the room.

"Thanks." I took a long drink that was more like a gulp.

"It started with an innocent game of strip poker and several more shots. For about forty-five minutes we drank and played poker. Looking back, I realize that it was foolish. I should have known where it was going. There wasn't going to be a winner of that game. I was down to my bra and panties when he removed his underwear. He was erect, and I figured, what the hell, who does it, hurt? We're both over twenty-one. Besides, he held the keys to my career."

I didn't know this, but Davis knew the name of the prospective agent without any disclosure by me. Davis knew the modus operandi of Roscoe Carmichael III. His reputation preceded him.

I continued, "Roscoe, sitting there naked, wanted me to dance and strip my panties and bra, and go all the way. I figured, who's going to know? No one. And, if it gets me an agent and possible work."

Talking to these lawyers wasn't as bad as I thought. I could tell that my audience was listening intently and Sammie was making notes as I spoke.

"I'm not proud of what happened next." I paused, trying to recreate a picture of what happened in my mind, so I could put what happened into words.

"I started to strip and dance. And then I saw the pole. My old fiancée gave me pole dancing lessons for my birthday. I think the gift was more for him than for me but, I learned a trick or two and was pretty damn good. I was a little rusty, but after a few minutes, my skills came back and I put on quite a show. I ended my routine with a split, completely exposing myself. After that workout, I was perspiring profusely. My entire body glistened from sweat. He took me into the bedroom, tied my feet and hands to the bedposts and screwed me good."

She laughed and added, "He screwed me in more ways than one."

Davis said, "We've all been screwed over at one point in our lives. You're not alone."

Again, he made me feel better. I took another drink and continued, "Because my body was wet from the routine, he kept slipping and sliding all over the place. He then flipped me over and entered me from behind. It may have been the drugs and/or the liquor, but it was the best sex I ever had. I remember it so vividly. Sorry for the vulgarity, but we didn't make love. This was something different. It was primeval. It was down and dirty, and while we were doing it, he said the filthiest things. I showered afterward in his bathroom. I needed one."

She paused, and Davis took the opportunity to comment, "It sounds like you have a pretty vivid memory of the night despite the drugs and liquor. It was memorable, but like you said, two consenting adults."

I burst out in a long guttural response, "The bastard recorded everything, from the beginning with our poker game, my dance, and right up through his orgasm. My entire routine on the pole is preserved for everyone to see. The sex from the front to the back is all on tape. I knew what I was doing, but I didn't agree to have it videoed."

Davis was a little confused, so he stopped me and had me back up.

"It was a setup. The exercise room, the bedroom, even the shower had two-way mirrors. Like you see on the cop shows, where they interrogate criminals. From the inside of this secret little room, you could see out. There was a camera set up on a tripod and a stool. The police are convinced there was a cameraman. I've watched my video from beginning to end. Someone knew what angles to shoot. I'm disgusted with myself. How could I have done what I did? I'm not like that. What I thought was a private moment was preserved forever."

I paused, and Davis cleared his throat. "So, you had consensual sex, but were unaware he was recording the act. Let's put aside whether a crime was committed. A tort against you has occurred."

"What's a tort?"

"A tort is a wrong by one citizen against another. It can be intentional, reckless, or negligently inflicted. You own your image. Mr. Carmichael took that image without your permission. That's an invasion of your privacy. You're entitled to damages."

"I've been damaged, and I've been humiliated. I don't know who's seen my video, but can you imagine being called to the police station and have to sit with two detectives and be shown a videotape like that? They figured out who I was from one of my real estate ads. One of them said that the only difference was that I was wearing clothing." I nervously laughed.

Davis began, "This was an intentional tort. He knew he acted without permission. A jury could award punitive damages in addition to compensatory damages. Sammie and I will need to do some research. This isn't the type of case that walks in our door every day. I think you have a winning lawsuit. Let us do the research free of charge, and then we'll sit down with the results. "

"That seems like a very reasonable way to proceed," I replied.

"One of us will get in touch with you after we've completed our research and schedule an appointment."

The meeting ended, and I exited the office, saying goodbye to the secretary as I left. My sense of hopelessness diminished. Somehow, I knew that these people could help me, or at least they were going to try. For now, that was enough.

CHAPTER FIVE

THE TEAM'S FORMED

Wednesday, October 23, 1996

(Same Day)

(ROSCOE CARMICHAEL'S VOICE)

Vincent Gray and two others presented themselves at my Music Row prison cell. According to the court order, my lawyers could come and go as they pleased. Gray made the introductions, "Roscoe Carmichael, this is Richard Tate, a trial attorney from our DC office."

He pointed to the shorter man in the navy suit. "Dick's on the firm's management committee. When I circulated a summary about your case, he convinced me that he should be co-counsel."

Surprised, I asked, "I thought you were my lawyer. Why do I need some fancy lawyer from DC if I have you?"

Gray was quick to respond, "I'm primarily a criminal defense attorney. Mr. Tate brings other skills to your defense. I'll act as local counsel. I know the judges, the local rules, and can help in picking the jury. I'm from Nashville, but Mr. Tate is one of the best trial lawyers in the country concerning protection of companies' copyrights and trademarks. He's sued defendants who have infringed on Elvis' as well as Mickey Mouse's image. He's represented Elvis' estate and the Disney Company for years protecting their marks. Those cases were about invasion of property rights. He's also sued tabloids when they've wrongfully taken pictures or videos of celebrities. He's the reason you retained Covington & Burling rather than a small Nashville firm, we anticipate a client's needs."

Gray did have a point, I did retain an international law firm for a reason, they were the two thousand-pound gorilla. He must have seen me shaking my head in agreement so he continued, "We're lucky to have him on board. He's an ex-Marine major, up at five, exercised, showered, and at his desk before seven. When he comes to town, he'll stay at our company apartment, and he'll give you at least fourteen hours a day, six days a week, if necessary. He takes Sundays off to go to church and then to decompress for a thirteen-mile run. He'll put up one hell of a defense, and he's got a good chance to dismiss any lawsuit that might be coming from the women you videoed. He'll provide you with the best defense that money can buy. He charges $500 an hour.

"Hold on here!" I directed my words at Gray, "I thought you were the most expensive lawyer in the firm at $400 an hour?"

Tate was the one who answered, "That's true for the Nashville office, I'm from DC and I'm worth every penny I charge."

Cocky little bastard!

"When Gray circulated your name and a brief summary of your case, I immediately realized that my services would be needed. In less than a week after your arrest, I'm standing in front of you prepared to defend you with a general strategy already planned out. Gray knows the courts here, but I bring to the table twenty years of very specific experience. That's why you retained Covington &

Burling. We're the best. Just think of us as a team and we each bring certain strengths to our team."

"What team? Why do I need a team? Bucky Lee was one lawyer, and he got me off for statutory rape and many other legal problems I had. What will your firm do for me that he can't?"

Tate's response was easy, "For some reason, Mr. Lee wants nothing to do with you. I'd have no objection of adding him to the team. He sounds like one hell of a trial lawyer, but he was willing to let you rot in jail. You're lucky he calld Gray. He gave you such a strong recommendation, it convinced Gray to take your call."

"I ask again, what is your firm going to do for me?"

Tate responded unapologetically, "In a few words, keep you out of prison and prevent these women from getting too deep into your pockets."

Tate pointed to the short, slightly overweight young woman with mousy brown hair, brown eyes, and glasses. "This is Ms. Sara Browne, an investigator with our firm. I had her pull two memos from our firm's archives, and asked her to update them. The first one concerns whether you have any criminal exposure for videotaping. The Tennessee legislature hasn't recognized a crime for invasion of privacy. Only eleven of the fifty states have passed statutes making an unauthorized videotaping of another, a crime. If the DA files criminal charges for the videotaping of these women, we should be able to get those charges dismissed. We need to hope that the drug charges overshadow the sex tape story. The less publicity those tapes cause, the better. If civil suits are filed, the plaintiffs' lawyers will push the DA to file criminal charges. Hopefully the DA will come to the same conclusion as this memo and see no percentage in pursuing criminal charges for the taping. If not, we're on solid ground and we'll fight hard, even an appeal if necessary."

I wasn't completely convinced, "What about the drug charges? Gray said I could be looking at thirty years. Who cares about the tapes and the possibility of civil suits if I'm facing that much prison time for the drugs?"

Gray answered, "We're going to have to attack the validity of the search warrants, and we're going to have to neutralize the informant, or he needs to become unavailable. The TBI and judges screw up search warrants all the time. Tate's presented me a ten-page memo 'How to Invalidate Search Warrants'."

I read the first two paragraphs, "The parcel of land, book 432, Page 11-13, on which the airstrip was recently constructed is not within the scope of the Cheatham County warrant issued by Judge Wyatt. Therefore, the plane and cash were illegally confiscated and the recording of those events should be held inadmissible."

Ms. Browne had cited several cases in support of this proposition. The second paragraph stated, "The TBI's seizure of the drugs, or at least part of the shipment should be held outside the scope of Wyatt's search warrant. The order, specified the farmhouse. Half the drugs were confiscated on the porch and the other half were still in the Jeep. The drugs weren't found in the farmhouse, but outside. The state can argue that the porch is part of the farmhouse, which leaves about half still in the Jeep and outside the scope of the warrant. We should be able to keep that portion of the seized drugs out of evidence, reducing the amount of drugs found. The charges would then become a Class C felony, rather than a Class B felony; and we should be able to exclude the recording of the seizure because it depicts the TBI's confiscation of the drugs in the Jeep."

Tate broke in, impatient by my reading.

"Ms. Browne is still looking for case law, which would exclude from evidence the drugs on the porch, arguing the porch isn't in the farmhouse. If there's a case she'll find it. We also will argue that there was no reason for agent-in-charge Pyle to request a second search warrant for the camera equipment and tapes from Judge Howard. That was private property and should never have been seized. Our biggest problem is your old friend Anthony Estes, who you thought you could trust. You were very wrong."

Thanks a lot asshole, don't think that thought hadn't crossed my mind.

I didn't need Tate to remind me about what that bastard June Bug had done. I'd already made some phone calls about locating that bastard. I'd discovered he been working with Weaver for three months, from an inside source. My two guys were kept in the dark. Weaver played it close to the vest, ironically June Bug had been secretly arrested with a minor and an ounce of my product. Only Weaver and two local deputies knew of the arrest. One of my inside men learned of his arrest and betrayal only an hour before the raid, and he jumped the order and his actions may have invalidated the farmhouse warrant. My agent knew nothing about the traitor's whereabouts. The TBI had him under wraps, in witness protection.

I shared with my lawyers what I'd found out from my sources. They listened and then Tate pointed out, "Be very careful who you confide in, any conversation could be taped and the person on the other side of the line could testify against you in court. Let's not complicate our situation by adding a charge of witness tampering or obstruction of justice."

I didn't need this lawyer to tell me to be careful. My grandfather already taught me well.

Tate turned to Browne, "Find out everything you can on the two judges who issued the warrants, Wyatt and Howard, and their families, soup to nuts, opposition research, any dirt you can find."

I perked up,

"I may be of some help concerning our judges. Everybody's got some skeletons in their closets, and I have access to inside people in both counties.

Browne asked, "Our informant, what can you tell me about him?"

This time I absolutely knew the answer, "Anthony 'June Bug' Estes. I've known him since middle school. We went to Ashland City High School together, and played on two state championship teams. He was one of my tackles on the Bulldogs. My frontline was Estes, Oz, Candy, Thomas and Miller. I played quarterback and still hold several school records, and maybe still a few state records. In the state championship one year I threw seven touchdown passes. We owned the high school and had our choice of girls. Those were glorious days, I can't believe after a lifetime of fun that bastard turned me in. In my youth, I ran afoul of Sheriff Weaver often. Thankfully my granddaddy, Mr. Mike and Bucky got me out of those childish jams."

Gray chimed in,

"So that's why Weaver testified so strongly against you at the arraignment? He was seeking revenge for all those times you got off"

"Yeah, he has a real hard-on for me. I've made some enemies in Cheatham County, but I also have plenty of friends there too. We need to get the case moved from Davidson County to Cheatham. I can better maneuver there..."

Tate cut me off,

"The judge already denied that motion. If necessary we'll raise the denial of change of venue on appeal but I suspect an appellate court will affirm the trial judge's discretionary ruling."

He added, "Remember, anyone can be working for the TBI. You need to choose your friends carefully and this firm can't be complicit and shouldn't be told the source of any information you might bring us. Carefully, find out what you can."

"I know everything Estes has done wrong since he was ten years old. Problem is, I was standing next to him every time he got caught."

Browne, a top investigator and researcher made the obvious observation, "The police know every time he got caught; what I want to know is every time he didn't get caught. That's what's valuable."

"I know when that's happened too."

Thinking of that bastard made me angry and exhausted. I suggested,

"Can we continue this conversation another day, I'm pretty tired."

Tate reminded me,

"Those seven women aren't going to simply go away. They'll file suits against you and they'll complicate matters."

"Maybe so, but it can wait till another day.

Tate could see I was becoming agitated and to avoid an argument, he agreed to leave.

Good riddance.

I was sick of lawyers.

CHAPTER SIX

WHAT'S THE LAW?

Friday, October 25, 1996

(SAMMIE DAVIS' VOICE)

I was intrigued by the Swann case and my assignment on the issue of personal privacy. I'd taken Torts 101 at Vanderbilt Law School, but little attention was paid to what poor Elizabeth "Lizzy" Swann went through. I knew that Carmichael had acted intentionally. He'd also acted fraudulently and callously. But, I quickly realized the controlling question was whether his actions constituted a tort, a civil wrong by one citizen against another; and if it was a tort, then was it done maliciously with bad intent? I did remember my professor referencing a new tort recognized in Tennessee called "outrageous conduct", but I couldn't recall all of the elements of the cause of action. Malice was just one of the elements.

I sat at my desk trying to remember what had to be proved to recover damages. I did know that the Tennessee Supreme Court in 1992 had elevated the burden of proof for a plaintiff to prove an intentional tort from a "preponderance of the evidence," the tipping of the scales of justice to a higher standard, "clear and convincing evidence." This made it more difficult to recover for an intentional tort than for negligence. However, a plaintiff could, within the discretion of the jury, be awarded not only compensatory damages but punitive damages.

I spent the entire day in our library, using books rather than my computer, researching various issues and potential causes of actions, making notes on a legal pad and copying cases. My efforts were limited to Tennessee law and federal law because our bookshelves did not include other jurisdictions. Morty complained all the time about the cost of maintaining our collection of books. If I wanted to determine the law of other states, I had to go to the Vanderbilt law library or use Lexis Nexis, a computer legal research service, which I lobbied hard for and acquired when I began law school.

I spent the afternoon using Lexis Nexis to expand my research into other jurisdictions. I determined that only eleven states considered what Carmichael did to be a crime and Tennessee wasn't one of them. That information wasn't available on our library bookshelves and would have taken five times longer at Vanderbilt's law library if the firm hadn't purchased Lexis Nexis.

As I was deep into my task, my uncle stuck his head in the doorway and asked, "How's it going?"

He was very demanding and wanted everything yesterday.

"I just started. What I've found is very interesting. This isn't something that was covered in school, so I'm starting from scratch."

He ignored the complexity of what he'd asked me to do.

"I've filled Morty in on the facts. You need to get us a memo on the applicable law. I've scheduled a meeting with Morty at noon tomorrow. Have the memo on my desk by ten and slip a copy under his door. The document should also include a client-friendly explanation of the Fifth Amendment because Carmichael is facing criminal charges and he'll probably invoke it."

I could have argued that was an unreasonable demand but, instead I told him what he wanted to hear, "I'll get it done."

With that said, he was out the door. He knew I'd stay at it all night. I lived in the building, one floor up, on the ninth floor. Morty lived on the sixth. He was my landlord, and my rent was one dollar a month. Not a bad deal for a student working part-time.

I didn't leave the office until 1:00 a.m. The memo was a solid piece of work, ten pages summarizing potential causes of action against Roscoe Carmichael. I took it home to proofread one last time in bed. At 8:00 a.m. I placed my work product on my uncle's desk. I also slipped a copy under Morty's door. Being the senior partner and semi-retired, he rarely came to the office before ten. *Seniority has its benefits.*

At noon, the three of us gathered in the conference room. Morty opened the meeting with a burst of energy.

"I've tried two invasion of privacy cases. One was against a newspaper, and the other involved wiretapping. This case has real sex appeal, no pun intended. Damages will be hard to quantify. It could be one hell of a jury verdict if you pick the right jury. We don't want older women on the jury. In fact, we want young people in general. Older jurors aren't going to approve of our young client having sex with a man ten years her senior, while on drugs and dancing around naked and doing a routine on the pole. That's not sympathetic behavior. No question it's an intentional tort, so we'll have a shot at punitive damages. This guy Carmichael sounds like he's got some money. Discovering his financial statements will become important."

The old man's mind was moving too fast. He was raising issues independent of liability and the controlling law. My uncle tried to bring him back to the purpose of the meeting, "Let's slow down, we're getting ahead of ourselves. Let's review the memo first. Then we can address ancillary issues, like damages and what type of juror we want on the jury."

I'd never seen Morty so excited about a case. He usually was so methodical. It was unusual for my uncle to have to rein him in.

My uncle turned the meeting over to me. I was a little nervous, but this was a friendly audience. This entire project was a learning experience for me. Both Morty and my uncle were my mentors, grooming me to join the firm as its third partner. I learned a lot in the classroom, but because of my work schedule, I cut a lot of classes. With assigned seats, my professors were bound to notice my being AWOL. I kept my mornings free for work and the afternoons and evenings for class. I knew that my real education occurred at Steine & Davis. Bella Rosario, our trusted secretary, a jack-of-all-trades, also took me under her wing and taught me the practical aspects of running a law office. She instructed me the way she trained my uncle twenty years earlier.

I took a deep breath and began, "As you know, the leading textbook on torts is Prosser & Wade."

Wade had actually taught my uncle torts at Vanderbilt twenty years earlier. He was a tough old bird who cross-examined his students mercilessly.

"Tennessee has adopted what both Prosser & Wade and the Restatement of Torts have identified as four types of privacy claims: appropriation, false light, intrusion, and publicity.

"One who gives publicity to another that places them in a false light is subject to liability for invasion of privacy if the false light is highly offensive to a reasonable person, and the speaker acts in reckless disregard to the falsity of the publicized matter."

I paused to let what I was saying sink in, no questions. I continued,

"The distribution of the videos of our client would be offensive to a reasonable person. The defense will argue that the TBI and the police, not Carmichael, published and publicized the videos. I think there are more appropriate types of invasion of privacy."

Morty suggested we should consider false light and let the defendant blame the TBI. He thought it wouldn't play well with the jury. I didn't agree but, he was the boss and I'd have time to respectfully object later on. I assumed by my uncle's silence he agreed with me but also decided to withhold his objection. I moved on to the next type of invasion of privacy.

"One who intentionally intrudes, physically or otherwise, upon the solitude or seclusion of another of his or her private affairs or concerns, is subject to liability to the other person for invasion of privacy if the intrusion would be highly offensive to a reasonable person. I think we should allege intrusion in the complaint."

I presented the next form of invasion of privacy; appropriation, which is "the unauthorized commercial use of a person's appearance, such that it unfairly exploits a person's property rights or his or hers right of publicity. I added, "I don't think appropriation is applicable unless Carmichael was selling tickets to watch the video. We simply don't have a commercial use."

No disagreement from either Morty or my uncle, so I described the last form on invasion of privacy; publicity.

"One who gives publicity to a matter concerning the private life of another is subject to liability to the other person for invasion of privacy, if the matter publicized is of the kind that would be highly offensive to the reasonable person and is not of legitimate concern of the public. Tennessee case law hasn't reported a lot of successful invasion of privacy actions on appeal. Most cases result in either a directed verdict by the judge at the close of the plaintiff's proof at trial or a summary judgment before trial. The most promising Tennessee case is Dunn vs Moto Photo Inc. 828 SW. 2d 747 (Tenn. Ct. App 1991). In Dunn, the Court of Appeals reversed the trial court's dismissal of the plaintiff's claims of outrageous conduct and invasion of privacy. The court held that the case should go to a jury to determine the facts. The plaintiff was a cocktail waitress, and together with her boyfriend, she took revealing photographs. She took them to Moto Photo to be developed. When she went back to pick them up, a Moto Photo employee claimed that the film could not be developed because of the provocative nature. The film was returned to the plaintiff. In reality, the Moto Photo employee developed the photos into a smut book which he maintained of the plaintiff and other unsuspecting customers. The Moto Photo employee showed the smut book to fellow employees and third parties. The trial court directed a verdict for the defendant. The Court of Appeals reversed and found that there were factual issues for a jury."

I stopped and took a drink of water. My mouth was dry from taking so much. Neither Morty nor my uncle had contributed much to the meeting.

I was winding down, "I'm exploring other possible torts, trespass of chattel, conversion (theft), constructive fraud (by omission) and promissory fraud (no intent to perform). There will be a section on each tort in the final version of the memo."

My uncle and Morty had tried many fraud cases. In the 1980s they were involved in the cases where the Tennessee Supreme Court recognized the torts of constructive fraud and promissory fraud.

My uncle pointed out, "Proving promissory fraud is tougher; you must prove at the time the promise was made there was no intent to satisfy the promise."

I spoke up, "I like constructive fraud better. It will be easier to prove. I'm also concerned about alleging outrageous conduct. It requires malice or ill will, which is a difficult thing to prove."

Morty asked,

"Expert testimony is required to prove intentional infliction of emotional distress. Did Ms. Swann mention that she'd sought psychological therapy? I think you'd need a therapist to establish outrageous conduct."

I corrected him, "That's not true. In Wheatly vs. Towers, the Court of Appeals for the Middle Section held that expert testimony is not required, but she did see both a psychiatrist and a therapist."

He retorted, "That might be technically correct, but from a practical standpoint, to get a jury award, they'll want to hear from an expert, if you want them to award damages."

I wasn't going to argue with him. Morty didn't like being corrected. So, rather than argue I insisted that,

"Our most important cause of action is to allege a conspiracy. Remember, we know there was a cameraman. Right now, his name is James Smith, but we'll eventually figure out who he is. I've really enjoyed reading the conspiracy cases; conspiracy is defined as combination between two or more persons to accomplish by concert an unlawful purpose not in itself unlawful by unlawful means; and the unlawful acts cause injury to a person or property. We've got a good claim that Carmichael and the cameraman entered into a conspiracy. All we need to do is find out who the cameraman is. The defendants' liability will be joint and severable, meaning each will be responsible for the full dollar amount of any judgment."

I waited for a question and neither of them asked one or made a comment, so I continued.

"You asked me to try to boil down for our client the rights and obligations of the Fifth Amendment. This is what I came up with."

I handed them a sheet of paper with the following:

"The United States Constitution protects citizens from being forced to incriminate themselves by requiring them to testify exposing them to criminal prosecution. Witnesses after acknowledging their identity and contact information must assert the privilege or the privilege is waived. In our case, the Fifth is a two-edged sword. Carmichael has drug charges pending and he will be taking the Fifth in that case. Until he either negotiates a plea deal or a jury passes on his guilt, he'll be taking the Fifth in our case. In order to get sworn testimony in our case the criminal case must be resolved. For that reason, our trial date needs to be set after the criminal trial and it is very probable that he could take the Fifth in our civil case. If the making of the videos is held to be a crime by the DA's office, that will only reinforce Carmichael's need to take the Fifth. The amendment specifically provides that no negative inference may be drawn against a criminal defendant for invoking the Fifth. However, if Carmichael takes the Fifth in our civil case, then the judge at the end of the trial will specifically instruct the jury that they can draw a negative inference because Carmichael took the Fifth. This most definitely would reflect badly on Carmichael with the jury."

Morty smiled and complimented the straightforward explanation I prepared. My uncle joined in. I decided it was time to give them the bad news.

"Carmichael's actions don't fit easily in any criminal statute. I'm sure in other states, his conduct was criminal, but Tennessee's pornography and obscenity statutes don't seem to cover this. Neither does the Peeping Tom statute. We'll need to try to work out an agreed order, and we probably won't get any discovery out of Carmichael for a long time. Carmichael will be forced to live with taking the Fifth until the drug charges are resolved."

Morty lit his cigar, which he'd been chewing on during the entire meeting, and said, "What a great job, I'm proud of you. I suggest that we let your uncle take a shot at a first draft of the complaint, and then we'll meet again. When do you think you'll have it done, Ben?"

"Give me a week or so. I've got a lot on my plate."

It was obvious that Morty was excited about this case.

"How about three days? Put your nose to the grindstone."

My uncle made a face, but there was no arguing with Morty Steine. We both had too much respect for him. It was nice to see my uncle struggle with a deadline.

Maybe he'll think twice and be more generous to me as to my deadlines the next time.

With that, we broke for the day. It was after six. We'd spent six hours meeting, and my uncle pointed out we worked through lunch.

CHAPTER SEVEN

DRAFT COMPLAINT

Friday, October 25, 1996

(Same Day)

(THIRD PERSON)

Davis walked in his front door to be greeted by his pugs, Abbott and Costello. He reached down and scratched each of them on the top of their heads and then under their chins, Costello's leg involuntarily moved back and forth rapidly. "Hello, my little monkey boys." The two fawn-colored animals with their smashed in faces and constant wheezing were an important part of the family. He found his wife, Liza, in the kitchen preparing eggplant parmesan, one of Davis' favorites. The aroma filled the room, and Davis enjoyed a deep breath as he squeezed her around her waist and gave her a husbandly kiss. His mind raced about what might happen after dinner and he became aroused.

She turned around, smiled, and questioned, "That's all you got?"

He pressed his lips hard against hers and slipped her the tongue. She enjoyed a good French kiss. Liza was no prude, but didn't share her husband's interest in further romance. Satisfied with the slight amount of passion, she went back to the task of preparing dinner. She buttered and sprinkled garlic powder on the bread and wrapped the French loaf in tin foil in preparation for the oven. As he left the room, he rubbed his hand along her backside gently. Her glance back communicated, without words, as understood between a husband and wife, "We'll see. It depends how I feel later on."

He heard music upstairs and went to investigate. He politely knocked on his daughter's door. Caroline was thirteen and going through a rebellious stage.

"Who is it?"

"Your father, and I come unarmed."

Davis thought he'd try to open up with levity, and it worked.

"You can come in, but be very careful, I've set land mines."

Father and daughter were going through a rough patch. She was asserting her independence; which Davis knew would happen at some point. He just hoped it happened at thirty rather than thirteen. Regardless of when she reached this stage, it was going to be painful for all concerned. Trying to be understanding and patient, Davis was making a concerted effort to reach out and spend as much time as possible with the teenager. He suggested, "After homework, how about a quick game of backgammon?"

Realizing she had her old man where she wanted him, she suggested, "How about a movie? We'll pick one that Jake can watch too."

Davis thought that was a reasonable alternative. Better they include the entire family. Caroline was two and a half years older than her brother, but much more mature. It was Sabbath, so the Davis family gathered together to say the tradition blessings over the candles, wine and bread. Dinner went quickly. The Davises as a family ate fast. Davis loved food. It was more than sustenance. It was a pleasure. It was his legal drug of choice, and it was just as unhealthy for him. At six feet two, he could hide some of the weight, but at forty-two, it was beginning to show. At two fifty, he knew he'd gained weight, always reminded when he wore his good suits because they were tight. They'd been custom made when he weighed two thirty, and now they fit somebody else. He hated exercise and had tried every fad diet without success. He was a Weight Watchers dropout three times. He even tried diet pills and had some success until they were taken off the market for causing irreparable damage to a few patients' heart valves.

They let Jake pick the film, a comedy of course. It was the second *Pink Panther* movie, not the first with David Niven. Peter Sellers kept them laughing for almost two hours. After he kissed his children and sent them to bed, Davis approached Liza, who without saying a word, made it clear that tonight just wasn't his night. He took defeat without a response and decided rather than sulk in bed, he'd go down to his home office. Davis did some of his best work at night at home. It was a place he could get away from the telephone and meetings with clients and really think.

Not enough lawyers take the time to *think. Everybody wants their questions answered immediately. Quick is not always right. A smart lawyer should take the time to consider the facts, and the law before giving advice. Often you need to look up the law and reflect on the circumstances before answering a question.*

He started with a yellow pad, and while he read, he removed a grape Tootsie Pop from his desk. Neither he nor the much older Morty Steine knew how to type or use a computer. All their work was dictated and then transcribed by the ever-faithful Bella. She was the lifeblood of the office, taking care of the other three members. They were a true team, and Davis' role tonight was to prepare a draft complaint. Using a green felt-tip pen, he started an outline.

Davis could identify two of the parties. One was the plaintiff, Elizabeth "Lizzy" Swann. He liked the name Lizzy. That's how he'd refer to his client in the courtroom, its kind of rolled off the tongue, and he hoped the jury would see her as a sympathetic figure. The other known party was the defendant, Roscoe Carmichael III. There was at least one other defendant: the cameraman. For the purposes of the complaint he'd be referred to as "James Smith." Davis realized there could be many other defendants, a second cameraman, individuals who watched the tapes and failed to report their existence to authorities. Davis decided to refer to this yet unknown group of defendants as "James Browns."

The big question is whether to use our client's real name or refer to her by an alias such as "Jane Doe." That will be the client's decision, but despite her decision, there is no guarantee of anonymity. A lawsuit is a public matter, and this lawsuit because of its sex appeal will garner a greater amount of news coverage than the average case. Even if I file the case under seal, courthouse gossip will feed the press. We could file a motion for a gag order, and the judge might order certain documents filed under seal, but eventually the plaintiff's identity will be revealed in open court, if we go to court. So, what's the point? The judge isn't going to bar the public from the courtroom. It's a public place.

Better to be courageous from the start was his position, but he wasn't the plaintiff exposed to humiliation and embarrassment.

The videos would be kept secret till trial, but the fact that Lizzy Swann was videoed would not. Davis wondered whether Steine & Davis could secure some of the other victims as clients. There was strength in numbers. You had more leverage for negotiation, and there was economy of scale from an expense standpoint. That was in all of the clients' best interest.

Davis prepared a skeletal statement of the facts. That portion of the pleading would have to come from Swann. Only she and Carmichael were there on the two nights of their intimate contact, and he wasn't going to talk to Davis. Sammie and Davis would interview Swann and re-interview her several times before finalizing the complaint. This document started the lawsuit, and the defense would try to pick it apart. It was critical that it not contain any mistakes. Many a plaintiff lost their case because of a poorly drafted complaint. It was better to say less than more.

The next section of the complaint was jurisdiction. There was no constitutional issue or federal statute protecting the plaintiff. For that reason, the case could not be filed in federal court, and it was required that it be filed in state court. Swann and Carmichael resided in the state of Tennessee, so which state was clear, but which county? Swann lived in Nashville, Davidson County, one of the more progressive counties in the state. Carmichael lived, and the wrongful conduct occurred, at his townhouse on Music Row in Nashville, Davidson County. The Tennessee legislature by statute directs "that a plaintiff shall file a civil lawsuit where the tort occurred or where the defendant resides." Jurisdiction could not be questioned.

Using Sammie's memo as a guide, Davis applied each of the causes of action listed in his outline to the facts of the Swann case. When the draft was completed, there were three types of invasion of privacy claims: constructive fraud, outrageous conduct, and civil conspiracy. Completing this task took quite a bit longer than Davis anticipated. When he looked up, it was 3:00 a.m. He decided to plow ahead.

The next section was simple to plead, but difficult to quantify, damages. Davis knew he would allege both compensatory damages and punitive damages. The purpose of compensatory damages is to compensate the plaintiff for her loss. In a business transaction, usually that loss is fairly easy to calculate. There may even be a reasonable formula. But the Swann case was different. No question she'd been damaged, but how much? Davis left the dollar amount blank. He'd discuss the dollar amount with Morty and Sammie, and then try to explain the dollar amount to the client. Managing the client's expectations was very important, or you'd have a disappointed client. You must explain to the client that the dollar amount of an award could vary dramatically from jury to jury, depending upon the jury pool and who eventually served on the jury.

Another reason not to demand too much in damages was if you got greedy in the complaint and your demand was too much, then the defense could have a field day with the plaintiff at their deposition or even worse, at trial in front of the jury, "for being about the money". What the hell, money was all that could be recovered at this point. The trick was not to ask for too little and under-value your case.

He next alleged punitive damages. The purpose of punitive damages was to punish a defendant for his intentional, fraudulent, malicious, or reckless conduct. Punitive damages couldn't be awarded for mere negligence. None of the causes of action of the draft Swann complaint alleged negligence. All counts were for intentional or fraudulent conduct, and Davis had to prove his case by clear and convincing evidence, not a preponderance of the evidence. The determination of whether to award punitive damages was up to the jury, who may or may not want to punish a defendant. The amount of punitive damages depended on the financial condition and net worth of a defendant and how he or she conducted themselves at trial. Davis left the dollar amount blank. The amount sued for was a tricky thing. Punitive damages were rarely awarded. Juries generally just wanted to compensate. A jury really had to dislike a defendant to award punitive damages.

Davis was in the home stretch. All he lacked was to dictate the prayers for relief, what the plaintiff wanted the court and jury to do for her. The first two were easy: to have the defendant served by the sheriff's office with a copy of the complaint and to require him to answer the allegations against him. Carmichael's lawyer, whoever that might be, would have to go paragraph by paragraph and respond to each allegation. He or she would probably deny everything in the initial pleading and raise certain defenses. The plaintiff wanted compensatory and punitive damages in unknown amounts at this point. That determination would be made by the team and then approved by the client.

Finally, a motion would be filed to restrict further distribution of those tapes. It would ask for them to be placed under the court's control and limit who had access to them during the proceeding. Davis would eventually have to decide whether to agree to play the tapes at trial. He was reserving judgment until he'd seen them. They might be too much for a jury to digest.

It was 5:00 a.m. Fortunately it was Saturday morning, and Davis slept till 10:30. Liza let him sleep, recognizing how late he came to bed. After he took a steam shower, he felt renewed, ready to polish his complaint and spend the rest of the weekend with his family.

CHAPTER EIGHT

SERIOUS PEOPLE

Friday, October 25, 1996

(Same Day)

(ROSCOE CARMICHAEL'S VOICE)

I could tell I was in trouble the minute I walked into the room. The faces of Tate, Gray, Ms. Browne, and two Covington & Burling Nashville associates said it all, "let's get down to business". They sat there with yellow pads in front of them, ready to record my every word.

Introductions were made to the associates and Tate started right in, "I hope you're ready to do some serious work, Mr. Carmichael. We've got a lot of ground to cover. I'm flying home to DC on the five o'clock. Let's get right to work. Let's start with the juvenile record. We've already prepared a motion to exclude your juvenile record, but we need to know the specifics."

"I don't have any regrets about my high school days. The Bulldogs, that was the name of our football team, we ran the school. We drank a lot and smoked a little pot. That fat bastard Weaver was the sheriff even back then. He began harassing my front line and myself after we got caught having a grain alcohol punch party with three or four girls. He was right, we were up to no good. After that he was on our ass and it was one thing or another. Before I turned eighteen, I had a DUI and two pot arrests. Both dismissed due to Bucky and my granddaddy, Mr. Mike."

Gray commented,

"So that's why Weaver was so adamant in his testimony at the arraignment. We can keep all of that out in your drug case. I want to go over your 1989 arrest. It's sure to come up, and they'll try to use it against you at trial."

I knew Tate was right. The state would raise the issue of my past bad behavior and convictions. I would take the Fifth. That wouldn't matter if my conviction was a matter of public record.

Tate confirmed,

"We've got your rap sheet but it just reports the two convictions. I'm getting copies of the court's order after sentencing. We probably should get a copy of the whole trial transcript. What happened?"

"I was charged with two felonies and two misdemeanors. The most serious charge was statutory rape. It carried a minimum sentence of twelve years. The girl, Maggie Kennedy was sixteen. She looked at least twenty-one. I asked her twice how old she was, once in the bar and once in my office, and twice she told me nineteen. She even had a driver's license that claimed she was nineteen, which the cops confiscated at the time of my arrest. None of that mattered. The law was clear that a sixteen-year-old was incapable of giving consent for either intercourse or any type of sexual contact to an adult male. If I had been a teenager, the same age, my charges and exposure would have been very different. This girl was no virgin. She was experienced, and despite the law, she had consented many times before to various sexual acts before she ever met me."

I paused to take a breath, "The other felony I was charged with was aggravated sexual battery, aggravated because she was a minor. There was no question she was a minor, despite the fact that she lied to me. All the state had to prove was that I touched her in an inappropriate way on any part of her body, and it had a guilty verdict. The two misdemeanors were a real problem because I had no defense. The first was casual exchange, exposing a minor to a small amount of drugs. When I was arrested, I was playing strip poker with the girl, and there was less than a gram of cocaine on the coffee table in front of us. She was in her bra and panties, and I was stark naked. She'd just beat me badly on the last hand. I had three Jacks, and she had a flush. The other misdemeanor charge was contributing to the delinquency of a minor."

I insisted, "I never touched the girl. I intended to screw the shit out of her, but I never got the chance. The TBI came in too soon. If they'd waited fifteen minutes longer, they would have caught me doing the dirty deed, and I'd have been guilty as hell on all counts. They simply jumped the gun, and that was my defense. I had plenty of evil intent, but not enough time. Bucky figured that the jury wasn't going to like me so, we had to simply tell the truth and not try to paint me as anything other than what I am, a horny bastard who wanted to take advantage of a young girl, but I didn't enough time. He argued that the jury had to judge me on the facts of the case, not what I wanted to do. He argued that the TBI screwed up. He also told the story of Maggie Kennedy through the eyes of her father. She was rebellious and had a history of drugs, alcohol abuse and sex. The father shared with the jury his daughter's admissions as to her sexual exploits. That was confirmed by Maggie Kennedy's testimony, which directly contradicted the affidavit she gave to the TBI the night of my arrest.

"That's quite a tale," remarked Tate, "please continue."

"From the beginning, Bucky warned me that I'd be found guilty of both misdemeanors and that I would serve probably a year in prison. He repeated that over and over. He didn't want me to have unreasonable expectations. He predicted my future and through his excellent legal defense, he made it happen. I helped my defense by remaining silent and taking the Fifth. Do you know which of our founding fathers suggested that the Bill of Rights include the Fifth?"

Tate knew, "Thomas Jefferson. He insisted that it was intended to protect both the innocent and guilty. He felt the state should be under a heavy burden to prove a citizen convicted a crime and that citizen shouldn't be required to help."

This guy Tate may be as smart as he claims to be. I hope so, my freedom depends on him.

"The night of my arrest, I said nothing to the TBI. I took the Fifth. I kept repeating it over and over. The only thing I said to the agent was that I wanted to call my lawyer, Bucky Lee. After the TBI read my Miranda rights, they tried to sweat a confession out of me for dealing drugs, even though they'd only found a gram. The drugs weren't the problem, but the girl sure was. They teased me about being found naked, 'with my dick in my hands'. I kept relying on my right not to self-incriminate myself. They said I was going to prison for more than ten years for screwing that little girl. I didn't take the bait. I just yelled back I was taking the Fifth.

"When they realized they were getting nothing, they called in Metro police to make the arrest for the statutory rape. Other sex charges were a state matter, outside the TBI's jurisdiction. Metro police screwed up the investigation. They failed to do a rape test because they thought the TBI had already done one. They didn't get their own statement from the girl, but rather relied on the TBI's secured statement, which was ambiguous. Maggie Kennedy never stated in writing that I penetrated her vagina. That was a critical mistake by the TBI and it was relied upon by Metro. Penetration is a required element of proving statutory rape. The TBI wasn't generally in the business of investigating statutory rape cases so that essential element went missing."

I took a sip of water and then continued, "Bucky got me out on bail. I think it was $100,000. He argued I'd never been arrested as an adult before and had ties to Middle Tennessee. He pointed out that I owned businesses and real estate property and wasn't a flight risk. Upon my release, we got in his car and drove to the home of Lester and Ginny Kennedy of Topeka Kansas. They were the parents of Maggie Kennedy. No charges were brought by the Kennedy's. Bucky was perceptive, Maggie went running home to her parents after the horror of our ordeal. Bucky brought a court reporter with him, who recorded the entire interaction with the Kennedys so there'd be no misunderstanding as to what was said and what transpired. Bucky would later introduce the transcript of our meeting at the trial as part of our case to prove that no pressure was applied to the parents or their daughter to influence their testimony. That's what I liked about Bucky Lee. He was always thinking six steps ahead of the prosecutors. I hope you're as capable as he was. I sure wish he was part of our defense team."

Tate confidently replied, "Let me assure you, Mr. Carmichael, I bring to the table not only my vast experience, but a firm of more than eight hundred lawyers. We're more than a match for anyone. Mr. Lee would have made a good addition to our team, but his services are not critical. Continue with your story."

I wasn't certain that Tate's little speech made me feel confident, but I decided to press forward, "Mr. Kennedy, who owned his own insurance agency, had tried to bring Maggie up properly, but they'd hit some bumps along the way. She used drugs and had already been in two rehabs and was sexually promiscuous. She'd been a singer in a rock band, and Lester shared that he knew, by Maggie's own admission, that she'd slept with every member of the band. For some reason the Kennedys confided to us that they were at their wits' end. They felt like they were losing their daughter to drugs and sex. Mr. Kennedy turned to me and admitted, 'I know my daughter lied to you about her age. I think you're a sleaze ball, but I know you didn't rape my daughter. She was prepared to have sex with you, but the cops just came in before you had time. For that I don't think you should be convicted for rape and go to prison for more than ten years. You need to be punished, but that's too severe.'

"Hearing all that, Bucky took charge. He suggested to Mr. and Mrs. Kennedy that they had an opportunity to gain control over their daughter's life because they now had leverage. Did they want her to go to rehab? Did they want her to finish high school? Did she want to take singing lessons, dancing lessons, and hone her entertainment skills? Did they want her to pursue her dreams and be happy?

"I remember Bucky asked them if those were the things that they wanted, and of course, they said absolutely yes. Then he asked them about the things that they thought their daughter wanted. Did Maggie want a two-year agency contract, a paid-for condo in Nashville and a guaranteed monthly salary? We all agreed that the answers to all of those questions were of course, yes. Well, Bucky proposed that Maggie, the Kennedys, and Epic Talent Agency enter into a contract that required Maggie to go into a thirty-day rehab, submit to biweekly drug tests and then random drug testing and obtain her GED. Upon her completion of those goals, Epic Talent would put Maggie up in a one-bedroom apartment in Nashville and provide singing and dancing lessons for the next two years and a salary of $2,000 a month. At first, I questioned Bucky's judgment and generosity. After a brief off the record conversation I realized the cost of what Bucky was proposing was more than reasonable in contrast to twelve years in prison. Bucky explained to me that the costs of the contract would be a business expense, all tax deductible."

I turned to the 1990 trial, "Mr. Kennedy testified that his daughter used drugs and had sex with many men prior to meeting me. He explained to the jury that his daughter felt intimidated by the TBI and the police and that they coerced her into giving a false statement. He testified that when she got home, she confessed that I never touched her. The state had to put Maggie on the stand, but she was a terrible witness. She contradicted her own statement. Bucky tore her apart on cross-examination. In his closing argument, he insisted that Maggie Kennedy's testimony alone created reasonable doubt as to the two felony charges. There was reasonable doubt as to whether I ever touched her. Bucky's defense was brilliant. He put three of my clients on the stand, and all of them admitted they played strip poker with me that ended in my having sex with them. All of the women testified that I furthered their careers. Their testimony corroborated that my conduct was within the standard of care for the music industry. Everyone knew it and accepted it. I came off looking sleazy, but Bucky argued I wasn't on trial for my past wrongdoings. The question was whether I penetrated or inappropriately touched Maggie Kennedy on that specific night beyond a reasonable doubt. He almost gleefully proclaimed the cops came in too soon. The final crux of Bucky's defense was to put the cops on trial. They failed to get a rape test. They failed to secure a solid statement from the minor girl, without counsel, and most important, it didn't include the word *penetration.* He also roughed up the TBI agents and Metro cops pretty good on the witness stand as to how they treated a sixteen-year-old scared little girl, who by the way, was high on cocaine. One of those agents was Arnold Pyle. It was a four-day trial, and the jury stayed out less than five hours. As Bucky predicted, I was found not guilty on the two felonies and guilty on the two misdemeanors. A month later Judge Howard sentenced me to the maximum imprisonment for my convictions of eleven months twenty-nine days. I served nine months. I got the rest of for good behavior. Prison was no picnic, but I learned a few things, so it wasn't a total waste of time."

When I took a breath Tate spoke, "We've got the same objection against this TBI raid, they failed to properly execute the warrant."

I had been talking for more than two hours and my mouth was dry, so I took a drink of water. Everyone else in the room put down their pens. They'd filled their yellow pads with notes and also needed to rest. They all sat there for a moment relishing the silence.

Tate decided to speak, "Let me assure you that your conviction will be part of the discovery in any civil cases filed and something that will be the subject of several motions. We need to try to keep the details of your arrest, trial, and convictions out of evidence. That will be difficult, but not impossible."

CHAPTER NINE

CONDUCTING THE INVESTIGATION

Monday, November 4, 1996

(THIRD PERSON)

Davis kissed his wife good-bye, got into his silver, twenty-fifth anniversary Vette, drove less than twenty minutes, parked at the Commerce Street Garage, walked up Printer's Alley to the back door of the old Steine's Department Store, and took the elevator to the eighth floor. He almost ran to the coffee machine to get his first cup of Joe. It was too early to make or return calls. Most lawyers got in at 8:00, but Davis was in before 6:30. He looked over his yellow pad to-do list, then at his calendar and tried to plan his day. The handwritten list, a task learned from the old man, was the key to his efficient performance and attentiveness to detail. The list certainly helped, but the real reason nothing slipped between the cracks was Bella Rosario. She'd been with Morty since 1959 and had seen and done it all at least twice.

Davis took out his green felt tip pen and a cherry Tootsie Pop and began his review of the two-page document, starting a new list, reorganizing the old by reprioritizing the items. He rearranged a few of the tasks, moving two items closer to the top of the list. At 8:00 he called Katie Stone, court reporter, "Hello, Katie, how are you, darling?"

"I'm doing fine, Ben. You're calling awfully early. I'm still in bed in my night gown."

Davis couldn't help picturing the pretty thirtyish in bed. His thoughts weren't that pure. *Don't go there,* he told himself. Katie Stone with her short black hair and deep blue eyes was a stark contrast to his blonde wife, and she was at least a dozen years younger. Like most men, Davis allowed himself the luxury of fantasy and rationalization. The court reporter broke into his thoughts, "If this call isn't strictly business, how about I talk a little dirty?"

Shaken back to reality, he kept his flirtations within reasonable limits, "Not quite, but I'm sure that would be a pleasant experience. I'm calling strictly about business. I want to order the transcript and the sentencing hearing of Roscoe Carmichael's 1990 statutory rape trial, Bucky Lee was his attorney. I'm sure you remember the case. Do you think you can find your notes so you could transcribe the trial?"

Stone feigned disappointment. "I should be able to find them, but I'll have to look and see. What do I get if I find them?"

Davis's response was a little curt, "Paid."

"I need a little more than that for my time. I'll be making an extra special effort, and I'll need more than my regular fee for my effort. I'm going to spend a weekend digging through files from six years ago. I don't have an organized filing system in my attic or a legal assistant. What's going on?"

Davis lowered his voice like he was telling a secret,

"I'll be filing a new case against Carmichael, and the transcript will be helpful in my case. I'll be asking Carmichael questions about that trial during the discovery, and if I have the transcript, I'll know if he's being truthful in his answers. The transcript will also help me structure my questions."

Stone paused and didn't say anything for a good thirty seconds. "So, this transcript is pretty important to you? I could be motivated to look really hard for that transcript if I get all the work generated by the new case and one romantic dinner."

"You've got the work and a lunch, but I can't promise any romance. I'm happily married. Do we have a deal?"

"Deal."

Davis abruptly said good-bye and hung up.

That's trouble. Stay away from her. How many doctors did I help out of a jam for forgetting they were married for a flirtation and ten minutes of excitement? I know better than that, or at least I'd like to think so.

Davis made several phone calls that were at the top of his to-do-list. He reported to the president of a manufacturing client that he'd settled an EEOC complaint for age discrimination. A business decision to settle rather than go through the cost of discovery and trial. Davis argued that it was better to settle quickly since the president referenced the man's age at time of his discharge.

The next call was to Charlie Forrest, who represented the seller of an insurance agency. Davis asked to be transferred to Charles Forrest. Davis opened with

"Morning, I've got a counteroffer, $3,450,000."

Davis's radio type voice was so recognizable that he didn't even bother to identify himself. There was silence at the other end, Forrest was a tough negotiator.

"That's not enough, I can sell a deal at $3,750,000, remember I'm down from $4,100,000."

"Let's say we meet in almost the middle, $3,500,000?"

"That's not in the middle!"

Davis snapped back, "That's my final offer. You'd better think about what's best for your client. You don't want to tell him this deal blew up over a couple of $100,000. He's been trying to sell this agency for over a year and he's tired and wants this done. My client is ready at $3,500,000. What else do you have?"

"Deal", and Forrest hung up, knowing Davis was right.

Meanwhile, Katie put everything aside and located the trial transcript and sentencing hearing. Within forty-eight hours of the Davis/Stone phone call the documents were in Sammie's hands with the assignment to read the documents and summarize the transcript for the rest of the team and the client.

CHAPTER TEN

THE DEMAND LETTER

Thursday, November 7,1996

(THIRD PERSON)

Davis arrived at the office precisely at 6:00am and quietly worked on his to-do-list. By 9:00 he was returning calls to clients and adversary counsel. By 10:00 he buzzed Sammie, but got no answer. He buzzed Bella, "Has Sammie come in yet?"

"She called in. She had a class this morning and then she's working from her apartment. Said she wanted to hide from the telephone and clients." Bella didn't say it but implied that she was hiding from Davis. "She's summarizing the Carmichael transcript for the meeting with Ms. Swann at three today. Give her some breathing room. You gave her a short deadline. Let her get the work done in her own way. Don't try to micromanage her. She'll get the job done. Have confidence in her. She deserves your confidence."

As usual Bella's right. I need to let go and trust her, she'll get the job done!

Bella knew what was going on in her office. Her reach was everywhere. Every written communication drafted by either Morty or Davis went through Bella. She knew everything they did and a lot more because she was the heart of the administration of the office, which neither of them substantially participated in. She wrote out all checks, and Davis simply signed them. She maintained the accounts payable journal and the accounts receivables journal. The firm didn't have the required checks and balances that Davis would insist upon of his clients. She also controlled the revenue collection. Some bills were paid within ten days, most within thirty. Hourly clients were expected to pay within thirty days. If they hadn't made a partial payment within sixty, then they got a letter from Davis demanding payment. If no payment was received within ninety days without good explanation, then Steine & Davis would resign or if necessary file a motion to withdraw as counsel.

Morty Steine was a jack-of -all- trades, who over the years did both criminal and civil work, a generalist. Davis, for the most part limited his practice to civil cases.

Although the firm did transactional work, like representing a purchaser of an insurance agency, most cases taken by the firm were on a contingency basis, usually at one-third. The firm's fee was contingent on obtaining either a jury verdict or a settlement. Often these cases took years to be resolved and were subject to the further delay by an automatic one time right of appeal and the possible second appeal to either the state or United States Supreme Court. The firm's longest running case had taken nine years, and several cases had taken four or five years. During many of these lengthy cases the firm advanced tens of thousands of dollars in expenses for experts and depositions on behalf of injured or defrauded clients. These clients were unable to fund their lawsuits. It was Bella's responsibility to keep track of how much the firm advanced in expenses in each case. At times the firm had as much as $1,000,000 advanced on behalf of clients imposing cash flow problems on Steine & Davis. When necessary, Morty loaned the firm the funds to survive those difficult times. Upon recovery, his note would be repaid, and all would be well. He looked at it as an accounting thing, nothing more.

Davis dictated a draft letter to Roscoe Carmichael. Afterwards he reread the draft complaint and then turned his attention to other matters. He called two clients and gave them status reports of their respective cases. Bella had given them an update, but Davis felt the need to give them the personal touch.

The day flew by, and at 2:00 p.m., Sammie strutted into his office and threw a fifteen-page summary of the 1990 Carmichael trial on his desk. "I delivered a copy to Morty, and he says he's coming to the meeting with Lizzy Swann."

Davis finished reading the summary in forty-five minutes. He was a fast reader. As a child, he'd taken an Evelyn Wood speed-reading course, so he moved his two fingers across the pages quickly, getting the gist of the trial. He'd later read it slowly and carefully making detailed notes. When Sammie returned to his office, he said, "Great job. I know you put in a lot of work."

"I've done nothing else the last two days. I've got a few dozen phone calls to return." Her to- do-list was on her computer. Unlike her uncle and Morty, she'd rejected pen and paper.

Prompt as usual, Elizabeth Swann arrived at three, and Bella greeted her with open arms. "Afternoon, Ms. Swann. Can I get you a cup of coffee and a prune or peach Danish?"

"Please call me Lizzy. All my friends do. I'd love a coffee and a peach Danish."

Bella was off to the kitchen. Over her shoulder, she called back, "One cup of black Joe coming up." She brought back two cups, and the two women sat down and got to know each other over a peach and prune Danish. Lizzy had never married, one bad engagement and a few boyfriends.

"I'm so embarrassed for what I've done. Has Mr. Davis filled you in?"

"Darling, I'm the one who typed and retyped the complaint. I do all of Mr. Davis's typing. He wouldn't know how to turn on my computer. He dictates everything."

It sounded arrogant, but sometimes the truth can sound that way. Married to Tony, Bella had two children, Tony Jr. and Angela. Her husband and children ran an Italian market and bakery that sold specialty groceries and made delicious sandwiches during the lunch hour. Bella supplied the office with pastries every morning. Clients had come to expect them if they had a morning appointment and were disappointed if the appointment was in the afternoon.

Sammie interrupted the conversation and escorted Lizzy into the conference room. Morty and Davis were already seated at the table. They stood when the women entered the room.

Morty began, "Ms. Swann..."

She interrupted, "Please call me Lizzy. I'll still call you Mr. Steine out of respect, but can the rest of us be on a first name basis? I've told you the most intimate details of my life. I think at the very least, you should be able to call me Lizzy."

Morty, who hated surprises asked,

"Lizzy, you're about start something that's like an avalanche, it starts quickly and once it starts moving it's hard to stop. So as your lawyers, we don't want to discover any surprises. I need you to tell us all your dirty laundry, anything negative that the other side could dig up."

It took Lizzy fifteen minutes to tell them everything; all of her boyfriends, how her fiancée ditched her and her one experimental relationship. No arrests, one or two parking tickets. At the end of her rendition Morty peppered her with a few questions and was satisfied she was telling the truth."

"I know that was difficult, but it's nothing like how bad your deposition will be. I took it easy on you."

She didn't thank him.

Morty continued, "Well, Lizzy, we've brought you in today to discuss three documents. The first is to review the current draft of the complaint." He handed her the pleading and the summary of the transcript of the 1990 Carmichael rape trial.

"Take the complaint home, put your feet up, and make any notes you want to in the margin. Write down what you don't understand and any questions you might have. This is a working document. We need your input and expect that the final document will be materially different from where we've started. The second document is a summary of Roscoe Carmichael's 1990 criminal trial. Sammie spent two days reading the transcript and creating this summary. She did an incredible job. She cut class to get it done."

Lizzy turned to Sammie, "Thanks for your efforts."

Morty wanted to keep on track, so he broke in, "The last document we've prepared is a letter to Roscoe Carmichael." He slid the document across the table, and she read the document to herself.

November 7, 1996

Certified Return Receipt Requested

Roscoe Carmichael III

Epic Talent Agency

223 16th Avenue South

Nashville, Tennessee 37203

Re: Elizabeth Swann

Please be advised that this office has been retained by Elizabeth "Lizzy" Swann to represent her in connection with your invasion of her privacy, outrageous conduct, and fraud, in conspiracy with an unknown cameraman in making a videotape without her knowledge or permission. Ms. Swann was shocked by your breach of her intimacy when confronted by the Metro police with the videotape of her engaging in sex acts with you.

On behalf of Ms. Swann, I call upon you to identify the name of the cameraman who conspired with you to video Ms. Swann. This party is equally liable for your intentional wrongful conduct.

Please either contact this office or have your legal counsel contact this office by November 14th at noon, or appropriate legal action will be taken.

Please be advised that you should refrain from trying to contact my client. I represent Ms. Swann, and all communications must go through this office.

Yours very truly,

Morty Steine

Lizzy put down the correspondence and said, “That’s quite a demand letter. What do you think he’ll do?”

Morty was the signatory, although written by Davis, out of respect. Davis almost always conceded to his teacher, because of Morty’s stature in the legal community. That was why Morty controlled the meeting and would start off answering the client’s questions.

“He might try to contact you. If he does, assume he’s taping every word you say. It’s best to hang up when he identifies himself. Don’t worry about being rude or extending common courtesy. Call us immediately if he tries. Most probably before the tenth, we’ll hear from his lawyer. What I don’t know is whether he will give up the cameraman. We’ll get the name eventually, if necessary, under threat of contempt. I want you to be prepared for the fact that Carmichael’s disclosure of the tape isn’t limited to he and the cameraman. There could possibly have been an audience of persons who have viewed the tapes. For all we know, Carmichael had sex shows. We just don’t know the extent of the distribution. You also need to be prepared for all of this to be picked up by the media. I want you to think about whether or not to file the suit in your real name or under an alias.”

“What do you recommend?”

Morty was trying not to influence the client, “It’s a personal choice. No one can make that decision but you. I should point out that even if we file the complaint under an alias, there’s no guarantee that the court will agree with your decision of amenity or that despite our efforts we’ll be able to keep the press from finding out your identity. Just guessing, I’d say eventually your identity will come out.”

Despite the Carmichael setback, Lizzy was a strong woman. “Screw it. I’m not going to hide. He did this to me, and I’m entitled to be compensated for what he did. If I file this document, I’m eventually going to have to stand in front of a jury, so I might as well reveal my identity from the start."

Morty smiled and said, "I think that's the right decision. It won't be an easy one, but it's the right one."

The old man turned to Davis and asked his partner to explain to the client a little bit about their trial strategy.

Davis began, "This isn't a negligence case. This is going to be an ugly case. I don't see how to bring it any other way. All counts of our complaint allege intentional torts, and we're even alleging his behavior was outrageous. That allows me to jump up and down and act dramatically in the courtroom, but it sets a bar pretty high up there. We've got to prove that Carmichael knew or should have known he was going to cause you damages, including mental anguish. We're saying Carmichael and his friend, the cameraman, acted with malice and ill will. The distinction between negligence and intentional conduct gets to be important when talking about who's going to pay the damages. The Tennessee Supreme Court requires negligent defendants to share liability. Because our action is for intentional torts, we can collect all our damages against one defendant, and then that defendant can go over other defendants. It's actually in Carmichael's best interest to identify the other defendants. The law provides that each defendant has joint and severable liability. In our case the entire burden can fall on either defendant."

Morty added, "We'll just have to wait and see. I'm working on a game plan."

He pulled out a Cuban and started chewing. Davis and Sammie prayed he wouldn't light it. *I could light it if I wanted to. I own the whole damn building.*

Morty asked, "Do we have your permission to send the letter?"

"Absolutely," Lizzy replied.

He lit the cigar. "You don't mind, do you, Lizzy?"

The client shook her head out of respect.

"It's a bad habit I picked up during the war. Winston Churchill offered me my first one, and I've been smoking them ever since."

She thought he was kidding, but he wasn't.

CHAPTER ELEVEN

NO WAY

Thursday, November 7, 1996

(Same Day)

(THIRD PERSON)

Professor Bucky Lee looked out at his class as he explained the concept of reasonable suspicion, "My definition of reasonable suspicion is when an aggressive police officer announces that he smells liquor on a suspect's breath or when he or she smells the sweet aroma of pot coming from a suspect's car. That determination will satisfy most judges that reasonable suspicion has been established. Some cops have a better sense of smell than others. Some police officers' noses are so sensitive if the suspect is a person of color."

The class laughed. They were almost all white, and about a third were women. Bucky figured more than half of them had smoked a joint before his lecture. After the laughter died down, Bucky noticed Roscoe Carmichael in the back of his classroom. Sheriff's deputy Larry Flood was standing next to him.

Bucky wondered, *what the hell's Carmichael doing here.* After seeing him, he continued to lecture for another fifteen minutes and then dismissed the class.

Bucky truly enjoyed teaching at the Nashville School of Law. It was a night school, so he had his days mostly free. Twice a week, he set aside two hours in his cramped office for his students who might be struggling or just wanted to shoot the breeze. He was always available by cell phone unless he was trout fishing, where cell coverage was spotty. He was much happier with his rod and reel than practicing law. He also loved to play golf. Before teaching, he was limited to Sunday rounds after church. Since his retirement, he played two or three times a week on one of two public courses, McCabe or Harpeth Hills. He still played with his regular Sunday foursome, but during the week, he joined pickup foursomes and enjoyed meeting new people. He also loved poker, but teaching curtailed that. He still stuck his head in once or twice a week for the last two or three hours of those late-night games. He had no one to run home to. He'd never married, and his dog Jasper had died five years earlier. Despite all his other interests, teaching had become his passion.

After the students rushed to their next class, Carmichael worked his way to the front of the classroom.

"Hello Professor, that was very interesting insight into police tactics that you shared with your class. As you know they can rely on reasonable suspicion and wind up with egg on their face. Thanks for the referral to Covington & Burling, those blue bloods are bleeding me pretty good. I guess you've heard the details of my drug bust?"

"The word was you were restricted to your Music Row residence, how the hell are you standing here?"

"I've only got a few minutes. That deputy has reported a malfunction with my ankle bracelet and that bought me thirty minutes of freedom. He did me a favor and removed my ankle bracelet so I could meet with my lawyer. He's charging me three times your hourly rate, and I've only got an hour. I used half of that time getting to and from Music Row."

Bucky wasn't impressed with the effort Carmichael made to see him, "I heard they have the whole transaction on tape."

"We're going to try to keep it out of evidence. The cops screwed up the search just like they did in the rape case. We'll argue they didn't have reasonable suspicion." Carmichael said it in a mocking way.

Bucky took the bait. "The police had a search warrant. They had more than reasonable suspicion and they convinced a judge that they had probable cause. That's a lot higher standard, and they were right. I'm glad I'm not your criminal lawyer, and remember, I teach this stuff. It will be very difficult to keep that evidence out. Who's working with Vincent?"

"I've got a team of lawyers. They've brought in this guy, Richard Tate, from DC. They insist that I also retain a local counsel. How about it?"

"You have a short memory, Roscoe. Have you forgotten about two years ago calling me a lying cheat over a fee I earned? I told you then, and I'll tell you now, get another lawyer. We're through. Besides I recommended Vincent Gray, he's your local counsel. You don't need me."

"Bucky, don't be like that. I need your help. Gray isn't half the lawyer you are, and you know it. I'll pay you $25,000 to sit there and watch my DC lawyer do all the work."

"No way. I don't care how much you offer me. I said we were through professionally, and I meant it."

The deputy announced, "Roscoe, you've got five more minutes. I'll be right outside the door. Make it quick. It sounds like this man's not going to represent you, and I've stuck my neck out for you."

Carmichael lowered his voice and whispered, "I really need your help please, I'll make it $35,000."

Bucky couldn't control his anger, and his voice went up two octaves. "You need my help, so here you are. You've got a lot of nerve. Look, I'm a teacher. I don't have a private practice. You need to find someone else. Gray will do just fine. He'll know the local rules and have some experience before whichever judge is assigned your case."

"What the hell are you so mad about? I called you a liar, big deal. You're a lawyer. That rhymes with liar. Why are you being so sensitive? You did promise me part of that fee."

Carmichael's last comment pushed Bucky over the edge. He almost yelled, "That's bullshit. You brought me a case. I never split fees with non-lawyers. You're entitled to a thank you, maybe a dinner out. If a lawyer brought me a case, I'd give him a five or ten percent finder fee, but you're not a lawyer. Under the Rules of Professional Conduct, ethically I was prohibited from fee splitting with you."

"That's discrimination."

"You know, Roscoe, you're an idiot. Not only did you get arrested on tape for drugs, but the cops found those tapes in your office that I know you've been bragging about in public. Yeah, I heard about your little studio. What type of imbecile are you anyway? After you get off for rape and sexual battery, you keep on playing strip poker and screwing women? Didn't you learn a lesson spending nine months in prison? And you videotaped it. What's wrong with you?"

"What do you mean? I was just following your advice."

"My advice? What the hell are you talking about?"

"You must remember that a few months after I was released, I came to see you about setting up a new corporation, that convenience store on Gallatin Road. We were drinking beer in your office, and I asked you how to hedge my bets with dating women so that I couldn't get accused again. We talked about how some women were fickled and could have second thoughts after we did the dirty deed, particularly if I decided to dump them and didn't call them again after they'd put out."

Bucky vaguely remembered the night. They drank quite a bit as they celebrated Carmichael's purchase of the store. He brought three six packs of beer, and they consumed all of them.

"I specifically asked you how I could protect myself and prove beyond a reasonable doubt that my partner proceeded voluntarily. Your first response was to have the women sign a waiver. We laughed and agreed that wasn't very romantic or likely. Then you suggested that if I recorded the encounter, there'd be a visual record of what happened. I remember you saying, 'A video would be absolute proof of consent and absolute protection. They'd back off once they knew you had the tape.'"

"I said what? I never gave you any such advice. I'd never say anything like that. You're a liar."

"Now, who's calling who a liar?"

Bucky in a fit of rage exploded, "Get the fuck out of here, and don't be putting words in my mouth. I never told you to build a secret room with two-way mirrors and hire a cameraman."

"Maybe I worked out some of the details on my own, but the idea of protecting myself from date rape came from you. You may even have mentioned a two-way mirror and camera."

"That's absolute bullshit and untrue." Bucky put his hand on Carmichael's shoulder.

"That's battery," Carmichael yelled.

Bucky drew his hand back. *Technically, the son of a bitch was right.*

Both men stared at each other with hate in their eyes and hearts.

Bucky thought about clocking Carmichael and weathering the lawsuit. “Get the hell out of my sight, your filthy piece of shit. You leave me alone. I won’t represent you under any circumstances. Don’t repeat that fantasy story about me to anyone. I never gave you that advice. If you repeat it, you’ll have a third lawsuit to contend with.”

Carmichael and Bucky squared off. Bucky at five eight was four inches shorter than Carmichael. The balding middle-aged man wasn’t physically intimidating, but his tone certainly was.

Carmichael, whose blood pressure had risen significantly, retorted, “You’re going to be so sorry for turning me down. I’m not someone you want to cross. This is the second time you’ve done that. You’ll be hearing from my lawyer.” Then he stormed out of the classroom and left with the deputy, who must have heard at least some of the exchange.

It was past ten. Bucky decided he’d seek advice from an old friend. He drove to his old Tuesday night poker game, where his friend and attorney, Jack Barnes, was losing more than he cared to. Bucky walked into the room and was warmly greeted by the half-drunk crowd. He leaned over and whispered in Barnes’ ear, “I need some advice about an issue that’s come up.”

Barnes threw his cards on the table and said, “I’m out and will be out for the next few hands.”

They left the room and walked outside for a smoke. “What can I do for you, my old friend?”

"I've got a problem. I need your advice."

Bucky recounted his conversation with Carmichael and then revealed what he remembered of that night. He also described the breakup of their relationship and provided details of his most recent actions. He explained how they almost came to blows and that technically he did touch Carmichael without permission.

Barnes tried to calm his old friend, "Don't worry about that bluster. It's his word against yours. He has no marks on his body and no damages. I'm more concerned that he's trying to establish a defense in the lawsuit filed by a woman who might file a civil suit. He knows one is coming. He doesn't really need you to help in the defense of the drug charges. He can find able local counsel for his criminal charges. He was feeling you out to see if you'd help him in those yet-to-be-filed civil suits. That's why he came to see you. He'd made a decision that you're either going to be on his team or be his scapegoat."

"What should I do?"

Barnes thought a few seconds, "The only thing you can do is wait and see. You've created not only an ethical problem but a legal one as well. I'll take a dollar retainer, and I'll keep this conversation privileged. You might want to bone up on the attorney/client privilege. You can benefit from the research and also teach a class on the subject."

CHAPTER TWELVE

UNWELCOMED PUBLICITY

Friday, November 22, 1996

(BENJAMIN DAVIS'S VOICE)

By the time Sammie showed up at the office, it was past three. We passed each other in the doorway of the kitchen. I had a black cup of coffee and the last of a dozen crullers Bella bought to the office from Rosario Market, lovingly created by Tony Jr. Sammie gave me a dirty look and I smiled right back.

I wasn't going to have my food intake monitored at the office. I got enough of that at home. Besides, I didn't want such a delicious work of art to go to waste.

Avoiding the issue, I asked, "where have you been?" My tone was inquisitive, not at all reprimanding.

"I went to class this morning and then worked on my senior paper. You forget I'm a student and I have to pass."

"You'd better pass. You'd better finish in the top half of your class if you expect to be an associate at Steine & Davis. We don't allow just any riff-raff to practice with this firm.

She was about to answer when Bella buzzed in, "We've got a problem out here. I need you in reception."

I asked, "which one of us?"

"Both of you, now!"

Bella's voice sounded shaky, which I couldn't remember ever hearing. She always had matters under control.

I led the way down the hallway to reception with Sammie on my heels. What we found not only surprised me, it left me speechless, which didn't happen often.

Bella stood toe to toe with Alice Krieger of Channel 5 News. The investigative reporter with the local station had brought a cameraman with her. Krieger couldn't have been much more than five feet. Her red hair laid on her shoulders and bright green eyes were unforgettable.

She had spunk, and I hated spunk in a reporter. It meant she was a pain in my ass. I knew the Swann case would garner publicity, so I should have been better prepared. The press couldn't invade the courtroom because under Tennessee law, cameras weren't allowed in the courtroom, but there was no restriction on my office, except to scream trespass. I don't know why I didn't expect the press to barge into my office like this.

"Mr. Davis, is Elizabeth Swann the same Elizabeth Swann who lives at 2354 Grady Place?"

I certainly wasn't going to confirm my client's address. The only biographical information in the complaint was that Lizzy was a resident of Davidson County.

The camera's red light was on, which meant the camera was rolling. I had to say something, or I'd appear as stupid as I felt.

"Ms. Krieger, can we go off the record first? This is a place of business, and you showed up without an appointment."

"Mr. Davis, I'm not a client. I don't need an appointment. I'm here to report the news and to interview you about the lawsuit that you filed. Better yet, I'd like to interview your client, Elizabeth Swann."

"My client will not be giving any interviews to the press. She'd appreciate your respecting her privacy. The complaint filed with the court spells out in detail our position. I suggest you quote from the document. Will you please turn off your camera? That's the second time I've asked you nicely to do so."

"Mr. Davis, your client filed a public document accusing Roscoe Carmichael of hideous deeds. Her accusations are newsworthy. Your client threw her allegations out there. The public is entitled to know more, and I can't simply quote from a document. This for television not for print. You can appreciate I need images."

"Look Ms. Krieger you have her allegations clearly stated in the complaint. The document speaks for itself. I have nothing further to say, other than what's stated in our pleadings. She's been injured by the wrongful conduct of the named defendant and at least another defendant, the cameraman, who's yet to be identified."

"The public deserves more information."

"Please turn off the camera."

"What's the next step in the lawsuit?"

"The suit is just beginning. There's a process that must be followed. The defendant will file an answer, which must respond to our specific allegations. He'll also need to identify his co-conspirator."

"How do you know there was a cameraman?"

"It's apparent from the video."

"So, you've viewed the video?"

Stop talking. Get her to turn off that damn camera.

"Look, Ms. Krieger, please turn off your camera. I've not agreed to conduct an interview. There will be a time and place for that to happen, but this is not it. I don't mean to be rude, but you and your viewers at this point will have to be satisfied with the allegations of the complaint."

"The public has a right to know, Mr. Davis. Ms. Swann has brought this matter to light, and your firm filed the complaint on her behalf. That's news."

"I'm not going to answer any more questions. This is private property, and you've been nicely asked to leave. The complaint is your story. For now, you've got to accept that fact."

Krieger was persistent. She made no move to leave. Her cameraman kept filming, and I was coming off as an uncooperative jerk. I wasn't handling the situation well, but I didn't want to comment on the complaint. Finally, I turned and started walking back to my private office. Amazingly, Krieger and her cameraman followed me down the hallway. I closed and locked the door behind me.

This is ridiculous. I look like I'm running away.

I heard her yelling questions as I turned the lock. I picked up the phone and asked information for the number of Channel 5 News.

"Channel 5 News, can I help you?"

"This is Ben Davis. I need to speak to your station manager right away, please."

"What does this relate to?"

"I'm a lawyer, and if you don't put your station manager on this phone in the next two minutes, I'm filing a lawsuit against your station. Alice Krieger and your cameramen, who refuse to leave my office. Now, I'm done talking to you. Get your damn station manager on the phone."

Two minutes later, the assistant station manager was enduring my wrath.

"Look, this lawsuit is about stealing my client's image. You can review the tape. I asked Ms. Krieger politely several times to turn off her camera. Despite my insistence that I was unwilling to be interviewed, Ms. Krieger kept peppering me with questions. I reminded her she was on private property, and she continued to invade my space. I sue people for a living. I know how to file a lawsuit. If you don't get her out of my office and allow me to confiscate the tape, you, Alice Krieger, her cameraman, and your station will find out exactly how good I am at my job. I also want an assurance from you that Ms. Krieger will not harass my client, Ms. Swann."

I remained silent, allowing the assistant station manager to digest my rant and the possible consequences.

The next words from him were exactly what I wanted to hear. "I'll call her on her cell phone, get her to back off, and leave the tape with you."

"Thank you. She needs to be put on a leash. I admire determination, but she's going to get your station in big trouble."

I intentionally put a nail in her coffin. She'd gotten under my skin. A few minutes later I could hear her arguing with her assistant station manager on the other side of the door. She got louder and louder as she realized that she'd lost the argument and would have to relinquish the tape. Her last words as she left the office were "You're an asshole."

I emerged from behind my office door and peeked down the hallway. I strode into reception and saw the tape on Bella's desk. Sammie and Bella stood there gaping.

Sammie asked, "What the hell just happened?"

"I made an enemy for life."

Sammie agreed and then asked, "Why didn't you give her a limited interview rather than make an enemy?"

"Anything I said would be used against us by the defendants. Our lawsuit alleges that our client has been damaged by the publication of the video. Any publicity that we extend to the case is further publication and arguably further damages our client. We can't be seen as compounding our damages. We made a big mistake filing the lawsuit under our client's real name. We should have used an alias and admitted that the plaintiff's identity was being hidden to protect her from further publicity. Both of us should learn from that mistake. Either Morty or I should have caught that one. We thought using her own name was the brave thing to do and the right thing to do, but, it was a mistake. If we used an alias we could have delayed the impact of publicity for Lizzy."

I went back to my office and called Lizzy to warn her about Alice Krieger and my hope that her employer had restrained her, "don't engage her. Simply call me, and I'll take care of her."

I generally tried not to make enemies. Most adversary lawyers and I were able to shake hands at the end of a case and do battle again down the road. Most business defendants whom I sued understood that it was just business and that I was just doing my job, representing my client. Sometimes my performance impressed the other side so much that the next time they needed legal representation they hired Steine & Davis as their counsel. That wasn't likely to happen in the Carmichael case. It had gotten very personal, and emotions were running high, even mine. I wondered how I could have handled Krieger better than I did. I'd have to ask Morty. He might have a suggestion. I always tried to learn from my mistakes.

I decided to call it a day and go home. I walked to the Commerce Street garage, put my top down, grabbed a grape Tootsie Pop, and drove home.

CHAPTER THIRTEEN

A FRESH START

Monday and Tuesday, November 25th & 26th, 1996

(AMY PIERCE'S VOICE)

I looked up from the brief I was writing, and the clock on the wall of my small office indicated it was 5:15 p.m. I needed to pick up my son, Carter, at afterschool care. School policy imposed a $50 fine for every ten minutes you were late after 6:00 p.m., and I no longer had the luxury of my guaranteed salary and bonus as a partner in a prominent law firm. I was now flying solo, renting a ten-by ten-office with access to a conference room and receptionist as part of an association of lawyers, some of whom were struggling to get by.

I didn't have anything to complain about. I wasn't starving because I kept my expenses down. I had work. It wasn't glamorous, mostly divorce or other types of domestic relations issues and some criminal stuff. I no longer represented doctors, lawyers, or successful businesspeople, the high society of Nashville. That work disappeared after my three-month suspension dished out by the Board of Professional Responsibility courtesy of my friends at Steine & Davis.

I fought those bastards for three years in those Plainview cases, tried one of those medical malpractice lawsuits before a jury, lost, settled the remaining cases, and then leaked the settlements to the IRS, who placed a lien on the proceeds. The Board found my leaking a breach of the confidentiality clause of the settlement agreement and suspended my law license for three months. My employer didn't understand, and I was fired from the law firm, leaving me the only alternative: hang out my own shingle.

I'd been on my own about eighteen months, and I missed the challenge of complex litigation. I knew I'd eventually have the right case walk through the door and grant me redemption. I desperately wanted to regain my status in the Bar. I was tough and confident in my ability. What I didn't know was that opportunity would come knocking at 5:15 p.m. and cost me $50 every ten minutes I was late. I needed to talk quickly.

The phone rang, and I picked up. The caller said, "Ms. Pierce, Vincent Gray. We've never met. I'm with Covington & Burling. Do you have a moment?"

I hesitated then told him, "I'm so sorry, Mr. Gray. My secretary just left for the day, and I have a client about to walk into my office. I was going to put the phone on my voice mail recording when you called. I can only give you a minute or two."

"I'll be quick then. My firm represents Roscoe Carmichael in a civil suit, and the other to be named defendant is Phillip Oz, a good friend of my client. Mr. Oz hasn't been sued yet but he will be."

Gray gave a five-minute summary of the videotaping and the the raid. Then he got to the point,

"Mr. Oz hasn't hired counsel yet, and we were hoping he'd hire someone we could work with under a joint defense agreement. Your name came up as a possible co-counsel. At Mr. Oz's request I'm making this call. We're hoping you'll join the team. We have some interesting theories and defenses that might even provide both defendants with insurance coverage if we work together."

Gray then set the hook.

"Steine & Davis are on the other side. Are you interested?"

"Sounds interesting. Look, I really have this client waiting. Have Mr. Oz call my office and make an appointment."

"Do you have any availability tomorrow?"

I didn't want to seem too anxious, but what the hell. "How about 2:00?"

"He'll see you then."

The phone call cost me fifty bucks. I hoped it was worth it.

Carter and I ate at Wendy's, his choice. We watched a little television, and then before he fell asleep, I read him two chapters of *The Hobbit*. I was getting better at altering my voice from character to character.

Once alone in my bedroom, I replayed my conversation with Vincent Gray in my head. Covington & Burling wasn't calling about some insignificant matter. That firm practiced big-time law. I'd have to wait until 2:00 p.m. tomorrow to find out more when I met with my prospective client, Mr. Oz.

I was wrong, I didn't have to wait until the next afternoon. When I walked into my office, spilled all over the floor were twenty or so attached fax pages sent from Vincent Gray. As I read the complaint filed in Circuit Court, Elizabeth Swann vs. Roscoe Carmichael, I appreciated the role of my client Phillip Oz. When I got to the end, I realized why Vincent Gray called me. The two attorneys who'd filed the complaint were my old nemeses, Morty Steine and Benjamin Davis.

That was the reason why Gray chose me to represent Oz, Gray

knew that I'd take this case and I'd fight harder than most, because of my deep resentment for Ben Davis. I'm sure my reputation as a tough and dirty fighter also played a part in my selection.

I reread the complaint. It was quite a story, and I could be a part of it. I was ready to sign on.

Mr. Oz was right on time. He was tall, six feet five, bald, and soft spoken for a man his size. I explained that Mr. Gray had faxed me the lawsuit, and I asked him to provide background information. I was surprised to learn that he and Carmichael had been childhood friends in Ashland City, and he was very proud that their high school football team for two years were state champions. He ran the pharmacy on the town square, which he'd inherited from his father. As I evaluated his appearance, I wondered, what the hell was he doing behind the camera in a secret room with a two-way mirror videotaping his best friend having sex with women? The question needed to be asked, but I had to work up to it.

"Mr. Oz, may I call you Phillip?"

"Sure, if you're going to represent me, then you're going to get to know a lot about me, right?"

"Absolutely. Everything you say to me is confidential."

"Attorney/client privilege, right?"

"That's right, so I need complete honesty. Do we understand each other?"

"Yes."

"I mean the nature of this case requires me to make inquiries different from ones I might with a client in a car wreck case."

"I understand."

We discussed the complaint in general. He admitted that he was involved in the construction of the secret room and that he was the cameraman. Oz was pretty open about what he'd done. He explained that Carmichael assured him that his lawyer, Bucky Lee, advised Carmichael, who'd been charged with statutory rape, would be protected from date rape by videotaping. He claimed that the women knew they were being videotaped despite the fact he was behind a two-way mirror.

"There was a camera in plain view. All of the women knew that Roscoe was taping them having sex. I remember Elizabeth Swann. She danced around the room and did a routine on a pole for the camera. She talks about it in her complaint."

We discussed the complaint in more detail. I pressed Oz on several points, and he answered right away and didn't seem to be withholding information. I decided it was time to get personal, "You're married?"

"Married twenty-four years, no children. My wife, Susan, couldn't have kids."

"Do you and your wife have a normal husband/wife relationship?"

"I love Susan, but she's lost interest in that sort of thing. I wouldn't cheat on her with another woman, so I needed to find another outlet. I tried pornography, but it didn't feel right and quite frankly, didn't do it for me. I confided to Roscoe, and he suggested that I film him. It's hard to explain, but watching Roscoe with those women satisfies my sexual urges. I get to live my sex life through him and he lets me."

I felt compelled to ask, "Did you masturbate while you filmed?"

It was the first question that he hesitated to answer, "I watched them afterward and did."

"Alone?"

"Sometimes, and other times with Roscoe."

"Were you and Mr. Carmichael ever romantically involved?"

"Absolutely not."

I handed Phillip Oz my standard contract. It provided that my hourly rate was $300 and requested a $15,000 retainer. I was a member of the defense team. I called Vincent Gray, who congratulated me and advised that he'd be sending over the joint defense agreement for my review.

CHAPTER FOURTEEN

INSURED OR NOT TO BE

Friday, December 27, 1996

(THIRD PERSON)

Sammie brought the mail into Davis's office, and remarked, "You got a pretty good-sized envelope from Covington & Burling. I'm sure it includes Carmichael's answer, but there's obviously a lot more."

Tate's document dump was clearly timed to have an impact on the Davis team's upcoming holiday weekend. The documents contained several surprises intended to screw with the heads of the Davis team. It was a cruel attempt to ruin Davis' family time. Instead, Tate interfered with the working weekend because the team felt compelled to at least read his fillings.

Davis examined the package and without opening it, he commented to Sammie, "I've got to give Tate credit. His timing is perfect. He knows we've got the long weekend ahead of us, and he gave us just enough time to read his pleadings and fret about them all weekend. What a bastard."

Tate was responding to the discovery early, trying to impress the Davis team. Such psychological games wouldn't work. Using his letter opener, Davis slit the top of the package and dumped the contents on his desk. He picked up the document on top. It was the answer to the complaint, but it wasn't solely an answer. It included a counterclaim against Elizabeth Swann as well.

That son of a bitch has sued my client. Tate's employing the strategy of a good defense is a strong offense. That's stupid, suing the victim!

The second document was a declaratory judgment action (a lawsuit that asked a judge to answer a legal question) against Carmichael's insurance company (his homeowner's insurance) demanding that it provide a defense in the Swann lawsuit.

The next three documents were almost identical. They were third-party complaints, lawsuits against others. The first was against Arnold Pyle, Karl Moore, Evan Tuke and Carlos Ramos; the TBI agents involved in the search of the Music Row office. It also named Officer Michael Sanchez, who pushed the play button at the police station of the VCR when the tapes were first viewed; Detective Robert Sanders, Detective Keith Rogers, and Chief Gerry Neenan of the Metro police department. The second complaint was against District Attorney Johnson Tory and three of his assistant DAs who viewed the tapes confiscated from Carmichael's office. Tate was taking no chances of leaving anyone out. The third and last complaint was against any unknown Metro police officers, Davidson County assistant DA, or any third party who may have viewed the tapes after they were wrongfully confiscated or who might view them in the future.

The last document was a motion for a protective order to delay the defendant Carmichael from answering all written discovery and from giving a deposition until the adjudication of the criminal case pending against Carmichael.

As Davis flipped through the documents, he came upon a lawsuit against Phillip Oz, who ran the local pharmacy in Ashland City. The Oz pharmacy was three doors down from Carmichael's family jewelry store on the town square. The pleading named Oz as the cameraman and stated that he videoed the seven women with their knowledge. The tone of the documents was very matter of fact, according to Carmichael the decision to videotape was upon the advice of counsel. Carmichael identified Bucky Lee as the attorney giving that advice. Davis didn't believe Lee would have given such advice. From Davis's standpoint, Oz was part of the conspiracy to defraud the victims because the complaint admitted that Oz was involved in the construction of the secret room and the installation of the two-way mirror.

At the time Davis opened the package, he was unaware of the long-standing relationship between Carmichael and Oz. All he knew was that the police had sweated the identity of Oz out of Carmichael.

Davis stopped mid-sentence, and he looked upset. "You won't believe this," he handed Sammie one of the documents.

She stared at it hard and asked, "Why so upset? We know who the cameraman is. We can amend our complaint and name Oz as a defendant. We'll only need to substitute his name for the man behind the two-way glass."

Davis directed her to the person who accepted service for Oz. She dropped the pleading on the desk. "Holy shit, Amy Pierce is the counsel for Phillip Oz."

Davis bitterly remarked, "I hate that bitch."

Davis had dealt with Pierce in the Plainview cases, and neither Davis, nor his niece could stand her. At the end of the Plainview cases, not only could Davis declare victory, but Pierce's license was suspended for three months for disclosing the settlement terms of the cases to the IRS, which put a lien on the settlement proceeds because of back taxes owed by Davis's co-counsel.

Davis went back to the first document and looked at Carmichael's answer. When he came to the end, the affirmative defenses, he was shocked by the assertion, "In late 1994, the defendant sought the legal advice of his attorney, Bucky Lee Esq., as to how to avoid claims by female companions that his sexual relations were not consensual. Lee suggested that Carmichael tape these sexual encounters to document the voluntary nature. Lee advised that such a recording would preserve his safety and make sure sometime before penetration that he was proceeding with a willing sex partner."

Davis turned to Sammie, "Make five copies of these documents. Give one to Bella to put in the file and distribute a set to Morty, you, and me. The fifth is for the client. See if you can get her in here today, as soon as possible. We need to explain these lawsuits to her and why we didn't sue Bucky Lee and discuss whether we should reconsider that decision."

At four o'clock. Lizzy Swann walked into the office. Smartly dressed in a blue business suit, she greeted Bella. They'd become friends. Bella was like that, immediately forming an almost motherly bond with clients. In most cases the clients of Steine & Davis became their friends. They provided a very personal service. People, for their own good, were forced to tell the team the truth, no matter how awful that truth may be. As Sammie took her back to the conference room, she said, "Lizzy, we've got a lot to talk about, so I won't waste time."

Davis handed her Carmichael's answer and counterclaim. "He's not only answered your allegations. He's countersued you."

"For what?" Lizzy actually yelled out loud.

"Let's just read through it together." Davis got to paragraph seven, the first response in the statement of the facts section, which read in part, "Defendant alleges that at all times material hereto, the plaintiff knew or should have known of the videotaping during sexual encounters. Defendant states that the plaintiff may not have known the identity of the person who was behind the two-way mirror, however, the two-way mirror was designed to provide privacy for the persons engaged in the sex acts as well as the cameraman. The plaintiff knew this privacy aspect of the two-way mirror."

In a response to a later paragraph, the defendant alleged that the plaintiff consented to being videotaped and that the plaintiff actually watched several videos of the defendant and other women. The defendant claimed that these viewings aroused the plaintiff, and immediately following such viewing, they had sex.

"He's sued you because you agreed to make the tape, and you have now sued him, causing him damages. He claims you're abusing process or the legal system. That's outrageous. The man is desperate, and I think he's getting bad legal advice from his lawyers. His aggression only adds to our claim that he's acted outrageously and is continuing to act outrageously, causing further damage. I'll argue to the jury they should increase their award because of such subsequent conduct."

Davis directed that the affirmative defenses were Carmichael's excuses for his conduct and that the third-party complaints were Carmichael's attempt to shift blame and collect damages from Bucky Lee to the third-party complaint against Bucky Lee, the TBI and the police. Carmichael was claiming that all these other defendants caused the tapes to become known and published.

"The TBI was on a drug raid and found the tapes. They had a lawful right to be there and discover the tapes. The police had to look at the tapes to see what was on them. As it turned out, the tapes were made unlawfully and in violation of your right to privacy. These lawsuits, except the one against Phillip Oz, need to be severed from ours, and these affirmative defenses need to be struck."

Perplexed, Lizzy asked, "I don't exactly know what that means, but I trust you. I've got no choice. At some point, you're going to see me dancing around a room naked."

Davis replied candidly, "Lizzy, everyone in this office is going to watch you having sex with Carmichael. If we can't settle, a jury and a courtroom full of people are going to see the same thing. The judge isn't going to bar the public from the trial, and there won't be an empty seat in the house. You'd better get used to others seeing that tape."

Morty added, "We hope it won't come to that. This case is more likely to settle than most."

"Why is that?" asked the client.

"This case is not certain as to liability than it is as to how much we can prove of damages. No one can tell you what this case is worth. The answer to that question probably varies from jury to jury. Once the jury is picked, I'd have a much better feel, but not an absolute certainty as to dollar amount. I'm worried about what a reasonable Nashville jury would consider an appropriate amount to compensate you. It's a difficult question. The second question that must be answered is whether the jury will award punitive damages. That depends on how Carmichael acts during his testimony. He's going to take the Fifth Amendment if his criminal charges are pending unless we work out a non-objectionable scope of that testimony."

That was the beauty of Steine & Davis, as trial lawyers, they looked ahead seven or eight moves, like chess masters, about how an action would look or impact at trial.

Davis turned to Lizzy, "This is the last lawsuit. It's against Carmichael's insurance company. It's filed in our case, which is the wrong court. Tate just did that as an annoyance. It will be moved to another court. It doesn't attach the policy as required by the rules.

Gray should have told Tate of that requirement. This misfiling is a cheap manipulation to slow down our case. Without the policy, it's hard to comment on the merits of the lawsuit, but intentional torts as a matter of public policy shouldn't be covered by insurance. It encourages people to commit intentional torts. I'll be objecting to this lawsuit on many grounds, and that will be one of them. It may take us as long as six weeks to clear this up, so they succeeded in their delay. This isn't right, and our judge will tell these guys so."

"I'll make notes in the margin." With that said, Lizzie was out the door. When she was gone, Morty commented, "That was very impressive. That many pleadings would usually confuse most clients. She handled it well. I think she'll make a good witness."

Davis, always the realist, said, "I'll let you know after I review those tapes."

That last comment made Sammie pretty angry at her uncle, *what a typical male thing to say*. She decided to quit for the day. It was almost six, and she needed a drink. She said her good-byes and was out the back door onto the alley and marched directly into Boots Randolph's, a bar she frequented. She knew the bartenders, "Hi, Larry, double shot of Jack and a light draft."

"Bad day?"

"Not bad, just complicated." Sammie, like her uncle, didn't like the fact that they'd pulled Amy Pierce as Oz's attorney. She was tough and sneaky. You couldn't trust her, and that made litigating the suit much more difficult. Tate was an unknown, but the team had already agreed they had bad vibes about him. Pierce was a known commodity, and what they knew wasn't good. Sammie downed her shot glass and took a slug of her beer mug. "I'll take another double, Larry, please."

Larry complied.

Sammie realized that the appearance of Pierce and her strong personality meant that Gray would play a lesser role in the defense. Tate would quickly realize that between the two, Pierce was the far more effective advocate and would hitch his wagon to her. Despite the suit between them, as is often the case, the defendants unite against their common enemy, the plaintiff.

Pierce and Tate will be working hand in hand. Just you wait, when Pierce starts playing games, the one who's going to have to deal with her will be me. Not the great Morty Steine or Benjamin Abraham Davis, but me.

While deep in thought, Sammie was interrupted. "Can I buy you another round?"

She looked up and saw a man in his late thirties, dressed in a business suit. He sat next to her without her noticing.

Sammie began to size him up. *Tall, good-looking, well dressed, well spoken. What's the harm of a few drinks and where they might lead?*

They had two drinks and then walked across the alley to Sammie's loft. He didn't spend the night. He wasn't a very good lover. Sammie already had a date for New Year's, so at 2:15 a.m., she ushered him to the elevator and out the back door into Printer's Alley.

CHAPTER FIFTEEN
BAD NEWS
Friday, December 27, 1996

(Same day)

(THIRD PERSON)

Professor Lee was teaching his last Criminal Procedure class of the year, exam day, when a Davidson County sheriff appeared in the doorway and said in a serious tone, "Bucky Lee, I have a summons to serve you."

That got everyone's attention. Everyone's eyes came off their tests as Bucky accepted service by signing, and the deputy quickly exited the classroom. Bucky was convinced that Carmichael's lawyer had slipped the deputy an extra fifty bucks to serve him during class to heighten his embarrassment. As the class finished the test, Bucky read the allegations of Carmichael against him. The more he read, the madder he got.

What a crock of shit!

Bucky considered what to do next. This was a public document available to anyone, including his students, as long as they were willing to go down to the Davidson County Circuit Court Clerk's office. He knew that several of his students would do just that after the holiday.

Who am I kidding? This will be on the news and in the paper tomorrow morning. I might as well come clean.

It would be better to deal with this now than after his class had read the lies alleged in the document. On the other hand, his lawyer, whoever he or she might be, wouldn't want him making public statements. Arguably, he could make his students material witnesses if he spoke up.

Bucky told his students, "As lawyers, you will be drafting civil complaints and hopefully not getting served with them."

The class nervously giggled.

"Other times, you might accept service on behalf of your clients rather than have them be embarrassed by getting served in front of co-workers, family, or this class. This is not one of those occasions. Unfortunately, I'm a named defendant in this lawsuit. As a lawyer, you should try to avoid that from happening. I guess I failed miserably."

Again, laughter.

"This document was served here to try to maximize the impact on me. It's an effective technique. I've used it on occasion. This is a public document. Rather than force you all to scramble and go downtown to the courthouse to read about your professor, I'll make a copy available after class for your review. I haven't retained counsel yet, so I can't say anything more. If I did, those statements would be admissible and all of you could be made material witnesses. There's no point in subjecting you to that. After I retain counsel and file an answer, I'll make that responsive document available to you so you can appreciate my position. I hope you did well on your exam. See you next year. Class dismissed."

As promised, Bucky went to the administration office, made a copy of the document, and posted it on the classroom door. Almost every student remained after class to read the complaint and see what trouble their professor was in. Bucky watched as they swarmed around the document. He couldn't take it. He couldn't let his class go on holiday break thinking the worst of him. He marched through the crowd, yanked the document off the door, pushed the door open, and invited his class back in.

Despite the fact that Barnes or any other lawyer would have advised him to stop there, Bucky pressed on, "those of you who want to stay, let's go through this document. It will give you a real-life insight into a lawsuit."

Only three students left, thirty- one remained.

"I'm being sued for allegedly advising a former client to use a two-way mirror to establish that his sexual encounters with women were voluntary. He alleges, based on my advice that he build a secret room at his office, and he asserts that I advised him that by taping these sex acts, he would be protecting himself from a charge of date rape. He alleges that my advice was unethical, tortious, and possibly criminal. It's all a lie. I never had any discussion with the client about that subject, and I never advised him to secretly videotape unsuspecting women to protect himself."

Bucky paused to let the substance of the lawsuit sink in. "Let's call it quits for tonight. For those of you who must know the details of the suit, the initial lawsuit is styled Swann vs. Carmichael, and this document is entitled Carmichael vs. Lee, docket #96-1243. Again, I'll see you all next year." Because they'd been held late, the students left quicker than usual.

Bucky sat down and tried to organize his thoughts. He knew his first phone call should be to Jack Barnes to determine if his old friend had any insight into Carmichael's actions. Bucky picked up his cell phone, "hello, Jack, I've been sued by that son of a bitch."

"Which son of a bitch?"

"Don't play games with me, Jack, I'm not in the mood."

"I already knew, bad news travels fast. There was quite a scene at Ben Davis's office."

Barnes described the scene as he heard it secondhand from Morty. "Sorry you're being dragged into this. You need to call your malpractice insurance carrier in the morning. Does the claim allege negligence or intentional acts?"

"I'd say both. The charges against me aren't what I'd say 'run of the mill'. It will get even more complicated as Carmichael's criminal case proceeds, or when I'm put under oath. I dread having to testify."

"For what? You did the right thing. I'd have done the same. This story he's spinning is a desperate attempt to explain away his wrongful conduct. He got caught, and he's trying to make you the fall guy. Didn't he turn you over to the Board of Professional Responsibility, something about a fee dispute?"

"Yeah, about two years ago. About a year after he got out of prison, he brought me a new client on a real estate deal. He complained to the Board that I didn't give him part of the fee. I never promised anything. We had a heated argument, and when I wouldn't budge and pay him part of the fee, he filed charges against me. The Board investigated and dismissed the charges. It was a real pain in the ass. I'd practiced law for more than twenty-five years and never had a complaint before the Board. I told him I'd never represent him again."

"Yet he tried to hire you when he got busted."

"Well, he did that out of ignorance. If he knew the truth, he'd spit in my face."

"What are you talking about?"

"I'm the one who told the DA that Carmichael had been videotaping himself having sex with women."

There was a dead silence on the line. Bucky's revelation took Barnes by surprise, and Bucky was waiting for his lawyer's reaction. Finally, after a long pause, Barnes spoke up, "Why would you do that?"

"I've got to take you back about six months ago. I was eating dinner at Sperry's, and Carmichael showed up drunk. I tried to ignore him, but he came over and sat down uninvited at my table. I was sitting alone and wanted to keep it that way but he forced himself on me. He wanted to talk about our fee dispute. I wouldn't take the bait. I told him to 'go to the bar and order another drink.' He was already pretty drunk. Jokingly I said, 'Maybe you'll pick up a woman,' but I snidely added 'Make sure she's over eighteen.' That really pissed him off. What he said next shocked me. He claimed, 'Don't worry about me. I've got plenty of videos of naked women, and I can watch them whenever I want. I took your advice and videoed myself with every single one of them. If I still liked you, I'd give you a private showing, but you're not invited to the Oscars.'"

Barnes thought a moment, "When was this meeting at Sperry's, and when did you go to the DA?"

"It was about June. I waited more than two months before I went to DA Johnson Tory. I kept playing what Carmichael said over and over in my mind. I debated about what was the right thing to do. Was he just bragging, or was he telling me the truth? Was he videotaping women having sex with him, and if so, did they know what he was doing? I wondered whether he'd been violating these women's trust by acting surreptitiously. I also thought about my obligation to him as a former client. The information wasn't given to me in a confidential manner or in connection with legal work I did for him. I considered all aspects of the attorney/client privilege and weighed that against what I thought he was doing to these women."

Barnes had a quick comeback, "Yeah, but you waited months. Bucky, they'll use that against you. If it was right to report him to the cops, it should have been done much sooner."

"I was struggling with my conscience. It took that long to reach a decision."

"Well, it's going to be uncovered in your deposition, maybe even in response to written discovery. It's intentional conduct, which isn't going to be covered by your carrier. If he brings disciplinary charges against you, they won't be covered by insurance either. There's no question when you went to the cops, you were acting intentionally. Let's stop speculating. I say we see what your carrier says. You must be completely honest and disclose the fact you went to the DA even though that allegation isn't included in the complaint. At the same time, you must be firm and demand coverage."

"I'm going to proceed as if I have coverage. I have coverage for negligent acts. The pleading right now alleges only negligence, that I gave negligent advice. That never happened." Bucky knew that Barnes was not only his friend but a solid lawyer.

Barnes hesitated and then offered, "I'd be willing to represent you. To accommodate both you and your carrier I'll even charge half my usual hourly rate. I think I should be on the call with you and the carrier. Better yet, we should set up a meeting instead. I think you're better off telling its representative in person. If they insist on a lawyer in their rotation, then I'd recommend John Dulles Henry. He's a fighter, and he'll believe in you. Those are the two most important requirements for good counsel."

CHAPTER SIXTEEN

DEMAND A DEFENSE

Thursday, January 2, 1997

(THIRD PERSON)

After the New Year, Bucky decided there was no point in putting off the call to his carrier. Whether or not his malpractice insurance carrier would provide a defense and coverage would impact his financial security and semi-retirement. He took a deep breath and called his contact person at Equity Insurance Company, one of its corporate counsel, Mindy Hart. She'd helped him when Carmichael filed his disciplinary charges against him less than two years earlier.

As a member of the Tennessee Bar Association, Bucky had purchased his malpractice insurance from Equity through the association. It was the preferred carrier of the association, and many members of the Nashville Bar used Equity because of its discounted rate. Bucky maintained $2,000,000 of coverage, which included the cost of defense. Because Bucky had only the one claim in almost thirty years his annual premium was only $3,600, lower because of the economy of scale of being part of a larger group.

"Hello, Mindy, it's Bucky Lee. How've you been? Happy New Year."

"Hey, Bucky! Happy New Year too, what can I do for you?"

Bucky swallowed and then sheepishly said, “I’ve been sued, and the plaintiff is our old friend Roscoe Carmichael.”

Bucky waited for a response.

“What’s his complaint this time? Is it fee related?”

“No, I wouldn’t represent that SOB. It’s complicated. Let me fax you a copy of the complaint, and then I’d like to meet with you. Do you have any time this afternoon?”

“I could see you at the end of the day. Could you be here at four?”

“That would be great.”

“Aren’t you teaching? How come you’re getting sued?”

“I bought a three-year tail policy covering me for three years from my last day of practice.”

“I’m curious. Why the need for the meeting?”

Bucky really didn’t want to give the specifics over the phone. “The complaint doesn’t tell the whole story. I’d rather explain the unstated in person. I’ll see you at four.”

Bucky hung up and immediately called Barnes to confirm his availability at four. He hadn’t mentioned to Hart that he intended on bringing Barnes to their meeting. He didn’t want to go to the meeting alone. He needed not only moral support. He needed good, solid legal representation.

At four, Barnes and Bucky were sitting in the reception area of Equity Insurance Company, nervously waiting for Mindy Hart. She joined them and took them to a small conference room with a circular table and five tall blue leather chairs. Bucky had spoken to Hart at least half a dozen times previously in connection with Carmichael’s earlier claims, but the two had never met. She was much younger than Bucky envisioned, mid-thirties with short black hair and gray eyes. She wore glasses and dressed very professionally. She was licensed to practice law, but went to work for Equity directly after graduation from law school. She'd been with the company almost ten years.

Bucky opened the discussion, "It's a pleasure to finally meet you. This is Jack Barnes. He's a friend and an attorney. I called him first when I got served with Carmichael's lawsuit..."

Hart interrupted, "Does Mr. Barnes represent you?'

"That depends on you and Equity. I'm here to request coverage, and if possible, I'd like Mr. Barnes to be appointed as my counsel. He's an experienced trial lawyer and I trust his counsel."

Hart commented, "No offense, but Mr. Barnes isn't on our rotation, I'm sure he's more than competent, but we have our own pool of legal talent. I've read the complaint. It's a third-party action. Do you have a copy of the original lawsuit filed against Carmichael that prompted him to sue you?"

Bucky came prepared. He gave Hart a copy of the Swann lawsuit.

"Give me a minute. Why don't you gentlemen help yourself to a soft drink or coffee over there on the credenza."

Bucky and Barnes picked up Diet Cokes, and sat back down as Hart read the sixteen-page Swann lawsuit. It took her more than twenty-five minutes, and Bucky became more impatient by the minute. He should have anticipated providing Hart with a copy of the Swann complaint prior to the meeting. She read slowly, or at least Bucky thought she did.

Hart put the document down, took off her glasses, and rubbed her eyes. She didn't look happy. "This is a unique case. I see a lot of lawsuits come across my desk, but this is my first invasion of privacy case. The plaintiff, Ms. Swann, is about to have a life-changing experience. Her lawsuit puts her life under a microscope. You didn't advise Carmichael to build a secret room and use a two-way mirror, did you?"

"Absolutely not. That's total bull. I know it's my word against his, but who would give such inappropriate advice? If those were the only allegations that I had to defend, I'd be happy with whoever Equity assigned to my defense. About six months ago, I was at Sperry's eating alone, and Carmichael came up to my table and sat down." Bucky recounted the conversation with his former client and his months long self-debate as to the veracity of Carmichael's claims of videotaping young women. Bucky got very emotional as he explained to the insurance representative that he truly balanced competing interests and finally decided that protection of innocent victims and the future victims was more important than a former client who was acting maliciously and badly. So, he disclosed what he'd been told to the DA, nothing more.

Hart's demeanor completely changed. She got aggressive, "Why would you do that? He was a former client, and you knew that as a result of your breach of confidentiality, he'd be arrested and criminally prosecuted."

Barnes answered the question, "Ms. Hart, I think you're missing some very important points. The TBI and Davidson County police were already planning on raiding Carmichael's office and home before Bucky went to the DA. They would have found the tapes anyway. Unfortunately, Bucky didn't know that. Second, you said it yourself, Carmichael was a former client, and the information that Bucky disclosed to the DA wasn't given with the intent of confidentiality. It was blurted out in a restaurant. If you've ever been to Sperry's, you know that one table is right on top of the other. Most important, Bucky as a lawyer had certain obligations to those poor women who were videotaped without their consent and future victims. After Bucky came to me, I sat down and reread the Professional Code of Conduct. Right at the beginning, in the Preamble, in the first paragraph it states, 'that a lawyer must conduct himself ethically, with integrity, dedicated to justice and the public good.' It goes on to say, 'that sometimes a lawyer's responsibility to his client may conflict with that of his or her responsibilities to the legal system and the lawyer's own interest of remaining ethical in his conduct. Such issues create a conflict, and the lawyer must resolve these issues through the sensitive exercise of professional and moral judgment guided by the basic principles of the Rules of Conduct.'"

The tone of Barnes's response was just as aggressive as Hart's. He softened and said," Bucky struggled for months with this problem. The rules are self-governing. In retrospect, he probably should have called either me or another lawyer for guidance because the code makes it clear that he's held to a standard of care of a reasonable attorney. Accordingly, the opinion of a competent ethical attorney would have been helpful. I'll tell you what, if he called me for my opinion, after reading the code cover to cover, I would have told him that under the circumstances and based on his obligations as an officer of the court, with responsibility to protect the public and to further justice that despite whatever obligations he had to a former client, he had to go to the police or DA. Rule 1.8 allows an attorney to reveal a confidential communication to prevent a client or for that matter, a former client, from committing a serious crime that would cause substantial injury or financial loss. It goes back to his general obligation to protect the general public."

Hart was not buying any of Barnes's argument, "What crime was committed?"

Barnes didn't have an answer for that one. Before the meeting, as Bucky had, he tried to fit Carmichael's conduct into the existing criminal statutes, but it didn't work.

Hart taunted Barnes, "Cat got your tongue? He perpetrated a tort. A wrong against another citizen. She might have a valid cause of action against him, but Mr. Lee had no right to interfere."

Barnes was ready with a retort, "That's simply not true. Rule 1.8 allows a lawyer to reveal a confidential communication to prevent a fraud that will cause substantial injury and/or financial loss."

Again, Hart was playing devil's advocate, "The fraud had already been committed. He wasn't preventing anything."

"What about other women and future wrongful conduct? Bucky was protecting future unsuspecting females from having their lives turned upside down. Come on, Mindy. You're a woman. Put yourself in the place of a woman who thinks she's having consensual sex and finds out the person she's been intimate with has made a fool of her."

Hart did just that and made an executive decision, "All right, he's got a defense for now."

She liked Bucky, and it was a close call subject to her discretion. A supervisor would eventually review the case and her decision probably in six months, and she'd defend her decision then.

"The complaint at this point in time only alleges negligence. There is no allegation of intentional wrongdoing. However, this complaint will eventually be amended, probably when Bucky testifies under oath and his intentional conduct is discovered. I'll allow the company to defend with a reservation. I'm making no guarantee that the defense will continue after the complaint is amended. I will reevaluate my decision in ninety days. Let me assure you when your disclosure to the DA is revealed, Carmichael will bring disciplinary charges against you. We will not defend that action. Bucky, you went to the DA knowingly. You said it yourself, you thought about it for months. I agree it was a close call, but I don't know that you made the right decision."

Barnes, by his silence conceded that point.

"Mr. Barnes, do you want the job of defending your friend and colleague?"

"Absolutely."

"I think that's in our insured's best interest because if we drop the defense, Bucky won't have to start over with a new lawyer at that point. We pay $175 per hour. Is that acceptable?"

"My usual hourly rate is $300, but I'm willing to accept your company's proposed fee."

The two men walked out of Hart's office, not completely satisfied, but satisfied enough that they thought they'd gotten the most they could get under the circumstances.

CHAPTER SEVENTEEN

INSUFFICENT INFORMATION

Friday, January 31, 1997

(THIRD PERSON)

As promised, Steine & Davis filed a motion to dismiss Carmichael's claim against his homeowner's carrier, American Insurance Company, and motions to sever all of Carmichael's claims asserted against the law enforcement personnel and the district attorney's office. Davis also asked the court to sever the claims against Bucky Lee. Davis argued that each action brought in by Carmichael was separate and should be tried by different juries. Davis refused to accept Carmichael's alleged fantasy story that he acted based upon "advice of counsel." The team worked through the first month of the year. Davis wasn't going to let Covington & Burling push their little firm around. The defense pleadings did delay the pursuit of the Swann case.

Before recommending to their client to sever Carmichael's claims against Bucky, the Davis team sat around a table and debated the pros and cons of either making Bucky a defendant or a witness against Carmichael in their case. In the end it was easier to call

Carmichael a liar and present Bucky as a credible witness. Bucky was articulate, far more believable than Carmichael. It helped that he was telling the truth and that the team recognized Carmichael for what he was, a desperate liar.

Davis also filed a motion to amend the complaint to name Phillip Oz as "James Smith". Davis wanted the only defendants in the case to be Carmichael and Oz. He emphasized to the court that any cross claim by Carmichael and Oz was between the two of them. They could sue each other all they wanted. He argued that intentional tortfeasors were each liable for the full amount of damages. How his client's damages were apportioned was a separate fight between them. Once a judgment was awarded, his client could collect from either of them or both. It was the victorious plaintiff's choice. There was no comparative fault when addressing liability for intentional torts, unlike a negligence claim where the jury was required to apportion the damages among the defendants, like dividing a pie.

The defendant's motion for a protective order to delay discovery was denied. Judge Howard picked up the phone and called General Tory and inquired if the DA had any intent to charge Roscoe Carmichael with a crime for videotaping any of the women.

Tory's response was,

"I can't fit his actions under any existing statutes. It should be a crime, but it's not. The legislature needs to pass a law, but Carmichael isn't going to be prosecuted."

In his order, Howard warned the plaintiff, "discovery needs to relate to my second search warrant and the videotaping of the women; the scope of discovery shall not include any reference to the other two warrant and the drug arrest of the defendant."

This was the long-awaited day of the receipt of the defendant's discovery responses. Davis had twice agreed to extensions beyond the deadlines provided in the rules. He'd refused a third request and told defense counsel he'd seek legal fees if the responses weren't received by the close of business today. Normally, Davis wouldn't be so harsh, but Tate and Gray had tried his patience. Morty had taught him as a young lawyer that at the beginning of a lawsuit, and in general when dealing with other lawyers, to extend common courtesy. It was the best policy until an adversary counsel gave you reason to conduct yourself otherwise.

I suspect by the end of the Swann case, courtesy will be thrown out the window.

Davis didn't know what time to expect the answers, so the three agreed that Davis would stay late. They would all go up to Sammie's loft, and she would cook dinner.

Davis argued, "You can't even boil water. What are you going to make?"

"I can so boil water. We're having spaghetti."

"Make five copies of the responses, put one in the mail to the client, and distribute the others. I'll see you at six."

Sammie didn't resent being asked to make the copies. She was low man on the totem pole. Bella, who ran the office and did all of Morty and Davis's typing, was much too busy to make copies. Her uncle would make copies before asking Bella to do so. Morty didn't know how to operate the copy machine. His gift was his mind and his ability to speak. He wasn't a Renaissance man, but that only made him that much more special.

Davis spent the rest of the day trying to address problems and returning telephone calls. He even had to make efforts to collect a fee. Bella had sent three letters and the $34,000 fee was 120 days past due.

"Billy, I sent you three letters and not even a partial payment..."

William Diamond interrupted,

"I need more time business is bad."

"That doesn't explain your ignoring my letters and remaining silent. I'm going to make this easy and non-negotiable, I want $10,000 on my desk by tomorrow at 2:00 p.m., another $10,000 a week later and the final $10,000 the next week. That's a $4,000 discount if you follow my payment plan. You miss a payment by a minute and I sue you for the entire balance and attorney fees of one-third. Do we have an agreement?"

"I guess I'll have to live with that."

"If you want this firm to continue to represent you, you'll have to live with it."

Davis knew Morty would have handled the call differently, that's why Bella assigned the task to Davis, because it was his steps that saved Williams' business. Davis was intimately familiar with his company's financials. The company because of Davis's actions avoided a judgment that really could have put it into bankruptcy.

Sammie delivered Davis's copy of the responses at five, so he had only an hour to review them. He put his hand in his desk drawer and pulled out a grape Tootsie Pop, put his feet on his desk, and dug in. Carmichael identified Phillip Oz as the only cameraman. That was good; Davis didn't want to add another cameraman as a defendant. He denied showing the videotapes to any third party other than Oz and some of the women. There was a debate as to whether or not any of the viewing women should be named. Quickly it was agreed that it was better to consider the women victims and witnesses. Davis wondered if the two men masturbated when they watched them together. The thought disgusted him. He suspected that Carmichael used the tapes to excite himself as he watched them with his sex partners.

He chewed on the Tootsie Pop stick, as was his practice, and continued to read. Carmichael identified four of the seven women including Elizabeth Swann. When asked, "Please identify the name, address, and telephone number of each and every unsuspecting female who engaged in sexual relations with the defendant and was videotaped," the answer was very disappointing.

"The defendant did not video any 'unsuspecting females.' The defendant does not have any videos of him engaged in sexual acts with women. The defendant has not viewed the videos taken by the police in some time. His best recollection of the identity of the women includes Elizabeth Swann, Carol Strong, Dominique Watson, and Sydney Ingram. The defendant has insufficient information to identify the other three women who engaged in consensual sex and knew they were being videoed. If the defendant is afforded an opportunity to view his personal property, he may be able to further identify his consensual partners."

The plaintiff had asked about the defendant's assets and requested any financial statements be prepared and provided to anyone. There was a long narrative at the beginning of the responses signed by Tate, which spelled out a long list of objections to the discovery. The pronouncement stated that these remarks were specifically made to preserve the defendant's rights on appeal. "As to the production of his financial records, the defendant objected on the grounds of relevancy and that "this information was more properly produced in a post-judgment proceeding after a jury verdict. The plaintiff is trying to short-circuit the justice system. The defendant moves for a protective order preventing the plaintiff from seeking such confidential and proprietary information." A motion for a protective order accompanied the responses.

CHAPTER EIGHTEEN

A BAD MEAL

Friday, January 31, 1997

(Same Day)

(THIRD PERSON)

At six, the group assembled on the ninth floor. Morty opened the discussion, "We need to find these women identified in the response. We need to first determine who should make contact, our client, Ben, or Sammie. I think I'd prefer having a woman open up the conversations with them. There was no consensus on the solution."

Sammie asked, "What about the other three yet unidentified women in the videos? Do you think the judge will allow him to play dumb?"

Davis answered, "No way. He had sex with them, and he says they consented to being videoed. You just don't forget the first and last names of somebody like that, maybe he doesn't have their address or telephone number. He's failed to identify half of the women. I think the judge will order him to review the videos to see if that review refreshes his recollection. He'll deny knowing their identity, and we'll be able to cross-examine him on his lack of recollection. It won't play well with a jury, but if he was to identify them, they are potential plaintiffs and definitely witnesses against him. What concerns me more is why he identified the ones that he did. My guess is that he silently settled with them and bought their testimony. I suspect that Strong, Watson, and Ingram are going to testify that they knew they were being videoed and that they watched some of the others screwing Carmichael. The testimony won't be truthful. It will be bought and paid for."

Sammie couldn't believe her uncle was right. She wasn't tainted and didn't think the worse of people. Davis had formed an opinion of Carmichael and what he was capable of, and Morty agreed with him, "He's had months to get to them. It's a cheap solution to a lawsuit that not only solves a problem but also buys supportive testimony. Why don't Ben and I contact these women? It may be too tricky for either you or Lizzy."

Davis agreed. He thought that was the best approach all along.

Morty continued, "He states in his answer that he doesn't know the current addresses and telephone numbers for these women. That's a lie. We should be able to find them on our own. If necessary, we can hire a PI to help us find them. If both you and Bella run into a brick wall, we'll spend the money to get the job done."

Dinner was terrible, as expected. The spaghetti was undercooked, and the sauce was thin and runny. Davis remarked, "You sure didn't inherit your Nana Shelly's ability to cook."

Morty was smart enough to keep his mouth shut.

Davis continued, "How are you going to get a husband by cooking like this?"

Sammie struck a sexy pose, "Don't worry about me. Men care about other things than cooking, and in that department, I more than satisfy."

Sammie was a beautiful woman. When she dressed up, she was always the most attractive woman in the room. Not only were her looks impressive, she was smart too. She breezed through the University of Florida and paralegal school without breaking a sweat. As a party girl, she had been with many men and was sent to live and work with her uncle Ben by her grandparents, Davis's parents, Larry and Shelly Davis. They were concerned about their granddaughter's partying and hoped to get her on the straight and narrow.

When she got to Nashville, she changed. She was a dedicated employee, capable, and hardworking. Morty noticed her efforts and offered to send her to Vanderbilt Law School, where she was about to graduate in June. She still had her urges, which she scratched every so often on her terms.

"I'm going home. I'm not going to argue about your power over men. I've witnessed it many times. It still wouldn't hurt you to learn how to cook. Think of it as a bonus. You can seduce them and then feed them. Just don't videotape yourself having sex with them."

"Bad joke, but that's good legal advice," she retorted. With that, Davis and Morty were out the door. Morty to the sixth floor and Davis to his home, which bordered Hillwood Country Club.

When he arrived home, the ever-faithful Abbott and Costello greeted him. "Hello, boys, where is everyone?"

He heard the TV on in the den and followed the two pugs. Seated on the couch were his two children, Caroline, age twelve, going on thirty, and Jake, who just turned ten. He bent down and kissed them and asked. "Where is your mother?"

Jake answered, "She's upstairs. She had a big fight with Caroline."

"Shut up, you little worm!"

Davis got mad quickly. The dramatic change from loving father to litigator occurred in a matter of seconds. His voice was controlled but firm. Some might say menacing. "I don't know who you think you are, young lady, but I don't want you talking to your brother like that. He's a part of this family, and I won't have you disrespecting him like that. I don't know what happened with your mother, but I'm going to get to the bottom of it. I suspect she was waiting for me to get home to deal with you. It sounds like you're in big trouble. I suggest you not dig yourself into a deeper hole. Your brother may be the only friend you have left in the house including the dogs, who will always side with your mother."

Caroline tried to explain the argument, but Davis cut her off. "I'm going upstairs and getting your mother's perspective first. I'll hear you out afterward."

He went quietly up the stairs, not knowing what to expect. His wife was in bed, a Cape Cod on the end table, only one-fourth full. "I heard you had a rough day. If it makes you feel any better, my day sucked too."

She responded, "All you had to deal with were adversary lawyers and clients. I had your daughter to contend with. Well, your daughter has a new demand for her list."

"I thought we agreed she could have a cell phone for emergency purposes?" That was code for they'd agreed under pressure to get her a cell phone because they were tired of listening to her complain and beg for one.

"What does she want now?" asked Davis.

"She wants her ears pierced and some cheap earrings."

Davis knew what the problem was right away, Nana Shelly. His mother, whose ears weren't pierced, wouldn't like the idea of her granddaughter desecrating her body. To quote her, "Pierced ears were for gypsies."

Liza took a sip of her drink and offered it to her husband. He gulped it down, finishing it, ice and all.

"She claims she's the only one in her class who doesn't have pierced ears, except the nerds. I know how your mother feels, so I said no. When I did, she threw a temper tantrum like a six-year-old. It got pretty heated, so I escaped to the bedroom."

Davis asked the right question, "Putting aside her disrespecting you, do you care?"

"If I were twelve years old, I'd want my ears pierced too."

"Let me handle it. I'll be the bad guy."

Davis went downstairs and asked Jake to leave the room.

"Can't I stay for the fireworks?"

"Go to your room or another room in the house. This is none of your business. I want to have a private talk with your sister."

Once Jake was out of earshot, Davis began, "First thing that's going to happen is you're going to apologize to your mother. You're twelve years old, soon to be thirteen. You're past throwing temper tantrums. For your information, your mother doesn't really care if you get your ears pierced. It's your grandmother who thinks it's wrong. If you can convince Nana Shelly, then you can have it done. But you can't disrespect your mother and act like a child. That's not the way to get what you want. We use persuasion. Haven't you figured out that using the right words can get you what you want? You're going to have to sit down and think about what you need to say to your Nana Shelly to persuade her to allow you to pierce your ears. If she agrees, or you can live with your Nana's heartbreak, then you can go ahead and get your ears pierced. I warn you she's going to be very much against it."

"Do you know why?"

"It has to do with the fact that you can't be buried in a Jewish cemetery if you have a tattoo or piercing."

"Is that true?"

"Yes."

"I'll give her a call, and we'll talk about it. I still get my cell phone, right?"

"Absolutely."

Davis returned to his bedroom to find Abbott and Costello sprawled across the bed.

"Do you think your friends could be made to move so we could have a personal conversation?"

"Is there some reason you can't tell me whatever it is from there?"

"I need to whisper it in your ear."

Liza nudged the dogs off the bed, and Davis jumped on. He spooned his wife and began kissing her on her neck. They'd been married more than fifteen years, and they knew how to arouse each other. Both satisfied, they fell asleep in each other's arms, putting their problems behind them, and didn't wake up until the next morning at six o'clock.

CHAPTER NINETEEN

A CRITICAL COURTROOM APPEARANCE

Friday, February 14, 1997

(BENJAMIN DAVIS' VOICE)

Bella located the three women identified in Carmichael's response to interrogatories, who he claimed knew they were being videoed. It wasn't hard to find them. Carmichael provided their addresses and telephone numbers in his response. They all lived in Nashville and were cordial and pleasant on the phone. Steine & Davis hired ex-boxer turned private eye, George Hopper to find the other three yet unidentified women.

Morty and I visited the women at their homes, figuring they'd be more comfortable there than at our office. The women were nervous, but that was to be expected because of the personal subject matter of the interview. We hoped these women would corroborate Elizabeth Swann's testimony, but in the back of our minds was my prophetic prediction to Sammie that they'd been "bought and paid for." As each woman was questioned, the lawyers became more and more disappointed. Although their stories varied slightly, the similarities seemed almost rehearsed. Each confirmed that she had consented to being videoed, and each acknowledged that she watched videos of other women having sex with Carmichael to arouse him. When shown Lizzy Swann's photo, all three women, Strong, Watson, and Ingram, denied they'd seen videos of Swann. That denial was detrimental to the case because its limited publication to Carmichael and Oz. The failure of the women to identify Swann was explained by Strong, who admitted, "I wasn't looking at their faces. Within minutes of the tape rolling, Carmichael was on top of me, directing me, making our own movie."

"Did you know that Phillip Oz was behind the mirror?"

"I knew there was a cameraman behind the mirror. Sometimes Roscoe would yell instructions to him. I didn't know his name, but I definitely knew he was there."

The whole exercise was a bust. The women supported Carmichael's story. Not perfectly, but that's what made it perfect. When presenting your case to the jury, you want consistency but not perfection because that usually meant collusion.

After meeting the three witnesses, I insisted that Carmichael had gotten to them, "They'd cut a deal for their silence. Hopper's got to find those other yet unidentified three women. I bet Carmichael, if he knows where they are, has at least approached them and didn't get what he wanted. I hope they spat in his face."

Despite our failure, Steine & Davis managed to get a quick hearing date in front of Judge Howard. The pending motions to be heard were a motion to dismiss the lawsuit against American Insurance Company because it had been filed in the wrong court. A motion to sever the lawsuits against law enforcement personnel, the district attorney' s office, and Bucky Lee because they were separate actions and should be adjudicated by separate juries. I also filed a motion to amend that added Phillip Oz as a defendant in light of his identification as the cameraman.

Tate filed a motion, and it was a remarkable one. When I read it, my reaction was, "Holy shit!" Tate moved for Howard to recuse himself as the judge and have the Supreme Court appoint a replacement.

That takes guts! If you lose, which is likely, you have to appear in front of that judge for the duration of the case. Risky move. He's creating a substantial issue on appeal by jeopardizing his relationship with the judge at the beginning of the proceeding. It's a jury trial. The judge doesn't determine liability or damages, so Tate decided the risk outweighed the risk. Has Gray agreed with this strategy?

Howard set all of the motions at the end of his Friday motions docket. He made me, Tate, Gray, Pierce, Barnes, and the rest of the lawyers wait more than three hours until he finished every other matter. He'd hoped the courtroom would empty, but he was wrong, instead the crowd grew. The lawyers who finished their business stayed, courthouse regulars showed up, and uninvited interested parties swelled the courtroom to capacity. The press, without cameras, was there in full force. Under Tennessee law, cameras weren't permitted in the courtroom. Alice Krieger was there minus her cameraman.

As his clerk announced Swann vs. Carmichael, Judge Howard looked out at the lawyers and said, "I see some unfamiliar faces at counsel tables. Maybe it would be best if we start with introductions. I'm Judge Barry Howard. This is the Third Circuit Court, and for those of you who don't know me, I'm in charge. Mr. Steine and Mr. Davis, I know who you are. You represent the plaintiff. Mr. Gray, and Mr. Tate represent the defendant Carmichael. Mr. Barnes, who do you represent?"

"I represent the third-party defendant, Bucky Lee Esq."

"Ms. Pierce, who do you represent?"

"I represent the proposed defendant, Phillip Oz."

"Ms. Alper, who do you represent?"

"I represent Chief Neenan, the DA and the other Metro officers and assistant district attorneys sued."

"That leaves two gentlemen who I don't know."

"If you're Honor please, I'm US attorney Larry Wells. I represent the TBI agents named as third-party defendants."

The last lawyer stood and announced, "If Your Honor please, I'm John Whitefield. I represent American Insurance Company. I'm licensed to practice in Tennessee, but I've not yet been admitted to your court. I'm from Memphis."

"Welcome to the Third Circuit, Mr. Whitefield. Well, the gang's all here. Our court reporter is Ms. Katie Stone, and she's taking down every word we say. Let me start with Mr. Tate and Mr. Gray, since you congested my docket with your pleadings. Mr. Gray, as local counsel, I don't appreciate the little game you're playing. You know the Rules of Civil Procedure and how we do things in my court. As Mr. Tate's local counsel, your most important job is to guide him as to how we do things in my court, which may be done differently in Washington DC. We don't stand for sharp practices here and wasting judicial resources. Mr. Tate, didn't I make myself clear at our last hearing that the Chancery Court had jurisdiction for the lawsuit against Mr. Carmichael's insurance company?"

"I took that as a suggestion, Your Honor, not a directive. The principal place of business of American is Little Rock, Arkansas, so I have diversity of citizenship. I could also file in federal court."

"That may be true, but you didn't file in federal court. You filed that action in my court, clogging my docket with a lawsuit for which my court did not have jurisdiction. Explain to me why you filed the insurance case in my court."

"I thought it would accomplish judicial economy to have all the issues decided by one judge and jury. All of these claims are related to the original complaint filed by Ms. Swann."

"You presumed wrong. The plaintiff's motion to dismiss Mr. Carmichael's claim against American Insurance Company is granted, and the lawsuit against American Insurance Company is dismissed without prejudice. Mr. Whitefield, you are excused. Mr. Tate, refile your lawsuit in either federal court or the Chancery Court of Davidson County. The next time you file a frivolous pleading in my court I'll hold you in contempt, and Mr. Gray, your fine will be twice that of Mr. Tate's."

Tate asked, "With respect, shouldn't you address our motion to recuse first before ruling on anything of the motions? If you're removed from the case, your successor should rule on the pending matters."

Annoyed, Howard replied, "That's where I was going next, Mr. Tate. I'm going to rule on the motion to recuse and the motions to sever at the same time. I've read the briefs of the parties. It seems that only the defendant Carmichael objects to my handling this matter, the plaintiff filed a detailed response, and the other parties simply stated they had no objection to my hearing their case. The two reasons given by the defendant Carmichael for my recusal are, first that I sat as judge on his criminal trial in 1990. The second reason is that I was the judge who issued the search warrant where drugs were found, and a second search warrant that confiscated the videos. Am I correct, Mr. Tate?"

Tate rose, "The defendant thinks those reasons are enough.

The 1990 trial was a sex crime. This case is about sex. We'd ask that you recuse yourself. There is a third reason as stated in the brief. You're friendly with the chief of police, the DA, the others in the district attorney's office, and Bucky Lee. You deal with all them on a professional level on a regular basis, but your relationship is more than just professional. You respect and like them. They are more than mere associates. They're your friends. Can you deny that those third-party defendants are your friends?"

Howard paused and then answered, "I said I was taking the two motions together, the motion to recuse and the motion to sever. I'm going to grant your motion to recuse in part and deny it in part. First, I'm going to sever the three third-party actions, the first against Chief of Police Neenan and the other police officers, the second against the TBI officers, and the third against District Attorney Tory and the district attorney's office. I'm going to recuse myself from those actions because of my past association with the DA's office and the law enforcement officials. I'm not going to transfer these matters to another Davidson County judge. Most likely, he or she would have the same conflict that I have because they would also have regular contact with these public servants. Instead I'm going to ask the state Supreme Court to appoint a special judge from another part of the state to preside. I'm also going to sever the third-party complaint brought against Bucky Lee, an attorney, who for years practiced before this court and others in this county and is known and liked. I'm also going to have the Supreme Court appoint a different special judge in that case, who will have no familiarity with Mr. Lee. So, who's left? The plaintiff, who I don't know, Mr. Oz, who I don't know, and Mr. Roscoe Carmichael, who I know professionally from his trial in 1990. I think the record would reflect that I gave him a fair trial. Ms. Stone was the court reporter on that trial. I'm sure she'll be happy to make you a copy of the transcript for a price. Mr. Carmichael must have thought that he got a fair trial. He didn't file a motion for a new trial nor did he file an appeal. So, the case that I will preside over will have one plaintiff and two defendants."

Tate questioned, "What about the fact that you issued the two search warrants?"

"That fact doesn't automatically disqualify me to sit on this case. I'm open-minded. You'll be able to file whatever motions you want attacking the search warrants. However, the drugs and videos were found, so what was sought was there."

Tate rose again and asked, "We'd like to appeal the court's decisions to the Court of Appeals under Rule 10."

"I'll take that under advisement. Put your request in writing."

Rule 10 is extraordinary relief, not often granted. It allows a higher court to review a lower court's decision, freezing the case, so a case could proceed without error. The case is frozen because if the issue is material, then an error by the trial judge would require a time-consuming and expensive new trial. The point of Rule 10 was to avoid the need for a second trial. Everyone in the courtroom knew that Tate's motion was an attempt to delay the beginning of depositions. However, everyone also knew that no one wants two trials.

Howard continued, "Mr. Davis is asking to strike certain affirmative defense. Those related to Mr. Lee and the ones relating to the police and TBI intervening by their search and seizure are struck. He's also moved for those affirmative defenses blaming the police and district attorney's office for publishing the tapes be struck. I'm not going to strike those defenses, but obviously the defenses relate to publication of the tapes and is permissible, but obviously the burden is on the defendant to prove those affirmative defenses."

Judge Howard moved on. "I grant the motion to compel interrogatories 5, 6, 9 and 19. Mr. Carmichael, Mr. Oz and their clients shall watch the tapes. I hope that will refresh Mr. Carmichael's memory. I'm going to let Mr. Davis and Mr. Steine view all of the tapes. I also order the defendants to produce the financial documents responsive to Requests 12, 13, 14, and 15. These documents shall be placed under seal, and a copy shall be given to plaintiff's counsel, who shall use those documents in a second deposition limited to the defendant's financials. The plaintiff shall be excluded from the room and shall be precluded hearing or reading that deposition. I'm allowing this discovery so the testimony could be used in a Toof hearing. (a punitive damage hearing) I want to make it clear that this ruling is limited to discovery only; I've not ruled that any of this financial information is admissible. I'm reserving that decision to a later date as to whether or not a jury ever sees these documents."

A Toof hearing is a mini-trial with witnesses and evidence if the jury renders a verdict for compensatory damages and within its discretion elects to consider punitive damages. If the Toof hearing proceeds, then the jury hears proof as to thirteen factors, one of which is the net worth of the defendant. The defendant's net worth is relevant because the purpose of punitive damages is to punish the defendant and the same dollar amount awarded against each defendant would not adequately punish them. Because Carmichael had a significant net worth reflected on his financial statement and an even greater net worth unreported, Tate was desperate to keep that information away from the jury.

Tate rose and announced, "We'd like to add that to the motion under Rule 10."

Howard casually said, "Put it in writing. Court's adjourned."

Pierce worked her way over to the plaintiff's counsel's table, in a clearly sarcastic manner, she said,

"It's going to be a pleasure working against you again. I've been looking forward to this day."

I glared and whispered at my adversary,

"Don't flatter yourself Amy. I haven't given you a second thought since we kicked your ass. Let's not pretend here. I don't trust you and I won't be cutting you any slack, so don't ask for any. I know who and what you are and I'm not letting my guard down for a minute."

Pierce didn't have a good come back, so she walked away, angry.

I was satisfied with the court's rulings. As I turned to leave the courtroom, I noticed Alice Krieger seated in the corner, without her cameraman. She glared at me when I passed her.

CHAPTER TWENTY

SURPRISING RULING

Tuesday, FEBRUARY 18, 1997

(THIRD PERSON)

Tate and Gray were true to their word. They filed their Rule 10 motion within two business days of the hearing. The motion argued all of the previous reasons for recusal and two new ones that hadn't been mentioned at the hearing on the 14th. Besides Howard's presiding over the 1990 criminal trial and the issuance of the search warrants for the Music Row office, Tate argued that the judge had recused himself in another case involving the defendant, and second, that Howard had lost $4,000 in a poker game hosted by the defendant.

The defendant asserted in the motion, "Rule 10 of the Code of Judicial Conduct 'imposes an affirmative duty upon judges to avoid even the appearance of impropriety.' Rule 2 provides that 'the actions of a trial court would at all times promote public confidence.' Rule 2 further provides that 'a judge would disqualify himself in a proceeding in which impartiality might reasonably be determined, including cases where the judge has a personal interest or is prejudiced by his past association with one of the parties.'"

All of the other parties, except Phillip Oz, filed pleadings supporting Judge Howard's decision not to recuse and to sever all of the parties except Carmichael and Oz. Within four hours, Judge Howard ruled, "The court does have a strong professional and respected relationship with Chief of Police Neenan and District Attorney Johnson Tory, which does rise to the level of friendship, although the parties do not socialize with or without their wives. Because these personal relationships exist, I have recused myself from those third-party actions and have asked that the Supreme Court appoint a new unrelated judge. Bucky Lee has appeared in my court on many occasions. I have always found him competent and honest. He is not a friend, but I respect him and hold him in high esteem. I do not believe that my opinion would cloud my judgment, but out of an abundance of caution, I have recused myself and asked the Supreme Court to appoint a new judge to adjudicate the claims against Bucky Lee brought by the defendant. I did sit as the judge on the defendant Carmichael's 1990 criminal trial. A copy of the transcript is attached to this order. This transcript makes it clear that this court treated the defendant fairly without any prejudice. Neither party appealed the jury finding or the sentence imposed by the court. Mr. Carmichael must have been satisfied of my fairness in his trial."

Judge Howard continued, "In this case there was three search warrants issued. I issued two of those warrants. The defendant Carmichael has indicated he intends to challenge the validity of all three warrants. I am more than capable of reviewing whether or not there was sufficient evidence for the issuance of my two warrants and the scope of each warrant. If I am wrong, then the defendant will seek and get relief in the Court of Appeals. Judge Peck will have to address Judge Wyatt's warrant of the farmhouse."

Carmichael had challenged the search warrant issued by Judge Peck. The videotaping by the airstrip and outside the farmhouse was argued inadmissible because it was outside the scope of the warrant. Peck's warrant extended to the "farmhouse" and the recording weren't within the "farmhouse." Tate further argued that because the drugs and money were seized outside the "farmhouse" that such evidence was outside the scope of the warrant. The motion was pending in the Carmichael's criminal proceeding. Peck and his two law clerks were researching the issue.

In the civil case Judge Howard paused before he continued with new information, "The defendant for the first time raises the fact that in 1994, I recused myself in a case involving Bart Simmons and Roscoe Carmichael. This was a breach of contract dispute involving the failure of Mr. Simmons to close on the sale of certain real property. Once a month, I play bridge with Bart Simmons. He's one of eight players, and because of that casual association, because of the appearance of impropriety, I recused myself. I do not know the defendant Phillip Oz or the plaintiff Elizabeth Swann. I have no bad feelings towards the defendant Carmichael and can sit on the case of Swann vs. Carmichael and Oz fairly and instruct the jury properly. The jury rather than I is the finder of fact. I will be responsible to instruct them on the law, but it will be the jury who determines whether to award a judgment to the plaintiff and, if so, for how much. The last reason given in the motion for recusal is a $400 loss at a poker game twenty years ago. There were six players, and my loss was spread among three or four players. I was angry about losing such a large sum of money, but at myself. I never blamed Mr. Carmichael. I learned a valuable lesson that night. I'm a terrible poker player. I switched to bridge after that. I've not played poker since that night. The decision to recuse is within my discretion, and I do not feel compelled to recuse myself."

The order made it clear that Judge Howard would hear the

Swann case with three parties, however, there was a twist to his ruling. He also ruled that he was going to refrain from setting the case for trial. Howard recognized that he wanted Carmichael's criminal trial to be adjudicated first, so he could exercise his Fifth Amendment right in his criminal case. He did indicate that he wanted the parties to attempt to reach a settlement through mediation, and that mediation should take place prior to the anniversary date of the filling of the Swann complaint.

Howard left the door open for the Court of Appeals to reverse him if it was willing to act quickly, which would have been extraordinary, but a Rule 10 motion, by definition was extraordinary relief.

"The court is going to grant the defendant's Rule 10 motion to allow the Court of Appeals to reconsider my rulings but shall accelerate the appellate briefing schedule and would ask that the Court of Appeals set oral argument within thirty days, and rule on the motion within ten days of the hearing. The defendant has ten days to brief the issues, and the plaintiff shall have ten days to respond. The defendant shall have ten days to file a reply brief. I hereby suspend discovery in Swann vs. Carmichael and Oz for seventy days to afford the Court of Appeals an opportunity to rule. The court shall have thirty days to rule after receipt of all briefs. After seventy days, if there has been no ruling from the Court of Appeals, then discovery shall proceed."

Howard had pressed the Court of Appeals ruling on the defense's Rule 10 motion, and it was his superior court. Trial judges didn't do that. It was a bold, very presumptive thing to do. He'd reduced the briefing schedule from seventy days to thirty and imposed a deadline for a hearing and ruling to another forty days. The ruling bordered on judicial indiscretion.

Tate's Rule 10 motion sought to reverse Howard, but at the very least it would delay the civil case. Tate wanted the criminal case set for trial first, so Carmichael if necessary could take the Fifth and then defend himself in the Swann case. Howard thought Tate was manipulating the judicial system, so he expediated the schedule. The order went on to set a very specific discovery schedule if the Court of Appeals affirmed or failed to rule within Howard's self-imposed deadline. It identified the order in which depositions would be taken and the order of which attorney should ask questions. Despite the fact he'd granted their Rule 10 motion, Howard wasn't going to let Tate hijack the case and delay discovery while it sat waiting on a lengthy appeal. Either the Court of Appeals affirmed or reversed within the seventy days or the case proceeded and according to Howard's schedule.

It more than made up for lost time. Howard had set the tone.

The plaintiff had to respond to the defendant's first set of interrogatories and request to produce. This required several meetings with Lizzy Swann. The plaintiff answered certain questions and objected to others. She identified the persons who had knowledge of her sexual encounters with Carmichael and the allegations of the complaint. This included the police officers, the TBI agents, and DAs sued, five of her close friends, her therapist and psychiatrist. She did not identify her parents. Davis thought it was a big mistake not to tell her parents about the suit.

A series of questions was intended just to embarrass the plaintiff.

1. Please identify all of the men you've had sexual relations (defined as oral, anal, or vaginal) with in the last thirty days, one year, and five years.
2. Has the plaintiff ever had a venereal disease? If so, which ones and when?

3. Has the plaintiff engaged in unprotected sex? If so, with whom and when?
4. Identify the name and address of any physician who has examined you in the last fifteen years.
5. Please identify all of the sexual positions you engaged in with the defendant Carmichael.
6. Did you use a condom when you had sex with the defendant Carmichael?
7. Did you climax when you had sex with the defendant Carmichael?
8. Please identify your first sexual partner and how old were you?
9. Have you ever had sexual relations with another woman? Have you ever watched pornography? If so what was depicted?

To each of these interrogatories, the plaintiff responded, "Objection. The information sought by this interrogatory is not discoverable under Rule 26 of the Tennessee Rules of Civil Procedure. The information sought is neither relevant nor reasonably calculated to lead to the discovery of admissible evidence."

The plaintiff admitted she had sexual encounters with the defendant. When asked about specifics, the plaintiff stated that the videos spoke for themselves. She denied consenting to being videoed and denied watching videos of other women with the defendant. The plaintiff or Davis described in detail why each count of the complaint was alleged. When it came to describing damages, Lizzy identified her psychiatrist and therapist as professionals who could describe how the defendant's conduct affected her life. In her answer, Lizzy elaborated, "I've lost all confidence in myself as a person and as a woman. Before this incident with the defendants, I had self-confidence and considered myself to have a bright future. Now, I'm depressed, feel desperate, and question my judgment. I feel like a fool. I had a dream of becoming a performer. I knew I had talent. All I needed was a break. Roscoe Carmichael convinced me that he was that big break and could open doors for me. All I had to do was to be nice to him. I believed him, and based on those promises, I behaved out of character. I did things I'd never done before. Sure, I'd smoked pot, but I'd never snorted cocaine. He offered, and I was afraid to turn him down. We drank too much, and I danced around like a damn fool and degraded myself. Those two nights are burned into my memory. I'll never forget that embarrassment.

But, those thoughts do not compare to the day I was sitting in the police station along with the detectives and police officers, and I watched the video of myself and learned of the existence of the cameraman. It was one thing to know what I'd done and that Roscoe Carmichael had gotten the better of me. It was quite another to discover it was memorialized on tape and that others had viewed it. The decision to file this lawsuit was not made lightly. I was warned that there'd be publicity and that the news coverage would intensify my embarrassment and the impact on my depression and negative impact on my reputation. It has, but the defendants need to answer for their intentional fraudulent conduct, or else they'll continue to destroy the lives of other unsuspecting females."

Sammie and Lizzy worked hard on her answers to interrogatories. Sammie knew that Tate and Pierce would try to twist every word set down on paper when Lizzy was deposed and at trial, but it was a pretty compelling story and it needed to be told in response to the discovery request.

CHAPTER TWENTY-ONE

LET'S GO TO THE MOVIES

Sunday, March 2, 1997

(BENJAMIN DAVIS' VOICE)

I often worked on weekends, rarely in the office, usually from the comfort of my home office. It was secluded from the rest of the house, and the family knew that room was off limits and respected my confidentiality with my clients. Morty and Sammie lived in the old Steine's Department Store, so it wasn't unusual for them to stick their heads in the office on a Sunday to tie up a loose end or to get something done that eluded them during the week. Today was movie day.

The defendants' objection to the plaintiff's motion to view six out of the seven videos was only half-hearted. Tate, Gray, and Pierce knew the court would allow the plaintiff, her counsel, and her designated representatives the right to examine not only her tape but those of the other women. I had reminded the court that the defendant Carmichael alleged that he'd watched some of the videos with other women. I also argued that the defendants had failed to identify three of the videoed women, and that they were important witnesses who needed to be found. I represented to the court I'd hired a private investigator to locate these yet unidentified women.

Finally, I pointed out to the court that I expected the defense to call Ingram, Strong and Watson as witnesses.

The court ordered; "counsel could sign out the videos from the Metropolitan Police Department, but all seven needed to stay together and shall be viewed in counsel's office and nowhere else. That the tapes are to be kept in a locked drawer or file cabinet at plaintiff's counsel's office when not in use. That counsel shall identify all persons who are to see the tapes, and that the court shall approve those persons. That the parties and their identified agents in their effort to locate any of the yet unidentified women who were videoed shall use reasonable care not to further publicize the identity of these other women."

In response to the court's order, I filed a notice that identified myself, Elizabeth Swann (plaintiff), Morty Steine (lawyer), Bella Rosario (legal secretary), Sammie Davis (paralegal), George Hopper (private investigator) and Elizabeth Swann's psychiatrist and therapist, as persons who would view the tapes. Hopper, the former middleweight knocked out by Tommy Hearns and twice by Sugar Ray, had been retained to track down the missing women and see if they would corroborate Lizzy's denial of the existence of the cameraman and videotaping. He was also hired to find out as much information about the seven women as possible. The proposed testimony of Watson, Ingram, and Strong was quite damaging.

On Friday, Sammie picked up the seven tapes from the police department and they were placed in the firm's safe. The team agreed that because there were seven tapes of unknown length, rather than lose a workday, they'd reconvene on Sunday for the showing. Bella agreed to cater the affair. Lizzy Swann wasn't invited because the team determined that discussion could be more open if she wasn't present at this first showing.

We elected to begin early at 8:00 a.m. in case the tapes were lengthy and it was going to be a long day. Bella brought an egg casserole, various pastries, rolls, and Italian cookies. A hot pot of coffee was placed on a trivet in the middle of the coffee table. The team was gathered around the conference room table, and Sammie was ready to pop the video into the VCR. Everybody was waiting on Bella, when she buzzed in, "Amy Pierce is on the phone. Do you want to take it before or after show time?"

What the hell does she want, and how the hell does she know I'm working on a Sunday?

"I'll take it now."

I pushed line two.

"Hello, Amy, it's Sunday. Don't you know today is a day of rest?"

"Well, you're at work."

"Yeah, but my people's day of rest is Saturday. How'd you know I was at the office?"

"Isn't today movie day? I went to check out the tapes and discovered Sammie checked them out on Friday, so I figured you'd be watching them today. I'm on the list to get them next. I'll write a letter to Metro Evidence that you're transferring the tapes to me. How long do you think you'll need them?"

I gave the question a moment of thought before answering, "Five days tops. I'll call you when I'm dropping them off with the police, and you can be waiting for their return. I'd prefer to follow the court's order on this issue, return the tapes directly to the police, and then let you check them out and not break the chain of evidence of the tapes."

I knew if I didn't follow the court order to the letter, Pierce would challenge the chain of evidence. She was just baiting me, but I was too smart to fall for her ploys.

Everyone at Steine & Davis hated Pierce because of her involvement in the Plainview cases. Morty had taught me, and we were in the process of teaching Sammie, that litigation was a war, but when it was over, the generals (the lawyers), shouldn't hold a grudge. When a case was over, there would be other battles in other wars, and the victors and the vanquished should shake hands and wait for the next war with new armies, with different names and different issues. Somehow Pierce had become the exception to the rule. Morty even felt that way about her. She'd made each litigation a personal battle rather than professional. She was dishonest, sneaky, and very good at her job. Each time Morty and I managed to achieve a verdict, but it was painful. She left a bad taste in our mouths.

The positions she'd taken on behalf of Phillip Oz confirmed my concerns about her as an advocate. In her answer, she stated, "On two separate occasions, Oz videoed the plaintiff having sexual intercourse with Carmichael at Epic Talent Agency. The plaintiff was aware that her sexual relations were being videoed. The defendant demands strict proof that the plaintiff didn't know she was being videotaped."

The defendant Oz denied that he entered into a conspiracy to tape "unsuspecting females." He claimed the women knew of his presence and what he was doing. The defendant denied that the plaintiff suffered emotional distress and humiliation.

Pierce needled me and gloated,

"This guy Tate delayed you for a good two months with his Rule 10 motion. Tate's motion could get lost in the Court of Appeals for who knows how long? You got outmaneuvered. You must be slipping."

"He achieved a seventy day delay, and then Howard imposed a pretty tight deposition schedule. I think he did me a favor. I think

Tate pissed Howard off with that motion to recuse. Just between us girls, I bet you think so too."

"I have to admit it took balls. It probably will keep Howard honest on his rulings, and I suspect he'll even lean towards the defendants on certain motions to avoid appearing biased."

I hadn't thought of that possibility. She might be right.

I ignored her and pressed my original point, "Don't count on it. I can put your client in a bad light with the judge if you make me file these cleanup motions. Let's enter an agreed order."

The two lawyers worked through the answer and Pierce insisted that Oz's conduct had to be compared with that of Swann.

"My complaint alleges only intentional torts. Where do you come off asserting comparative fault? You claim my client was somehow negligent in having sex with Carmichael and allowing your client to video tape them. I don't see how..."

Pierce broke in, "She got drunk and did cocaine. No one held a gun to her head. She's got some responsibility here. She voluntarily and intentionally consumed the alcohol and drugs."

"You're crazy. At best she was negligent, and the law is clear, negligence never negates an intentional conduct; no comparison is permitted."

"Howard didn't rule on that defense. The Supreme Court decision in Breault is not clear about contribution among tortfeasors."

Pierce was right. Carmichael hadn't raised that defense, so I dropped my objection, and we agreed on how Pierce would amend her answer. Pierce also agreed to produce the financials under the same terms as Howard ordered at the February hearing.

I hung up.

What an asshole.

I wrote a confirming letter to Pierce just in case she tried to squirm out of what we'd discussed. I got up from my desk and joined Morty, Sammie, Bella, and George in the library. The decision not to have Lizzy at the first showing of the tape was a good one. The men particularly needed to orient themselves to seeing their client naked, performing her dance and having intimate sex acts with Carmichael. Before the viewing, I marched over to the credenza where there was a pot of coffee and assorted pastries. I wolfed down an apple strudel and took a second to my seat at the table.

The tape rolled, and the crowd saw Lizzy Swann lose at strip poker, dance around naked for ten minutes, climb the pole and then perform various sex acts with Carmichael. They could see Carmichael interact with his cameraman when Lizzy wasn't looking in the mirror's direction because her back was to the camera, or she was orally satisfying Carmichael. A reasonable observer could conclude that she was unaware of the taping and that Carmichael was attempting to conceal his directions to the cameraman from her.

The videos sickened and embarrassed the two women. Bella spoke first, "You don't want women of my age on the jury. They'll conclude that our client is a slut. Some of those acts simply are not part of my generation's repertoire."

Morty, who was more than ten years older than her, lit a cigar and agreed. Smoke filled the room, which annoyed both Bella and Sammie, but he was the boss. Each had tried to get the old man to quit, or at the very least restrict his cigar smoking to his office, but had failed. The only one who could control Morty Steine was his wife Goldie, but she died in 1991.

Sammie commented, "She doesn't look like a victim. You're going to have to humanize her before you play that video. We've got to strategize how we're going to handle this delicate matter. Maybe we introduce the other women's tapes first before the jury sees our client's tape."

Morty listened carefully to the female members of the firm before saying anything more. He knew that their opinions were important since in all likelihood, the jury would be composed of at least half women. He concluded, "This case needs to settle, not go to court. We just need to put the defendants in a box, and settle at that point."

George Hopper made a photo of each of the clothed women to circulate as part of his investigation. Davis gave him specific instructions of what he could do and say, and what he couldn't do and say if in fact he found any of the missing women. Hopper left with his marching orders, "Find those other three women. Always be mindful that the defendants will characterize your efforts as further publication of the tapes."

Later that day, Sammie brought Lizzy in to watch her movie. Bella, and Sammie sat with her and watched her reaction. The effect was horrific. She cried the entire duration of the tape.

After her tape ran, I joined them in the conference room to speak with the client. Lizzy's eyes were red and puffy.

"Pretty rough. Do you think you could sit in a courtroom with a hundred people watching? Every eye looking at you as the tape is shown?"

"I don't think so. It was bad enough in the police station with four policemen present. It helped having Sammie and Bella here for moral support but only a little bit. Do we have to play the tape at trial?"

"Carmichael and Oz's attorneys will insist on it. The judge might clear out the gallery, but the jury's going to see it. We brought the lawsuit and alleged that you were damaged because they made the tape and that because of Carmichael, others got to see it. The jury's got to be shown the tape. It's unavoidable."

"I should kill that son-of-a-bitch," Lizzy blurted out.

She didn't like my answer, but it was the truth, and she knew it. She left our office in a state of fury.

I thanked Bella and Sammie for watching the Swann tape twice and for being there for the client. It had been a long, hard day, and all I wanted was some good family time. I walked up the Alley, got in my Vette with the top down, an orange Tootsie Pop in my mouth, the radio blasting and drove home, listening to the Moody Blues.

I got lucky, there was no drama waiting for me, and I was able to spend the night watching TV with my family. By the time I went to bed, between the seven tapes at the office and the two movies at home, I'd stared at a TV screen for more than twelve hours. I closed my eyes and fell asleep.

CHAPTER TWENTY-TWO

TODAY SHE BECOMES A MAN

Saturday, March 8, 1997

(THIRD PERSON)

It was a beautiful spring day in Middle Tennessee for an outdoor reception at the Davis home. The service would happen in the morning at the Temple, Congregation Obabai Sholom. The cantor and Morty had been working on Caroline's Torah and Haftorah portions for months. She had a beautiful voice, like her mother, and would chant, rather than simply read the Hebrew words. She was also required to give a speech in English at the end of the ceremony to the congregation She'd worked on this task under the watchful eyes of Morty Steine. A master communicator, who could turn any juror's head. He'd been her speechwriter, and for the last two weeks he'd worked with her every night on her delivery. She had her speech memorized, but he didn't want her to simply say the words. He wanted her to move her audience of more than two hundred friends, family, and business associates of her father to ponder the absence of brotherly love in the world.

Finally, two days before the event, he declared her ready. Morty insisted to Liza, "She's going to be great. The congregation won't know what hit them. You'll both be proud, and they'll pee in their pants, she'll be so funny."

Liza's stressed voice asked, "You've got me concerned. You know your homespun humor isn't for everybody. This is supposed to be a solemn occasion. A rite of passage from childhood to womanhood. Maybe I should read the speech to make sure you didn't include something inappropriate. I wouldn't want to offend the rabbi or the cantor. Her grandparents and Uncle George are coming down from up north. Are you sure those Yankees will appreciate your humor?"

Slightly offended, Morty responded, "Funny is funny, no matter where you're from. Relax, please. Don't lecture me about the solemnness of a Bat Mitzvah. Remember, you used to be a shiksa (gentile girl or woman)." Liza the daughter of Dr. John and Patsy Caldwell was born into a religious Methodist family.

Liza, who converted to Judaism prior to marriage, just wanted everything to go perfectly during this lifecycle event. She'd raised her children Jewish, and a Bat Mitzvah of a thirteen-year-old woman was part of the tradition. They went to Temple on an irregular basis, but she made sure they kept a Jewish home. Candles were lit on Friday nights, and the Kiddush, the blessing over the wine, was said every week before the blessing over the bread. Davis loved breaking a piece of challah (cakelike bread) and dipping it in a little bit of honey.

Caroline would be the first woman in the Davis family to be Bat Mitzvah. Because of her nomadic childhood, Sammie had little religious education. Larry and Shelly Davis never had a daughter, so when Sammie finally came to live with them, they didn't press her to attend Hebrew school or become a Bat Mitzvah. The new Jewish Reform Movement had recently encouraged equal treatment of men and women, including the important rites of passage. Fifty years earlier, it would have been unheard of for a woman to read from the Torah. Both Davis and Morty saw this as progress. Morty truly had a passion for humanity and equality. He'd proved it time and again, first as a CRAF pilot over the skies of Britain, and then at the front of the picket lines with Reverend Martin Luther King Jr. He also doubled as their counsel, working closely with Thurgood Marshall and the NAACP, bailing protestors out of jail and defending those arrested. He was known and well-loved among those members of the black community involved in the movement. Earlier in his life Morty experienced prejudice as a young Jew growing up in a southern city during the depression. Sometimes he was required to physically defend himself to respond to bigotry. He often recalled an incident along the shores of the Cumberland River, where his two gentile friends came to his aid.

Davis grew up in the North, and personally didn't experience anti-Semitism because Jews were a significant minority, tolerated by the majority. This quiet truce in the North, the passage of time, and the evolution of the Jewish Reform Movement embraced and included women in the process. Davis selflessly wanted his daughter to have all the same advantages of his faith as his son, Jake. Davis wasn't overly religious, but he was definitely proud of his Jewish heritage.

Davis was looking forward to the ceremony. Morty actually made suggestions that the rabbi approved. He had a flair for the dramatic, which was fine for the courtroom, but not necessarily acceptable in Temple. It was Morty's suggestion that the traditional prayer shul be passed from the grandfather to father to the Bat Mitzvah girl.

The Davis' hired an event planner, Jayne Meadows, to execute the perfect party. Davis insisted on a wide variety of food stations, two carving stations of prime rib and turkey, and at least two bars. Davis knew how to throw a good party. He looked at the budget and then kept his mouth shut. Meadows made excellent suggestions but added to the expense, exceeding the budget. Davis was fine until Meadows brought up charger plates. He said, "If you can explain to me what they do, maybe I'll pay for it." Meadows had a prepared answer. She was very good at her job, "It protects the linen tablecloths."

"I don't own the tablecloths."

"But you want to keep them clean."

"I don't care if they stay clean or not. Let the linen company spend the $2200 to have charger plates. He's the one who has a vested interest in keeping those tablecloths clean. No charger plates."

Davis couldn't have been happier about Caroline's big day. His extended family, friends, and associates came to the big event. His mother, Nana Shelly, his dad, and his brother George, left their three cleaners in the hands of their managers. Liza was the hostess all weekend, catering to Davis's family, who she enjoyed and loved. Davis fell further behind in his work as the big day drew near. His legal pad of things to do was four pages long, but with his best efforts, everything would get done.

His daughter's performance was perfect. She entertained the audience of more than two hundred people. She read in Hebrew about the story of Joseph and his brothers, "Joseph, his father's favorite, mocked, danced around, and annoyed his brothers so badly that they threw him down a well. Left there to die for his vanity. They returned home with Joseph's colorful coat, lying to their father, Jacob, telling him that animals had killed their brother."

Caroline warned, "Be careful, Jake, the Torah is a prophetic document. We don't have a well, but we do have a swimming pool." The audience broke up. She had to pause to let them regain control. She reminded them that in the end because there was famine in Canaan, Joseph's family wound up in Egypt, where Joseph had become a powerful advisor to Pharaoh, and he benevolently helped his family. "Jake, I've been told by our Dutch Uncle Morty that history does repeat itself." More laughs from the congregation.

"So, from this moment forward, I'm going to be nicer to you, Jake because someday I may run out of food and be at your doorstep looking for a hot meal. Who knows? You may become some powerful person, and I'll need your help. Anything's possible, I guess." She shrugged her shoulders and held out both hands. Another Morty one-liner. The people found that hilarious.

She ended on a serious note by thanking the rabbi and cantor for all their help and guidance in understanding her Torah portion. She then turned her attention to Morty. "I'm a lucky girl. Morty Steine helped me prepare for this day. He made the experience fun and memorable. We spent a lot of time studying, but we also spent a good bit of time just talking. I learned a lot from those conversations with someone I love and respect. Thanks, Morty, for all your help."

She looked directly at Jake, "I've wondered what it would be like to be an only child, and although the silence would be intriguing, I'm glad I have you, my little brother."

She thanked her parents for all the time, effort, and money they put into this day. "Today I am a man, I mean, woman." She invited her guests over to her parents' home, on the seventeenth hole of Hillwood Country Club.

The Davis family lived only a few miles from the Temple so the valet parkers were overwhelmed. As the guests arrived, the band, headlined by a friend of the Davis', Jimmy Hall, of Wet Willie fame, played rock & roll classics and the blues. During the night, Morty got up and sang three Motown songs, one by Smokey Robinson and two songs by Marvin Gaye. He brought down the house, or more accurately the tent.

The food was amazing. Davis took pride in his parties. His July 3rd party and holiday party were big events of the year for many people. The two bars remained open all night, and some guests partook a bit too much. Davis controlled his drinking but not his eating. His attitude was; *I'm enjoying myself, it's my party, and I'll cry if I want to.* He had multiple servings and then got up and danced with his beautiful wife and then his daughter.

The family loved being together. Grandpa Larry and Nana Shelly actually raised Sammie for seven years before she went off to college. Her parents divorced, and after a few years with her mother, she grew up in Woodbury, Long Island, and she was spoiled. *Spoiled badly, but she'll be one hell of a lawyer. I sure am proud of her,* Davis thought.

Davis slow danced with his daughter. They were alone as he whispered to her, "You know you're still my little girl?" He hated her response, "At least for a few more years, but then watch out."

Davis knew she was right.

CHAPTER TWENTY-THREE

THE APPEAL

Monday, May 5, 1997

(THIRD PERSON)

Tate began the appellate briefing process with a vengeance. On the tenth day following the entry of Howard's February 18th order he filed his twenty-eight-page brief with the Court of Appeals. The document had several exhibits including affidavits from three of the card players from the poker game where Howard lost $400, the 1990 trial transcript, the two search warrants of the Music Row office and Howard's recusal order in the Simmons case.

With expert precision Tate picked apart the 1990 statutory rape transcript and questioned every ruling Howard made. Most issues he raised weren't relevant because Bucky didn't object to them at trial. On those issues previously raised, Tate was far less respectful than Bucky was. Tate's arguments amounted to nothing more than a bunch of complaining about nothing. Almost all of the rulings were correct in accordance with the Rules of Civil Procedure and Rules of Evidence and those that were questionable were harmless error, having no impact on the jury verdict. More important, after the verdict, Bucky didn't consider them material because he failed to file an appeal. Both he and Carmichael were more than satisfied with the verdict. In fact, Carmichael was ecstatic to be acquitted on the two felony counts and only found guilty on the two misdemeanors. The failure of Tate to explain why Bucky didn't file a motion for a new trial or failed to appeal the jury's verdict was fatal to this issue.

The second basis for the Rule 10 motion to recuse was equally problematic for Tate. He argued that Howard didn't have probable cause to issue the two search warrants. This argument was flawed because Agent Pyle had an inside informant, Anthony Estes, who reported that a drug shipment was end route. June Bug was accurate as to the farmhouse. A large shipment of drugs was confiscated consistent with the information relied upon in Peck's warrant. A much lesser number of drugs was found at the Music City address as sworn by June Bug Estes, Pyle's informant, it yielded almost an ounce of cocaine. There was a reasonable basis for the first warrant.

The second Howard warrant related to the videotapes and camera equipment and again, Pyle claimed it was based on agent Tuke's discovery of the secret room, camera, and videos. Pyle himself got on the phone and explained to the judge the need for the second warrant. That portion of Howard's warrant that directed that the tapes be reviewed by a limited number of persons and that an effort be made to contact the women in the videos. Was the responsible thing to do? The police and DA Johnson Tory's office needed to view the tapes to prosecute Carmichael. Tate argued the tapes were a private matter, relying upon the testimony of Watson, Ingram and Strong. He further claimed that the testimony of those witnesses proved that there were no damages sustained by the women. Tate claimed that no publication occurred until the police and TBI seized the tapes, and it was the acts of law enforcement that caused the plaintiff and the other women damages.

Tate argued that Howard's refusal to recuse was inconsistent with his recusal in the Simmons case. He insisted that Howard's relationship and nexus to Carmichael was at least as close to Howard as Bart Simmons, a mere associate, with whom he occasionally played bridge. Tate claimed that Howard couldn't distinguish why he recused himself in one case and not the other.

The last reason asserted by Tate addressed Howard's poker losses in 1982 at a game hosted by Carmichael. The three affidavits filed by the other players made it clear that Howard was pissed when he lost the $400 and that he never played in the game again. Tate in his reply brief couldn't explain why Bucky didn't ask Howard to recuse himself from the 1990 statutory rape trial because of Howard's alleged bias because of his poker losses.

On May 5th the attorneys for all the parties in the Swann case appeared in the Court of Appeals for oral argument. Tate and two associates from DC came in for the hearing, Tate had been previously admitted so he could argue for the defendant Carmichael. The Court of Appeals consisted of a three-judge panel. A decision could be unanimous or by a majority of two of the three. If the decision was split, the minority usually wrote a dissenting opinion. The Court of Appeals for the Middle Section, which sat in Nashville, consisted of nine judges, who rotated to make up three different panels. The presiding judges today were Clark, Clements, and Todd. Each judge had received and reviewed a summary prepared by their clerks and if the case interested them, they'd read the three briefs in their entirety. The clerks would also provide their judge with proposed questions for counsel. Judge's relied heavily on the clerk's work so that the docket could move ahead. Sometimes clerks had too much influence on their judge's rulings. It all depended how industrious or how lazy the judge was.

The format for argument was that Tate, the moving party, had fifteen minutes, Davis, the respondent, had fifteen minutes, and Tate had fifteen minutes for cleanup. Both Tate and Davis prepared remarks but both expected within minutes to be interrupted by one of the judges with a question, and then the balance of their time would be responding to one question after another.

Tate stood and walked to the podium. He cleared his throat and began, "This is a Rule 10 motion, which by definition seeks extraordinary relief..."

Judge Todd interrupted, "Wouldn't you agree that the fact that Judge Howard granted your motion and allowed you to appear in this court shows his lack of bias?"

"To the contrary, Your Honor. I think he granted the motion because he recognized that the issue of his recusal was a close call and wanted guidance from this court to make sure he was doing the right thing. Remember the test under the Judicial Code of Conduct is does his failure to recuse give the appearance of impropriety?"

Judge Clark shot back, "I've read the transcript of the hearing. He didn't sound like he was hesitating as to his decision at all. He stated he'd considered your arguments carefully and rejected their merits. He sounded pretty sure of himself. Judge Howard isn't new to the bench. He's an experienced trial judge. Although motions to recuse are rare, I bet this isn't his first. Doesn't our Supreme Court holding in the Manning case clearly stand for the principle that the decision of whether to recuse oneself is within the discretion of the trial judge? Only the judge knows what's in his or her heart and mind?"

"That's true Judge Clark, but Judge Howard's issuance of the search warrants and the fact that the defense will hinge in part upon an attack on the issuance of those search warrant places Judge Howard in a difficult and awkward position of reviewing his own actions."

Judge Clark stood her ground, "Are you saying Mr. Tate, that Judge Howard is incapable of reexamining his own rulings? How many times during a trial does a trial judge reverse a preliminary ruling based upon the evidence introduced at trial? Documents are admitted and excluded based on the evidence. Witnesses are permitted and prevented from testifying based on the evidence. Cases are dismissed by directed verdicts by the judge and are never considered by the jury based upon a lack of evidence. Isn't reconsidering his own ruling what a trial judge does as a basic function of the job?"

Tate knew he was in trouble. Clark wasn't giving him time to breathe. The fifteen minutes seemed like an eternity. He was given his two-minute warning, and he did the best he could to wrap things up.

Davis stood and replaced Tate at the podium. He was allowed to speak for ten minutes without interruption. His argument was quite a contrast to the attack leveled against Tate. Finally Judge Clement asked, "Do you think that Judge Howard might be prejudiced by Mr. Carmichael's statutory rape trial?"

"Only Judge Howard can answer that question for certain. I'm sure he searched his conscience and weighed his decision. The law leaves the determination to his discretion because only he can make that judgment. I can state as an officer of the court that Judge Howard is a fair and honorable jurist, and if he felt any bias for or against a party he'd recuse himself on his own motion."

Davis handled another four questions from Judge Clement, who stayed silent during Tate's argument. Davis ended, "if there are no further questions I've completed my argument and ask that the court deny the Rule 10 motion."

With no further questions, he sat down and smiled confidently. Davis took a lack of questions from two of the judges as a good sign.

Tate returned to the podium, and all three judges pummeled him. He couldn't wait for the torment to end and sit down. He tried to fight back, but there was no point in poking the judges on the panel. He might find himself facing them next time on an appeal of the merits of the case. No point of burning any bridges. The next day the Court of Appeals issued its order.

ORDER

The appellant's motion under Rule 10 is denied. The trial court's order denying the motion to recuse is affirmed. The decision whether or not to recuse is within the sole discretion of the trial judge. This court does, however, reverse the trial court's deposition schedule, which it imposed upon the parties and the witnesses. This court is unaware of any obstructive behavior by any party in the scheduling of discovery, which would justify the trial court interfering with the discovery process. Without such obstruction, this court directs that the parties rather than the trial court should determine when and which depositions should be taken.

The court further orders that the scope of discovery of the defendant Carmichael, including answering interrogatories and giving a deposition, shall be limited to the second search warrant issued by Judge Howard and the camera and videos seized. No reference to the other search warrants or the drugs may be questioned and no answers or questions should relate to the other warrant and or the drugs.

The court further notes that under the laws of this state in 1982, poker for money, even in a private home, constituted illegal gambling. The court admonishes Judge Howard, who at that time was a member of the Bar for participating in such illegal conduct but levies no charges because the statute of limitations has expired and the court will not recommend either criminal or ethical prosecution. Discovery should proceed.

The unanimous opinion, authored by Judge Clement affirmed Howard on the law, but definitely slapped him in the face.

CHAPTER TWENTY-FOUR

DISCOVERY

Thursday, May 8, 1997

(SAMMIE DAVIS'S VOICE)

Red-faced and angry, I burst into my uncle's office and yelled, "She's a bitch, and that Washington asshole isn't any better. I can't work with either of them. You've got to take over getting the discovery set. They're pushing me around. I can't get anything done."

"Language young lady, what would Nana Shelly think?"

"I want to be reassigned. You deal with them."

He knew I'd run into a road block. He'd sent me on this fool's errand half expecting me to fail. He'd dealt with Pierce before and could easily imagine what Tate was like. Yet, I sensed his disappointment that I gave up so quickly. He expected more determination and gumption from me.

Ready with solid advice, he reminded me, "Don't let those bastards get to you like that. If they do, then they've won. You need to remain stoic and unperturbed. If they believe they can't get to you, then they'll begin to compromise, and you can push back harder to achieve what you want. You've got to stand up to them and be persistent. Then you'll start to make headway. The most important rule is to document all of your communications with those vultures.

Often a previous written word will trip up the other side and force them to make a concession. What's the specific problem?"

"They keep switching dates on me. Every time I think I have a deposition schedule worked out, they become unavailable. It's like trying to hit a moving target."

"Do you want me to show you how this is done?" he asked arrogantly.

"You bet," I replied.

He asked Bella to set up a conference call with Tate, Gray, Pierce, and with Katie Stone on the line, "Tell Katie I need her to record and transcribe a multi-party telephone conversation."

He couldn't possibly have completed that feat without assistance because he was technologically challenged. So was Morty. "I've got everyone on the line," she announced.

He put the group on speaker so I could hear.

"Good morning." He identified everyone on the line and then mentioned, "Katie Stone's on the line so she can record this conversation and type up a transcript if necessary to be given to the judge."

"I object. Why do we need a transcript?" Tate yelled.

My uncle quickly responded, "Katie read that back."

She did, "Mr. Tate, 'I object. Why do we need a transcript?'"

"You can object, you can hang up the phone, and I'll get you right back on the phone, except this time I'll have the judge on the line. I don't think..."

Tate cut him off, "Who do you think you're talking to? Do you know the type of pull my firm can exert? Let me..."

I watched my uncle's demeanor dramatically change, he'd had enough of this nonsense.

"Look Dorothy, you're not in Kansas anymore. You're in the Third Circuit Court of Davidson County, not DC. We do things a little differently. First, we treat each other with respect and don't pick unnecessary fights. We certainly work out discovery schedules, and if we can't, then the obstructive party pays a heavy price with the judge. Gray and Pierce should have told you that. I'm making a record that will show Judge Howard that I made a good faith effort to get these depositions set. I will comment for the record that Ms. Davis, my paralegal, has already spent more than three hours trying to complete this task and reported to me an intentional lack of cooperation. Judge Howard prematurely anticipated you'd act like a horses' rumps, so he set our deposition schedule. The Court of Appeals admonished Howard for doing so. I suspect he'll be happy to hear he was right about your obstructive behavior. He might even award my client attorney fees to further prove his point."

He waited for a response. None was made, so he continued, "My two experts are available on either the June 2nd, 3rd or 4th at my office. They've cleared their calendars and are waiting for me to call them with a date certain."

We'd discussed that we wanted the defense to set and take those expert depositions because we didn't want Tate and Pierce to have the ammunition of Swann's deposition when they were deposed.

"Dr. Little, Swann's psychiatrist, charges $300 an hour, and the therapist, Beverly Newman, LMT, charges $100 an hour. That's what I'm paying them, so you're getting my rate. I certainly am not going to let them charge you less."

Tate asked, "How much do they charge a patient for a session?"

"Why, are you in need of therapy? You can pose that question to them at their depositions. I'm not under oath. Pick one of those dates. I don't want to hear that you're unavailable. You can send someone else from your firm. Mr. Steine and I are the only two lawyers for the plaintiff. You've got eight hundred in your firm. I'm sure you can find someone competent to attend."

Sammie was impressed by how her uncle controlled the conversation and pushed it forward to get the job done.

Pierce volunteered, "I'd prefer the 2nd, rather than the 3rd or 4th."

Davis pressed, "Any objection?" Silence.

He interjected, "Done. Ms. Pierce, does ten o'clock suit you? Okay. The next group of depositions we need to set up involves the three women identified in the videos. I need a full day to complete all three depositions. You control Strong, Ingram, and Watson..."

Tate tried to cut him off. "We don't control any of them. They're fact witnesses, that's all."

"I'm looking forward to deposing them. Mr. Steine or I will be available on June 10th, 11th, or 14th. You pick, Tate."

We could hear whispering between Tate and Gray,

"I'm not available on any of those dates, and neither is Mr. Gray."

A quick response, "These are your witnesses. You already know and like what they're going to say. Ms. Pierce, your pick. The defendant Carmichael will manage to have representation present?"

"I have the afternoon of the 10th," Ms. Pierce replied.

"We need more than an afternoon to take three depositions. I'll need either a full day or two half days. Let's agree on two dates, and before I issue subpoenas, you'll confer with the witnesses and determine their availability on which date and at what time to best accommodate their schedules.

Pierce was trying to squeeze my uncle for time. He knew exactly what she was doing and wasn't going to let her succeed.

I knew he wasn't taking any chances relying on the good faith of defense counsel. Despite the transcript, once a deposition was agreed to, he intended to have either Bella or I issue a subpoena to that witness compelling attendance on the date and time. If the witness failed to appear, he or she would be subject to a contempt ruling by the judge.

Pierce suggested the 11th, as the second date. Tate remained silent, not wanting to indicate any agreement or concession to any of the dates.

Recognizing Tate's lack of participation, my uncle commented, "Mr. Tate, if you think silence will be golden, you are sadly mistaken. Vincent, I'd suggest that either you or Mr. Tate speak up when I propose these deposition dates. Your lack of participation in this conversation only evidences your lack of cooperation. I assure you that Judge Howard and the Court of Appeals will view silence as obstructive behavior.

I admired how my uncle controlled the conversation and got the job done. I know he thought this confrontation would be a learning experience.

He continued, "Now let's address the important depositions of our client. I'll make it easy. Lizzy Swann will go first at my office. I'll offer you June 22nd, 25th, or 26th."

We'd discussed how we wanted Lizzy's deposition taken early in the discovery process before defense counsel had the benefit of full discovery. She would read the depositions of her experts to help in her damage testimony and the testimony of the three women, who contradicted her version of the facts. We already knew that defense counsel would insist that our client be deposed before the defendants and that if pressed, Judge Howard would agree.

"We'll take all three," Tate spoke up. "At the very least I'll need a day, and Ms. Pierce will need a day." Pierce agreed.

"Okay, I can see this isn't going to be easy. I'm filing a motion for a protective order to limit my client's deposition to the federal rule of seven hours."

The Swann case was pending in state court where the federal rules didn't apply, but the circumstances warranted some time restraint, or Tate and Pierce would depose our client for days. In other matters he'd convinced other state judges to limit deposition lengths to the seven-hour federal limit before.

Pierce spoke up, "I'm not agreeing to seven hours, but the best of those dates for me for Ms. Swann's deposition is June 22nd."

My uncle jumped on the selected date, "Agreed, 9:00 a.m. at my office. Now what about your clients?" He directed the question at Tate. "I think we'll need two dates for Carmichael's depositions on the factual issues, and then a much shorter time for discovery of his financials."

Tate very aggressively responded,

"I don't want to set my client's deposition until after his criminal case has progressed. If you don't agree Roscoe Carmichael will be taking the Fifth in this case and your deposition will be a waste of time. Howard doesn't have the right to waive my client's constitutional rights."

My uncle didn't like that answer. Everyone knew that Carmichael wasn't at risk for criminal charges for his videotaping, but the Fifth amendment was a powerful right protected by the Constitution.

Tate's position wasn't unexpected. My uncle begrudgingly agreed to delay setting the deposition and then changed gears.

"What about your client's deposition Ms. Pierce? He's not under criminal indictment, and under the Constitution he doesn't have a Fifth Amendment right. When's he available? Mr. Steine and I are available on June 29th or July 2nd."

Pierce refused to set her client's deposition based upon the possibility that criminal charges might be brought against Oz.

Frustrated my uncle said," I'll be submitting an order with this transcript attached and will issue individual subpoenas consistent with the order. When are you going to disclose your experts so we can schedule them?"

Pierce answered the question, "Our deadline isn't for some time. We'll want to first digest what your experts and client say, and then we'll notify you about our experts and what they have to say. If I don't like your order, I'll submit my own. You know our expert will need to examine your client before he or she forms their professional opinions. We'll be filing a motion seeking court approval of that examination under Rule 35."

"That's your prerogative, we won't object to such an examination. As to your unwillingness to set your client's deposition, the judges will have the transcript and when appropriate he'll order the deposition. Katie, type it up and get me a copy as soon as you can."

"It will be my pleasure, Ben."

Pierce and Gray requested a copy as well. Katie Stone was making a killing. She charged $3.00 per page for the original and $1.50 per page for each copy. The scheduled depositions would be at least seven or eight full days of testimony, and depending on the number of pages, she'd make more than $10,000. The parties hung up with a series of clicks.

Sammie looked at her uncle and said, "I'm impressed. In less than an hour, you set six depositions, that was six more than I was able to. Tate turned out to be the difficult one."

"Pierce knew better. She realized there would be a record reflecting the conversation. She knew, regardless of what I said, that I was going to file that transcript. As soon as I identified Katie

Stone on the line, she was on her best behavior. Don't trust her. If you do, she'll screw you in a minute."

We'd set six depositions, that was a good start. I left his office with one difficult task off my plate.

Now all we have to do is take these depositions and survive the questioning of Lizzy Swann.

CHAPTER TWENTY-FIVE

INSIDE MEN

Thursday, May 15, 1997

(ROSCOE CARMICHAEL'S VOICE)

I wasn't impressed with my legal representation so far. Judge Howard for the most part ruled against me and he got the stamp of approval by the Court of Appeals. That didn't sit well with me. I wasn't taking any chances in my criminal case. I had an associate make some inquiries, expressing my willingness to expend some funds to approve my position. I decided not to discuss my efforts with my lawyers, as tough as they claimed to be, they weren't real tough guys, just men in expensive suits.

I was given permission to leave my house confinement to appear in the First Circuit Criminal Court, Judge Peck presiding. Scheduled to be heard were my motions to hold that the drugs seized under the search warrant of the farmhouse issued by Judge Wyatt was outside the scope of the warrant because the shipment and cash were confiscated outside the house, taken from the jeep, while a larger amount was seized on the porch. The motion also sought to exclude from evidence the cash and airplane taken because the airstrip was constructed on a different parcel of land, as well as excluding the recordings of the events of that evening. Obviously, this was a critical motion. If successful, my criminal problems would be greatly reduced, limited to the less than one ounce seized at the Music Row townhouse. A much more manageable amount and a Class C felony, not Class B.

My motions, pending over a month, were ripe for a ruling, and today was the scheduling conference at 2:00 p.m. The hearing was to take place in chambers outside the prying eyes of the media. The court's ruling would be released to the press when filed.

In preparation for his ruling Judge Peck tasked both of his law clerks to generate detailed memos on the pending issues. Unlike any of the lawyers on the case, I'd get to read the memos in advance because I'd paid for them. I elected not to tell my lawyers of my investment of $100,000 to influence the outcome of the motions. I kept my lawyers in the dark for fear they'd cry my actions violated their ethics or was some type of tampering crime.

Neither of Peck's law clerks went to law school on a scholarship and faced with mounting debt, saw an opportunity to make a quick $50,000. The key was what other state law to cite in support of the ruling. What was said in each document didn't require any direction on my part. Each young man drafted a document which narrowly defined the scope of Judge Wyatt's warrant. The common conclusion was "farmhouse meant the house, not a jeep in the yard or the porch." Each memo cited some of the same cases and some different cases in support of this proposition. Both documents argued that the recordings had to be excluded from evidence because they were the "fruits of and depicted an invalid search warrant."

Peck had been on the bench twenty-four years and had recently been reelected to a seventh four-year term. After twenty-five years the judge was tired and probably relied on his law clerks more than other trial judges. His age was to my benefit.

My inside person reported to me that these documents were delivered to the judge a week before the status conference, according to my associate, who delivered payment, Peck read them and then the three met to discuss the clerk's findings. Peck challenged his staff on a few issues but in the end because of their consistency adopted their arguments.

At 2:00 p.m. my lawyers, DA Tory Johnson, two Assistant DA's and I all appeared simultaneously in Peck's outer office. Peck's law clerks entered the room and the group proceed into chambers. There was no court reporter present.

Peck announced,

"I've ruled on the defense's pending motion, the clerks distributed copies to everyone in the room. The order held that all drugs, cash and the airplane seized at the farmhouse are inadmissible. The plane was confiscated on another parcel, and the cash and drugs were not seized in the house. The videos of these events that were illegally seized is inadmissible. I see no need for a court reporter, my order speaks for itself."

The state representative's demeanor completely changed from one of confidence to defeat. The court's ruling destroyed the best part of the state's case. No one said anything, but I could tell that Tate and Gray were ecstatic, sure they thought it was their brilliant lawyering that saved the day. I knew better at a cost of $100,000.

Peck waited, silence, so he continued,

"That leaves the 26 grams found at the townhouse seized under Judge Howard's warrant. Less than an ounce; that reduces the charge from a Class B felony to a Class C felony, a much more manageable amount. Anyone interested in a plea bargain?"

Again silence.

"Well, maybe you all need time to think about it. I'm setting a trial date for December 14th at 9:00 a.m. Maybe you can come to an agreement by then. Let's set another status conference in thirty days and see where we are then."

I walked out of the judge's chambers floating on air, I was so happy. Then I was reminded of my Music Row jail cell and my confinement. As I was getting in the van to return, Tate proudly said,

"See what Covington & Burling can accomplish for you."

I laughed to myself the entire ride back.

CHAPTER TWENTY-SIX

A SECRET CALLER

Friday, May 16, 1997

(BENJAMIN DAVIS'S VOICE)

I arrived at the office at 6:00 a.m., I'd already reviewed my to-do-list and knew exactly what I wanted to work on first. Before I began, I grabbed a cup of coffee, and was disappointed there were no left-over pastries. I told myself I could wait another hour until Bella arrived. I read a two-hundred-page deposition, dictating a summary. The summary would become part of my trial notebook. The trial would be a one-day bench trial in Probate Court. I'd been associated as trial counsel, by Robert Rutherford, another attorney, who didn't like to try cases, and who in this case would be a key witness. Robert and I had worked together successfully on four other cases for the same purpose. We'd made some good money together and I valued our relationship.

After I completed that task I put my feet on my desk and outlined in my head my opening argument in the Will and Trust contest. Rutherford had prepared the Will and Trusts, which distortional distributed the estate between three children. The estate, worth just under $2,000,000, made certain charitable gifts and then divided the estate into thirds, but two of the children's shares were placed under a trust controlled by an accountant and the third child as co-trustees. The two children named beneficiaries of the trusts resented the supervision of the trustees and challenged the Will and Trusts on the grounds of undue influence by the third child and Rutherford, who drafted the Will and Trusts.

The case was a simple one. The father didn't have to divide his estate equally, a child had no right to inheritance. The testator father could give all of his money to charity if he so desired. I was about to list the reasons Rutherford gave me the father considered when he placed two thirds of his estate in trust when the phone rang. It was a few minutes before 7:00 a.m., Bella hadn't arrived yet so, I picked up,

"I thought you'd be in the office. You work all the time, must be hard on your family?"

"Let's just keep my family out of this," I said, maybe a little too aggressively. I was unhappy to hear the voice of Amy Pierce, not only because she interrupted me in mid-thought, but I just didn't want to talk to her before my second cup of coffee.

"What do I owe this unexpected call, Ms. Pierce?"

"Have you read Judge Peck's latest order, you might find it quite interesting."

She proceeded to read me the order. I felt sick to my stomach. DA Tory had lost a substantial amount of his proof. I quickly tried to think of a response.

"It sounds like Carmichael still has to worry about almost an ounce found at the townhouse. Besides, I don't think anything in that ruling helps your client. He's going to be held liable, the big question is for how much?"

"Has anyone ever told you that you're much too sure of yourself?" With that said, she hung up.

I tried to go back to working on my opening statement but had lost my focus. Instead I dictated a fax to Robert Rutherford suggesting two possible days and times to meet to prepare him for his trial testimony. The trial would have five witness', but I knew the judge and that he'd insist we squeezed the proof into one day. He'd insist that we go as late as necessary to complete the trial. He wasn't bluffing; once in a similar situation he finally ruled at 10:00 p.m.

The morning flew by. I continued to whittle down my to-do-list. I decided to eat my lunch at my desk, even though I'd much prefer to dine out. As I eat my chicken salad sandwich, I opined how proud my wife, Liza, would be, who was constantly putting me on some type of diet. Today, I was too busy to eat, so I rationalized my action as dieting. Bella knocked and said, "Pick up line three. It's one of the mystery women."

I put down my sandwich, wiped my mouth, pushed the record button on the Dictaphone and the speaker button on my telephone. It was legal to tape a phone conversation in Tennessee if one party was aware of that taping, and I was the aware party. In some states recording the call would be illegal.

"This is Ben Davis; can I help you?"

"I don't know. Can you help me?"

"Well, I'm licensed to practice law in the state of Tennessee, and if I do say so, I'm pretty good at what I do. Would that be of some help to you? Maybe if you tell me your problem, we can figure out if I can be of some assistance. I'm a good problem solver."

"I'm an acquaintance of Roscoe Carmichael, but I regret that I ever met him. I believe he's taken videos of the two of us being intimate, and the police, when I inquired, told me you represented another woman in my situation."

"I do. Her name is Lizzy Swann..."

The caller with a soft but insistent voice said, "I've read about her. I wouldn't want to read about myself in the newspaper. I've seen you on television. That Alice Krieger is very persistent. I'm not looking for publicity. In fact, that's the last thing I want. If I was to get involved, I wouldn't want to use my real name in any lawsuit. I do feel like I'm entitled to be compensated for what that bastard did to me."

While I was contemplating whether the caller was genuine, or just a crank, she broke my train of thought, and said softly, "Maybe this is a bad idea..."

I didn't want to lose her, so I tried to keep her talking. "Hold on. Let's talk about this. You could sue under an alias, something like Mary Doe, to protect your identity, at least on the front end before trial. These cases in all likelihood will never go to trial. All of the parties are motivated to settle. Nobody really wants to drag these facts through the media. I can't make any absolute promises of anonymity because eventually you'll be deposed, the lawyers will get to meet you, and depending on the judge, they may learn your real name. Whether they learn your name at the deposition will be up to the judge. The public will know you only as Mary Doe. We haven't scheduled Carmichael and Oz's depositions yet."

There was a long pause before she asked, "Who's Oz?"

"He was your cameraman. Carmichael claims you knew that you were being filmed and knew there was a hidden cameraman."

Noticeably louder, she responded, "That's bullshit. Sorry, but I'm mad as hell. I didn't have a clue there was anyone else involved other than the two of us. I read about the secret room and two-way mirror. I consented to sex, nothing more. I had no idea that I was being videoed. I realize I'd made a fool of myself, and decided it was best to get out of town."

"Where are you?"

"Safe, and I'm going to stay that way. You can meet me in St. Louis."

I wasn't surprised that this mystery woman had left Middle Tennessee. Hopper had been looking for the three yet unidentified women locally. I wasn't going to let her locale interfere with my gaining representation of this new client.

"I can drive there pretty easy, or fly up on a direct flight. How about Friday?"

I was unfamiliar with St. Louis, so we agreed I'd get a conference room at the airport. We agreed on a time, and she hung up.

I walked into Morty's office and played the tape.

Morty informed me, "I'm going too. We'll take my plane."

"We'll fly commercial. Liza won't let me fly with you. She's been with you in a car, and she doesn't want me riding with you."

"That's ridiculous. Driving is far more difficult than flying."

"That may be true, but it's the landing part that she's worried about."

"I was flying more than twenty years before you were born. I flew against the Germans, and they were shooting at me. I certainly can get us off and back on the ground to St. Louis. What are you, a mouse? You tell your wife we're flying to St. Louis. Just leave out what airline we're taking. I doubt she'll ask. If she does, tell a little white lie. I'm flying us up there."

Morty got his first plane on his sixteenth birthday from his grandpa Abe and was taught to fly by the father of his friend, Albert Wilson, who was a World War I ace. In 1939, Albert and Morty left Nashville and joined the Royal Canadian Air Force and fought the Nazis in the Battles of Britain and Dunkirk. Today his plane of choice was a Cessna, which he kept in mint condition for his last opportunities to fly. At seventy-seven, he should have been grounded years ago, but he had a friend at the FAA, who helped him keep his license. He didn't get to fly very often, and he jumped on every opportunity. Liza's concerns about the old man were justified. His eyesight was well below FAA requirements, and his hand/eye coordination was shot. I'd once confided this information to Liza, which was why she knew he was incapable and I wasn't in safe hands.

CHAPTER TWENTY-SEVEN

THE SECOND CLIENT

Tuesday, May 20, 1997

(BENJAMIN DAVIS'S VOICE)

On Tuesday, like an idiot, I got in the passenger seat next to my old friend. I came clean to my wife, who chastised me from the moment I told her.

I should have waited till the morning I was to leave. My mistake.

The flight was uneventful. Morty sang most of the way. He loved piloting his Cessna again. I chewed one Tootsie Pop after another. I was truly nervous. Morty chewed on the same Cuban throughout the flight. We landed at the private airfield and had to take a bus to the regular terminal where the rented conference room was located.

George Hopper, the investigator we'd hired, flew commercial, earlier in the day, and had stationed himself outside the meeting room, so he could follow the mystery woman to her home or place of business if necessary. Hopper, about five years ago embarked on a second career. He'd been a successful middleweight fighter with a 22-4 record. All of his losses had been to Tommy Hearns and Sugar Ray Leonard, two of the best middleweights in the last thirty years, arguably the best of all time. One of his fights with Hearns was a title fight. He got knocked out in the fifth round. When she arrived, Hopper confirmed that she was in fact woman #3.

As we entered the room, women # 3 stood. I introduced myself and said, "We spoke on the phone. I'm Ben Davis. This is my law partner, Morty Steine. You are?"

"Just call me Sara for now. I'm not sure I want to get involved with you, your partner, or your lawsuit until I figure out what's in it for me."

I immediately recognized Sara as woman #3. I'd seen a lot more of her than she realized. I put her at mid to late thirties, shoulder-length blonde hair and brown eyes. I didn't think she was a natural blonde, neither was my wife. I detected her brown roots. Average height, nicely dressed, with no indication of a wild streak, she was nervous, as she should have been.

I considered myself a good judge of character, I liked this woman. She got to the point right away so, I figured candor was the best approach. "You could be a plaintiff or a witness. As a witness, you would have no financial gain, but if you testified, you'd be supporting a woman who went through the same ordeal that you did. Your testimony might even put Carmichael back in prison."

Sara, or whatever her name was, was noticeably surprised and asked, "When was he in prison?"

"He served less than a year in 1990 for contributing to the delinquency of a minor, for providing her cocaine and intending to having sex with her. He was charged with statutory rape, but he got off because of sloppy police work."

That got a reaction. "He never mentioned that."

I continued, "This guy is dangerous, and unless you help me, he'll get to do it again to some future unsuspecting woman. Now if you want to become a plaintiff and client, I'm confident I can promise you a judgment."

The mention of a judgment got her attention.

"How much?"

"How much do you think a jury would award to compensate you for having your privacy invaded and for being lied to? What do you think would be a reasonable amount?"

She thought for a moment,

"More than $100,000."

"Under Tennessee law, a jury can award not only compensatory damages but also punitive damages. However, the award of punitive damages depends on how a defendant conducts himself or herself in front of the jury. We're kind of hoping Carmichael acts like a jerk."

She asked a thoughtful question next, "What would be the extent of my involvement as a witness or a plaintiff?"

I knew the answer to those questions.

"You're going to be deposed by the defense either way. We can videotape your deposition and play that at trial if not a party and you're unavailable. As a plaintiff, you'd have to testify in front of the jury. Obviously as Mary Doe, you'd have far greater contact with my office."

Sara took it all in. She was looking hard at Morty and I, trying to decide if she should trust us, and if so, should she retain us? She nervously kept cracking her knuckles.

"I'm going to sleep on it, and I'll get back in touch with you one way or another."

I worried I was losing her, but I had to be honest with her. I explained that Carmichael had lined up Strong, Ingram, and Watson. "We're pretty sure he bribed them for their testimony. We've got their depositions scheduled and hope to crack them."

Sara angrily insisted, "I certainly didn't know that I was being videoed, and I didn't know there was a cameraman."

She paused, deciding whether to reveal something. I waited, and then she exposed the truth, "I suspect this is important. I can testify that Carmichael offered me $50,000 if I'd testify in your case that I agreed to be videoed. He didn't use your client's name specifically, but he claimed that he thought somebody might sue him, and that he figured he'd done the same thing to me and wanted to do right by me without the involvement of lawyers. He argued against me sharing my recovery with a lawyer who did nothing for me. I was broke so I listened. As the discussion progressed, he kept adding conditions for the payment. When he suggested that as part of the deal I might have to testify that I knew I was being taped and that I was aware that there was a cameraman, I'd had enough. It got pretty heated after that and the negotiations broke down."

Morty asked, "When was this conversation?"

"About six months ago. I came clean with my husband. He threatened to tell him and I didn't want to be blackmailed. David was hurt, he even threatened to leave me. In the end we decided to move my family to Bowling Green, just over the Kentucky line. My husband commuted an hour to his job in Gallatin, Tennessee. Somehow Carmichael tracked me down. I thought I'd covered my tracks pretty well, but I guess he found me through my mother because she was the only one who knew where I was. Two days after I visited her, he showed up at my new home. One of my son's was there. He stood in my kitchen and in a very menacing way made the offer. I wanted to spit in his face. I did tell him to go to hell. He got very angry and with a death stare, 'told me I was making a life changing mistake.' I got scared, told my husband what happened, and we left Bowling Green in a hurry. My husband had a good job with seniority, and he left without giving notice. I don't live in St. Louis. I hope he won't find me where we live now. My marriage is pretty fragile, and I can't let my family break up."

Morty asked, "How did you meet Carmichael?"

"I'm a songwriter, like every third girl in Nashville. I can also sing and dance. I've got some talent, but in Nashville, there are thousands of girls like me. We met at a party, and I went back to his office to play some of my songs, with the hope of representation. We shared a bottle of wine, and he suggested we play strip poker. I figured, this could be my big break. I forgot my family and who I was and made a life changing mistake, I wish I could take it back. Look, the sex was voluntary, but I never agreed to be videotaped. That was a low blow. What we did was intended to be personal between the two of us. The sex wasn't half bad. The betrayal of my husband was wrong, that was my mistake and my responsibility. He's pretty hurt but claims he's forgiven me. I hope he has, but we're rebuilding trust."

Morty insisted, "If you testify against him, you'll return the favor. If you hire our firm, you can be compensated for what he's done to you. A jury will put a price on his betrayal, which I admit is a difficult thing to predict. Quite frankly, the strength of your testimony will be the determining factor. The jury will need to identify with you and have sympathy for you. Also, how the jury perceives Carmichael and Oz will be equally important. If they come off as creeps, which I think they will, then the jury is much more likely to award a greater amount of damages. What do you think?"

"I'll sleep on it."

We agreed to keep in touch, or she agreed to keep in touch. She left as abruptly as she appeared, with Hopper on her tail.

The next day, Hopper called me, "I owe you fifty bucks. You were right. She's living and working in Branson. I've got her address and telephone number."

"Good job."

"You'll get my bill."

CHAPTER TWENTY-EIGHT

A NEW MEMBER OF THE TEAM

Monday, May 26, 1997

(THIRD PERSON)

Davis picked up the phone and called the number Hopper provided him. It rang twice before she answered, but said nothing. Davis waited for some comment from her. Finally, he said, "Sara, it's a friend calling."

"Who is this?" she asked cautiously.

It's Ben Davis, hopefully your new lawyer."

"How'd you get my number?" Her tone was almost angry.

"It wasn't that difficult. You're not as safe and hidden as you think. If I can find you, don't you think Carmichael can? He threatened you, and you obviously took him seriously. Mr. Steine and the rest of my firm can provide you with some protection, but your best protection would be the umbrella of the justice system. Bringing suit against Carmichael shines the light of public scrutiny on him. That places the greatest restrictions on him. I admit the process isn't perfect, but it's better than trying to deal with Carmichael on your own."

"I want to know how you found me."

Davis was reluctant to tell her that he had Hopper follow her. "You're going to have to trust me or run again. You'll be running the rest of your life. You don't want to live like that. Let me help you. I'll help you whether you want to file a suit or not. I'm concerned for your safety."

"What the hell are you talking about?"

"I think that Carmichael is a dangerous person. He's told me he's not going back to prison. You've told me he threatened you. What did he say?"

Davis chided himself for not asking that question during their first interview.

"He told me if I didn't take the $50,000, I'd never work in the entertainment business again. When I told him to go to hell, he promised me I'd get there first."

Davis weighed Carmichael's words, trying to figure out whether they amounted to an assault and concluded that a court would require more.

"Look, you're already involved in this mess, so you might as well be compensated for your inconveniences and injuries. The defendants owe you something. The exact amount will be up to a jury. Tell them your story, and I'm confident they'll do the right thing."

After a long pause as she weighed her options, Mary Doe, aka Sara, agreed to file a lawsuit.

"What's your real name?"

"Melissa Fields, but my friends call me Mel."

"Well, Mel, when can we meet and where?"

She didn't answer right away, so Davis took charge, "You don't live in St. Louis. You're closer to Branson, aren't you?"

He surprised her by targeting her relocation. He kept going, "I'll come in your direction. I'm going to bring a court reporter with me to take a detailed statement. We'll meet twenty or so miles away from your home. I'll make sure I'm not followed."

"Who's this court reporter?"

"She can be trusted. I'm going to need help documenting your story, and my staff is committed for the next week and isn't available to accompany me."

Sammie was studying for finals, hoping to graduate, and Bella had to remain back in Nashville to run the office. Davis had Katie Stone in mind. He rationalized that it was better to use an actual court reporter, who was independent of his office.

"I'd like to file your complaint after I take the depositions of Ingram, Watson and strong. I want to get their testimony before we reveal your lawsuit. We should be filing by mid-June. The preparation of the complaint will be quite intensive. What we say in the document needs to be correct. We'll spend whatever time is necessary to get the job done."

Davis first explained his contingency fee arrangement of one third and that he anticipated that his firm would be reimbursed for the expenses it advanced on her behalf. He could not be specific as to how much those advanced expenses would be, but he anticipated tens of thousands of dollars.

The conversation ended with the law firm of Steine & Davis being retained by a new client. A very happy Davis called Katie Stone. He was pretty proud of himself for getting Mary Doe on board. He was downright cheery when she answered the phone.

"Hello, Katie, how are you doing?" he asked in his smooth, deep voice. Sensing his good mood, she flirted, "I'm watching pornography. Do you want me to describe what's going on?"

"Lucky you. I'll pass. I have to go back to work after this call and I shouldn't be in an excited state." He thought she was just playing with him. He decided he shouldn't flirt and turned to business. "Do you have two days this week you could travel by car to take a sworn statement and help me draft a complaint? Sammie's studying for finals, and Bella can't come. I need your help."

"I like that you need me. Forty-eight hours is a pretty long job. What's the sleeping arrangement?"

"It's a long trip, and car is the best way to get to the witness. It takes about five hours to get there by car, and it will be a long statement involving several hours of prep before we actually obtain the statement. There's no direct flight, we'd have to connect either through Atlanta or Chicago. Whether we go by car or by plane, I don't think we can get it done and get back home in one day. It might be possible, but we'll both be beyond tired, and I'm not the best driver when I'm tired. It's a safety issue."

There's always the old man's plane, but I'm not sure that would be a safe trip if attempted in one day. You'd probably have to fly back in the dark and Morty was no longer capable of flying at night.

"Safety first," she said, emphasizing the word *safety*.

"I also may need you to take some dictation."

"I'm happy to take your dictation. I'm available any two days this week."

"How about we leave on Friday 6:00 a.m. before traffic gets backed up. We'll get there about eleven, eat lunch with the witness, and then get to work until it's done. We may need to do some cleanup on Saturday and then drive home."

"It's a date."

"Behave yourself, Katie. I've invited you because I promised you all of the work in the Swann case. This statement will be used in the Swann case and may form the basis of a second suit against Carmichael and Oz. This will result in quite a bit of benefit for both of us."

Technically this sworn statement wasn't in the Swann case. If Davis was being honest with himself and Katie, he enjoyed her flirtation and her attention.

Davis set to work on drafting the Mary Doe complaint. He converted the Swann document to a different, yet similar document. The facts were different, but the legal theories were almost identical. The conspiracy count was expanded. It now alleged that "In furtherance of the conspiracy, the defendant Carmichael, within a short time after receipt of the notice from Steine & Davis of the claims of Elizabeth Swann, contacted the plaintiff Mary Doe. The defendant Carmichael first offered her $25,000 to testify in the Swann case that the plaintiff Mary Doe had prior knowledge and gave permission to videotape them having sex. He also wanted the plaintiff to testify that she knew the defendant Oz was the cameraman. The plaintiff told the defendant 'to go to hell.' The defendant then upped the bribe to $50,000. The plaintiff again rejected the defendant Carmichael, who then threatened the plaintiff. The plaintiff, in fear for her life, fled Nashville."

CHAPTER TWENTY-NINE
A TOUCHY SITUATION
Friday, May 30, 1997
(BENJAMIN DAVIS' VOICE)

Katie and I drove to Big Cedar Lodge, twenty-six miles from Branson, Mo. The trip took over four hours. Katie was very professional the entire ride, our discussion covered many subjects, none were inappropriate. She was dressed in a white blouse, two buttons undone, and a black skirt that came a few inches above her knees. I did peek a few times.

Bella had birddogged the location. There was a main lodge surrounded by deluxe cabins. Bella had reserved one for the client, one for Katie, and a larger one with a kitchen and a large table for me. I figured we'd work in my cabin. There was a printer and copy machine off of the kitchen. There was a dining room in the main lodge with a half decent restaurant.

Mary Doe arrived first and, as instructed by Bella, checked in and waited. The bellboy escorted her to her cabin, I'd said that I'd call her when to join us in the restaurant for lunch. I carried my blood-stained briefcase and luggage. Once in my cabin I called Mary Doe and asked her to join me in my cabin; I wanted to have a private conversation. I sat with her for sixty minutes, first presenting my one-and-a-half-page employment contract. Doe read it and signed with her real name, Mellissa Fields. I then provided her with and she reviewed the draft complaint, with the statement of the facts omitted.

I interjected, "I'm here to fill in the blanks," pointing at the fact portion. I need to hear what you say happened, and we need to get it right. I have a court reporter who will take down your statement."

I wanted to know what Mary Doe was going to say before she told her story in front of Katie Stone. Katie wasn't my employee and therefore not protected under the attorney/client privilege and therefore subject to being questioned by the defense as to the development of the document. I had no intent to volunteer Katie Stone's participation in the process, but it could be discovered. I would make sure that all earlier drafts of the complaint were destroyed so that the defendants couldn't use them against my client through Katie's testimony. During our interview I questioned Doe about the current state of her marriage.

"David's agreed to this move to Branson, so I could pursue my singing career. I think he did so because he knew I wouldn't succeed. Don't get me wrong, I enjoy performing but my family is suffering. The boys miss their friends and their school. David was in management and now he's a commissioned sales person, needing to make a sale to put food on the table."

"Under the law your husband has a claim against Carmichael and Oz as well. It's called loss of consortium and he can recover for the impact their intentional conduct had on your marriage. He could be a party to the lawsuit."

"No way absolutely not. I don't want him involved. You need to keep David out of this."

"That's not very likely. The defendants will want to depose your husband. Your suit will allege that you've been affected emotionally because of the defendants conduct, your husband's testimony about a change in your mental state is relevant and discoverable. The defendants will insist on taking his deposition and I bet they'll insist on playing your video at that deposition."

Mary Doe excused herself to call her husband and give him the bad news. I wondered whether I'd talked myself out of a client. She came back fifteen minutes later, and announced,

"He'll be deposed and if necessary watch the tape, but he doesn't want to be part of the lawsuit. He claims he doesn't want people to think that he's profiting from my sleeping with Carmichael. He told me that this was my mess and that I had to clean it up. He insisted that our boys play no part in this, and I agree."

I assured her there was no reason her sons had to be involved.

I then called Katie and asked her to join us for lunch. It was one o'clock, and I was pretty hungry, so I ordered a ribeye, French fries, and a wedge salad with blue cheese dressing. The two women ate much lighter than I did, club sandwiches.

After lunch, it took four hours to get the first draft complaint completed, it was just before 6:00 pm and we agreed to meet for dinner back at the restaurant. I took my shoes off and laid on the bed and reread the document, while sipping on a Jack Daniel's over ice. After an hour of making notes I called home and checked in with Liza. After a few bourbons, I went over to the main lodge for dinner.

I had a shrimp scampi appetizer, a large piece of swordfish, sweet potatoes, and apple pie. Katie and Mary had roast chicken. After dinner, we went back to my cabin to go over my notes. Mary approved most of my changes, and I explained to Mary that over the next few days I'd be polishing the complaint and get it ready for filing.

At 9:45 p.m., Mary Doe excused herself and went to her cabin. I poured Katie and I a double Jack.

"Good job. Thanks for all your help today. I told you it would be hard to get this done in one day and get back home."

Katie called bullshit, "I don't know. It was fifteen hours of work and travel. You work fifteen-hours days in Nashville all the time. It's almost an average day for you. You just wanted to stay overnight with me, right?"

"That's not fair. I don't like driving long distances, particularly at night. Ten hours is a lot of driving in one day for me."

"We could have split the driving between us. No, you just wanted to stay overnight. You like flirting with me, Ben. I like flirting with you. We've got a strong animal magnetism between us. Don't be afraid to admit it."

I was sitting at the table and she moved to my side of the table and leaned over and kissed me, to my surprise I kissed her back. I stood and we locked arms around each other, her breasts pressed hard against me. I'd not embraced another woman like that in more than fifteen years. She placed both her hands on my ass and pulled me toward her. I became aroused, and she began to move her hand from behind to the front of my pants. She grabbed hold of my erect penis through my trousers and began rubbing it hard. I jumped back.

I realized I was about to make a big mistake. I'd represented many men who'd been in this position, proceeded, and regretted what they did, both emotionally and financially. I thought about the possibility of destroying my marriage. I needed to think quickly. *What would I tell a client to do in this situation? That's probably the right move.*

"Katie, I've put you in a very unfair position. I apologize for flirting. I'm happily married. You're a beautiful woman. Somebody is out there for you, but it's not me. I jeopardized our professional relationship, which is my doing. I promised you all of the depositions in the Swann case, and that's going to require us to work closely together, just not in that way. Friends." I stuck my hand out.

She grabbed my forearm, drew me close, and kissed me again, her tongue swirling around in my mouth. I returned her effort and my tongue shot into her mouth. It was a natural reaction beyond my control. Katie bit down hard. I jumped back and wiped my mouth and examined my bleeding tongue. I moved to the far side of the room, my penis erect. My brain tried to maintain control over the rest of my body. I turned to walked into the bedroom, and over my shoulder said, "Katie, you can see yourself out. We'll have breakfast at seven and leave when we're done. Good night."

After she left I took a cold shower. I got into bed and started watching a pay-per-view movie. About halfway through, I got hungry and ordered room service. I felt like having breakfast, so I asked for a three-egg western omelet, well-done ham, hash brown potatoes, and two pancakes. I always ate under stress. Being with Katie had become stressful.

CHAPTER THIRTY

THE EXPERTS

Monday, June 2, 1997

(THIRD PERSON)

While Davis was away with Katie Stone and Mary Doe, Morty and Sammie met with Lizzy Swann's therapist and psychiatrist to help them prepare for their important depositions. These would be important depositions because they would set the tone for Lizzy's claim for emotional distress. On the ride home, Davis called Morty and insisted that Mary Doe also needed to be seen by mental health professionals and since Swann's people were already on board, Doe might as well be seen by them. Not every decision that appears to be a good idea, at first, is in fact a good idea. The fact that Lizzy sought psychiatric care before seeking legal advice supported her claim of emotional distress. The defense couldn't argue she sought professional care simply to support her claim of damages. Her pain was real, and she was entitled to be paid for her suffering. The critical question was how much? It was a problem that Doe didn't seek care after learning of Carmichael and Oz's actions. The defense will argue that the treatment was an afterthought, and that Doe was just trying to build her case. The counter argument was that she was too busy running away from Carmichael and that her delay to seek help was because she had limited funds, and her immediate goal was to save her marriage.

The defense challenged for more than an hour Dr. Adam Little's credentials. Dr. Little, a board-certified psychiatrist, did not regularly testify in court, and he'd only been deposed once. At first, he was both uneasy and reserved. However, the more Tate attacked his opinions, the more confident Little seemed to grow.

He was a skilled professional who treated all types of psychiatric and distressed patients, from alcoholics to ones suffering from post-traumatic stress disorder and depression, such as Lizzy Swann. Little obtained his undergraduate degree from Tufts and then went on to get his medical degree and completed his fellowship at Vanderbilt University. As her psychiatrist, Dr. Little prescribed and managed Lizzy's medication. He started her on Prozac and over time increased dosage of Ambien to help her sleep. He testified that he saw Ms. Swann "during the first month following her discovery of the video, weekly, then biweekly, and now once a month." Tate asked,

"So, the fact you're now seeing the patient less frequently indicates that she's doing better?"

"Not really, all it indicates is that for the time being I think she's on the right dosage of her medication. Lizzy is suffering from post-traumatic stress disorder; that diagnosis doesn't get better with medication. The patient, through therapy must confront the traumatic event. My sessions with Lizzy are not therapy, my role is medication maintenance. I guess you don't understand the disorder."

"Doctor, don't lecture me about stress disorders, I led men into battle. I watched men die in agony and I've seen them blown to bits. I've also seen how the realities of war affect some men. Most soldiers are forced to cope, while others can't and are medically discharged. I've seen dozens of men with post-traumatic disorder, probably more than you, sir."

Tate ended the deposition on that rough note. Next up was Lizzy's therapist, Beverly Newman, who had a master's degree in social work. She testified that following Lizzy's viewing of the video, Lizzy required that their sessions be in her home, three times a week because Lizzy was so depressed that she couldn't leave her condo. Newman described a woman who was "near bedridden, petrified to leave her home." Her fear was based on shame of having conducted herself as she did, but more so because others had seen her behave as she did.

"The treatment was to have her realize that although she may have acted out, even foolishly, it was your client who betrayed her and he was responsible for the existence of the tape, not her."

When it was her turn, Pierce attacked Newman, claiming that her opinions were subjective, based upon what Ms. Swann told her. Pierce then asked, "You realize that your testimony is being used to establish Ms. Swann's damages and that she has a vested interest in convincing you of her trauma and depression?"

Newman's response was defiant, "Lizzy could hardly get her ass out of bed on those days I came for my one-hour session. She wouldn't shower, and her personal appearance and hygiene by the second week deteriorated so badly that I seriously considered hospitalizing her. I had to continue to see her at her home until she was well enough to drive a car. That breakthrough came in the fifth week into our therapy. At first, she cried most of the session, but with time, we began to address the issue of the video. Ms. Pierce, Lizzy Swann isn't that good an actress. I'm a trained professional, I can state with certainty she was damaged by your client and Mr. Carmichael."

Newman testified that after twenty or so sessions, by the seventh week, Lizzy began to better cope with the fact that others had seen the video.

"She's no longer downs on herself. She recognizes that she's a victim and that your client violated her trust."

"So, she's doing much better?"

Davis knew exactly where Pierce was going, but he had to remain silent. He hoped that the therapist would recognize what Pierce was doing.

"She's doing better, but everything is relative. She's turned her frustration and anger away from herself toward your client and Mr. Carmichael, which is much healthier."

"Ms. Swann never met my client. She must blame Mr. Carmichael more so?"

"No, after Lizzy discovered the existence of Mr. Oz, she hates him and holds him equally responsible, possibly more so. He made the tape. She never intended for him to see her dance routine, and she never intended for him to be part of the sexual experience. He invaded her privacy even more than Mr. Carmichael did. Fortunately, as she improves, her anger and hatred seem to diminish. Being too angry is an unhealthy thing. She's trying to return to a more productive life, and this lawsuit has replaced her personal anger."

"So, you've encouraged Ms. Swann to hate my client?"

"I've not done that. It's human nature to hate someone who betrays your trust. The lawsuit is a vehicle to channel her anger. I'm hoping that a jury verdict will bring Lizzy closure."

"So, you think this lawsuit is therapeutic for Ms. Swann?"

"Absolutely, and I hope that it will be financially beneficial as well."

"So, you're rooting for Ms. Swann to win her suit?"

"As her treating therapist, I think it's in her best interest, and as a person, I think that justice requires a jury to hear the facts and award what they deem appropriate."

"So, you'd concede that you're biased?"

"I guess I am."

Pierce asked Newman, "It was the police who discovered the tape at the Music City office, right?"

"Yes."

"It was the police who showed the tape to everybody?"

Davis objected, "The judge had already separated the claims against the police. The last thing Davis wanted was for his witness to blame the police rather than Carmichael and Oz."

Pierce insisted that the witness answer. The judge would rule on the objection at a later date. Under the rules, all objections were reserved, except an objection based on a privilege.

"The police found the tape, but Mr. Carmichael and Mr. Oz made the tape. If not for them, there wouldn't be any tapes. I can't blame the police for viewing what they found and showing it to the DA's office."

Pierce didn't like that answer, but she continued, "Lizzy Swann has confided in you her greatest fears about these tapes?"

"Yes."

"So how much?"

"How much what?"

"Is this case worth? Haven't you been hired to give an amount?"

"No, I haven't. I professionally treated a woman in pain, and that pain was caused by the defendants, not the police."

Thank God, Davis thought.

"On a scale from one to ten, ten being the greatest pain, where did Lizzy Swann fall?"

"It doesn't work like that."

"It's hard to put a number on pain. Isn't that right, Ms. Newman?"

"The patient does that. It's a question of tolerance as to physical pain and mental pain. Two different patients will react differently to an event depending on the circumstances and the personality of the patient. In part it's genetics, and in part it's situational."

"Pain is subjective then?"

"No, it's objective, but the patient determines the tolerance of the pain."

"You don't know how much a jury should award Ms. Swann to compensate her for her pain, do you?"

"Not a dollar amount. That would be up to the jury."

"Well, if you don't know, how will they know how much to award?"

Davis thought that was a stupid question to ask, and he was right.

"They'll just need to figure it out, through discussion, mutual agreement and come to a dollar amount. They'll listen to Ms. Swann's testimony and her description of her depression and trauma, the experts' professional opinions, the testimonies of Misters Carmichael and Oz and judge everybody's credibility. Then they can collectively come up with a dollar amount. That's how our system of justice works. You went to law school. You should know how our jury system works."

That last answer made Pierce furious.

"Do you have a law degree?"

"No."

"How many times have you testified in court?"

"None. I've given two depositions. Both cases settled."

"How many juries have you picked?"

"None."

"Despite your lack of experience, you would agree that picking the jury will be very important in the outcome of the case and if Ms. Swann succeeds, the amount that might be awarded?"

"I think the outcome is very clear. Mr. Carmichael and Mr. Oz betrayed Lizzy Swann by secretly videotaping her, and they should be required to compensate her for the embarrassing situation they put her in."

"I'm amazed about your certainty of the outcome without knowing all of the facts, but at least you're uncertain about the amount?"

"Yes."

Pierce had laid the groundwork for a speculative damage's argument. "If the experts can't put a price on her damages," Pierce would ask, "How can the jury calculate damages?"

Davis, of course, would have given a much better answer, "The jury listens carefully to the testimony, has an opportunity to view the witness's demeanor and judge the witness's credibility. After weighing all the evidence, the jury decides. That's what reasonable people will do because the judge will instruct them to do that."

Much better answer, insisted Davis.

Davis asked very few questions. Both experts had agreed to testify at trial, if one became necessary. Everyone ordered a copy of the depositions. Tate and Pierce would provide them to their experts to counter and to prepare cross-examination in the event of trial. It had been a long day, Davis sat there and had very little control of the testimony and the outcome. He was tired and hungry. He hoped Liza would have dinner ready when he got home. On the drive home he contemplated the day's events as he sucked hard on a cherry Tootsie Pop. All in all, it had been a pretty good day. They'd set out their expert testimony for damages.

CHAPTER THIRTY-ONE

THE LIARS' DEPOS AND CONSOLIDATION

Tuesday, June 3- Thursday, June 5, 1997

(THIRD PERSON)

The day after the defense discovered the professional opinions of the plaintiff's experts, it was Davis' turn to take the depositions of Carmichael's cheerleaders, Ingram, Strong, and Watson. He'd held off filing the Doe complaint. The experienced litigator wanted these witnesses to commit to their positions before they knew that he represented another one of the videoed women, one who would testify that Carmichael tried to bribe her.

He began his questioning of Ingram slowly, getting to know her, with Ingram providing background information about her family, her education, and her work history. He was friendly. No reason not to be, and he tried to put her at ease. He only partially succeeded. Ingram hesitated before answering every question and gave short, precise responses. She had been schooled by either Tate, Gray or Pierce. Davis could tell from her demeanor and body language that defense counsel had coached her and that she anticipated his questions. Recognizing that the witness had been prepped, Davis chewed around the edges of the issues, waiting for Ingram to drop her guard and make a mistake.

Twice divorced, she was thirty years old, tall, attractive, with short brown hair, and a dark complexion. Her glasses made it hard to see her brown eyes during the depo, but she was calm and was well spoken. Davis knew from her video that she had a rose tattoo on her right shoulder and a leopard tattoo on her left.

"I have received interrogatory responses from the defendant Carmichael that indicates that you consented to being videoed?"

"Yes, sir."

"That was on September 23rd and 30th, October 4th and 6th, 1995?"

Her tape identified each date Carmichael and Oz videoed her. It was written on the face of the tape.

"It was in 1995. I don't remember every date."

"I thought you signed a document that identified each date you had sex with our friend Roscoe Carmichael? They provided you with those dates?"

"I guess so."

"Who typed your statement?"

"I don't know who typed it."

"But it was provided to you and you just signed it?"

"I told the lawyers what happened and they typed it up."

"Which lawyers?"

She pointed to Gray and Pierce.

"Let the record reflect that the witness pointed out Mr. Gray and Ms. Pierce."

"These words are their words, not yours?"

"I told them what happened and they prepared the document and I signed it."

"But this isn't the whole story is it?"

"I don't understand."

"Didn't you sign a second document that released Mr. Carmichael and Mr. Oz from any liability regarding the making of the video and were paid $50,000 for your signature?"

Davis was taking a shot in the dark, trying to get Ingram to either lie or admit to the bribery. Tate objected to Davis' question, "facts not in evidence."

Davis shot back, "that's an improper objection. The fact this statement leaves out vital information is not a basis to object." Sydney Ingram obviously now nervous, didn't answer. Defense counsel had not prepared her to be confronted with her contract/release. Tate and Pierce had not produced the release and did not anticipate Davis asking a question about the hidden contract.

Breaking the silence, Davis asked, "Didn't Mr. Carmichael at first offer you $25,000 and then upped it to $50,000?"

Ingram was so flustered she didn't know what to do. Tate jumped in and objected, but before he could state the basis for his objection, Davis turned on Tate, "Do you deny the existence of such an agreement?"

"I'm not under oath, and this isn't my deposition."

Davis got snippy, "I'd be happy to schedule your deposition, and if you interfere with my questioning of this witness, you may just become a witness, possibly a co-conspirator, if you drafted that agreement."

Looking at the Mary Doe complaint, Davis started quoting to the witness how Carmichael approached her to get a release in exchange for cash. He gave Ingram the impression he was reading from either her agreement or a similar agreement. Tate kept objecting, and Ingram, confused and pressed, eventually denied the existence of any such contract with Carmichael.

The ploy failed to secure an admission, but the lie was even better. He'd eventually prove the existence of the Ingram/ Carmichael agreement, and Ingram's credibility would be irreparably damaged.

Davis wasn't deterred. He started the Carol Strong deposition immediately following the conclusion of Ingram's. He demanded an immediate start because of the late hour in the hope of completing the second deposition by the end of the day. He reminded Tate and Pierce that their schedules dictated that the day begin at 1:00 p.m. rather than 9:00 am. The shortened workday turned out to prejudice defense counsel, rather than squeeze Davis. Tate didn't have time to warn Strong that Davis knew about her release and that Ingram denied its existence.

Davis didn't take the chance of Tate getting too strong at a break, so he started right out of the box by asking Strong about her release agreement rather than getting her background information. He again used the Mary Doe complaint as a prop. Unaware of Ingram's testimony, Strong, after being confronted, admitted to executing a release with both Carmichael and Oz in exchange for a payment of $50,000. On the record, Davis asked Tate why the Carmichael/Strong agreement wasn't produced in discovery. Tate didn't answer but indicated he'd look into the matter and "get back to him." Like Ingram, Strong testified that she knew she was being videotaped and that she knew Oz was acting as the cameraman. Davis would stick the defendants' failure to produce the releases in response to discovery down their throats, first in front of Judge Howard and later at trial before the jury.

On Thursday, he took the deposition of Dominique Watson. She was a better witness than either Ingram or Strong. She admitted right away to the existence of the release and testified that neither Tate nor Pierce was involved in the negotiation of the document.

"I made the deal with Mr. Carmichael and nobody else. We talked, agreed on a price, and then he drew up the document."

"Was it typed?"

"Yes."

"Do you know who typed it?"

"I never asked, but I assumed Mr. Carmichael did."

Davis was pleased that Ingram's testimony was inconsistent with Watson's and Strong's testimonies as to the existence of the release. Although the three women lied about the creation of their videos, Davis still thought he had two good days of discovery. He flushed out their testimony and knew what he had to deal with.

Katie Stone expedited the transcription of the videoed women's depositions at Davis' request. She worked through the night. She was highly motivated, both financially and romantically. She hoped that Davis would reward her effort and that they'd connect.

CHAPTER THIRTY-TWO

THE JUDGE SPEAKS

Friday, June 6, 1997

(THIRD PERSON)

Davis filed the Mary Doe complaint the next day, as well as a motion to consolidate the two cases so they could be tried together for "judicial economy." He argued that "all of the fact discovery, except the plaintiffs' depositions will be identical." The defendants opposed the consolidation.

Judge Howard heard the motion two weeks later. The court wanted to address the new lawsuit right away. Howard opened the hearing by asking, "Mr. Davis, I expediated this hearing; I'd like to know whether you want to envision filing any more complaints relating to the videos?"

"Judge, I don't have any other clients at this time. I've hired a private investigator in an effort to find the remaining two women."

"I want you to let the court and defense counsel know if your PI finds either of them immediately."

"Yes sir."

Davis had filed the inconsistent testimony of Strong, Watson, and Ingram concerning the releases, "I submit to the court that

Ms. Ingram committed perjury, and that she has a release with the defendants.

Judge Howard turned to Tate and Pierce, "Is there a document between your clients and Ms. Ingram?"

Pierce threw Tate under the bus, "My client didn't negotiate one."

Tate responded, "I'm trying to determine if one exists. It appears Mr. Carmichael on his own, without my knowledge, may have negotiated these documents."

Howard had definitely read the transcripts and was upset with the false testimony of Ingram and the failure of Gray and Tate to produce the documents identified.

"Well, Mr. Tate; Ms. Watson and Ms. Strong admitted that they executed releases with your client. Why weren't they produced?"

"I was unaware..."

Howard cut him off, "Your client knew the documents existed?"

"He didn't tell me about them."

The judge got angry, "It's a yes or no question. You've got twenty-four hours to produce all of the agreements, that includes those of the yet unidentified women, if they exist. It's 2:00 p.m. Ms. Strong and Ms. Watson have admitted the existence of these contracts. Get copies from Mr. Carmichael and produce them. If the Ingram document exists, turn over all three documents by tomorrow at 2:00 p.m. If an Ingram release exists, Ms. Ingram will answer to me for her false testimony. Mr. Tate and Mr. Gray; I warn you not to play games. Your client should have produced these documents in response to Mr. Davis' document request. We know who women # 2 (Swann), # 3 (Mary Doe), # 4 (Ingram), # 5 (Strong), and # 6 (Watson) are. Does your client know the identity of women # 1 and # 7? Do those women have agreements?"

Gray, who had been sitting, stood and assured the court he'd find out what was going on, including any information about women #1 and # 7. The court then turned to whether to consolidate the two cases.

Pierce argued that each plaintiff was a separate event and deserved their own day in court and that her client was entitled to a separate defense. The defendants preferred three women's testimony on their side on the issue of consent, and only one on the other. Consolidation allowed Davis to argue that Mary Doe corroborated Lizzy Swann's testimony, and Lizzy Swann's credibility improved.

Pierce argued that the Steine & Davis law firm had a conflict of interest representing two plaintiffs accusing the defendants of the same wrongful acts. She argued that the defendants had limited funds and that Davis' clients were therefore competing for the same dollars.

Davis produced two documents, one signed by Swann and one signed by Doe waiving any possible conflict by the firm. Judge Howard responded, "Nice try, but no way. No conflict."

He ruled, "Look, there's no question we need to consolidate discovery. Except for experts, any depositions taken can be used in both cases. Mr. Davis, does Ms. Doe have any treating professionals or have you retained any testifying expert witnesses?"

Davis answered, "No, sir. She chose to run away to another city out of fear of Mr. Carmichael but didn't have the funds to seek professional help. She has not been treated by a psychiatrist or a therapist. I intend to have her examined by Ms. Swann's treating psychiatrist and therapist, Dr. Little and Ms. Newman."

"In paragraph 32 of the Doe complaint, you describe the contact by Mr. Carmichael and Ms. Doe as an attempted bribe. Is that an attempt of Mr. Carmichael to secure a release?"

Tate jumped up, "I object to it being called a bribe. We executed a legal document that speaks for itself."

"Have you produced it?"

"It hasn't been asked for. It was never executed. In my understanding it was a failed attempt at a release."

"That's not true, Your Honor. We asked for the document but didn't get it. We asked for "all correspondence and other documents with any woman in the videos." The defense didn't know Ms. Doe had retained me so they didn't produce it. They were playing fast and loose with discovery and the court."

"Produce it, Mr. Tate, to plaintiff's counsel by 2:00 p.m. tomorrow, and any other releases or any other attempted releases that may exist. The court also wants to see these documents. Mr. Tate and Mr. Gray; I have real concerns you may have committed an overt act and joined the conspiracy with your client. I am going to reserve judgment as to whether or not contempt charges should be brought against Mr. Carmichael and his counsel for failure to produce. I reserve the right to bring perjury charges against Ms. Strong for her deposition testimony."

Extremely upset, Tate stood and started turning red. "That statement is completely uncalled for, sir. You're just showing your bias against the defense. I object to that comment. I renew my motion to recuse."

"Again, I deny your motion. The Court of Appeals has already answered that question."

The week before, the Court of Appeals denied the defendants' Rule 10 motion and directed that the Swann case proceed to trial. Howard pushed Tate, "What about settlement? Any discussions?"

Davis answered, "None yet. We'll finish the depositions of the parties and then we can address settlement. May I ask for a clarification of one of the court's orders?"

"What's your question?"

"Mr. Tate and Ms. Pierce have refused to set their clients depositions. Neither are going to be criminally charged for the videotaping, so there's no Fifth Amendment basis for refusing or delaying from testifying..."

"Stop right there. Mr. Tate, I've previous ruled on this matter. in one of my order's I described the scope of the deposition of your client; stop being obstructive. If you don't there will be consequences. Ms. Pierce, ditto, or else."

Hesitant to interrupt Howard, Davis sheepishly asked,

"Do I have a right at the defendants' depositions to ask them about the financials they produced?"

"What do you say, Ms. Pierce?"

"I signed an agreed order to produce my client's financials because you ordered the other defendant. Your order says nothing about answering questions at a deposition."

"I'm amending my order. I hereby direct the defendants to answer questions about their financials at their depositions, except the plaintiffs cannot be present for that part of the depo, and that part of the deposition shall be placed in a separate deposition and shall be filed with the court under seal. Ms. Pierce, you draw the order."

Tate didn't like that ruling or the fact he wasn't heard on the matter.

"Anything else?"

Davis, who was on a roll asked,

"Judge, the plaintiffs filed a motion for a protective order limiting the length of their depositions to seven hours in accordance with the federal rules."

Howard did not hesitate,

"The depositions of the plaintiffs and the defendants shall be limited to seven hours and an additional one hour shall be granted the plaintiffs' to ask each defendant about their financials. I also rule that prior to the anniversary date of the Swann case being filed in November, I'm ordering mediation. This case should be settled, and I want all of you to work together to get that done. Trial in the Carmichael criminal case is set for when?"

Tate responded,

"December 14th."

"Trial in the Swann case is set for February 3rd. If the mediation fails, I'll let you know if the Mary Doe case will be tried on that date. Discovery is consolidated and should proceed as quickly as possible. I'm waiting to see if any other lawsuits are filed. Mr. Davis, you'll let the court and defendants know immediately if you stumble upon any of these other videoed women."

"Yes, sir."

Davis still regretted offering to do so, but the words had already gotten out of his mouth. His only solace was that Tate was very upset. And he noticed that Alice Krieger was in the back of the courtroom making notes and would report on Tate's disappointment later on that evening newscast.

CHAPTER THIRTY-THREE

A HAPPY FAMILY DAY

Saturday, June 14, 1997

(SAMMIE DAVIS' VOICE)

I came to Nashville a party girl after spending four years at the University of Florida and another eighteen months studying to be a paralegal in Miami. I wasn't much of a student, but I was bright and with minimal effort I earned both degrees. I was tall, blonde, tan, beautiful, and I spent those six years in Florida having a real good time. Prior to going off to college, from ages six through sixteen, I lived under the watchful eyes of my grandparents, who kept me on a pretty tight leash, in Woodbury, Long Island. Off to college a year early, I developed a taste for drinking, drugs and learning a lot about the opposite sex. During the five and a half years away from my grandparents, I'd forgotten many of the values they taught me. My grandmother, Nana Shelly, aware of my lifestyle change, was at her wits end and was on a mission to save me. She wanted me to relocate to a more stable family-oriented environment. Hence the phone call to her younger son, Ben, and her daughter-in-law, Liza. The old woman was convinced that her son held the key to my success through employment, "I want you to take her in and under your wing. You're a lawyer, and she's a paralegal. You can help each other. More important, you're going to do this for me. I need to know she's on a good path and moving in the right direction. I want you to consider yourself Sammie's mentor, the way Morty mentored you. Teach her your work ethic."

My uncle never had a chance to turn her down. No Davis man could win an argument with Nana Shelly.

In 1992, I came on board as a paralegal. Morty had no objection. He liked the idea. I was family. Not only did he give me the job, he gave me a place to live in his building and he only charged me a dollar a month rent for a one-bedroom loft one floor above the office. My first task was the Plainview cases, ten medical malpractice lawsuits against the same two doctors and a community hospital. The firm of Steine & Davis was strained to the limit prosecuting those ten civil actions against those criminals with medical licenses.

After I spent two years as a paralegal, Morty suggested that I go to law school. I leapt at the challenge, having been inspired by the Plainview cases. I went to Vanderbilt Law School at Morty's expense, no strings attached. He insisted that during the school year I continue to work at the firm part time and also work during the summers. Three years of hard work, and graduation day had arrived. The entire family had traveled to town to attend my graduation ceremony on Vanderbilt campus. Morty was especially proud of me, his ward.

I was barely in the top half of my class because I had a full-time job, not a part-time job as originally agreed. My professors must have mentally taken attendance, and it counted toward my grades. I'm sure my test scores would have earned me a much higher class ranking if my seat wasn't empty half the time. Steine & Davis needed me, so I was at the office rather than in class.

My real education didn't come from lectures or case studies

presented in the classroom. It came from observing my uncle and Morty in the office, depositions, and in the courtroom. For five years, as a paralegal and then as a law student I was in the trenches right alongside them, handing them documents and watching them cross-examine witnesses. That's how I learned.

Morty, who was generally very serious, became even more so. He was my benefactor, so he had a right to give sage advice, "I have high expectations for you. You'll get the benefit of my years of experience as well your uncle's. We plan on molding you into a better lawyer than either of us. I expect great things from you before I go out. You know Goldie and I never had children. I think of your uncle like a son. When you joined this firm, you became part of my family, like Ben and Bella. I want a legacy after I'm gone. Let me make you the best female lawyer Nashville has ever seen."

"Why shoot so low? How about the best lawyer Nashville's ever seen, including you?"

Arrogant little imp. That would be something, better than Ben or even me. She's already learned arrogance from both of us.

"I accept the challenge. You're up against some tough competition. You know I've been in the law for more than fifty years, and in all due modesty, I've achieved quite a bit."

"That only means you've got a lot to teach me, so you need to stop smoking those damn cigars. They're not good for you. I need you to stick around."

"Don't worry, I'm not going anywhere." In an act of defiance, he took a Cuban from his inside jacket pocket and lit up. Morty could care less who might be offended by his smoke. He figured he was a big donor to the school, and the Board of Trustees would overlook his indiscretions.

After I walked across the stage, my family, including my grandparents, went back to my uncle's home for a celebration. Liza, the perfect hostess, had everything ready. As always on social events my uncle rode on her coattails. My uncle operated the grill, but my aunt did everything else. We met at the grill and I proudly said, "I've made it."

He corrected me, "you're just starting, but what an education you got at Steine & Davis. You could prepare and file a lawsuit. Most of your classmates won't get to do that for two years."

I agreed that there were many advantages of a small firm. "You should be noticed for your effort and results.

"Can you watch these steaks for a moment? Your aunt likes hers well done. That's hers in the corner."

He was back in a moment. He had two gifts, "One's for now, and the other for later."

I opened the now present. It was a tan briefcase with my initials, "SAD." Sammie Adele Davis. I hated my middle name.

I commented, "It's just like yours without the blood stain." Five years earlier, in association with the Plainview cases, he was severely beaten, and some of his blood made its way onto his briefcase.

He handed me the second present, "When we hang this depends on you. I suspect it won't be a long time."

I unwrapped a bronze plaque that read, "Steine, Davis & Davis."

He gave me a big hug and while doing so whispered, "You'll be the second Davis listed, by the way."

Always ready with a quick response, I said, "For now."

"You're a real smart-ass."

I drove my grandparents to the airport and helped them with their luggage.

Larry Davis put his arms around me tightly and he said, "You're playing with the big boys now. You've got two incredible legal scholars as teachers, but let me give you some non-legal advice; don't let anybody push you around because you're a woman. Men are going to try. Stand your ground when you think you should. Ninety percent of the time your gut reaction is the right one. Keep the partying to a minimum. I know you'll need to blow off steam, just use good judgment. When in doubt, ask your Aunt Liza or Bella. As women, they will have insight your uncle and Morty couldn't possibly give you."

I gave my grandfather a hug. As I did, he slipped me an envelope with ten one-hundred-dollar bills and said, "For an emergency. God forbid you have one."

Nana Shelly's advice was quite different, "You're a beautiful, smart young lady. Find a nice boy and settle down. It would be good if he was Jewish, but I'm willing to waive that requirement."

"Nana, I'm not ready to make such a commitment. I haven't found that special someone. But when I do, you'll be the first to know."

She kissed me and said good-bye. Nana Shelly got a little teary eyed, "I'm so proud of you. Keep up the good work."

I met friends for drinks and a late night of celebrating my graduation. I brought a male friend back to the loft for an evening of pleasure, I felt entitled.

CHAPTER THIRTY-FOUR

DEPOSITION OF ELIZABETH SWANN

Tuesday, June 17, 1997

(ELIZABETH SWANN'S VOICE)

I spent two days getting ready for my deposition under the guidance of Mr. Steine. We worked out of his sixth-floor apartment rather than the eighth-floor office. Bella would periodically visit and bring us a fresh pot of coffee and various homemade pastries. Throughout the long ordeal, Morty, who I finally became comfortable calling by his first name, at his insistence, spent hours chewing one black cigar after another, never lighting them. He refrained as a courtesy to me, who could not tolerate the smoke. I finally protested his bad habit and being a gentleman, he acquiesced.

He explained from the beginning of our marathon session that the strategy of the defense team would be to embarrass me, in an effort to force me into a cheap settlement. "They will try to make the deposition an intense experience, hoping that you will relapse into depression and fear the possibility of trial. You need to remain strong and can't let them succeed. Don't let them take away from you the progress you've achieved in therapy. Remain sympathetic, but be strong."

I was determined to be thick skinned and cope with the ordeal. I conferred with Beverly Newman, my therapist, and she agreed with Morty that my deposition and the trial were opportunities for me to tell my story. Yes, I acted foolishly, but that wasn't a crime, all I did was agree to consensual sex. It was Carmichael and Oz who acted deceitfully and should be embarrassed by their conduct.

Morty also explained that my deposition would get very personal. Under Rules 26 and 35 of the Tennessee Rules of Civil Procedure, the defense counsel had a right to have me examined by their own psychiatrist and to inquire into my sex life both before and after my encounter with Carmichael. He anticipated that Pierce would do most of the questioning because she was a woman and wouldn't be embarrassed talking about sex from the women's perspective. Morty insisted,

"You need to listen to the questions and give short responses, except when asked about your damages."

I could tell I was being prepped by the very best. Morty's fifty years of taking depositions was invaluable. He also was a kind man and made me feel like a victim rather than a tramp who acted foolishly. He instructed me on how to dress and present myself at the deposition. We discussed all aspects of my testimony and he indicated when it would be appropriate to become emotional. He assured me that how and when to get emotional would come naturally to me.

He knew all the pitfalls and all the little tricks. He instructed me, "Don't let them bait you into a banter back and forth. If they do, you'll say something you'll regret. An expanded answer gives the questioner his next ten questions to ask. A short answer; yes, no, I don't know, I don't recall or I don't remember, gives him or her nowhere to go."

The old man and I went over every word of my complaint and interrogatory responses. He explained that one of the purposes of the taking of my deposition was to obtain inconsistent answers from those documents.

"If they can obtain inconsistent answers then at trial, whatever answer you give they can impeach you. If in your sworn interrogatory response your answer to a particular question is "A" and at your deposition the answer to the same question is "B" then you're in trouble. No matter what your answer given at trial defense, counsel can confront you with a different answer. If you respond "A" he or she will jam "B" down your throat; if answer "B" consistent with your deposition then you've got to explain why you said "A" in your interrogatory response. It's a lose/lose situation."

Insisting on thoroughness, we also reviewed the depositions of my therapist, psychiatrist, and the three women who'd made their deal with Carmichael. We discussed each deposition at length. He also provided me with Sammie's summary of each deposition as kind of a cheat sheet so I had a quick reference of each witness's testimony.

He emphasized, "The one area where you want to go into specifics and talk in detail is your damages. I want you to describe your humiliation at the police station or when a friend asked you about an article or news report. It's important that you convince the other side that a jury will be sympathetic to your plight."

"I don't have to act. I'm going to cry!"

"Fine."

We'd rehearsed the damages portion of my testimony for several hours, but Morty insisted, "I don't want you to sound scripted.

Listen to the question, pause, and then testify and say whatever comes to you within the parameters we've discussed. When you describe what the defendants did to you, let loose, but don't get too angry. Juries don't like angry. The jury needs to identify with you. Get them to think, what if this was me or my daughter or someone I care about? If you do a good job at your deposition of explaining how this video affected your life and mental status, then we can get this case settled. You've got to scare them not to go to court."

Katie Stone was set up and ready to go. Pierce started the questioning as Morty anticipated. He was a smart old man. Pierce skipped the background inquiry and went directly for the gold.

"You weren't a virgin when you engaged in sexual relations with Roscoe Carmichael?"

"No."

"How many men did you have intercourse with before Mr. Carmichael?"

"Five." Morty had prepared me for that question.

"How old were you when you lost your virginity?"

"Seventeen."

"What was the boy's name?"

"Larry Papello."

Again, Morty had prepared me for both questions. I was feeling pretty comfortable and confident. Morty warned me that neither he nor Davis would object because under Rule 26, this line of questioning "could lead to admissible evidence." All objections in regard to relevancy were reserved for a later hearing before Judge Howard.

Morty must have been pleased so far with my short answers. They gave nothing for Pierce to use against me going forward.

Just keep up the good work.

"You're thirty-three, so in sixteen years you've had only six men, including Mr. Carmichael?"

"No, I said five men prior. I was twenty-eight when I met Mr. Carmichael."

"In the last five years, how many men have you been with?"

"Four."

"So, you've been with ten different men?"

"Yes."

"How many times have you been with each man?"

"I don't know. I was with Mr. Carmichael only two times. Both times were at his office. I haven't kept a record of my lovers."

That answer was a little snippy.

"Too many to count?"

"I just don't know the exact number."

"Well, how many times did you have sex with your first sex partner, Larry Papello?"

"We dated an entire summer."

"Did you see him day and night?"

"I guess so. We were kids on our last summer break before he and I went off to college."

"You were out of school about ninety days?"

"June 1st through sometime in August. At least seventy-five days."

"If I define sex as oral, anal, and vaginal intercourse, did you have sex with Larry Papello more than twenty-five times?"

"I suppose so, we were teenagers and sex were something new."

"The other four men before Mr. Carmichael, did you have sex about twenty-five times with each of them?

"No, two of the men were only once."

"One-night stands?"

"Just sex once. We dated more than one night. In one case, we had sex on our fourth date and then never saw each other again. That was my decision. We weren't compatible. The other one-timer, we dated six or seven times, and it also ended after one night of sex. Again, I felt we had no future. There was no chemistry. I saw no point in going any further. I was doing both of us a favor."

Much too long an answer, thought Morty.

Pierce digested the information and moved on, "Were the other two college boyfriends?"

"Yes."

"Did you have sex with those college boyfriends as often as with Mr. Papello?"

"I don't know an exact number for either man, but during college I was sexually active with both of my college boyfriends. The second boyfriend became my finance."

Pierce paused as if she was making a calculation, "So during the four years of college would you say you had sex as I defined at least fifty times?"

I thought for a minute, which seemed like a long time. That was once a month for four years, "At least that many times."

"How about a hundred times?"

"I really don't know."

"That would be only twice a month?"

"At least that many times."

"So, by my count, you had sex at least one hundred and twenty-five times before you met Mr. Carmichael?"

"You did the math."

I would regret that answer.

"You certainly weren't a virgin."

"I never claimed to be."

"Did you ever have sex, as defined, with a woman?"

"Twice, during college. I was drunk and I was experimenting. I figured out quickly I preferred men over women."

"So, you were with seven people, men and women before you met Mr. Carmichael?"

"Correct."

"How many times did you engage in anal sex?"

Davis spoke up, "This is going to stop. Put the complaint in front of my client, and ask her about her lawsuit. I'm sure Judge Howard would have called a stop to this by now. Rule 26 determines the scope of this deposition, and you've exceeded the bounds permitted by the rule. My client never had anal sex with your client. How does that question lead to the discovery of admissible evidence? Should we call the judge, Ms. Pierce, or will you proceed with this deposition by asking relevant questions?"

Pierce didn't take Davis' interference well.

"If you have an objection, state it. If not, get out of my way, and let me conduct this depo my way."

Davis picked up the phone and started dialing. He got the judge's secretary on the phone. He was in court and would call back when available.

Pierce backed down, "I'll move on to something else until the judge calls back."

Pierce pushed play on the VCR. It was cued to start with my routine on the pole. Pierce froze the tape at my split. I was completely exposed.

"Mr. Carmichael didn't ask you to perform on the pole, did he?"

"No. I did that on my own initiative. My financé Pete bought my stripper pole lessons and that was my old routine."

"You did see the camera on the tripod in the corner?"

"Yes."

"You were performing for that camera?"

"Absolutely not. No red light was on. I was drunk, and I'd done cocaine. I was trying to impress Mr. Carmichael. I wanted him to sign me to a contract. In retrospect I'm ashamed of the way I conducted myself."

"So, you admit the situation was at least in part your fault?"

"No. I acted badly. I drank too much and used drugs. I thought what happened was between two consenting adults. I didn't know Mr. Oz was hiding behind a two-way mirror, and I didn't know my bad decision was being recorded. I acted stupidly. The defendants acted intentionally and maliciously."

Pierce continued the tape. It showed my dancing around the room.

"That was for the camera?"

"No. I was trying to be seductive. As I look at it now, it makes me sick that I could act so foolish. Again, I was trying to get Mr. Carmichael to give me a contract."

Pierce let the movie roll. We were now in the bed, Carmichael on top, pounding away. Pierce turned up the volume just as I orgasmed.

"Were you faking?"

"No."

"So, he satisfied you?"

"Yes."

"Unlike those two men we discussed earlier, you agreed to go out with Mr. Carmichael a second time and have sex with him again?"

"We went out a second time. We had sex that night. I was trying to get him to take me on as a client. That was my interest in him."

Pierce ran the portion of the tape that showed the second encounter.

"You weren't drunk or on drugs this time?"

"No."

The tape showed my arching my back in pleasure.

"Looks like you had a pretty good time?"

"I did."

"Your big complaint is that you didn't get a contract, isn't it?"

I hesitated slightly, and Pierce said, "I withdraw the question."

"You're pretty angry at Mr. Carmichael and Mr. Oz, aren't you?"

"If they dropped dead, I wouldn't shed a tear."

Morty wouldn't like that answer.

Pierce changed directions and began asking me about each of the causes of action alleged in her complaint. I did an excellent job because of my preparation. The hard work with Morty really paid off.

Frustrated by my poise and demeanor, Pierce moved on to damages. We discussed my humiliation at the police station.

"I was sitting there with four policemen staring at me on the screen dancing around naked. When I did my routine on the pole, one of them commented that 'I hadn't lost my touch.' They were practically drooling when the video finished. I felt eight eyes staring at the back of my neck."

Bella walked in to announce, "Judge Howard is on the phone."

Davis pushed the speaker button. "Morning, Judge. The gang's all here. We're on the record. Katie Stone is preserving this conversation. Ms. Pierce has been taking the deposition of my client, Lizzy Swann. May I have Katie read a portion of the testimony that prompted our call?"

"Go ahead."

As directed, Katie started reading from the virgin questions.

It didn't take long for Judge Howard to rule,

"I'm not going to restrict defense counsel into their questioning of the plaintiff's sex life. Ask whatever you want except about work product and confidential communications with her counsel, but I'm limiting you to seven hours, like under the federal rule. I'm limiting all depositions to seven hours. That will make you focus, Ms. Pierce. If Ms. Swann's sex life is the most important discovery issue then have at it. Now, so there's no mistake, this ruling is no indication of what I may allow into evidence at trial. If you think who and how many times she had sex in high school are going to be relevant and admissible at trial, then you're delusional. A jury will never consider such proof, but if that's how you want to spend your valuable deposition hours, then so be it."

Pierce and then Tate used the full seven hours, but the questioning was much more relevant.

"I'd never been videoed before and didn't know that Carmichael had Oz filming me. I didn't know Oz was in the secret room. No, I never had sex with Oz."

Neither Davis nor Morty had any questions. They could talk to me whenever they wanted. No need for them to ask questions at my deposition.

Morty, Davis and Sammie congratulated me on the job well done. Sammie hugged me and whispered, "The hard part is over. They've got your testimony, and I think you scared them. A jury will believe you."

"I came off like a slut. Sex one hundred and twenty-five times seems like a lot."

Sammie assured me that I did fine, and that my sex life was normal. "We just need to keep old ladies off the jury. If Pierce tells that story to male jurors, all she's going to do is get them horny."

I looked Sammie in the eyes and said in a determined tone, "I don't want to go to trial. I want to settle. I'll let you figure out how we get there, but we've *got* to settle. I can't tell that story in open court."

Sammie thought, *both sides are scared. This case should settle.*

CHAPTER THIRTY-FIVE

DEPOSITION OF MARY DOE

Monday, June 23, 1997

(THIRD PERSON)

Davis expedited the answering of the defense's written discovery to Mary Doe. It wasn't much of a concession since Judge Howard consolidated the cases. The discovery was identical to the questions asked of Lizzy Swann, except there were four additional interrogatories concerning the alleged bribe and threat by Carmichael.

Morty worked with Mary, converting Lizzy's answer to hers. They wanted the two discovery responses to be as similar as possible. Of course, there were some differences. Mary fled while Swann remained in Nashville. For that reason, the interrogatory relating to damages varied somewhat. Morty and Mary focused on the additional questions concerning the recent contact by Carmichael and his efforts to secure perjury. That testimony would be particularly important in addressing the depositions of Ingram, Strong, and Watson, even though Mary was never presented a release. Tate did produce the three releases Carmichael negotiated with the other women. Mary confirmed the terms of those documents were consistent with Carmichael and his efforts to get her to lie.

At Morty and Davis' insistence, Mary was examined and diagnosed by Dr. Little, who prescribed a small dose of Prozac to help Mary cope with the stress of the litigation and her return to Nashville. She also began seeing Beverly Newman as a patient and found those sessions helpful in coping with the emotional side effects of her dealings with Roscoe Carmichael.

The defendants insisted that Doe's deposition be scheduled within days of providing the responses to written discovery. They wanted her testimony before they were deposed. Davis figured it was a reasonable request in light of his request for consolidation. Again, Morty prepped the witness. He gave her much of the same instructions he gave to Lizzy. His hope was that Mary would do as well as Lizzy.

Another reason Davis was anxious for Mary to be deposed was that he hoped both cases could be settled at the court-ordered mediation that Howard had required before the November anniversary date of the filing of the Swann complaint. In order to settle, the defense counsel needed to meet and depose Mary Doe.
Finally, for Mary's sanity, the case needed to be settled. Because of the delay in seeking psychiatric help, Mary's post- traumatic stress went untreated, and she was in far worse emotional shape at this point than Lizzy. The fact that Lizzy's treatment was beneficial mitigated her damages.

Because of Mary Doe's paranoia, Steine & Davis took precautions to maintain the anonymity of their client. When she visited town, she stayed in a motel in Franklin, a bedroom community of Nashville. They prepped her away from the office at the motel and always took precautions to make sure that they weren't being followed. They didn't drive directly from their homes or office to the motel but took a roundabout route.

In prepping for her deposition, Mary had the benefit of reading Lizzy's deposition. That helped immunize her from what was about to happen. No matter how many times Morty role-played the sensitive material, they both knew that the stress of a trial would be tenfold. Morty wasn't certain she would ever be ready for the tension of a trial. He could role-play with her for years, but when she got to trial in front of the jury, it would be different. The closest thing would be the deposition, so that was another reason Davis pressed for an early deposition of Mary Doe.

Katie Stone set up while everyone drank coffee and ate the most delicious pastries from Rosario's Italian Market. As Morty often commented on, Davis consumed two and a half pastries before the deposition began and the other half during the deposition while he sat helplessly listening. Davis tended to stress eat.

Mary Doe took her chair, and Davis opened the record, "This is the deposition of my client Mary Doe. That's not her real name, and she will not be giving her real name. She's trying to preserve a life after this lawsuit. You can call her Mary or Ms. Doe, but that's as far as she'll go in giving information about her identity. She may also elect not to answer specific personal questions that may give away her identity. If you think a certain question she refuses to answer is critical to your discovery, put it in writing, we'll answer it, and file the written answer under seal with the court. Judge Howard will determine if you're entitled to that information. Don't worry. We'll let you ask all reasonable questions about Ms. Doe's sex life, similar to those asked of Ms. Swann."

Pierce went first. It was interesting that Tate and Gray were letting Pierce take the lead again.

Davis thought, *I bet they're afraid of committing overt acts in the conspiracy. Judge Howard scared them with that question about the bribe.*

"How old are you?"

Wow, Pierce surprised me with that one. I didn't expect that out of the box.

"I'm thirty-eight."

"You have a husband?"

"Yes."

Davis was ready to object if Pierce asked for his name.

"You have two sons?"

"How do you know these things?" the witness demanded loudly.

"This isn't my deposition. It's yours. Please answer my question."

"Yes."

"Your name is Melissa Fields, and your friends call you Mel?"

"I don't understand."

Davis could see his witness was rattled, so he spoke up, "You already think you know who she is. She's not going to admit or deny her name. She still wants to keep her name out of the record. She wants to minimize her injury and reduce the damages you'll have to pay for exposing Mary Doe, the woman you claim is Ms. Fields, so cool it. If you intentionally foil her plan to keep her name out of the press and the public record, I will ask the judge to instruct the jury that your actions are malicious and that you, Ms. Pierce, and your clients have subjected yourselves to punitive damages for further exposing her to unnecessary publication. Your purpose could only be to further humiliate her and not minimize your damages."

Pierce's response wasn't very professional or lawyerly, "Mr. Davis, I believe you've just threatened another member of the Bar with civil action. I'd be careful with loose allegations that you can't prove, or you could wind up a defendant in either a defamation lawsuit or an abuse of process suit."

Davis shot back, "I'd say the entire defense team has been skating on the edge of joining a civil conspiracy since they've been retained in this case. Judge Howard warned Mr. Tate and Mr. Gray at our last hearing that their conduct was suspect, and I'm putting you on notice as well. Your law license doesn't grant you immunity from becoming a co-conspirator right along with your clients. All you have to do is commit an overt act, and you're liable for all acts of the conspiracy. Don't forget your license was suspended three months for your actions in the Plainview cases. Don't think it can't happen again, possibly permanently."

Davis took a breath and smiled. *Eat shit!*

He really didn't like Pierce, and he hoped she'd make a false step.

"Thanks for the law and history lessons, professor."

Pierce asked no other personal questions. She already knew the witness's identity and had made her point that the alias was a charade. She called her Mary Doe, or Mrs. Doe. She was hard on her for the sex portion of the depo. It was very explicit. Doe was asked to describe her sex acts with other men and with her husband. Mary Doe was no Virgin Mary before she'd met Carmichael. She'd been with him only once and claimed that other than one occasion, she'd been married ten years. Her sons wouldn't understand why their mother wanted to be a singer so desperately that she'd degrade herself. "No mother would ever want her children to know about the existence of the tape or, God forbid, see it."

She did well when Pierce reviewed her complaint. When they got to the conspiracy count, she was firm and explained in detail how Carmichael and Oz were co-conspirators in perpetrating a fraud on her and invading her privacy. When asked about the bribe, she replied, "You had to be there. He offered me money, and I was insulted. I wanted an apology, not money."

"So, all you want is an apology. If the defendants apologize, will you dismiss the lawsuit?"

"Not bloody likely. I never agreed to be videoed. Those other women are lying. They sold their testimony for money. Carmichael asked me, I refused and told him to go to hell. He and his friend Mr. Oz, who I never met and was unaware of, ruined my life and I am entitled to be paid for what they did to me. I deserve money, and a lot of it..."

Pierce interrupted, "How much?"

Mary was prepared for the question. "That's up to the jury. I made a bad mistake. I was unfaithful to my husband. I was blinded by the possibility of moving up from the church choir to becoming a studio singer or even a star. I was foolish, and I'll regret my actions for the rest of my life. My husband threatened to divorce me and take away my children. I had to beg for forgiveness. Thank God, my husband is a loving, kind, and forgiving man. He took me back begrudgingly. He deserves the money. He forgave me, but he couldn't stay in our home, he insisted that we move. Moving was a condition of saving my marriage, he insisted that we leave town, so we moved to Bowling Green, about an hour drive to his job. After Carmichael threatened me, we moved again and David had to quit his good job, and we uprooted our family for a second time to another state. He lost his seniority he'd worked so hard for. He had to get a job with another company in a related field and start over. He blames me, and it has had a deep impact on our relationship. I admit I'm to blame because I was just stupid. But the defendants didn't just make a mistake. They weren't negligent. They acted maliciously with criminal intent."

Morty knew that was a bad answer.

Both Tate and Pierce objected, "There are no criminal charges pending, and based upon our research and conversations with the DA's office, there's no possible law violated."

Pierce asked, "So how much?"

"The complaint asks for $1,000,000 in compensatory damages and $5,000,0000 in punitive damages, but I'll accept whatever the jury gives me."

When pressed by Pierce about the camera and the presence of Oz, Mary stated, "I didn't know about the camera or Oz. When Carmichael approached me after his drug bust, he tried to get me to say that I knew about both the camera and your hidden client, but I wouldn't take his damn money, and then he got angry. You didn't look into his eyes when he said 'take it or else.' I believed those eyes. No words had to be spoken. He left me no choice. I was afraid for my life, and we had to leave town."

"He didn't threaten you with words?"

"It was a combination of words and body language, but the eyes said it all, 'take it or you're dead.' We ran, and my husband blames me."

"So, he doesn't blame the defendants?"

"He hates the defendants, but he didn't know and trust them. He trusted me. I'm trying to earn back his trust. I may never completely do so. That's my fault, and I'll have to live with that."

Pierce's next question was one that all jurors would be asking themselves, "Why'd you go up to the office with Roscoe Carmichael?"

"I was trying to break back into show business. I'd worked at Opryland as a teenager and then at the Grand Ole Opry. I sang backup for some acts on stage and worked twice as a studio singer in recording studios. After marriage, I sang in our church choir. I missed performing professionally, and I saw my chance of making my mark in the music industry at thirty-five. The night I met Roscoe Carmichael I'd been out with a few of my girlfriends celebrating one of their birthdays. After they left, I stayed for one last drink, to make sure that my husband had put the children to bed. I didn't want them to see me tipsy. Carmichael approached me and began flirting. We started talking, and I told him a little bit about myself and my aspirations. When he told me, he was a talent agent looking for singers and would love to audition me, I jumped at the chance. He convinced me that night to come up to his office and discuss studio time. Once I was up there, he pushed for me to perform a few karaoke numbers. He ooh'd and ah'd over me and made me feel good about myself. Vanity got the best of me, and I started flirting with him. I can't say he took advantage of me. It was consensual. I desperately wanted him to sign me. I still thought I had talent."

Pierce asked, "So you feel at least partially responsible for your marital problems?"

"Yes."

Davis figured out where Pierce was going, "Objection, if Ms. Doe feels guilty, it's for being gullible and stupid. You can't equate negligent conduct with intentional conduct."

That was a talking objection. Oh, well, Ms. Pierce deserves a little hard ball. She's a big girl and has certainly done worse.

Mary Doe figured out Davis' intention and testified, "I may have been stupid, but I didn't act intentionally. I didn't try to defraud anybody."

Pierce asked, "When you took off your clothing, that was an intentional act, wasn't it?"

"I was drunk."

"He didn't make you drink. You'd been drinking all night with your girlfriends?"

"He got me drunker and I wanted to get a contract."

"He didn't hold a gun to your head or a knife to your throat, did he?"

"No."

"You voluntarily put his penis in your mouth and then let him enter you from behind doggie style?"

"Yes."

"But you claim you were afraid of Mr. Carmichael despite the consensual nature of your relationship?"

"Yes, after he tried to buy me off, he got mean and very frightening. The Swann lawsuit changed him. He wasn't concerned about anything but protecting himself. I was an obstacle in his way. When I wouldn't take his money and be bought off, I became a big problem that had to be dealt with. He scared me so bad that I came clean with my husband, and out of fear, we left town. I lost the love and respect of my husband because of those bastards. How much is that worth? We gave up our home, our friends, and the life we knew. We live in temporary housing for the staff..."

Pierce stopped her, "The staff of what?"

Morty objected, but he knew she'd opened the door.

Pierce threatened to call the judge, "He won't like getting called again, and you know it. Your client opened the door, and you know it. Why get into an argument and lose? You're going to regret forcing me to make this call."

Morty whispered loudly in Davis's ear, "Let her make the call."

Pierce was right. The judge didn't like being called during a deposition. He'd ordered these lawyers to work out this case. He didn't want the case to go to trial. It would waste valuable resources of the county, and he'd have a lot to do. He didn't mind working. He loved deciding motions and conducting a two-day bench trial. *That was fun. Maybe as long as two weeks, and my small courtroom would be filled to capacity with one hundred fifty people.*

"What's the problem?" Howard said sternly.

Pierce had Katie read back the question and the partial answer to the judge.

"She opened the door about her living arrangement and who provides her place of residence, but not where she lives."

All Morty could say was, "I renew my objection."

Howard replied, "Noted."

Back on the record, Pierce established that Mary sang in two shows in Branson, Missouri. She testified that her family lived in a trailer provided by her employer, Deaton Amusement. She commented, "It isn't very nice. My two boys have to share a bedroom."

While Pierce was thinking about her next question, Doe added, "Not like our home in Bowling Green. I made a mistake, but those sons of bitches ruined my life, and my children are paying for it."

Pierce struck back, "How are your sons doing?"

She hit a nerve. "Don't you mention my boys. That's who this money's for. I want them to know..."

"So, you made a movie, sued, and now you expect to pay for your children's education?"

Davis stared down Pierce, "That was a low blow even for you, Pierce."

"No, my husband was an assistant store manager in a large retail store. Now he's working as a commissioned salesman because we had to uproot our family. He was on a good career path until all this happened. We had set up college funds for both of our boys. We would have had the money when the time came."

Pierce used almost six of the seven hours. She had an agreement with Tate to carry the heavy load. Gray asked a few questions and used the rest of the full seven hours.

When they stood to leave, Davis surprised them by saying, "I've got a few questions for the witness to preserve on the record."

Davis took out the agreement made by Carmichael and Ingram produced by court order. He didn't identify the document, but using it got Mary to document what Carmichael told her that night he tried bribing her.

"That was the offer, except he started at $25,000, and when I refused, he upped it to $50,000. He was trying to 'tie up loose ends.' I told him to drop dead. I didn't mean it literally. That was when he responded with his deadly stare, and he meant it."

"You thought Mr. Carmichael had threatened you?"

"Absolutely, I uprooted my family."

"What words did he use that scared you?"

"Mr. Davis, it wasn't his words that I remember so well, he said something like 'you'll regret not taking this deal or you'll regret not taking my money' but it was the deadly look he gave me. That look is what's burned into my memory. Carmichael's deadly stare was what scared the hell out of me."

Davis again directed the court reporter to type that portion of the deposition. Katie did type that deposition about the bribe and threat. Davis said, "I'm sending a copy to the judge."

Tate, Gray, and Pierce each made an objection on the record, but that made no difference to Davis. He was keeping the judge advised as ordered.

At the end of the day Davis walked down Printer's Alley to the

Commerce Street Garage to go home for dinner with his family. When he got to his car, he saw that his twenty-fifth anniversary Vette had three flat tires. He determined that each tire had been punctured with a knife or other sharp instrument. Someone was sending him a message. He spent the next two hours calling AAA and waiting on the tow truck.

When he got to his house, he went into his home office and called Police Chief Gerry Neenah and made an incident report. He didn't think the culprit would be caught, but he thought a record should be made, just in case.

CHAPTER THIRTY-SIX

ANOTHER SCARED WOMAN

Wednesday, June 25, 1997

There was no vacation time for the new associate of Steine & Davis. Her uncle instructed Bella, "Give all new clients to Sammie for their initial contact. She can summarize the case, and we'll decide if she's competent to handle the matter with supervision."

She still hadn't passed the Bar, so she could meet with clients but couldn't appear in courts. She would take the exam in July, and the results would be available in September. Sammie would then have to be admitted into state and federal courts separately. She'd negotiate time away from the office so she could study for that most important test. She'd already read through the material twice and now needed to cram to get the job done.

Davis, Morty, and Sammie had been planning Sammie's graduation for years. She was a member of most women's groups in town and had learned to network from one of the best, Morty Steine. Morty even began taking her up to the hill and introduced her to several state representatives. They were a bunch of leeches, and a beautiful woman easily turned their heads. Once she got their attention, she impressed them with her smarts. Several of them commented, "You've got a future in politics." She'd hung around the courthouse and knew everybody in the clerk's office by their first names. Morty instructed her, "Get to know the clerks and court officers. They're the key to getting in front of a judge when you need to, or get your phone call returned. They might also volunteer whether their boss is in a bad mood, or more important warn you away. Treat them the way you'd want to be treated."

Generally, the male members of the Bar looked down on the female members and they resented them. The female members, who'd made it were very protective of their success and often were inappropriately aggressive.

Over the years Sammie was prominent in the courtroom handing her uncle documents during trials. Her striking looks made her hard to miss. Now she would have a law license and would be coming off the bench and into the well of the courtroom, questioning witnesses and addressing judges. She'd make her mark in the courtroom using the same tactics employed by her uncle and Morty, "and look better doing it."

Davis thought his niece could be a real arrogant smart-ass. He couldn't complain too much. He knew she got that from him. He'd like to rationalize this flaw as "confidence".

With her new position came renewed effort; Sammie started coming in earlier, about the same time as her uncle. Her commute was just one floor down. Sammie buzzed in, "I've got one of the videoed women on the phone. She's pretty spooked."

Davis got on the line and introduced himself, "Miss, I'm Ben Davis, and I represent Lizzy Swann and Mary Doe, two young ladies who were taken advantage of by Roscoe Carmichael and Phillip Oz."

The voice on the line hesitated, "Are those your clients' real names?"

Now it was Davis' turn to hesitate, "The answer to your question is yes and no. Elizabeth Swann is the real name of one client. My second client, Mary Doe, elected to use an alias."

"I don't understand."

"Ms. Swann felt comfortable disclosing her identity to the press and public record. She wants to get in the defendants' faces. Mary Doe is trying to keep her real name out of the lawsuit. She feels it will allow her to return to normalcy after the trial. She won't be successful if we have to try her case. A courtroom is opened to the public. Anybody can attend a trial. The court has ordered mediation before we go to trial. Hopefully the cases will be resolved then. If not, a case can settle any time before the jury renders a verdict. Hopefully before you get to the courthouse steps, but I've settled cases in the middle of a trial. At that point, I'm busy trying the lawsuit, and you never know what a jury will do. The outcome will vary from jury to jury. That's why picking the jury is the most important part of any case. Look Miss, I can help you. I've dealt with two women who have been in your identical position. Off the record, what's your name?"

There was silence on the line before she replied, "Just call me Jane Doe for now. When's the trial?"

"The Swann case is going to trial on February 3rd, 1998. The judge hasn't decided if he's going to consolidate the Doe case with the Swann case for trial. He has consolidated the two cases for discovery purposes."

"What does that mean?"

"To save money and time, the depositions taken can be used in both cases, but the judge was waiting to see if you or another yet unidentified woman was going to come forward before he made a decision about whether to try the cases together. It's not too late to join the party. We've been waiting to hear from you. We've been looking for you and another woman. We thought your testimony would help our case. Have you read about the lawsuits or seen stories about the cases?"

"I've not read the lawsuits, but I've been following your stories in the local paper, which a friend of mine has sent me. She's also taped and sent several newscasts by Alice Krieger. She just Federal Expressed me a tape about the second lawsuit and the fact that Roscoe Carmichael tried to bribe your new client. Memphis is a different news market. I think there have been one or two stories about the Swann case."

"So, you're in Memphis. Is that home?"

"No, Nashville's home. You said you've been looking for me. Have you sent a bald tall man to Memphis trying to find me?"

"I'm not supervising the search. Our investigator, George Hopper, is in charge and he's hired the personnel in the field. He's average height and muscular. He's got a full head of hair. I'd have to inquire and see who he's hired to help him."

Jane Doe changed the subject, "If we met and I told you my story, and I agreed to file under an alias, say in a week or so, could I participate in the mediation, and if necessary the trial on February 3rd too? I don't want to be involved in an extended legal battle that lasts years."

Davis thought a moment before answering, "That's an interesting question and I don't know the answer. The only thing we could do is ask Judge Howard and push for those things to happen. It would be up to him. The defendants are sure to object. I'm confident he'd allow the discovery conducted to date to be used in your case. I'm equally confident he'd consolidate future discovery, so the three pending cases would share the cost of all depositions going forward. That certainly would save time and money. Logically all three cases should be addressed in the same mediation, but again that would be up to the judge. Trying all three cases at once would be my preference, but the defendants will object arguing that each case is a separate matter."

Davis took a breath and then asked one of the questions he was dying to ask, "Did you know about the camera or the cameraman?"

"Absolutely not."

Davis was relieved and then asked, "Did Carmichael try to bribe you?"

"He offered me $50,000 and like your client Doe, when I refused, he threatened me. He scared the shit out of me. I can close my eyes and still see that stare. I was so concerned he'd hurt or even kill me, that I left town. I had a friend in Memphis who put me up. I started drinking heavily, I was a borderline alcoholic before meeting Carmichael. After two months of being drunk, I checked myself into rehab. After twenty-eight days, I got out, and I've been clean ever since."

"When did Carmichael approach you?"

"Christmas, I left town before New Year's. I spent March in rehab, I'm clean almost four months. January and February are a real blur. I gave up my life, and I've been looking over my shoulder ever since. I'm afraid. I don't want to get directly involved. Why do you need my testimony?"

Davis explained the substance of the testimonies of Ingram, Strong, and Watson. "If you'd testify consistent with Swann and Doe, then the proof will evenly split, three women claiming knowledge of the videotaping, while three others denying knowledge of the tapes. Even if you didn't file suit or if your case wasn't consolidated for trial, we'd ask that you testify at the February trial."

Davis added, "You'd have to be deposed quickly, probably before we depose the defendants. They have already raised an objection to consolidation. We'll need to allow them to depose you first so Judge Howard's more likely to consolidate the cases and still feel like he's being reasonable. A wise old man once told me, 'You've got to give the judge something he can use to compromise and feel good about the ruling."

"I really need to be a part of that February trial. I can't wait around for years to get my day in court. I'm exposed. I want to get my money and then fade away. I'm in danger and you may be too."

Jane Doe really sounded scared with her last statement. Davis had been in danger before, so he listened carefully.

"As I said, I've read yesterday's coverage of the Doe case and her recent encounter with Carmichael where he tried to buy her off. He tried the same thing with me, but his offer had a twist. He insisted that I screw him one last time in exchange for a release and a $50,000 payment. He insisted that 'I should take his money, have one last roll in the hay, and shut up if I knew what was good for me. If not, I was a dead girl.' I believed him. He scared the hell out of me, so I moved to Memphis to get lost in the crowd. I don't think I moved far enough away. I think he's found me. I know I'm being followed, and I'm scared shitless. My landlord, who is also a friend, told me a very tall rough-looking guy was snooping around my apartment."

"Did he describe what the snooper looked like?"

"He said he was big and had a completely bald head and dead eyes, more than six foot four, looked like he'd played football."

Davis wondered whether the stalker was Phillip Oz. He fit that description.

"A week ago, I got severe cramps, and I was rushed to the emergency room and had my stomach pumped. My blood work revealed a high level of arsenic. I have no idea of how I was exposed, but I'm on high alert, and I'm drinking only from a sealed bottles and consuming food where I'm certain of the source."

Davis listened to Jane Doe sympathetically.

"I was in the hospital two nights after they pumped my stomach, and I'm still under the care of medical doctors. A counselor is also treating me for post-traumatic stress disorder."

Oz has knowledge of poisons.

"Carmichael's cameraman was Phillip Oz, who is a pharmacist. Avoid him like the plague. Can you come to Nashville, or should I come to you, or should we meet somewhere else?"

"I don't think I'm well enough to travel. Could you come here?"

They agreed to meet in Memphis, the next day, on Thursday the 26th, and Davis would get the document done over the weekend. He'd take Sammie with him rather than Katie Stone. She was trouble with a capital T. Memphis was about three hours away by car from Nashville.

Davis would use the trip as an excuse to go to the Rendezvous, a restaurant dating back to the 40's and eat some dry ribs. They'd stay at the Peabody Hotel, where the ducks conducted their twice-daily parade. He'd drink bourbon and listen to some blues on Beal Street. A nice plan, but other than the ribs, he'd be working the remaining hours.

Davis immediately picked up the phone and called Chief Neenan. He recounted his conversation with his caller. "I think Phillip Oz is going after Jane Doe, and the other yet unidentified woman. I hope Elizabeth Swann and Mary Doe are safe because they've filed suit, but who knows? I told them there was safety in disclosure. What do you think? Carmichael and Oz may be getting desperate. Do you have any suggestions?"

"A smart criminal isn't going to act when under the microscope if he or she believes there is an alternative. The person will weigh the risk/benefit and avoid arrest. I can't tell you what's going on in Carmichael or Oz's mind. If your clients are in danger, you can't prove it. You've called me. I'll prepare an incident report, so if something happens to a Nashville resident or someone visiting our town, then Carmichael and Oz will be the first suspects I interrogate. Jane Doe now lives in Memphis. I have no jurisdiction there. Have her call the Memphis police or the Shelby County Sheriff's Office and make an incident report of stalking, and have her allege that she suspects it was Phillip Oz. She'll have no proof, but at least there will be a record of her concerns."

"Can't you question Oz and see if he's been to Memphis?"

"You're the lawyer. Wouldn't Pierce jump up and down screaming harassment? Remember Carmichael and Oz have sued not only my department, but me personally."

Neenan made a good point. Davis decided to put George Hopper on Oz to determine his whereabouts during the last few days.

Neenan asked, "Don't you have an obligation to notify the judge that you've heard from your caller?"

Neenan was right. Davis was obligated to call the judge and defense counsel. "Ben, some friendly advice, I know you're casual about your diet, but be careful what you eat and drink."

Davis dialed Pierce first. She wasn't happy at all. He specifically asked her if she knew where her client had been over the last week or so. She claimed she had no idea but would look into it. He concluded the conversation, "You have three women bought and paid for on your side, and now I have the testimony of three victims. Things stand pretty equal. I can't wait to see you in court. You call Tate and Gray, and then if any of you want to be on the line, I'll wait an hour to call him."

"Don't you make that call without us. I'll not stand for you having any ex-parte conversations with the judge."

"Just call Tate and Gray and get back to me before the end of the day or you'll miss the call."

Within an hour, Pierce, Gray and Tate were on the line, Bella did her magic and the judge was on the line too, asking Davis, "Are you going to file a motion to consolidate?"

"Absolutely, and with the court's permission, I'd like to continue the depositions of the defendants to a date in the future agreed to by the parties, which would afford the defendants an opportunity to review the Jane Doe complaint, her responses to interrogatories, and her deposition. We will provide this information within the next week and will schedule Ms. Doe's deposition as quickly as possible."

The judge inquired, "Do you really think you can act that quickly?"

"My office and my client will perform as promised. The defendants are entitled to this information prior to deposing Jane Doe and prior to engaging in mediation. Give us the opportunity and we'll deliver."

Howard instructed Davis to proceed.

CHAPTER THIRTY-SEVEN

ANOTHER LAWSUIT

Monday, June 30, 1997

(BENJAMIN DAVIS' VOICE)

Sammie and I toiled over the Jane Doe complaint, only having time for ribs and a few hours' sleep. The complaint and discovery responses were not difficult to prepare since the allegations of one Doe was identical to the other. The words of the offer and threat were slightly different but the intent was the same and so was the women's reaction. Both clients suffered the wrath of Carmichael and his deadly stare, which struck fear into their hearts.

Neither the complaint nor the interrogatory responses referenced Oz's suspected stalking, the suspected poisoning, or anything about Jane Doe's hospitalization. I did have Jane Doe make an incident report with the Memphis Metropolitan Police Department. The emergency room and hospital records already xisted. The complaint could always be amended. Morty and I debated how real the Doe threat was. I protested, I'd had my tires slashed and had once been beaten up; I'd personally experienced a defendant who stepped outside the bounds of the courtroom's rules.

I got a little irritated with my old friend, "Have you forgotten the Plainview cases? Pierce was counsel of record in that case too.

It wasn't you who got head butted by a shotgun or whose shoulder was dislocated. Arsenic doesn't grow on trees. It has to be purchased and then mixed in a way for the victim to ingest it. A pharmacist would know how to do that."

Morty shot back, "Don't talk to me about threats. In the 1950s and 1960s, I had friends and associates who were hung from trees or found in ditches for just trying to register blacks to vote. I've seen threats made and acted upon."

Morty insisted,

"You're not thinking like a lawyer. I think your phone call to Pierce was a big mistake. If you're right, you've just alerted Oz that we're on to him. Rather than confronting him, we should be setting some kind of trap. You're approaching this all wrong. This is a time to show courage."

I hesitated. generally, I didn't like to argue with the old man. It was usually a waste of time but, I was pretty stubborn and rarely conceded a point.

"This isn't a question of courage. You proved your bravery when you beat the Nazis over in the sky over the English Channel and when you stood up against bigotry in the 1950s and 1960s in this country. This is the safe move. Shed light on the defendants so they'd have to be incredibly stupid to act against either our clients or us."

I knew that our clients and possibly the members of the firm were at risk, and I knew I shouldn't take any chances. The decision of what to do next weighed heavily on me as I struggled with how to proceed. I decided I'd try something unconventional.

I walked the complaint over to the courthouse. I opened the door to the Circuit Court Clerk's Office and after exchanging greetings with the two female clerks, filed the Jane Doe lawsuit. I then took a stamped filed copy together with a cover letter and delivered them to the court officer of the Third Circuit Court.

I knew that Judge Howard would refuse to communicate with me ex-parte, without the other lawyers. To do so would create an issue on appeal. I decided the best course of action was to give the court written notice of my concerns.

Honorable Barry Howard
Judge of the Third Circuit Court,
Davidson County Courthouse
James Robertson Parkway
Nashville, Tennessee 37219

Re: Woman#1 from the Carmichael videos

Dear Judge Howard,

This will confirm my voice message, that was court ordered, that I've been contacted by woman #1. I will refer to her as "Jane Doe", and I will be representing her. I will be moving to consolidate discovery and trial.

The other purpose of this letter is to notify the court that my new client believes, through information and observations of her landlord, Tommy Brothers, that a tall, bald man may be stalking her. Mr. Brothers has provided a statement to the Memphis Police Department that a suspicious tall bald man has been loitering around Jane Doe's apartment building. Attached is the entire incident report filed by Jane Doe with the local police.

The defendant Oz is tall, according to interrogatory responses, six foot four and a half inches, and shaves his head. Immediately after my client's landlord raised these concerns to her, that night, Jane Doe was hospitalized and had her stomach pumped. Her blood work revealed such a high level of arsenic that the only reasonable conclusion is poisoning. Attached are her medical records. The defendant Oz is a pharmacist.

I called Ms. Pierce, who represents the defendant Oz, and asked her to determine if her client had recently traveled to Memphis. In our conversation, Ms. Pierce informed me that she was unaware of her client's travels. She indicated she'd inquire and get back to me; she hasn't.

I know that ex parte communications are contrary to the Code of Professional Conduct, but I didn't feel right leaving you in the dark. I have not copied counsel of record on this correspondence. I wanted you to determine how best to proceed and to advise if I am required to disclose the stalking suspicions and poisoning to defense counsel.

Yours very truly,

Benjamin Davis

I knew the judge would be forced to take some action, better him than me.

CHAPTER THIRTY-EIGHT

JUDICAL DISCRETION

Monday, June 30, 1997

(Same day)

(THIRD PERSON)

Judge Howard called for a status conference that afternoon. The judge was concerned by the allegations in Davis' letter and he intended to find out what the hell was going on. He started his investigation by calling Chief Neenan to get his input before the hearing. Neenan and the judge weren't friends, but they had known each other for more than twenty-five years and over the years earned a mutual respect for each other. Regardless of their long-standing professional relationship, this was an unusual conversation, "Judge, I don't know what to tell you. Davis thinks that these defendants are dangerous. I have no jurisdiction in Memphis. Davis can't prove anything. It's just a hunch. Even if Davis could prove that Oz was in Memphis at the time of the poisoning, that degree of circumstantial evidence would not convict."

"I don't know, Chief. Davis stepped way over the line sending me this letter. I'm going to call the Judiciary Board and seek guidance."

Howard dialed an attorney whose sole job was to answer ethical questions for judges. The judicial ethics attorney asked a good question, "What do you want to do, Judge?"

"I'd like to do nothing. Davis has asked Pierce to determine her client's whereabouts. I'd like to hear what she has to say. I'd then like to let Davis take the defendants' depositions and hear their sworn testimony. I'd like to get the defendants committed on the record before I react. Davis will grill Oz about his familiarity with and use of arsenic. After that, I'll have a clearer picture of the problem and whether there's something to Davis's concerns."

The ethics counsel didn't hesitate, "That's a reasonable course of action. We'll follow your lead. Keep me in the loop. You realize if these cases go to trial, this issue concerning the alleged threatening conduct of the defendant and how it's handled by you will be part of the scope of the appeal."

Howard actually laughed and said, "It will be one of two dozen issues on appeal. These parties are each filing multiple motions which no doubt will be an appealable issue, no matter how I rule. I'm in a catch-22 no matter what." The call ended on that unhappy note.

At the status conference later that afternoon, the Judge was presented with three questions. The first came from Davis. He wanted to know if the three lawsuits would be consolidated for discovery and/or trial.

Judge Howard replied, "I'm consolidating for discovery purposes. I can't imagine there's a serious objection to saving money and time by taking these depositions once rather than three times. Later if the cases aren't settled and not tried together, if a party presents a valid reason to retake a deposition, I will certainly consider the argument. I'm also consolidating the three cases for mediation. Mr. Davis, I'm confident that you've explained to your clients that they do have competing interests, I suspect there's only so many dollars. There may or may not be insurance coverage, and that will be determined in another court. The question may be subject to years of litigation through appeals. They are competing for the available net worth of the defendants."

Davis stood and said, "Absolutely, all three clients have signed contracts acknowledging the conflict and waiving it. Ms. Swann, our first client, was presented with two later contracts that acknowledged the other two clients."

Howard had a simple response, "Good." He then moved on, "As to the February 3rd trial date, I'm concerned about the existence of this still yet unidentified woman # 7 who was videotaped. Has Mr. Carmichael provided any specific information as to her name or location?"

Gray responded, "No, sir."

The judge addressed Davis, "If I knew that there was going to be only one trial and that granting your motion to consolidate would end the civil lawsuits against these defendants, that no new plaintiff would materialize, I'd be inclined to grant your motion. My concern is the outstanding potential plaintiff. Because of her uncertainty, I'm going to withhold my decision on whether to try these cases together. All three cases should proceed to mediation. I want these cases settled. I'm counting on all of you to get the job done. What else do we have pending?"

Tate brought up his motion to change venue, "Nashville has been overwhelmed with publicity." Tate pointed to Krieger in the back of the courtroom and said, "She's here every hearing."

The judge pointed out, "This is a public place. Ms. Krieger has a right to be here, and our docket is a public record."

Tate argued, "To get a fair trial, the case should be moved to a rural courthouse somewhere outside Middle Tennessee. Alice

Krieger of Channel 5 News has run story after story about this case. Her viewership extends as far east as Cookeville and as far west as Jackson. The case should be moved to a rural courthouse outside of Knoxville or Memphis. We need to get outside the news market."

Davis objected. He argued that the defense was really trying to manipulate the court to move the case to a more conservative locale, where the jurors would be less likely to award a large judgment or punitive damages.

The judge denied the motion, "Mr. Tate, your motion is within my sole discretion, and after weighing the prejudice to the defense vs. the cost to the small rural county where you propose to move the case, I find that the burden must fall on the defense. I can't see placing that kind of expense on a county that has no nexus to the case. The torts occurred in Nashville. That's where the case should be decided."

Tate then asked that the jurors be sequestered during the trial. He argued, "If you think the publicity of this case has been extensive to date, just wait. I'm hounded by that newscaster Alice Krieger. Let me assure you that when we get to trial, she'll become even more relentless, and her reporting is very biased in favor of the plaintiffs."

After pondering Tate's request for a moment, the judge stated, "What you're proposing imposes a tremendous expense on the innocent county. That's more than fourteen hotel rooms and meals for as long as two weeks for jurors and sheriff's deputies. It's tens of thousands of dollars."

Tate persisted, "I ask you, Judge, what's more important: having a fair trial or saving a few bucks?"

"I'll take your motion under advisement. I don't have to decide that motion today. We still have the possibility of mediation. I'm expecting everyone to conduct themselves in good faith." The hearing broke up without another word.

Pleased with the court's decisions, Davis figured the rulings put pressure on the defendants to settle at the mediation. It looked that if they didn't settle, they'd have to try all three cases together in front of the same jury in Nashville. Neither Davis nor his clients relished the prospect of trial, but the defendants were far more afraid of that possibility.

When Davis got back to the office, he found a message from Jack Barnes. Davis knew that the Supreme Court appointed Clark Lundy, a retired Chancery Court judge from Knoxville, to sit on Bucky's case. The highest court of the state also appointed a Memphis Circuit Court judge, Leland Ray, to sit on the case against Chief Neenan, the DA's office, the TBI agents, and the other law enforcement officers.

"Hello Jack, I just got back from Howard's court. We now have three cases consolidated for discovery and mediation, and if mediation fails, he'll probably consolidate them for trial."

Barnes said what he knew Davis wanted to hear, "It would be a waste of resources to hold three separate trials. You'd be better off if you settled the cases."

Another vote for settlement. I bet Bucky would agree.

"Have you read Carmichael's complaint against Bucky?"

"It's basically the same allegations he made against Bucky in my case."

"Well, that's about to change once Bucky files his answer. You can expect Carmichael and Oz to amend their complaints within a day or two of their receipt of that document. Bucky was Deep Throat."

"What the hell are you talking about?"

"About a week before the raid on Carmichael's office, Bucky went to see Johnson Tory concerning his former client. He told Tory that based upon a conversation with Carmichael, he suspected that Carmichael was secretly videotaping unsuspecting females who were having sex with him."

"Holly shit, Jack," Davis said angrily. "Bucky should have shared that information with Morty and I. We elected not to sue Bucky because he swore to us that he didn't advise Carmichael to videotape those women."

"Well, Bucky didn't do that. Think, would a reasonable lawyer give such obvious negligent advice to a client? You know who Bucky is. Carmichael has raised this defense out of desperation. Bucky didn't lie to you."

Davis still uncertain responded, "But he turned Carmichael in to the DA. A solid argument can be made that Bucky's action proximately caused the publication of the tapes. At least we should have known that fact before we filed the Swann complaint. I suspect we still would have believed him and not have included him as a defendant, but I feel deceived."

Now it was Barnes' turn to get angry. "That's bullshit! The DA was already going to raid the office to search for drugs. They would have found the tapes anyway. Bucky didn't build the secret room, nor did he install the two-way mirror. He didn't promise these women stardom in exchange for sex. Don't buy in to the defendants' argument."

Davis considered what Barnes was saying. He was right. They were on the same side.

"Look, Ben, if it wasn't for Bucky, Carmichael's wrongful conduct wouldn't have been discovered and would have continued. Bucky struggled with his decision to report Carmichael. He's facing not only disciplinary charges but also an amended complaint alleging intentional conduct."

Davis regained his sympathy for his friend, "Does he have insurance coverage?"

"As to the Circuit Court action, he currently has a defense, with reservation to withdraw the defense. The insurance company at a reduction of my normal hourly rate has hired me. As to the charges before the Board of Professional Responsibility, he's on his own. Bucky's life is about to be turned upside down once the defendants get hold of our answer. We've decided to reveal Bucky's involvement with the DA's office in our first responsive pleading. There's no sense trying to conceal his actions. In fact, we're going to wear it like a badge of honor. Bucky acted not only to help your clients but also to protect future non-suspecting females."

With the revelation of Bucky's actions, the Carmichael/Oz cases became more complicated.

CHAPTER THIRTY-NINE

MORE PUBLICITY

Tuesday, July 1, 1997

(THIRD PERSON)

Barnes filed Bucky's answer in one day, because Barnes and Bucky had prepared his answer in advance. Barnes felt compelled to reveal Bucky's betrayal of Carmichael to Davis before it became public. Barnes filed an immediate response because he figured there was no point in putting off the inevitable. He hoped the filing just before the holiday would cause the filing to get lost in the trash. He was wrong. The press was monitoring the clerk's office, and every local television station ran the Jane Doe story and characterized Lee as the attorney who violated his confidential obligation to his client. That evening Alice Krieger reported the story, quoting extensively from Carmichael's complaint and Bucky's answer.

The next day, at noon, Channel 5 gave Krieger a half hour special report where she summarized not only the Carmichael/ Lee case, but the other six related pending lawsuits, including the insurance case filed by Carmichael and Oz. The report didn't put Bucky in a good light. Krieger also posed the question of why the women didn't sue Bucky Lee if he was the one who alerted the DA's office about the tapes. She speculated that the Steine & Davis law firm might amend their clients' complaints to add Bucky Lee as a defendant.

Tate would renew his motions for change of venue and sequester and file a video of Krieger's special in support of his motions. Davis knew he would need to meet with his clients to calm them down after seeing Krieger's report and explain again why they didn't sue Bucky.

Barnes' responsive pleading was very detailed on purpose. He and Bucky labored over every word for good reason. The pleading was Bucky's trunk speech for his deposition, and, if it became necessary, trial testimony. The document stated, "The defendant Lee learned, in an unsolicited non-confidential conversation with Roscoe Carmichael, that he was secretly videotaping women who had agreed to engage in consensual sex, but were unaware they were being videotaped."

The answer addressed why Bucky waited more than two months before he went to the DA's office. First, the defendant had to determine in his mind if Carmichael, while drunk, was merely bragging about his sexual exploits or telling the truth. The answer claimed that Bucky replayed the conversation over and over in his head. Once Bucky "determined he believed Mr. Carmichael that the videotaping had occurred, the defendant Lee had to consider his obligations to a former client." The answer explained the disciplinary dispute between the parties and how the Board dismissed all charges and found no merit in Carmichael's claim that he was entitled to a fee split. The answer assured that "the decision to disclose to the DA had nothing to do with the fee dispute." The answer asserted that "Mr. Carmichael clearly had terminated their attorney/client relationship approximately a year before their confrontation in Sperry's." Lee also considered it important "that the information shared did not involve any legal matter for which he had represented Carmichael."

Furthermore, Lee considered that "when Carmichael disclosed the information, Carmichael did not indicate that the conversation was intended to be confidential, and it was said where more than a dozen persons were within close proximity. The tables at Sperry's restaurant are right next to each other, and because the plaintiff was intoxicated, he spoke in a louder than normal voice. The defendant determined that the plaintiff didn't intend for the conversation to be confidential."

The documents asserted that "defendant Lee spent hours reviewing the Code of Professional Responsibility, which governs his ethical obligations as an attorney licensed in the state of Tennessee. The defendant Lee specifically focused on his obligations to the general public, the women videotaped, and future unsuspecting females who might be videoed by Carmichael. After careful consideration, the defendant Lee "concluded that disclosure was the right thing to do."

The answer concluded, "the defendant Lee went to see District Attorney Johnson Tory and explained the circumstance as to how he learned of the videos. It is the defendant's understanding that the police had already obtained warrants to search the plaintiff's residence and office for drugs. During the raid, the videotapes were found, and the police secured an additional warrant to confiscate the tapes. The police, regardless of the defendant Lee's actions would have found the tapes. However, because of the information the defendant reported to the police, the district attorney's office knew what they had found before they viewed the tapes. The defendant Lee, as a licensed attorney and officer of the court, had an ethical obligation to report the existence of the tapes to preserve justice and prevent future wrongdoing of the plaintiff Carmichael."

Barnes' phone was ringing off the hook from reporters, local, regional, and even the national publication, *USA Today*. Alice Krieger showed up at his office with a cameraman demanding an interview. Having heard about Davis' fiasco with Krieger, Barnes decided to take a different track. He figured it was better for him to give the interview, rather than fight her, or even worse, have Bucky do so. Barnes knew that he wouldn't be deposed or have to testify at trial.

Barnes thought the first question out of her mouth was an astute one. Barnes didn't want Bucky to say anything other than what was stated in the answer, but Krieger had taken him outside the document. "Do you think Ben Davis will add Mr. Lee as a defendant in the Swann and Doe cases?"

Barnes had been wondering the same thing, and he gave Krieger the best reason Bucky could muster, "My client was faced with a difficult ethical problem. If you ask ten lawyers that question, they'll each confirm the choices were all bad. He didn't seek the information. He didn't accidently discover it. Mr. Carmichael blurted it out. He got drunk and loud. The reason my client was even faced with the ethical dilemma was because of Mr. Carmichael's actions and then his disclosure of those actions. He had to weigh bad choices and, in the end, he decided to protect not only Mr. Davis' clients but also future young unsuspecting women who Mr. Carmichael was sure to hoodwink. Mr. Davis' clients shouldn't sue Bucky Lee. They should thank him. Ben Davis works with Morty Steine, an elder statesman of the Tennessee Bar. I'm confident he'll understand what I'm saying and not bring suit against my client."

Barnes was nothing short of a genius; by taking the Krieger

interview, he was forcing the Davis team off the fence and to take a wait-and- see approach, which, if he was Davis, would be his recommendation. Make them pick sides: Carmichael and Oz or Bucky. It was a fairly easy pick, and Barnes just spelled it out for them on television.

Tate would file Barnes' interview in February in support of his renewed motions for both change of venue and sequester. He'd argue that during the trial, the publicity would intensify supporting the need to first move the trial outside of Nashville and then argue the need to place the jury in seclusion away from all ties to the outside world.

Krieger continued the interview, "Mr. Carmichael and Mr. Oz haven't been charged with a crime in connection with the videotaping, have they?"

"Not yet. That's a decision for the DA's office. It's against the law to steal someone's property. It's also illegal to commit fraud on another person. Mr. Carmichael and Mr. Oz stole these women's images and Mr. Carmichael defrauded them by letting them think that the sex they agreed to would remain private and intimate. Applying the existing criminal statutes is confusing. The best solution would be for the legislature to pass new legislation that clearly states such an invasion of privacy will not be tolerated and is illegal."

"Your client had no prior relationship with any of these women?"

"That's correct."

"So, Mr. Lee put the interests of strangers over his obligation to his client?"

"Former client. Mr. Lee had represented Mr. Carmichael in a statutory rape case in 1990. Mr. Carmichael was found guilty of two misdemeanors and served a year in prison."

Bingo, that will play well with prospective jurors.

"Why did Mr. Lee end his attorney/client relationship with Mr. Carmichael?"

"I'm not at liberty to go into the details of their business relationship. They had a falling out over a fee dispute, which was resolved in Mr. Lee's favor and dismissed. It was a mutual decision to end their relationship."

"Were the two men friends?"

"When you're a solo practitioner, like me, you tend to form a relationship with your clients. It's usually friendly, some more than others. Mr. Lee represented Mr. Carmichael for many years. You tend to get closer to your civil clients than criminal ones. They did go through a serious criminal trial together. Once you've been through an experience like that, you're more than strangers. As our answer admits, Mr. Lee weighed his former relationship with Mr. Carmichael very carefully and agonized before he decided to act and go to the DA."

Krieger kept pressing Barnes on camera. Her questions were direct and difficult to answer.

I've got to keep reporters away from Bucky.

"Wouldn't you agree that Mr. Lee's actions proximately caused the publication of the tapes?"

"Absolutely not. Mr. Carmichael is an alleged drug dealer. Remember he's innocent until proven guilty. But it was two judge's findings that there was probable cause that Mr. Carmichael was dealing drugs that prompted the searches. Those acts by Carmichael caused his home to be raided, not the videotapes of the women. The district attorney didn't get a search warrant for the tapes until after the police entered the Music Row townhouse."

"Well, you'd agree that the women's case against the defendants Carmichael and Oz has been weakened by Mr. Lee's actions?"

"I wouldn't agree. I'd argue the opposite. If it wasn't for Mr. Lee's actions, the police wouldn't have known what was on the tapes. The police acted with more sensitivity because of the knowledge Mr. Lee provided."

Barnes and Krieger knew that the tape of their interview would be edited to Krieger's satisfaction. Barnes wished he could see the tape before it aired. *Forget it, there's no point even asking.* "Can we go off the record?"

Krieger directed her cameraman to put his camera down.

"Ms. Krieger, I hope you've found this interview helpful in understanding why Mr. Lee acted as he did. I think if you polled other lawyers who considered what had happened to Ms. Swann and the Doe's, and the risk to future victims, they'd have acted the same way."

The interview ended there. Before she aired the piece, Krieger did two things. First, she polled ten members of the Bar on air. She reported that all ten admitted it was a difficult ethical dilemma. Barnes got that right. The answer was six/four in favor of Bucky's actions and disclosure. That wasn't a clear answer to the question, but it did lend some support to Bucky's decision. Krieger's other investigative act was to call Davis for a comment. The rebuke from her editor during her last contact with Davis still stung. She intended to approach him carefully.

"Hello, Mr. Davis, I'm calling in regard to Bucky Lee's answer in the case filed by Roscoe Carmichael and the revelation that he turned in his former client to the DA's office. What do you have to say?"

"I take it these remarks are on the record?"

"I'm recording our conversation."

Davis was no fool. He knew he really couldn't sit on the fence.

If he'd been in Bucky's shoes, he'd have first gone to Morty, and then the two of them would have reached the same conclusion as Bucky, that disclosure was the right thing to do. How could he fault Bucky for doing what they would have done?

Davis replied, "First, it's important to remember that the claims by Misters Carmichael and Oz against Mr. Lee are pending in a separate lawsuit. Second, the police had decided to raid Carmichael's office before Mr. Lee reported the wrongful conduct. Third, Mr. Lee was in a difficult position. He weighed his bad choices, and in the end, he determined that his obligation to my clients and future victims outweighed his obligation to a former client regarding an unrelated matter to his prior representation. I think he was ethically bound to take some action. He certainly didn't have the right to do nothing."

"Will you be amending your complaints to allege that Bucky Lee was the proximate cause of the publication of the tapes?"

"Absolutely not. May I ask you a question?"

"That depends on the question." Krieger didn't trust Davis and was unwilling to commit to him.

"Are you single or married?"

"Single."

"Have you engaged in consensual sex with someone?"

Krieger hesitated before answering, "I'm no virgin. Why, are you looking for a date? You're not my type. You're a little on the heavy side."

That stung. Davis was conceited enough to think of himself as not only good looking and bright, but funny with a winning personality.

He shook it off and posed the question to Krieger, "My point is, what if you were in the position of my clients? A man you engaged in consensual sex with videotaped that intimate moment without your knowledge, and Bucky Lee discovered that fact. Wouldn't you want him to come forward and not hide behind the attorney/client privilege?"

Krieger didn't answer. Her response would be inconsistent with the hatchet job she intended to do on Bucky Lee.

Davis responded to the silence, "Before you go on air with this story, you should answer that question."

Davis hung up. He'd had enough of Krieger. He went directly to Morty's office and recounted the conversation with the reporter.

"Maybe your last question will get her thinking."

"I doubt it. She's not forgotten our last meeting, I think I made an enemy for life. I'm here for a purpose. I need you to make a trip to the state legislature."

Nashville was the state capital. Morty had played Democratic politics for almost fifty years. He was well liked by several members of the legislature and was owed many favors. He knew where most of the bodies were buried and had dug a few holes himself. He was very close with the Speaker of the House.

Davis continued, "They need to pass a new law that specifically defines the conduct of Carmichael and Oz as illegal. Let's get Sammie to research the criminal statutes of other jurisdictions and see how they've addressed such wrongful conduct. There's no point in reinventing the wheel. You've got the contacts in the legislature to get this done. It may be too late for our clients, but at least it will protect women going forward."

Seldom a man of few words, Morty simply said, "I'll get it done, and I think I'll bring Sammie along for the ride. I think I can get the Attorney General to support the legislation."

Davis had complete confidence that Morty could get the job done. Morty met with Sammie and gave her the research assignment to figure out what criminal statutes other states had passed protecting victims. When she completed her task, they'd walk over to the hill, and he'd contact some old friends in the legislature.

Unfortunately, there was a hole in the law, but Steine & Davis were committed to fill it in.

CHAPTER FORTY
ACADEMIC COWARDS

Same Day

(THIRD PERSON)

The summer semester began five days after tonight's exam. Class was at 6:30 p.m. At 8:30 a.m., Belinda Shaw, administrative assistant to Gregory Daniels, dean of the school, called and asked Bucky to come by Dean Daniels's office at 4:00 p.m. Bucky arrived a few minutes early and chatted with Ms. Shaw. She and everybody else in the school knew about the lawsuit against Bucky because of Alice Krieger's recent coverage. Barnes put the best possible spin he could on a bad situation. In a sympathetic tone, she asked, "How are you doing, professor?"

He responded, "I've been better, but I guess I could be doing worse. The fact is I believe I did the right thing and that gives me some solace."

Ms. Shaw liked Bucky, most people, students and faculty did. He wasn't an academic snob, who drilled and demeaned the students with the Socratic method, but rather, he was a lawyer with real life experience. The full-time faculty members projected an undeserved air of superiority when relating to the part-time staff. They felt that instructors, such as Bucky, lowered the standards of the school. They'd been pushing Dean Daniels to terminate all of the instructors and retain a full-time faculty to boost the school's reputation.

Bucky entered Dean Daniels' office and was offered a chair. The Dean opened the conversation, "How are you doing, Bucky?"

"I've got myself involved in a complicated litigation, with complex legal and ethical issues. If you've read my answer and seen Jack Barnes' interview, you'd know I was in a difficult position, with only poor options."

The Dean had been a trial judge in another life. "I saw Jack's interview. I thought he spelled out your predicament pretty well. I did a little bit of research on my own. If Carmichael had committed a crime and you believed he was going to commit another, I think you'd be on absolutely firm ground, and ethically you would have had no choice but to turn him in to the DA. But I can't seem to fit Carmichael's conduct into violating any existing statutes or arguably any case law. As I see it, that's a big problem. His conduct may have been immoral, but not illegal. If it wasn't illegal, your act of reporting him to the DA may have been unethical."

Concerned with the Dean's conclusion, Bucky remarked, "Jack came to the same conclusion. It seems Carmichael's action falls between the cracks. At the time of my decision, I thought he might have violated some kind of property right. I figured the women owned their image and Carmichael converted it without their permission. I also thought some kind of fraud charge might be appropriate. The DA doesn't agree."

The Dean opined, "So Carmichael's conduct was tortious toward these women and probably to future victims. You must have known that going to the DA could backfire and would have consequences."

Frustrated, Bucky responded, "Of course I knew, but I couldn't sit by and let Carmichael perpetrate a fraud on someone else. Tory shied away from prosecution because Carmichael and Oz are suing him and his office."

"I was glad to see that Ben Davis stood behind you."

"My lawyer didn't give him much choice. He had to side with me or with Carmichael. I'm clearly the better choice. He'll get to hear my version of what happened, Carmichael's version of what happened, and then he can make a final decision."

"When will you give your deposition?"

"In September. It won't interfere with my teaching."

"I bet it will be good for you to tell your version of what happened."

"I'd like to forget about this lawsuit. It's overwhelming. I'm looking forward to teaching again. These lawsuits have preoccupied my time, and I just want to get back in the classroom."

Daniels took a long pause before saying, "I'm under a lot of pressure to let you go. Our full-time faculty members have signed a letter demanding that I take action." He handed a document to Bucky.

From: The listed faculty members
To: Dean Gregory Daniels
Re: Bucky Lee

Dear Dean Daniels,

All of the full-time faculty members of the Nashville School of Law are gravely concerned that the continued employment of Instructor Bucky Lee besmirches the reputation of our school. The professional staff of the school find the allegations of the pending civil ligation and the ethical questions raised by probable Disciplinary Board charges sufficiently damaging. We request that Mr. Lee be put on administrative leave immediately before the commencement of the summer semester.

All three tenured professors at the school and three associate professors signed the document. The entire full-time staff signed the letter; the remaining staff members were part-time instructors like Bucky. Bucky was taken off guard by the petition and didn't say anything.

Daniels continued, "These six professors are pushing hard for your suspension. Each one called me and personally urged me to follow the request in the letter. They aren't concerned about the allegations of negligence. Their concern is that you acted unethically when you went to the DA and violated your oath of confidentiality. They've argued that you've set a bad example for our students by violating the attorney/client relationship."

"What did you tell them?"

"I told them you weren't charged with a crime but had been sued civilly. I reminded them that the claims against you were, in part, allegations of negligence, and those charges were for giving bad legal advice and that the claims were denied and unproven. I told them that they were professionals, and they should have a better understanding of our legal system. They should be more supportive of a fellow member of our staff. I pointed out that at the first pleading, you disclosed your ethical dilemma. I also shared with them that I didn't know for certain, but I hoped I'd do the same thing. That got their attention."

Daniels handed Bucky a second document, "I gave each of them a copy of this." It was a Petition in Support of Professor Lee, signed by each member of his Criminal Procedure class and Civil Procedure class, sixty-three signatures.

"You've taught your students well. They have a better understanding of our judicial system than certain members of our staff. I can't revoke tenure for the three who already have it, but the other three will never get tenure at this school while I'm Dean. I told each of them to mind their own business and wait for our judicial process to work through the lawsuit. I told them that I knew you as a man and as a lawyer and that I was confident the judge or the jury would dismiss these false claims of negligent advice."

Bucky was emotionally shaken by the betrayal of the faculty, but even more moved by the support of his students and Dean Daniels. "You won't regret your support. I'd never advise a client to secretly video himself having sex with unsuspecting women. These are desperate defendants who have made outrageous claims."

Two hours later, Bucky was standing in front of his Criminal Procedure class. He held up the petition and said, "Words cannot express the appreciation I feel by your outward support." He held the paper above his head. "I value your confidence in me. I'd never give the unethical and tortious advice that I'm accused of. Now, I want to wish you good luck on your exam."

About four miles away, Davis and Sammie were sitting down to dinner, a home-cooked meal with the rest of the Davis family. They never talked business at the table, but Davis felt compelled to ask, "Has anybody seen any strange characters hanging around the house, or any cars parked in front of or near the house for an extended period of time?"

Liza immediately became concerned, but she tried not to show it in her voice. "Why do you ask?"

Everybody at the table knew that Davis had been attacked in his office five years earlier and that two of the attackers had been shot dead and one of the culprits was still on the loose. The kids listened but both thought their father was being overly dramatic, Liza knew better. Her husband didn't make casual remarks like that. He must have been worried. Davis only shared with the family that his beloved Vette suffered a flat tire, not three, nor did he reveal the details, such as the fact that the three were man made.

Caroline and Jake went out after dinner. Their mother was glad to get them out of the house. As Sammie cleared the dishes, Liza asked, "What the hell is up?"

Her question was directed to her husband, "I didn't want to alarm the kids. What are you concerned about?"

His single-word response was, "Oz."

Liza's voice changed. It got lower, as if someone was trying to listen in to their conversation, "You think he punctured your tire? What haven't you told me?"

"Tires. This person may be trying to scare me into settlement. I've called Chief Neenan and made an incident report documenting that my Vette suffered three unexplained flat tires..."

Liza, who'd lived through the Plainview cases, pointed out, "Big deal, you documented the threat. What steps have you taken to protect this family?"

"I just warned everybody to keep their eyes and ears open. What more can I do?"

"You can settle those damn cases. Money isn't going to make those women whole anyway. You've made your point by filing suit. The community will never look at the two of them the same way. What more do you want?"

"I want the system to work. I'm not letting some thug intimidate me and broker a quick and low settlement. That wouldn't be fair to my clients."

"What about your family? Aren't we more important than the rights of your clients?"

They started yelling at each other, and Sammie, who'd never seen her aunt and uncle really fight before, wanted to interject but was afraid to.

"Don't worry, I can take care of both my family and my clients. That's what I do."

"You can sleep in the spare bedroom, tonight and for as long as you remain stubborn."

Liza stormed out of the kitchen without another word. Davis turned to Sammie, "She doesn't understand."

Sammie's response was four words, "I see her point."

Sammie and Morty left to return to their loft apartment. On the ride downtown, she kept checking her mirrors to see if she was being followed. It seemed all clear.

CHAPTER FORTY-ONE

HAPPY BIRTHDAY, AMERICA

Thursday, July 3, 1997

(THIRD PERSON)

Every year the Davis' hosted a July 3rd barbecue around their pool. The reason they celebrated the birth of our nation on the 3rd rather than the 4th was not out of confusion or irreverence to our founding fathers, but because the Davis home bordered Hillwood Country Club. Years ago, the country club's board of directors decided that the membership would celebrate the holiday on the 3rd, so that the employees could be sent home at 3:00 p.m. on the 4th and spend the evening with their families. The evening of the 3rd the club, using a professional company, treated their members and surrounding properties to a twenty five minute fireworks display. It was one of the best in the city.

The next day on the 4th, the club served a buffet/barbecue lunch and the golf course remained open, but after 3:00 p.m. the facilities and golf course were closed. On the 4th it operated with a skeleton staff usually supervised by the general manager, who graciously sacrificed his holiday so the other managers and most of the staff could enjoy the holiday with their families.

The Davis' party always had a diverse guest list including family, friends, clients, and members of the Bar and judiciary. This was the eighth year of the party. Most years, they had more than two hundred attendees. Davis spared no expense on the incredible menu of smoked and grilled proteins, side items, and desserts too numerous to count.

Larry and Shelly Davis, who had just visited a few weeks before for Sammie's graduation, came back to town. Davis' parents always made the journey from their home in Woodbury, Long Island for the party on the 3rd. It was the perfect opportunity to visit with grandchildren and see their Nashville friends. They'd make a week of it, and Larry would call his son George multiple times each day to check on the stores. Each time Davis' father called to get a status report from one of his locations, Davis asked, "What could possibly have changed in three hours?" The elder Davis and his son George operated three dry cleaners near Woodbury.

"You never know," replied the older Davis. "You're better off keeping a close eye on things when you own a business."

Davis knew he was right. The key to a successful family-owned business was staying on top of things by being at the business and controlling the cash flow. Davis had seen many small businesses fail because the owners got lax. The hardest part of running a small business was employees. They often weren't motivated and sometimes stole from a cash business.

It was a barbecue, so the dress was casual, and everybody brought an appetite. Davis, Liza, and their children greeted everyone in a receiving line. Davis felt strongly that he should personally welcome each guest. Caroline and Jake didn't agree with their father's view of southern hospitality. Caroline would remind her father, "You're from New York, not the South. Why don't we just mingle?" Despite her protest, she and her brother stood there stoically. Liza had taught them well.

The Davis home had an invisible fence to contain their pugs, Abbott and Costello, and an irregular tree line, which did not obstruct their view of the golf course. They bordered the seventeenth hole, which every year was where A-1 Fireworks set up its complex electronic board that controlled the firing tubes for the evening's festivities. A-1 was a family-run business. Three generations were involved in the elaborate show that lasted twenty-two minutes. The expense was borne by the country club at a cost of over $20,000. The founder of the company, Tom Miller, his son, Derek, and his fifteen-year- old grandson, Stevie aka Pinky, whose father Darrell was deceased, rounded out the A-1 team.

During the day, Davis watched the A-1 men set up their equipment for the evening's performance. He approached the grandfather and yelled between the trees, "What time do you anticipate starting?"

"It won't happen until after it gets dark. I'd say between 9:15 p.m. and 9:30 p.m. It's going to be one hell of a show, and you and yours are going to have the best seats in the house."

Davis' party started at 6:00 p.m. That gave his guests three hours to eat, drink and visit before the show. The fireworks would end before 10:00 p.m., and for most people that was their cue to go home. Davis knew, however, that of the two hundred guests, fifty or so would remain long after the last explosion, taking advantage of the two open bars. He didn't mind as long as there was a designated driver.

The first three hours of the evening went perfectly. Morty, as usual, got on stage and sang a few songs with the band. He liked

Motown. Liza and Caroline, who sang in the Temple choir during high holy days, belted out two Aretha Franklin songs. No one invited Davis to the stage. He was tone deaf.

At 9:15 pm, the fireworks began. Davis' guests could see everything from their vantage point. The night sky was illuminated by the bursts a hundred feet above the crowd. The spectacle brought them alive. After the explosions, different colored streamers fell to earth right at the tree line of the property. There were a lot of ooh's.

Wthout warning, about fifteen minutes into the program, one of the cannons that hadn't yet been used, for some unexplained reason turned downward, and its blast went eight feet off the ground straight through the tree line, just above the heads of Davis' guests.

The fireball struck the house, bounced off and set fire to the lawn. Secondary explosions dispersed the colored streamers, injuring more than a dozen guests standing in the immediate area. People ran in every direction. Liza's mother, Patsy Caldwell, was pushed to the ground, and if not for Davis' father, Larry, would have been trampled. The fire spread quickly over a thirty-foot by six-foot area. Several guests received third-degree burns to their arms, legs, and two of them to the face. Most people were wearing shorts, and everybody had on short sleeve shirts.

The crowd panicked, and several people either fell or jumped in the swimming pool. Davis pushed his own mother into the pool to protect her. Thank goodness, several doctors and nurses were present and could tend to the injured. That included Dr. John Caldwell and Davis' wife. Dr. Caldwell immediately called Saint Thomas Hospital on his speed dial, and five ambulances were dispatched. Then he organized a triage area and dealt with the more seriously injured guests until the ambulances arrived. The less injured would be transported to various hospitals by car. Even though it was the 3rd of July, and not the 4th, emergency rooms all over the city were crowded with children and adults who'd mishandled fireworks.

Someone grabbed a hose and directed the spray at the fire. The flames weren't far from the house. Another guest grabbed a second hose on the other side of the screened-in porch. The two together managed to stop the flames from reaching the house.

Frantic about the safety of his guests, Davis pulled his poor mother out of the pool. A moment later, he ran into one of the Metro detectives who'd been sued by Carmichael. Detective Robert Sanders, a longtime friend, had brought his family to the party, and they were standing next to him. Davis said, "Bobby, I need you to do me a favor. Somebody really screwed up on the other side of the tree line. We've got some pretty seriously injured people here. I can't leave until everyone who needs medical attention goes to the hospital. There are going to be insurance claims, and I'm afraid, some lawsuits. I'm sure this is already called in, but would you go over there and make sure things stay status quo until your bomb squad, fire department, or whoever is going to conduct this investigation can get here? I'm concerned that evidence could be altered or destroyed. Send your family home, and I'll get you a ride home later."

Sanders turned to his wife, "Janet, take the kids home. Ben needs my help." He hugged his kids and ran toward the problem. Sanders liked and respected Davis, but he would have helped even if he'd been a stranger.

The A-1 team, on its side of the tree line, was also in a panic. In twenty-seven years, nothing like this had ever happened. Sanders started asking questions, which the grandfather answered without hesitation.

"How could this have happened?" Sanders asked, louder than he intended. He was upset. His wife and children had been in the line of fire.

"We're checking. It could have been a programming error, but I don't think so. Something happened manually to make that cannon point in that direction. Those cannons are pretty heavy. Two of us have to lift them off the dolly and put them in place. Someone would have to be pretty strong to change the direction of one of them alone. All three of us were here when that cannon went off. I did see a strange tall guy at that end of the line just before the show started. He was talking to my grandson, Pinky."

The youngest Miller was standing about twenty feet away. His grandfather called him over. "Who were you talking to before the show started?

"I don't know. I'd never seen him before. He looked like a biker, big guy with curly hair and a beard. He asked a lot of questions. Seemed like a nice guy."

"Did he touch any of the equipment?" the older man asked anxiously.

"No, he just asked a bunch of questions. He didn't touch anything."

"Pinky, your stupid idiot, you know better than to let anyone near our equipment right before a show! The malfunction took place on your end of the line. Nobody's supposed to be near the panel during a show."

"He didn't get near the panel. He was at the end of the line. You were operating the board. Uncle Derek was at the other end, and this guy just stood next to me before the show started, asking questions. I don't see how he could have done this," the young man insisted.

Sanders asked, "Describe the guy again."

"He was very tall. I'm six foot, and he was at least three inches taller than I am. He had long curly brown hair over his collar and a goatee. I guess he was about fortyish."

"Did he have any distinguishing marks?"

"What do you mean?"

"Like a birth mark or a tattoo?"

"He had on a long sleeve denim shirt."

The fire department and the bomb squad arrived. The firemen addressed the fire, and the bomb squad took over Sanders' examination of the Millers. It was 9:45 p.m., twenty minutes after the misguided cannonball made its entry through the tree line onto Davis property. The transportation of the injured was completed, so Sammie and Liza went to Saint Thomas to sit with friends and families of the injured. Davis and Morty promised to join them as soon as possible.

This was a nightmare. Davis practically ran over to Sanders, and Davis didn't usually move that fast for anyone, "Bobby, what the hell happened? Do they know?"

"They're checking it out. It could have been mechanical or manual. There was a mystery man at the site. The bomb squad is doing its job. Say, do you have anybody who doesn't like you?"

Davis actually laughed. "You've got to be kidding. I've been making enemies for the last twenty years. Every time I enter a courtroom, somebody wins and somebody loses. I almost always win, so somebody's mad at me. Everybody loves their own lawyer but hates, sometimes with a passion, me. Most businessmen understand it's just business, and some of them are smart enough, after I kick their ass, to retain our firm. But I'm confident that there are dozens of people who hate me. I didn't think anybody cared that much to injure my guests, burn down my house, and ruin my party."

Davis didn't make it to the hospital until 3:00 a.m. He was interviewed by the bomb squad, the police and gave a handwritten statement. When he walked into the waiting room he found Caroline and Jake fast asleep on a bench. Sammie, Liza, and Davis' father and mother were sitting with about two dozen friends and family of the injured. Dr. Caldwell entered and Davis had never been so glad to see his father-in-law. "How bad is it?"

"It's not good, but it could have been far worse. Two persons have third-degree burns on their faces. They'll both need plastic surgery and skin grafts. Six others have third-degree burns on their arms or legs. We'll watch them carefully for infection. Several others have second-degree burns, but those will heal with treatment. We've admitted fourteen people to rooms. What the hell happened?"

"John, I don't know, but I'm going to find out. I don't think this was an accident."

CHAPTER FORTY-TWO

THE DAY AFTER

Friday, July 4, 1997

(BENJAMIN DAVIS' VOICE)

My family got home at 9:00 a.m. after spending the night sitting in the waiting room at Saint Thomas with the families of injured friends. It was a distraught group of people, whose children, husbands, and wives were disfigured and burned. We were tired, confused, and scared. Liza, a psychiatric nurse, kept busy, moving from one family member of an injured person to another. During the entire time, my children Caroline and Jake were traumatized and kept to themselves on a bench in a corner. They were pretty freaked out. As soon as the family returned to the house, Caroline and Jake went to their rooms, exhausted.

As I climbed the stairs, Liza began a heated exchange, "It's been quite a night. I hope you're proud of yourself. Several of our good friends were injured, and you don't know if it was an accident or not? In fact, you suspect it wasn't. You've got to live with the possibility that you exposed your family and friends to extreme danger, injury, and death."

"Nobody died. Let's not get too dramatic."

Bad response, I realized as soon as the words left my mouth.

Liza said angrily, "Well somebody could have. Many people almost did. You're being a selfish prick, always thinking about yourself. That's all you and that old man do. You've lost perspective, and you're setting a bad example for Sammie. She's learned your passion for the law and the need to protect and pursue the rights of your clients. Now you need to teach her the importance of family. Your mother sent her down here so you would do just that. You've got a family to protect, Caroline, Jake, and me. You even have obligations to those damn dogs. I know that a good lawyer needs to compartmentalize his personal life from his practice. Every time I've ever asked you about work, that's been your mantra, and you were right. There needs to be a wall. The family didn't elect to take on the Swann and Doe cases. You did. Your business decisions can't jeopardize the lives of your family. It's just not right, and you always try to do the right thing."

That struck a nerve. I knew Liza was right. In my heart I knew the fireworks malfunction was no accident, but proving that would be another story. I'd need all the help I could get. Liza didn't like the way I'd minimized the seriousness of the problem. Pissed at me, she couldn't go to sleep and elected to shower instead. In an effort to wake up and make up, I jumped into the shower with her. I turned on the second showerhead, and we stood there naked in silence until Liza finally broke it.

"Stop bullshitting me. People, friends of ours, got hurt. They could have been killed. Stop being so stubborn and settle those Carmichael cases before something worse happens."

My attempt at a romantic shower failed miserably. Liza showered and then laid down in our bed and closed her eyes. She made no invitation for me to join her.

Morty was waiting for me at the kitchen table. He was on his third cup of coffee. Everybody was struggling to stay awake. He began, "We need a game plan. You need to start by calling Chief Neenan and sharing with him all your suspicions about Carmichael and Oz and their connection with last night."

"Tell him that I think Carmichael and/or Oz was behind this tragedy?"

"Exactly. Oz is six feet five. Men of that size don't grow on trees. His height is strong circumstantial evidence."

"You can't arrest someone just because he's tall. Detective Sanders told me that the guy had curly hair and a beard. Oz is bald and clean-shaven. He doesn't match the description."

Morty questioned,

"What the hell's wrong with you? Haven't you ever heard of wearing a wig or a false beard? You can buy disguises like that at a million places. We need to get that kid together with a sketch artist."

As usual, Morty had a good idea.

I called Chief Neenan, "Gerry, Ben Davis. Are you aware of what happened at my home?"

"I'm the chief of police. What do you think I do around here? Of course I've heard about last night. That was one helluva party you threw. How come I wasn't invited?"

There was a long silence.

"I'm just screwing with you, Ben. When you play with fireworks, you've got to watch it, or you can get burned."

"I'd rather you didn't joke, Gerry. I'm not in a laughing mood. First of all, let's get something straight. I didn't touch, let alone shoot off, any fireworks, nor were they shot off from my property. Hillwood County Cub hired professionals to do the job, and, the cannon shot the fireworks onto my property, injuring my guests. I'm pretty shaken up. This wasn't any accident. Some serious people wanted to make a point, and they did."

"That's a serious accusation. You're the lawyer. You know for me to launch an investigation into Carmichael and Oz as suspects I've got to have reasonable suspicion, and if they are charged, the prosecutor must prove his case beyond a reasonable doubt in order to convict."

"I just want you to question them. Find out if they have an alibi."

Neenan tried to change the subject, "How many people were seriously injured?"

"Eight people received third-degree burns. Two will definitely require plastic surgery. Fourteen were taken to the hospital, nineteen injured in total. Have you talked to Bobby Sanders? He was there before the fire department or the bomb squad arrived. Who's the detective in charge?"

"Jay Turner. I did speak to Sanders and Bobby insisted on working the case with Turner. I didn't think it was such a good idea since he was a defendant in the Carmichael case, but he wouldn't take no for an answer. He claimed he had a dog in the fight and wanted to be a part of the investigation. I finally had to relent."

I figured it was a good thing to have Sanders on the case. He was motivated. "So, where are we?"

"The Miller kid is trying to cooperate. I'm told he's not real bright. Sanders described him as 'dumb as a rock.' He's sleeping right now, but we'll keep questioning him. I'm hoping this was just a bad accident. Sanders doesn't think so. He's convinced this 'big guy' somehow messed with the cannon purposely. He was near it, but so far, we can't prove access. The grandfather claims one man wouldn't have the strength to move the cannon by himself. How do we overcome that testimony?"

"I can't prove anything."

"I didn't ask you what you can prove. Stop thinking like a lawyer. What do you think?"

"I think it was that son of a bitch Phillip Oz."

"I think you're right. Okay, you're the lawyer. How do we prove it?"

"Morty's suggested a sketch artist."

"I like it. It's old school, but that's worked thousands of times before. I'll put the kid with an artist when he wakes up. If he's not up by noon, I'll wake him up personally."

I liked the fact that the chief was getting directly involved, Neenan then volunteered, "I hope this isn't related but Anthony "June bug" Estes is dead. It happened two days ago, Agent Pyle called me first thing this morning."

"What happened?"

"He was in witness protection living in Topeka, Kansas and he keeled over dead. There doing an autopsy, Pyle suspects poisoning. I don't think his death was just a coincidence.

I hung up, recounted my conversation with the chief with Morty and opined, "I wonder what Oz looked like with hair? He played football with Carmichael in high school. He must have been born in 1950 or 1951. He'd be eighteen in 1969. Let's see if we can find him in a high school yearbook."

We embraced for more than a minute. I truly loved this man. As we released the embrace, Liza walked into the room. "Did I interrupt something? Do I need to leave the two of you alone?" she said playfully. I was glad to see she hadn't completely lost her sense of humor?

I explained to her personal exposure problem as the sole owner of their residence.

Liza exploded, "So because I own the property, our injured friends would sue me, not you or us?"

I apologetically responded, "Technically that's correct, but of course the primary responsible party is the fireworks company A-1, and before you have any liability, Hillwood Country Club would be secondarily responsible because it hired A-1. We bought insurance, two policies, up to $5,000,000. I haven't read the policies since we purchased them about ten years ago. I don't remember any of the specifics. Charlie's bringing them over at noon. He's worried it may exempt coverage. Let's not overreact."

Charlie Roberts was right on time, and he brought two copies of each policy. The underlying policy was twenty-nine pages long, and the question of coverage boiled down to a simple definition:

> 1(g)(5) Not-a-Natural Event. This policy shall cover events, which are not natural in origin but are a result of human error, which cause property damage to the insured or personal injury to others.

Morty and I didn't have to be legal scholars to understand that Liza's policy provided coverage if the damage was caused by an accident, human error, or negligence. However, the policy was silent if the damage was a result of an intentional act. I needed to reconsider my allegations against Oz in light of these new developments. There might not be any insurance coverage if Oz intentionally caused the damage to my house and injured my friends.

This reality made me sick to my stomach. There were plenty of leftovers and I elected to take out my stress by eating two plates full. Morty smoked a Cuban to release his frustration. Liza shook her head in disgust at the two of us and got in her car to go back to the hospital to sit with the family members of our injured friends about to have surgery. Morty decided to drive to Ashland City and I elected to go to the office first and check in with Bella.

That was a big mistake.

CHAPTER FORTY-THREE

UNWELCOMED VISITOR

Friday, July 4, 1997

(BENJAMIN DAVIS' VOICE)

As soon as I got to the office I was really thrown off balance. Alice Krieger confronted me. She was waiting outside his office, so there was no avoiding her. I decided I couldn't duck her, even though I wanted to.

"Ms. Krieger, good morning. I thought we understood each other. At this time, neither my clients nor I am giving interviews."

"I'm not here about the Carmichael cases. I'm here about what happened at your residence the other night. Your injured guests and what happened are news."

I decided that an interview was the best course of action. I was confident I could handle Alice Krieger. "Let's do it, on the condition you won't harass my clients other than at the courthouse.

"I won't harass them."

I nodded and Krieger began, "Do you think that your guests will sue you?"

"You need to appreciate that everyone who attended my party was either a friend, client, and/or business associate. I knew every one of them well. Some are hurt badly. They were hurt at my house, at my party. Look, I fed them, offered them drinks, and told them there would be a firework show put on by Hillwood Country Club by professionals it hired. For seven years on July 3rd that's exactly what happened. I had no reason to believe that wouldn't happen an eighth time. Many of my neighbors were sitting in their backyards watching the same show, and they were lucky the fireworks didn't invade their property. I guess my friends and I weren't so lucky. At this point all I'm concerned about is the recovery of my friends."

I paused and became obviously emotional, I wasn't acting.

"So, my family and I feel helpless. We've been sitting at the hospital trying to comfort and offer what little support to our friends we can, but we realize nothing we say or do can really lighten their sorrow. Slowly as loved ones recover and their lives return to normal, the healing process will begin. I came to my office this morning to clear my head. It didn't work. My thoughts are still at the hospital. We're taking food to the hospital in shifts so we can be there 24/7. My wife, Liza, and niece, Sammie, are there now."

I hoped that explained why I wasn't at the hospital would be acceptable.

"To answer your second question, we're not thinking about a lawsuit. If we get sued, we get sued. A-1 Amusement held itself out to be a professional fireworks company. It is the primary responsible party under the law. Hillwood Country Club hired A-1, and the fireworks were shot off from its property. The club would be the secondary responsible party, as the principal for its agent, A-1 Amusement. Again, my concern at this time is not a lawsuit, but the health and recovery of my friends. I want to thank Ms. Krieger for allowing me to tell her viewers about what happened and how miserable I feel about my injured friends."

Krieger ended the interview with a few closing remarks, and the red light went dead.

"Nice job. How much of it is bullshit?"

"None of it. I'm not worried about a lawsuit. I'm really third in line. They both have insurance coverage, so I want my injured friends to be compensated."

Krieger left, satisfied she'd gotten her story. It would play tonight at six in the part B segment, I looked up and standing in the corner was Morty.

"How long have you been standing there?"

"Long enough to hear you make a pretty big mistake in that interview, which may hurt you later on."

"What the hell are you talking about? What I said was absolutely legally correct. A-1 and Hillwood are ahead of me in liability."

"You idiot, you don't own the property. All of those references to 'my property or our property' were misleading. You don't own shit. You may have now opened yourself up to liability where you previously had none. Nice going, smart boy."

"Nobody's perfect. It was from the heart. So, I made a small mistake. I'm not at my best. Maybe I should go to the hospital. Maybe coming here wasn't the smartest decision."

"You do that, but before you go, let me show you what I found." Morty went into his briefcase and retrieved four photocopies of a photograph of a much younger Phillip Oz from the 1970 Ashland City high school yearbook. Dressed in his football gear, except for his helmet, Oz had a full head of brown curly hair.

"How did you find it?"

"I asked a librarian to help an old man looking for his grandson's picture for his fortieth birthday party. I told her I wanted to blow it up to poster size. She was very accommodating. Maybe we should have it blown up anyway, so as to avoid making me a complete liar."

"No, I like you better as a complete liar. It makes me feel a lot better."

I looked at the pictures and pointed out, "These are awfully grainy. Couldn't she let you have the book?"

"If we need the book, the DA's office can subpoena it. These pictures should do the job. I'll take them over to Sanders so he can have the Miller kid look at them to make a positive ID. Anything you want me to tell Sanders?"

I wondered if pursuing Oz as the culprit was voiding coverage for my property damage and liability coverage for my injured guests. I erased that passing thought as irrelevant and decided it was critical that Sanders press on with his investigation. "Just tell him good hunting."

Morty left for the police station, a ten-minute walk. I slipped my to-do list in my briefcase and started to gather my work to take home. I figured I'd stop by the hospital, go home, and spend time with the kids. Caroline and Jake were not in school and couldn't be expected to spend July 4th in a hospital.

I was about to walk out the door when Bella buzzed in, "There's a Sara James to see you. She doesn't have an appointment."

"Who is she?"

"She's Randy James' mother. We've been talking. You'll want to see her in the conference room right away. I'll bring coffee and pastries, and I can take notes if you need me to."

I'd worked long enough with Bella to appreciate when she said "you need to meet with someone", I should take the meeting. I met Ms. James at the doorway of the conference room and extended my hand to a woman in her mid-fifties.

"Ben Davis."

"Sara James. My son's Randy. He was a bartender at your party the other night. He was injured really bad."

I thought for a moment and remembered a young black man working behind one of the two bars.

"How old is Randy?"

"He's twenty, a junior at Middle Tennessee State. He wants to be a lawyer like you. He was working this summer as a bartender at parties to pay for next semester's tuition. We need his income, and he's too hurt to work now. I don't know how he's going to pay for school."

"What are Randy's injuries, Ms. James?"

"Bad burns to his face."

I thought I knew the names of all the injured persons, all nineteen. Fourteen were admitted to Saint Thomas. I had a copy of a list.

"I'm sorry, Mrs. James, somehow your son's name didn't make it to my list of injured persons admitted to Saint Thomas. What room is he in?"

"He isn't in any room there. He was treated in the emergency room and then sent to General Hospital. He doesn't have any insurance. He was admitted to General Hospital, treated, and then released. He's got a bad blister on his face. It might be infected. Randy doesn't want to go back to General. He's stubborn like his late father. We don't have any extra money for medical care."

Thinking like a lawyer, I asked, "He was injured at work. Isn't he covered by worker's comp?"

"Nope, he's an independent contractor. The company that catered your party made him sign a piece of paper saying he was independent so it wouldn't have to provide him with medical insurance."

I knew exactly what he'd signed. I represented the catering company and I drafted that document for my client's benefit. I was feeling a little guilty about placing this young man without insurance coverage. I walked over to the credenza, picked up the phone, and dialed.

"Kim, Ben Davis. I'm sending over a new patient. He doesn't have insurance. How quickly can you get him in?" I knew Dr. Max's office would be open despite the holiday because it was the 4th and he was a plastic surgeon who specialized in burns and trauma.

Kim checked the schedule. "Looks like 5:30 p.m. tomorrow. How's that for service?"

"Thanks," and I hung up. Not only did I represent Kim's boss, I also represented her seventeen-year- old son, Billy, on drug charges and with Morty's help, got them dismissed.

I smiled and returned to the anxious mother waiting and said, "That was Kim Williams. She's the office manager for Dr. Peter Max, a plastic surgeon I represent. I helped Peter purchase his practice from a retiring doctor. He owes me a favor or two. He'll treat your son. Randy has an appointment tomorrow at this address at 5:30 p.m." I jotted down Dr. Peter Max's address.

"But, Mr. Davis, we don't have the money for a doctor."

"Mrs. James, maybe I'm not making myself clear. Your job is to help your son get better. Here's my cell phone number. I want you to keep me advised of his progress. If you need any further help, let me know, and I'll see what I can do."

Although there were ethical considerations and possible insurance implications for paying these medical bills, I wasn't going to let Randy James fall between the cracks. The woman started crying. I put my arms around her and gave her a bear hug.

When I released her, she gasped for breath, "Thank you, sir, for your kindness."

"It's the right thing to do."

Sara James left as quickly as she arrived. I grabbed my briefcase, said good-bye to Bella, who was hard at work deflecting the day-to-day problems of the office, and went straight to the hospital.

The Saint Thomas waiting room was a depressing place.

CHAPTER FORTY-FOUR

A BAD WITNESS

Tuesday, July 8, 1997

(BENJAMIN DAVIS' VOICE)

Sammie and I arrived at the police station at 9:15 a.m. just as Detective Bobby Sanders requested. We'd been invited to observe the questioning of Steven "Pinky" Miller, ironically through a two-way mirror. I brought with us the 1970 Ashland City High School yearbook to prod the young man's recollection. The hope was Pinky Miller could place Phillip Oz at the scene on July 3rd. We were placed on the other side of the two-way glass while Detectives Turner and Sanders met with Pinky in the cramped interrogation room consisting of a small table and four chairs.

Turner began, "Okay, Pinky, we're here today to see if you can ID the tall man who was hanging around the cannon the evening of the 3rd..."

"I've told you I didn't get a good look at him. I wasn't paying attention to him. I was getting ready for the show. All I did was answer his questions over my shoulder, and five minutes later he was gone."

Turner asked, "What questions did he ask you?"

"Typical stuff. Where do we buy our fireworks, do we make them ourselves? How long will the show last? How expensive is it to hire our company to put on the show?"

"Most of the questions I couldn't answer and I directed him to my granddaddy. He was gone in five minutes, left about ten minutes before the show began. I didn't get a good look."

Turner pressed on, "Well, yesterday, you worked with our sketch artist, and she came up with this." Turner handed Miller a charcoal sketch of the suspect.

"I could tell his hair was brown, curly and longish. He had a goatee. He was a lot taller than me, and I'm six foot. That's the best I can do. This generally looks like the guy, but I can't get more specific. I don't think the guy did anything. My granddaddy says it would be impossible for one man to move the cannon. My granddaddy would know."

I turned to Sammie, "It sounds to me like the kid's afraid of his granddaddy."

Sammie asked the right question, "Why wouldn't his grandfather want Oz to be responsible for what happened?"

The answer jumped out and hit me smack in the head. I said, "The same reason I questioned pursuing Oz. A-1 might lose insurance coverage if there was an intentional wrongful act. If the injuries were caused by negligence, A-1 has coverage. If someone intentionally caused the injuries, A-1's coverage could be voided. Granddaddy may have been advised by his lawyer that he's better off from a liability standpoint to let this go down as an accident."

Sanders showed Pinky the photo from the 1970 yearbook. Miller stared at it a long time. "Could be. He's got curly hair but no goatee."

"What do you mean, could be?" asked Turner. "That's not a good enough answer. We need a positive ID."

"The guy I saw was forty years old or more. This is a picture of a teenager. It looks like a high school football picture. I can't say the guy that night was the same guy. This picture is grainy, and I didn't get a good look at the guy. That's the best I can do. Could be is all you get."

I was disappointed.

Turner and Sanders left Miller to pow wow with the kid's lawyers. The grandfather made sure the company's insurance lawyer was contacted and available to Pinky when he was brought in for questioning. It was the lawyer who impressed upon the kid that an ID was not in A-1's best interest. He needed to be absolutely certain if he was going to make a positive ID. He shouldn't guess.

Turner and Sanders joined us. Turner spoke first. "He's slow-witted, but I think he's intentionally being dense. I don't think he's going to make our identification for us."

I added, "Even if he does finally make an ID, he'll make a terrible witness on cross. Pierce will destroy him on the stand. She'll find his weaknesses, and he'll have no credibility left with the jury."

I announced to no one in particular, but Sammie knew she'd be assigned the task, "Go buy six identical curly wigs and six identical fake goatees. Sanders, find five guys over six three, and ask Oz to come in for questioning. Have him participate in a lineup. Have the six men put on the disguise and participate in the lineup. If Oz refuses, arrest him on suspicion of what?"

Turner answered, "Aggravated assault and battery. That's the most serious crime I can think of."

Sanders responded, "Attempted murder in the second degree."

Sanders was reaching, no DA would indict Oz on the limited evidence to date. I'd never tried a murder trial. In fact, I'd never met an accused murderer. Morty had tried and won seven murder trials. He was very familiar with the elements of what the state had to prove beyond a reasonable doubt. He'd saved six black men and one white man from the electric chair. Morty thought corporal punishment was cruel and inhuman punishment in violation of the Eighth Amendment. I shared his opinion.

Turner argued, "I don't think you've got the elements to prove murder. How are you going to prove intent? You need to prove that Oz took actions intended to kill Davis' guests. If you can prove he was there and tampered with the line, you should be able to establish that he acted recklessly, without regard for the safety of your guests. Those actions could have caused death, but proving intent will be tough."

I tried to answer Turner, "Shooting off those fireworks into a crowd of two hundred is like shooting a gun into a crowd. To attempt murder, you just have to be reasonably certain someone is going to die. Look, do the lineup, and then get back to us. If the kid positively identifies him, we'll talk about how to pressure Oz."

We had a plan. The lineup might turn maybe into yes.

Two hours later, with Sammie and I behind the two-way mirror, Amy Pierce and her client were waiting for Detectives Sanders and Turner in the same interrogation room.

"We want your client to participate in a lineup."

Pierce questioned, "What for?"

"He fits a description of a suspect."

"Tall and bald?"

"Not quite."

He turned to Oz, "Put these on."

Oz froze. Pierce immediately recognized something was wrong by her client's guilty expression and body language.

"What's the crime?"

Turner was having a good time. He stated, "Attempted second degree murder."

Now it was Pierce's turn to get flustered. She fought to gain control. "Will everyone on the line be wearing these ridiculous wigs and beards?"

"Absolutely."

"My client's taking the Fifth Amendment on the grounds that by participating in the lineup, he asserts his right that he might incriminate himself and what he says may be held against him."

Turner corrected Pierce, "I'm not asking your client to say anything. I'm asking him to put on a disguise. No words, just stand in a line."

Pierce insisted, "Well, he's cooperating, but theoretically he could incriminate himself if he participates in the lineup. I'm directing my client not to put on that damn wig."

Turner didn't arrest Oz. He couldn't because he didn't have a positive ID.

Sammie and I left for the office. When we walked through the door, Bella told us, "You've got several calls from the spouses and parents of injured persons. They want to know where to send their bills. I told them you'd be calling and would get back to them as soon as you can. I smoothed things out for now, but I'm not sure for how long. Also Dr. Max called. He wants to give you an update on Randy James."

I went back to my office, glanced at my to-do list and called the doctor. "Peter, Ben, what's the status on the James kid?"

"Hello my friend, you didn't send me an easy patient. He's got a bad staph infection. I've got him on strong antibiotics and I've got him scheduled for surgery tomorrow. After he heals, in a month to six weeks, I'll have to do a skin graft. Ben, Kim tells me that the boy has no insurance and that you told her you'd stand for the boy's charges. For the two surgeries, my fees are going to be $15,000, and the ancillary charges are another $25,000. That's a total expense of $40,000. Are you okay with that?"

"Peter, this kid was working as a bartender at my house serving drinks. I can't let him go without getting medical care. I'll make sure these bills are paid. You have my word. Just get him taken care of."

I hung up and dialed Karl Goodwin, the manager of Hillwood Country Club. I'd been a member of the club for the last ten years. "Hello Karl, it's Ben Davis. I've been spending a lot of time at the hospital, and we haven't had an opportunity to speak. Could I stop by about five?"

Works for me, Mr. Davis. If we're going to talk about the 3rd, I should have the club's attorney present."

"That's a great idea. In fact, why don't you have the president of the club, old man Miller and his lawyer there as well."

"I can't guarantee that A-1..."

"Just make sure that A-1 Amusement is there. They'd be better off if they were represented at this meeting."

I hung up and began dictating documents I would present at the meeting. At five I arrived at Hillwood and was ushered into a banquet room. Present were Karl Goodwin, club manager; Gary Peller, club president; Hope Cash, club attorney; Queenie and Tom Miller, the owners of A-1 Amusement; and David Edison, A-1's insurance company's attorney. I knew both lawyers.

"Gentlemen, Ms. Miller and Hope, thank you for meeting with me so promptly. I won't take up too much of your time. I've been getting calls from my injured friends and clients about their hospital bills and expenses, and I need to know what to tell them."

Hope Cash, known for her aggressive demeanor, spoke up, "What do you mean? What exactly are you asking for?"

"Look, both the club and A-1 are insured; either the club or A-1 carriers need to step up and start paying the medical bills of my injured guests, and we need to identify what types of expenses will be reimbursed. Some of them have insurance, but some of them don't. Ultimately A-1 is going to be held responsible, and Hillwood is liable for the actions of its agent. I thought the two insurance companies might want to avoid the additional expense of litigation."

I handed the document I prepared to Hope Cash. It was titled Indemnification and Acceptance of Liability. The document provided that "A-1 and Hillwood's insurers indemnified Benjamin and Liza Davis from any and all liability for any and all injuries sustained in the July 3rd, 1997 to their guests and/or any workers at their barbecue." The document further provided that "A-1 and Hillwood's insurers would be responsible for all property damage to the Davis residence from the July 3rd event."

Hope Cash passed the document to Edison, the other lawyer in the room. Edison almost yelled, "We're not going to sign this. This leaves us no options. We're admitting liability. You're out of your mind."

"I may be out of my mind, but either you're admitting liability, or I'm going back to my office to prepare and then file suit on my behalf and the behalf of the other twenty plaintiffs free of charge."

Cash jumped in and declared, "You can't do that. As the property owner, you're in the line of liability and therefore clearly have a conflict."

I responded, "I suggest you check with the Register of Deeds. My wife, Liza, owns the property. I'll get each of the plaintiffs to acknowledge that Liza Davis is third in line for liability and waive that conflict. If necessary, I'll sue my wife. She has $5,000,000 of insurance. I'm confident the court will find that liability doesn't fall on her shoulders. Your two clients can fight out liability, and I'm confident that A-1 will lose that battle. Now, you can get involved in an expensive lawsuit, or we can minimize costs and orderly pay medical expenses. Ultimately, you'd pay those anyway. Take the document to your insurance companies and get back to me within seventy-two hours."

My tone was confident, and it was impossible to tell that Liza's coverage was an issue. I had a signed document before the deadline.

CHAPTER FORTY-FIVE

A REALLY TOUGH CUSTOMER

Monday, July 28, 1997

(ROSCOE CARMICHAEL'S VOICE)

My deposition had been postponed by agreement of the lawyers because of the filing of the two Doe complaints and Davis' desire that all three cases be addressed at the court-ordered mediation. Vincent Gray spent two weeks prepping me for Davis' onslaught. I'd been instructed to keep my answers short and when necessary to respond, "I don't recall." Gray insisted that was a perfectly good answer. Such a response placed an extreme burden on Davis to prove a negative, which was near impossible.

I would be questioned at Covington & Burling's office on the twentieth floor of the Crystal Tower office building in downtown Nashville. It would be sweet to be released, even temporally, from house arrest. I was tired of hanging around the Music Row townhouse, although it beat awaiting trial from a jail cell.

Tate and Gray worked out the scope of my testimony with Davis. He'd agreed to go nowhere near my drug arrest or the pending charges. This was the deal that was cut to allow discovery yet protect my Fifth amendment rights.

The Davidson County sheriff's deputy arrived at the townhouse at 8:00 a.m., removed my ankle bracelet, and drove me downtown. I stuck my head out the window and let the wind rush over me, like a dog who rarely got to travel by car. The Covington & Burling conference room was strategically located in the corner of the building. It had a two-story glass wall with a view of the majestic Cumberland River. The defense team waited for Davis and his clients to arrive.

Oz and I weren't supposed to be talking about the case. We'd been warned that our conversations with each other were fair game and not confidential and protected. Our lawyers felt that the best answer we could give was "that we hadn't discussed the pending cases." To their knowledge, all of our communications went through our lawyers and were therefore protected by the joint defendants privilege.

Davis, his niece, and Elizabeth Swann arrived a few minutes before the scheduled start time. Swann gave me a defiant look. She wasn't afraid of me. Gray told me that the Does elected not to come. I suspect they were afraid of me and for good reason. Davis poured himself a black cup of coffee and munched on a jelly donut. Katie Stone entered the room next, set up, gave Davis the once-over with her eyes and a friendly hello. I thought I detected a sense of familiarity between the two of them. I made a mental note to be observant and try to uncover any sordid details between them.

The court reporter introduced everyone in the room to Cary Edwards, the videographer. Davis had filed a motion to videotape Oz's and my depositions, which Judge Howard granted. Gray assured me that the tactic wasn't that unusual. He explained that the reasoning behind the request was to place additional pressure on the witness to tell the truth.

The deposition opened with Gray's prepared speech, "This is the deposition of the defendant Roscoe Carmichael. As per Judge Howard's order, this deposition shall not last longer than nine hours; eight hours of testimony, one hour on financials and there shall be a one-hour luncheon break at noon."

Davis didn't respond, so Gray continued, "Mr. Davis, I won't tolerate your abusing my client..."

Davis cut him off. He wasn't going to be bullied by Gray on the record, "Look, Vincent, stop with the speeches. My seven hours doesn't begin until you sit down and shut up. It is now 9:15 a.m. We will adjourn at 6:15 p.m. The court's order doesn't state when lunch will be taken, so it will be taken at my convenience at a good stopping point. This is my deposition, and I will control my time as I see fit. Do we have an understanding, or do we need to delay the start and call the judge?"

Davis didn't waste any time. He immediately attacked me on the issue of consent.

I insisted that all three of his clients knew they were being filmed, "They were looking at a camera in the corner of the room. It wasn't hidden."

"Then why the secret room and the cameraman?"

"That camera on the tripod in the room couldn't zoom in for the close-ups."

"My clients didn't know that Mr. Oz was behind a two-way mirror, did they?"

"No, but what's the difference? They knew they were being recorded. What difference does it make which camera recorded them?"

"Was the camera in the room on a tripod clearly visible to everyone?"

"Yes, when we had sex, I'd move a camera into the right position and focus on the bed and then we'd go at it."

"There's a video of Ms. Swann dancing and then doing a routine on a pole, right?"

"Yes."

"How was that filmed?"

"I held the camera and faked the video. Mr. Oz, not me, held the camera that was rolling. He was in the room behind the mirror. I couldn't possibly do as good a job, and I'm a perfectionist."

"Do you think Mr. Oz is a better cameraman than Mr. Edwards here?"

I didn't answer, Davis was only trying to throw me off. Eventually as I sat there for what seemed like a half an hour, he moved on, "So, it's your position that my clients knew they were being taped. They didn't know that Mr. Oz was doing the recording?"

"That's correct."

"Why didn't you tell them about Mr. Oz?"

I was surprised Davis asked such an open-ended question, but he was dying to know my reason.

"Because I didn't have to. That was the advice of my lawyer, Bucky Lee. He said as long as the parties knew they were videoed, that's what counted."

"It's your testimony that Bucky Lee advised you that it was legal to tape women without their permission?"

"No, he said that I had to get their permission, but I didn't have to tell them about Oz. He told me once they agreed to be videoed, it didn't matter that there was a secret room or a cameraman."

"When did you get this legal advice from Bucky Lee?"

"I don't recall the date, but we could figure it out. In 1993/1994, I purchased the Langford building. That night, after that closing,

Bucky and I shared two six packs of beer. We got drunk, and it was then that I asked Bucky how to protect myself against date rape."

"Was Mr. Lee impaired by alcohol when he allegedly gave this advice?"

"No, sir, our discussion occurred within the first half hour of us drinking our beers; we were on either our first or second. He wasn't drunk or impaired."

Davis changed subject matter. He questioned me about my sex life.

"I've been with about a hundred and twenty women."

"I noticed in the video that you never used a condom."

"I don't like them."

"Aren't you concerned you might contract some type of venereal disease?"

"No, I'm a gambler."

"What about the possibility of pregnancy?"

"I assumed all of them were on some form of birth control. I don't remember any of them asking me to put on a condom. They all enjoyed themselves. Not one of these ladies complained. That's why I made the videos. Look at those tapes. Everybody's having fun. That's the best evidence that nobody was forced to do anything. Bucky was absolutely right. The videos prove the sex was consensual."

Davis went over my answer and interrogatory responses. He got me to contradict the document. That was part of the purpose of the deposition. At trial if I testified consistent with the discovery responses, Davis would pull out my deposition testimony, creating an inconsistency, which Davis would characterize as a lie. If at trial I testified consistent with my interrogatory response, then Davis would pull out my deposition testimony. It was a win/win for him, either way.

It was 11:30 a.m., and Davis declared that he was at a good stopping point, "Let's take lunch."

Gray asked, "Are you halfway done?"

Davis's response wasn't satisfactory, "I don't know, but I've got seven hours more of testimony. We're stopping now. I've got five hours and fifteen minutes left. The order says I have nine hours, and there's a one-hour lunch. It doesn't say when we should take lunch. I'm going to lunch."

Davis stood, Sammie Davis stood five seconds later, and Davis walked out. She had a cute little ass. It didn't run in her family. As they were leaving, I overheard their stage whispers. Sammie asked, "Why the early lunch?"

Davis responded in an equally loud stage whisper, intending for me to overhear. "I wanted Carmichael to go more than five hours without a luncheon break. He's more likely to get tired. Besides, I was hungry."

After lunch Davis returned and without any discussion started right in, "Have you destroyed any videotapes? Do the police have them all?"

"I've burned a few still photos, but never a videotape."

"Why burn a naked woman's photo?"

"I guess it felt good."

"Was Mr. Oz there when you burned the photos?

"Yes."

"Did he take the photos?"

"Yes."

I'd been warned that Davis would want to establish the elements of a conspiracy. He questioned me about the details of my agreement with Oz to video the women.

"So, you made a deal with Mr. Oz. You agreed to allow him to videotape you having sex with women from your secret room?"

"We had an understanding."

"Was it in writing?"

"No. Why would I put that in writing?"

"So, when did you come up with the plan?"

"I think it was more than one conversation, but over a couple weeks, we came to our understanding."

Davis placed in front of me the evidence lists created by the police after the arrest. There was one for my farm and one for the office.

When Davis got to the drugs found at the farm, Tate directed me to take the Fifth Amendment against self-incrimination. "I take the Fifth upon advice of counsel."

Davis reviewed with me the releases with Strong, Ingram, and Watson.

"You paid out $125,000 to these three women?"

"Yes."

"Why did you have to bribe these women to testify that they gave consent to have Mr. Oz tape the video?"

"I didn't pay them for their testimony. The police raided my office and published these videos to others. I had the situation under control with them safely hidden in my office. No one other than myself would have seen them..."

Davis interrupted, "Let's make something clear. The police raided your farmhouse and office because you were distributing drugs and got caught?"

Tate objected, "My client has pending criminal charges, and I direct him to exercise his Fifth Amendment right to self-incrimination."

Davis had anticipated the objection and moved on.

"I want to get back to Mr. Lee and the advice you claim he gave you. Did he know you'd built a secret room?"

"He told me the camera didn't have to be visible. He told me that as long as I got the women to agree to be videoed, that was enough."

"How do you lie without any regret?"

"Don't call me a liar!"

I got halfway out of my chair. Tate had to restrain me.

"How dare you defame my client! He's answering your questions candidly except where you asked about the pending criminal charges." argued Tate.

Davis fought back, again questioning my honesty. "You must be lying. If Bucky Lee had told you to secure these women's permission prior to sex, then he would have insisted that you record them giving permission. Do any of the seven tapes show you getting the permission from these women?"

"No, not specifically, but you can tell from the tapes the sex was consensual."

"Isn't the failure to record consents of these women a significant failure to support your fabricated story?"

I didn't know how to answer that question, but I had to say something. The camera was rolling. "It would have been better to have done so. That was Bucky's fault. He never specifically told me to do that. His advice was negligent because he left out that detail. I guess he wasn't a very good lawyer because I have three lawsuits against me. That's the reason I sued Mr. Lee. His negligent and unethical advice is the proximate cause of your clients' claims."

Davis didn't like that answer. Fortunately, Tate and Gray had prepared me for that one. They instructed me to use the buzz phrase "proximate cause." It was the key to the lawsuit against Lee.

Davis went through all seven photos of the women that Hopper had been using to confirm identity. Davis pressed me as to the remaining woman # 7, who was yet unidentified.

"You had intimate sex with woman # 7, yet you don't know her name?"

"I preferred it if we didn't know each other's name. It made breaking up with them much easier."

"Did you break up with these seven women?"

"Most of them. A few caught me with another woman. I had to do a lot of juggling. Some of them were mighty jealous."

"They became an inconvenience, didn't they?"

"Two or three of them felt that our relationship had grown beyond sex. It was all about sex. I didn't want more of a relationship."

"Did you threaten any of them?"

"Absolutely not."

"Did you hire anyone to follow them?"

"Absolutely not."

"What about Mr. Oz? Ever ask him to follow any of these women?"

"Absolutely not."

"You tried to buy off Mary Doe and Jane Doe like the other women?"

"No, I tried to settle with them to avoid lawsuits. If it wasn't for Bucky and the police, I never would have to pay anything out. It was cheaper to end the problem quickly than deal with a money-grubbing lawyer like you."

"Did you threaten the Does when they rejected your bribe?"

"Are your clients saying I physically hurt them? I thought you were claiming only emotional distress?"

Davis got snippy, "I'm not here to answer your questions. Did you or someone at your direction hurt any of these women or attempt to?"

"No, I'm a lover, not a fighter. I wanted to settle these cases so we didn't get to where we are now. I never would have had to deal with any of this if Bucky Lee hadn't opened his big mouth."

'Wasn't it you who opened your big mouth at Sperry's?"

"Maybe so, but he was my lawyer, the person who gave me the bad advice. He violated our attorney/client relationship."

"Have you ever had contact with any person associated with A-1 Amusement?"

"No, sir."

"Are you aware of what happened at my home on July 3rd of this year?"

"I saw your pathetic interview with Alice Krieger and read a few newspaper articles. I didn't think you were very sympathetic."

"You felt nothing for my guests who were injured?"

"Not particularly. Their mistake was to associate with you."

Davis looked over his notes and then announced, "Katie, this is the beginning of the financial deposition. This portion will be placed in a separate folder as per the judge's order. Ms. Swann, you must leave the room. You can go to our office or home. I'll call you and the Does when we're done here."

Elizabeth Swann got up from the table, gave me a hateful look, and left the room.

Davis continued, "I have here your checking account statements for September, October, November and December 1996 at Sun Bank, account 34536871. There are some large withdrawals from that account. Did you, after receiving my letter in November, 1996, make two withdrawals of $50,000 and one for $25,000? Those were the payments to Strong, Ingram, and Watson for their silence?"

"Yes, those were the payments for the releases."

"On December 3rd and December 5th there were withdrawals of $25,000. What were those funds for?"

"I don't know. I'll have to get back to you."

"Are those payments to other girls?"

"I told you I don't know. I'll have to get back to you."

"What are these withdrawals of $10,000 on October 5th and 6th?"

"I'll have to get back to you."

"Are any of these payments to an accomplice who was following these women?"

"No."

Davis didn't ask a question for a good two minutes. The camera was fixed on me, and I was getting really antsy.

Tate asked, "Are you done?"

"No. I have a little less than an hour of my time left, and I'm going to use that time to explore Mr. Carmichael's financials."

For the next forty-eight minutes. Davis pried into my financial statements and net worth. When he asked about the $300,000 found in my safe, Tate directed me to take the Fifth Amendment against self-incrimination.

Davis stated, "I'm going to adjourn this deposition. I reserve the right to reopen this deposition based upon the testimony of Mr. Oz, Mr. Lee, Chief Neenan, and/or the testimony of DA Johnson Tory. I will be required to file a motion with the court, but I'm confident if I pose a good reason, Judge Howard would grant such a motion."

Tate had a quick response, "In your dreams."

Davis's response was equally quick, "No, in your client's worst nightmares."

CHAPTER FORTY-SIX

LET'S PUT TOGETHER A STRATEGY

Friday, August 8, 1997

(SAMMIE DAVIS' VOICE)

My uncle requested that Katie expedite the transcript of Carmichael's deposition so it could be reviewed before the deposition of Phillip Oz. Morty was very disappointed that he missed Carmichael's deposition. Morty grabbed the Carmichael transcript as soon as it came in. He didn't wait for Bella to make copies for Davis and myself. We didn't know it had arrived because we were busy with other cases. Morty went down to the sixth floor, got comfortable, and spent four hours reading. He may have moved slowly, but his mind was still quick and focused. When he'd read and digested the three hundred pages, he felt he was on equal footing with us.

Morty called a meeting in the conference room and began by saying, "Carmichael's argument against the police is silly. No judge is going to buy it. The cops had no option but to review the tapes. They needed to know what they'd confiscated, and once they realized what they had, they had to show them to whichever videoed women they could locate. They couldn't simply put the tapes in a safe and forget about them. The state will argue that they were obtained during a valid search under a properly issued search warrant. The weakness of the government's position is the chain of evidence. First, the TBI and Metro were looking for drugs and 'all matters related to their search for drugs and cash.' Tell me how videos of Carmichael having sex with women 'is a matter relating to the search for drugs and cash.' That's where Covington & Burling will attack. They'll go after the second search warrant they obtained from Judge Howard. They'll argue that he's biased from the 1990 trial, and he ordered a search that was overly broad. Second, they'll argue that the second warrant related to the tapes was issued based upon the unethical actions of Bucky, and therefore the fruits of a diseased tree are inedible and the fruits of the search are inadmissible. That may be the strongest argument for keeping the tapes out of evidence. We need the defendants to fear that a jury might see those videos. That's critical to settlement. We need them to want to settle more than risk a jury seeing those tapes. Truth be told, we don't want a jury to see those tapes. We can't let the defendants know that. We must give them the impression we want those tapes played in open court."

My uncle didn't disagree. I accepted their conclusion. I was assigned the responsibility of researching the issues related to both search warrants.

Davis said, "We need case law, preferably from the Tennessee Supreme Court supporting our position."

I took the command in stride and just as I was digesting my new task, he asked, "What's the status of your research concerning criminal statutes related to invasion of privacy?"

I smiled and handed them a copy of a memo on the subject

matter. I summarized the law for thirty-six states, the other thirteen, like Tennessee didn't have a criminal statute. I explained that the laws fell into three general categories. "I've drafted a proposed statute for you to consider."

UNLAWFUL PHOTOGRAPHING IN VIOLATION OF PRIVACY

A. It is an offense for a person to knowingly photograph or cause to be photographed an individual, when the individual is in a place where there is a reasonable expectation of privacy, without the prior effective consent of the individual, or in the case of a minor, without the effective consent of the minor's parent or guardian, if the photograph:

(1) Would offend or embarrass an ordinary person, if that person appeared in the photograph, and

(2) Was taken for the purpose of personal arousal and gratification of the defendant.

(a) As used in this section, photograph is defined as a photograph or photographic reproduction, still or movie or any video or live television transmission of any individual so that the individual is readily identifiable.

(b) All photographs taken in violation of this section shall be confiscated and, after use as evidence, shall be destroyed. Any law enforcement personnel, who view the photograph and/or show the photograph to the victim shall not be considered publication of the photograph.

(c) Any person found guilty of this section is guilty of a Class E felony. If he or she disseminates the photograph or if the victim is a minor, that person is guilty of a Class D felony.

Morty spoke first, "What an exceptional job. If it's a minor, should the penalty be increased?"

"I thought the judge can accomplish that in the sentencing. Each class has pretty wide judicial discretion of sentence length."

My uncle commented next, "Great job. If this statute existed last year, Bucky would have clearly acted ethically to prevent a crime."

Morty spoke up, "There's a hole in Tennessee law, and we're going to fix it."

Morty, a yellow dog Democrat, had been active in statewide politics for forty years. He considered himself a progressive, part of the New South. He started off a civil rights leader. He'd fought the good fight in the 1950s and 1960s. He'd marched with Dr. King and legally helped the Freedom Riders. After years of struggling, he figured out it was better to try to change the system from within than from the outside. From those rationalities, Morty worked his way into the system. At first by ringing doorbells for candidates, and then by giving speeches. He was quite an orator. After his father died and he inherited his fortune, he became a substantial donor and philanthropist. Finally, with age and experience, he served as a valued advisor. Over that time, he'd helped a lot of people and therefore was owed many favors. He'd helped most of the Democrats get elected to statewide office. As a distinguished member of the Bar and former president of the Disciplinary Board, he wielded influence with his fellow lawyers. Respected and proven, Morty Steine knew how to grab a project and get it done. He'd let me come along for the ride. He could use a little help.

I'd seen Morty go to the Hill to press for the legislation. Morty was pleased that I showed an interest in mingling with politicians. My uncle had no interest in legislative matters and Morty figured that I could succeed him as the firm's lobbyist. Over time he could transfer to me his legislative responsibilities.

I asked, "Do you think you can get your legislation passed before our February 3rd trial?"

Morty had spent years lobbying Democrats in the Tennessee legislature. "I'll get started right away. I'll make a visit to the Hill tomorrow and see what reaction I get. I've got a few friends who still owe me favors. Besides, who's going to oppose legislation that protects women from creeps who secretly videotape them? They may play with my language, but the concept will be unanimously accepted. The key to this case is credibility. Who would the jury believe? Jury selection will be critically important. We've got to figure out our optimum juror profile."

I reminded him that our goal was settlement.

He insisted, "We better be prepared,"

I insisted right back, "Answer my question. How long will it take to get the law enacted?"

After further reflection, Morty replied, "I should be able to get the job done before trial but not before mediation. It's difficult to predict time on something like that."

Morty got back to Carmichael's deposition, "He makes a case against Bucky. It will be a matter of credibility. Who will the jury believe, Carmichael or Bucky?" He said half-jokingly.

I interrupted, "We made that decision about who was telling the truth when we didn't sue Bucky and lend credibility to Carmichael's claims against him. I think we were smart. I don't believe Carmichael's story. It's much too elaborate. He never explains why there was a secret room. His claim that the women saw a dummy camera just doesn't fly with me."

Morty interjected, "We have two liquid defendants." He was referring to the financial information that Carmichael and Oz produced. "All our claims are for intentional torts. We've got to tip the scale if it's more likely than not then we win. That's how the jury resolves the credibility issue. Who do they believe? We tell our story and make them accept it. That's our job, bottom line. We can collect our compensatory damages from one or both conspirators. Punitive damages are a different story. If we're lucky enough to be awarded punitive..."

My uncle inserted, "That all depends on the jury and how Carmichael and Oz conduct themselves at the trial."

Morty proposed, "Well, I wasn't there, but he read like an arrogant putz."

Everyone in the room, being Jewish, knew that the word literally meant a penis, more accurately a prick. He went back to the claims against Bucky, "The jury will like Bucky Lee, and I don't think a jury is going to think he gave Carmichael such stupid and unethical advice. I've known the man for twenty-five years, and he's always done the right thing by me. I'll take him over Carmichael every time."

Bella walked in with documents in her hands. As she placed them on the conference table, she commented, "I've read them. You're not going to like them."

Tate and Pierce had been busy. They decided to double team our clients by filing a joint motion to have each of the plaintiffs examined by a psychiatrist of their choice under Rule 35.

My uncle, who'd joined us spoke first, "This was expected. They have every right to have their own expert evaluate the plaintiffs, but I'm not sure how to prepare our clients for this ordeal. There is no point in objecting."

Morty answered the question, "The first thing you tell them is to tell the truth. That way when the shrink asks, 'What did your lawyer tell you to say?' they can honestly say, 'to tell the truth.'"

We all laughed. Morty wasn't kidding, and continued, "I also suggest that when the shrinks examine our clients, they should go back to the day they first saw the video in that police station and relive it on the couch. The Does can testify as to the bribe, the threat, and then the fear that drove them to leave town, and the impact that decision to flee had on their lives. We have Swann's and Jane Doe's therapists who can testify professionally, but their doctors will be on the defendants' side. They're paid-for whores. We need to get Swann's therapist to examine Mary Doe. At least that will allow us to present contradictory professional proof. It's not a perfect solution, but it puts us in a better position."

Included in the package from the defense was a second set of questions for each plaintiff. After reading the plaintiffs' depositions, the defendants had some follow-up. Bella had made a set of documents for each of them, and the three followed along and reviewed the thirty-five questions. They all knew if they challenged the entire question and went to the judge, he'd order them to answer. Sammie chirped in, "The interrogatory I'd object to is protected by the attorney work-product doctrine. How we found the Does is none of their business."

Morty quickly responded, "Let's say you're right, but how does it hurt us for them to know the whole story? We'll make George part of the story. The men on the jury will love the fact he'd been a fighter.

When we put him on the stand, we get into he fought Sugar Ray and Tommy Hearns, and he could comment that he'd been knocked out by both of them. Besides it's not worth fighting about. Pick your fights. Always weigh the importance of evidence, its benefit versus its risk. That's especially true when you think you're winning the trial. Sometimes less is really more."

Morty paused and said, "We need to win a big motion before the mediation. Something that will set the defendants back on their heels."

I spoke up, "We'll move that the jury should visit the secret room. They'll argue that the tapes are enough, but we'll insist that being in the room is important. We should have the camera rolling as the jury walks through, let them see themselves like at Disney-world in those long lines. The defendants will shit their pants. Howard will understand what we're doing and will grant the motion if only to increase the probability of settlement."

Morty felt pride as he commented, "That's a pretty damn good idea. That will unnerve them. Good thinking."

We were a team, and we divided up the tasks. I needed to send the interrogatories to the clients and then meet with them together. Originally, Morty had insisted that we keep our clients apart. Morty feared their testimony would be influenced by each other, so he insisted that we keep them apart. They had a bond, their common Carmichael experience. Deposed, they could now meet together and coordinate. I prepared agreed orders, which the defendants would refuse to sign, so I also prepared a motion to have the jury view the secret room. These were battles to be fought so that there wouldn't be a trial. No one really wanted to try these cases.

CHAPTER FORTY-SEVEN

THE SHRINK

Friday, August 15, 1997

(THIRD PERSON)

The deposition of Phillip Oz was set but he asked to be released because his mother was in a car accident. Davis agreed to release Oz from his deposition subpoena obligation on certain conditions: "I want a sworn statement from the mother's doctor confirming the mother's medical condition, specifically stating whether the mother is hospitalized or in rehab and verifying that Oz visited his mother daily. I also want to reschedule his deposition for a date certain no later than September 1st."

Pierce told him, "You're a distrusting and demanding person. I've never talked to the mother's doctor so I can't promise his cooperation, but put your request for information in writing, and I'll submit it to her doctor. I can't control his response."

Davis didn't like her answer, but he'd been taught that certain courtesies should be extended rather than play hardball and force your adversary to go running to the judge. Phillip Oz wasn't going anywhere. He'd be deposed.

Two weeks went by without any word from Pierce regarding Oz's availability. Davis dictated a short note to Pierce, copying everyone as to the need to reschedule Oz. As he said, "End dictation on this tape," Sammie walked into his office and placed three documents on his desk. They were the responses of their three clients to the questions posed by the defendants so that the defense's expert psychiatrist could generate their psychological profiles to help when he examined them. Sammie did an outstanding job getting the three clients to carefully answer the thirty-five questions that delved into their psyche. Sammie also set up their respective examinations with Dr. Andrew Resnick, the defense's expert.

Morty came in smoking a Cuban and sat down next to Sammie. Davis handed him the completed questionnaires. As he read, he continued to puff away. Davis's office soon filled with smoke. Morty suddenly sat up straight as if hit by a lightning bolt and said, "Before they see Dr. Resnick, I think we should have our ladies take a lie detector test. We pick out some of the questions we know Resnick's going to ask, and after they pass, it will be like a shot of adrenaline for each of them. We can then look at Resnick's report and use the lie detector results to challenge him."

They all knew that under Tennessee law, lie detector results were inadmissible, but the rules of mediation were different. A lie detector result might be admissible in mediation to impeach an expert, who had examined a patient only once. Morty argued it was likely to be considered. He insisted it all depended on who was selected as the mediator. No mediator had been agreed upon, nor had a date.

Discovery was still being conducted, and Morty and Davis already had their smoking gun, the tapes. They were a blessing and a curse. They showed how Carmichael and Oz had deceived Davis' clients, but they also showed three sexually promiscuous women. The Davis team didn't want older conservative women on their jury.

They probably didn't want a female mediator either. Davis had been waiting on the defense to file a motion to exclude the tapes based on an invalid seizure under an inadequate search warrant.

Morty continued, "Sammie, call my old friend Billy Tanner. Billy's ex-FBI. We'll let him test our clients..."

Billy Tanner arrived with his machine and interviewed the three clients. They passed with flying colors. The girls, as Morty referred to them, at first were nervous, but as the tests progressed, they gained a sense of confidence.

A week later the Davis clients found themselves in the office of Dr. Andrew Resnick. There was no two-way mirror, just a room with four walls. Dr. Resnick was confident that he could finish his examination of all three women in one day. He was armed with their deposition testimony and two sets of written questions that Sammie helped them prepare. Resnick intended to use these documents to try to find inconsistencies in each woman's sworn testimony. He already knew a lot about each of these women. It would allow him to go deep into their background and sex lives.

Mary Doe was first up. Resnick made her and the other women sign a release. This document made it very clear that he was acting as an expert witness for the defense, and what was revealed in his examination would be testified to in court. He started right off with the reasons for her divorce. "Your actions caused a serious rift in your marriage?

"Yes.

"You need to take some responsibility for that?"

"I've blamed Roscoe Carmichael but between myself and my husband, I need to take responsibility."

"But you and your husband had problems before your infidelity?"

"We had problems like everybody else. We were one major disaster from being broke. Most of the time we paid the minimum on our credit cards, and we had four of them. Our kids were great, but being a parent is a tough job. We did our best. Our boys will grow up to be good men."

"So, your sons are okay. We don't have to worry about them. They've got bright futures."

Davis would have cringed if he heard that exchange. Under the veil of Rule 35, and his professional credentials, Dr. Resnick was conducting a far more effective deposition of Doe than Tate or Pierce had. The thought of Dr. Resnick reading from his notes in open court scared Davis. He'd get to pick and choose his biased highlights of the sessions.

No sense worrying about it. What's done is done, he thought.

Dr. Resnick was equally effective with the other two clients. Both were much stronger when they faced down Tate and Pierce at their depositions. The therapist kept pushing them on their problems before they met Carmichael. He pressed more than once about the camera on the tripod.

"I didn't see a red light, and he never mentioned that what we were doing was being taped."

"But you saw the camera?"

"Yes, it was in the corner. I saw it, and then I forgot about it. It had nothing to do with me. I certainly didn't agree to a cameraman and a two-way mirror."

"What difference does it make if it's a camera on a tripod or if there was a camera? The same result, a sex tape would be made."

"First, I never agreed to be filmed, period. But using your hypothetical, there's still a difference. With Oz secretly present, Carmichael brought another person into the sex act. I certainly didn't agree to a threesome."

Each held her ground on the camera issue. All in all, the examinations by the defense's expert could have gone better, but they could have gone far worse.

Morty turned to Davis, "Dr. Resnick will be a dangerous witness at trial. Who should cross-examine him?"

Davis answered, "I think we should give this tough one to Sammie. She'll learn a lot from the experience, and I know she'll do a great job."

Sammie perked up. She knew she was being given an opportunity, and she intended to make the most of it. "Thanks for the vote of confidence."

The two men couldn't have been prouder of their young protégée. They'd both guided this wild thing into a confident lawyer. Sammie wouldn't just go through the motions. She'd find out everything she could about Dr. Resnick and secure every deposition and trial transcript he'd ever given. She'd then find the inconsistencies and use them at either his deposition or trial to cut him up.

CHAPTER FORTY-EIGHT

A REALITY CHECK

Monday, August 18, 1997

(THIRD PERSON)

Bella, before the firm went home for the weekend on Friday, called a 7:00 a.m. Monday meeting. She'd let them ponder her agenda over that weekend. Usually, she sat behind her desk in reception and did her work of running the office without interference from the lawyers, playing lawyer when necessary. She was friendly with most members of the Bar and knew every judge's secretary's husband and children's names. She didn't have a law license but because of the firm's small size and limited resources, she was often the point person with other lawyers and clients. Recently she'd noticed she was playing lawyer too often. The Carmichael cases had taken a toll on the firm.

"I called this meeting to inform the three of you that your work is getting sloppy and backed up. Our clients aren't being properly served, and they're starting to complain to me. Ben, when was the last time you had a completed to-do list? Morty, when was the last time you prepared a to-do—list?"

Morty and Davis maintained handwritten to-do lists on yellow pads. The system established years ago required both men to look at their list each morning, and then as they performed the listed tasks, the completed items were struck from the list. The system had worked for more than twenty-five years. The system was broken.

Bella continued, "I've been here more than thirty years and can't remember the last time I called a meeting about the operation of this office. We're spending too much time on the Carmichael/ Oz cases. All three of you can't work on the same case. It's not economically feasible. No firm would assign all of its talent to one case. We need to meet the needs of our other clients, and we need to pay our bills."

Morty, who had a net worth of more than $10, 000,000 wasn't really worried about paying the bills. There had been many times when he carried the firm through rough patches. He argued, "We'll eventually get the expenses we've advanced back from Carmichael. He's got it. He's an arrogant bastard, the jury's going to award punitive damages, and the judge, under rule 54, is going to reimburse us most of our expenses."

Bella, who'd been around almost as long as her boss, responded, "You're awfully optimistic. Since when can you guarantee what a jury and judge will do? Haven't you always told me that they were the great unknowns? That you didn't have any idea what would happen in a jury trial until you picked your jury."

"Don't quote me to me. I've earned the right to work on whatever I damn well want to work on. You may be right that we need to redistribute the firm's talent, but Bella, I'd look to the other members of this firm. I'm having too good a time working these cases, and I intend to continue having a good time."

"You think so?" She held her ground. Do you know how much we've advanced in expenses?"

Morty had no idea. He didn't want to hear the dollar amount.

She pressed, "Take a guess."

He did, "$25,000?"

She turned to Davis, "How much do you think we're out?

Davis knew that Morty was way low, "$50,000?" She figured he'd be a lot closer.

"It's $87,000, and you still have four or five depositions, a mediation, and possibly a trial. Hopper is costing a fortune looking for that last plaintiff. We'd be better off putting him on salary. I like him. He's smart and could be a big help around the office if he was full time."

She took a different tack. She turned to Davis, "How many hours do you think you have in the three cases?"

Davis was embarrassed to guess and be low, so he went high. He tried to calculate his time; we started in October, that's ten months, say ten hours a week, forty weeks, that's four hundred hours. "I'd say I have four hundred hours, give or take."

The actual number was four hundred twenty-three, but Bella wasn't going to quibble.

I know your hourly rate varies, but you average more than $300 an hour, right?" You've charged as much as $400 an hour."

Davis agreed.

"That's a minimum cost of $120,000."

Davis was shocked. His time and the expenses exceeded $200,000.

He braced himself when she asked, "What about Sammie's time?"

He did the math. It was definitely more than his, probably by twenty-five percent, So a hundred more hours. That put her at five hundred hours.

"I'd say five hundred."

"I can go with that number."

"Part of that time she was a paralegal and part of the time an unlicensed lawyer. So, at $100 an hour, that puts the cost of her time at $50,000. So, your time, her time, and expenses are under $250,000."

Davis hadn't considered the total picture. To break even, the jury would need to award the three plaintiffs a total of $750,000, and the judge would have to award all expenses incurred. That didn't even take into consideration Morty's time.

Bella inquired, "How are we going to make anything on these cases?"

"We'll get some of that back from the defendants either at mediation or under Rule 54."

"Don't try to play me, Mr. Benjamin Abraham Davis. Remember, I was here long before you. I taught you a good bit of the practical practice of the law. You'll recover only part of the $87,000 of expenses. What about the other $200,000 of your time?"

Davis felt like he was being cross-examined.

Wait a second. That's my job, she's good. I don't like being on this end of the questioning.

"We've also got Morty's time."

Morty took a Cuban out of his breast pocket, lit it, and spoke for the first time. He financed the office. "I work on what I work on as long as I want to do so. But if you're going to charge for my time, it's $500 an hour. I bring a lot to the table."

Morty hadn't kept time tickets like the other two. He preferred to charge based upon the size of the legal problem. He felt it was far more reasonable and lucrative. Bella shot back,

"You don't even keep time tickets, and I'm trying to manage this business."

The parties were getting heated. Davis stepped in, "She's right, we can't ignore our other clients."

Morty didn't like being told what to do. "Don't worry about money. I can carry the firm. We've got to get our other work done, but I'm committed to these women. I'm not letting Covington and Burling win."

Tate's strategy was to try to break the small firm. He constantly covered them with paper. In response, Steine & Davis responded with even more paper. The judge was getting tired of reading all the motions and briefs. He was praying the cases would settle.

Bella, who was always practical, returned everyone to reality. "Well, this quarter, and probably the next, the firm's going to suffer significant losses. Forget about any member of the firm earning a bonus at the end of the year unless these cases settle."

Morty assured her that the cases would settle before the end of the year, and that everybody would get a healthy bonus.

"I said my peace. I'm only looking out for the firm."

Morty ended the conversation, "Just pay the bills, and I'll worry about our cash flow. Ben, I want you to turn more responsibility in the Carmichael cases over to Sammie, and you focus on our other clients. Make sure you're getting their work done with the usual high quality of Steine & Davis. I'll supervise Sammie in the Carmichael cases."

Stubborn to a fault, Morty could and would ride the cases out. It was the right thing to do. Bella left in a huff. She was as stubborn as her boss, but she was right.

Everybody stayed in his or her office. Nobody wanted to see one another. Morty started feeling badly and questioned his tone with his longtime friend and secretary. He walked out of his office to reception. He bent down, gave her a kiss and a check made payable to Bella Rosario for $5,000.

"What's this for?"

"A small token of my appreciation for all that you've done for more than thirty-five years. We're going to do better. Sammie and I will take the lead in the Carmichael cases and let Ben get our other work done. I don't admit I'm wrong often, but you were right, and I was wrong. We owe our clients the best legal work possible."

She thanked him for the check, and all was well again.

A few days later, Davis walked into reception to ask Bella a question, and he found Jack Barnes and Bucky Lee sitting on the couch. They'd made an appointment.

Davis greeted them and asked why they were there.

Barnes told him that he got a call on Tuesday asking them to come over to discuss strategy. Davis knew nothing about the call or the meeting. He wanted to invite himself, but he had three pages of a legal pad to address.

"You're meeting with Sammie and Morty. I have another commitment, but you're in good hands."

I should have been given the option to attend, he thought.

He went back to his desk, a little pissed. He attacked the items on his list. He was determined to be available to attend the next strategy meeting. He pulled an orange Tootsie Pop from his top drawer and started sucking away.

Sammie and Morty met with Barnes and Lee in the library. Barnes addressed Morty, "You called this meeting. We're all ears."

"You've read Carmichael's version of the facts..."

Bucky cut him off, "Lies. What idiot would give such advice? At the very least, even an idiot would have told him to get the women consenting to being videoed on the record."

Morty took back control of the conversation. "Hear me out. Your enemy is my enemy. I think transparency is the best policy. We didn't sue Bucky because we knew Carmichael was lying. He's trying to blame Bucky for his outrageous conduct. He's the one responsible for his own actions. He wants to blame everybody but himself; the TBI, the DA's office, and Bucky. That's a shotgun approach to a problem. I suspect that will backfire with a jury."

Barnes asked, "Do you think your cases will come to a jury trial?"

Sammie sat there watching and listening to the veteran trial lawyers. It was a real learning experience.

Morty addressed Barnes, "It will settle, maybe not in mediation, but before trial. I've come up with an idea for a motion, but it needs to be filed by you." He was talking to Barnes.

"Howard split the defendants' claims into four lawsuits. Bucky will be required to give a deposition in all four cases. There's a lot of chances for inconsistency. Bucky's the defendant in one of those suits and an important witness in the other three. I suggest you file a motion to consolidate discovery, one deposition of Bucky Lee to be used in all the cases. If your judge grants the motion, I'm pretty sure the judge in the Metro, DA, and TBI case will follow. Who knows? Maybe it could also be used in the insurance company case. If not, then Bucky only has to give two depositions instead of four."

Barnes liked the idea. He'd start with the case in which Bucky was a defendant. If his judge granted the motion, he'd file an intervening motion in the sex tape cases. The risk/benefit favored the benefit. He didn't want his client giving four depositions. It would be bad enough if they got two bites at the apple.

CHAPTER FORTY-NINE

WE'RE OFF TO SEE THE WIZARD

Thursday, August 28, 1997

(THIRD PERSON)

What happened on July 3rd was a major distraction and problem for the Davis family and the Steine & Davis law firm. The Davis team over the years was used to dealing with difficult cases and even personal physical attacks, but never had friends and family been affected. Although all of the guests who received second-degree burns completely recovered, four of the attendees who received third-degree burns and Randy James, the young bartender, weren't as lucky. Molly Arnold, a neighbor, had to undergo three surgeries and have skin removed from her thigh to graft onto her face. Lonnie Strump, a client, also required a skin graft, but the surgeon used artificial skin rather than his own. The other two friends, Mary Parker and Faye Weeks, suffered staph infections, which they more than likely caught at the hospital. Randy James' first surgery went well, and he was healing, waiting to undergo his second surgery.

The Roberts Agency did a great job keeping up with the patients and their families, making sure that their medical bills were being paid, and helping the families of the injured address other issues. Roberts stayed on top of Aetna, A-1's carrier, making sure it was responsive to these families. This took a tremendous amount of pressure off Davis, who knew that whenever those injured became dissatisfied or felt ignored, they'd retain a lawyer and sue everyone, including his wife, the owner of the property. Davis secured Aetna's cooperation in a heated telephone conversation in which he threatened to organize the injured and file a class action lawsuit and expose Aetna to hundreds of thousands of dollars of liability. After a few minutes of threats, Aetna came around and became reasonable and agreed to try to placate Davis's guests. In the long run they knew as A-1's carrier they had exposure and that they were better off if Davis controlled the situation rather than a dozen lawyers filing separate suits for damages.

Liza went to the hospital almost every day, going from room to room. She brought her friends food and videos, trying to make the injured families a bit more comfortable. Each night Davis stopped by the hospital and checked on his injured friends. Although he'd done nothing wrong, he still felt guilty. He didn't admit it to anyone but himself; he knew this was no accident, and he'd caused these innocent people to get hurt. Davis was tired. Work and life had become overwhelming. The last two months had been a draining experience. As usual, under stress, he turned to food. He'd probably gained fifteen pounds in the last fifty-five days.

The Davis team was small, and under normal circumstances, it was highly organized. They had to be. Davis and Sammie were the workhorses, and Morty, did whatever the hell he wanted. He brought wisdom to the table.

The Carmichael/Oz cases were progressing at an acceptable pace, but the rest of the firm's caseload was stagnated. Covington & Burling sent over another pile of paper that would require responses. The defense was trying to get ahead of and overwhelm Steine & Davis. The sight of the envelope only made Davis more determined. The extra work was the brainchild of Tate.

Pierce, who knew Davis, assured her co-counsel that the additional workload wouldn't discourage Davis, "Ben Davis is a stubborn son of a bitch, and your tactic will only make him work harder." She was right.

Davis and Sammie kept up and probably filed several motions they might not have otherwise if not for revenge. One of those motions was to prevent Carmichael from altering the secret room, rubbing in that Judge Howard had ruled that the jury would get to visit the room during trial. Another motion requested that Oz surrender his passport so he couldn't flee the country before trial. The motion made little sense and was denied, but the judge's order required Oz to notify the court if he intended to leave the continental United States. Each side was trying to disrupt the other. " A stupid game we shouldn't play," urged Morty.

Davis could be prideful. He worked fifteen-hour days, and his family paid the price. He tried to get his work done late at night, after ten, but then bedtime was at 2:30 a.m., and he was up again at 6:00 a.m. Those long hours allowed Davis to catch up and get the firm's business done.

Exhausted, Davis suggested to his partner, "What if we let Sammie depose Oz? She drafted the first outline of his examination, and I've polished her document all the way through. The worst she could do was read the questions we wrote out, but I expect much more of her. I think she'll shine if she'll listen to the answers and takes her lead from those answers. If she does that, and she knows to do that, she'll get her next three questions from Oz's answer. It's a deposition, not a trial. She'll do great."

Morty laughed and said, "You think I was going to argue with you? You're wrong. I think we should be pushing her out of the nest. There are a lot of things that need to get done around this office, and you're spending too much time on the Carmichael/Oz cases. They're going to settle in mediation. I've been pondering a plan."

"What's your mediation game plan?"

"All in due time. I'm still hatching it. You'll be the first to know. Tomorrow is Oz's deposition. When are you going to tell her that she's taking the lead with Oz?"

"Join me. This should be interesting to see how she reacts."

The two men walked down the hall to Sammie's office, much smaller than Davis' and extremely messy.

"For what do I deserve this honor? I'm usually summoned to your offices."

"You can clean up this pigsty."

No response, so Davis continued, "We've got a little assignment, and it has to be done tomorrow."

"No problem, what do you need?"

Good answer, thought Davis.

"I need you to depose Phillip Oz."

Morty and Davis waited on her next words. Her answer would reflect whether they were on the right track in grooming Sammie Davis into the lawyer they hoped she would become. They had high expectations.

"I'm ready. I outlined the deposition. I hope you'll both attend; I'd like to hear any constructive criticism."

Again, a perfect answer, confident, yet acknowledging she'd need feedback.

The next day the Davis team arrived at Pierce's office a few minutes early. The defense didn't know it, but a different Davis would be leading the team today. They sat in reception and were taken by a secretary to what she referred to as the Small Conference room. Katie Stone was already set up in one of the five seats at the sixty-inch circular table. Davis, Morty, and Sammie took a seat. That left one seat for the three other lawyers who were coming, Pierce, Tate, and Gray, and the witness, Oz.

There was an awkward moment, and then Pierce said, "I'll get three more chairs. Whichever one of you is taking the deposition can sit at the table, and the other two can sit in chairs in the corners."

When she started to get the chairs, Davis asked, "I know you've got a bigger conference room than this. I've taken depositions in it. What gives? How about using some pull and getting us the bigger room?"

"Sorry, it was reserved by another member of the association, and I like to follow the rules. It's the right thing to do. Isn't that your motto?"

Morty had taught Davis to always be respectful of another member of the Bar, but he felt like spitting in her face. He didn't but the thought made him smile.

With the chairs brought in, Morty grabbed his seat first. Davis took the other. Sammie sat alone at the table. There was a definite reaction by defense counsel, but nobody said a word. Davis scooted his chair closer to the table. Katie sat between him and Sammie. He got closer than he should have. He took a deep breath, and he smelled her. She smelled really good. He had to slightly crack his neck to refocus.

Set up in the corner was the videographer Edwards. He nodded to Sammie, who introduced herself and proudly stated she was an associate of Steine & Davis.

She began, "Mr. Oz, are you a licensed contractor?"

"No."

"But you were directly involved in the construction of the secret room, right?"

"Yes, I was helping a friend."

"The only workmen involved in the construction of that project were you and Mr. Carmichael?"

"Yes."

"Just the two of you did all of the physical labor?"

"We enjoyed working together, and we built something we were proud of."

Sammie was listening, "Proud! You're proud of your dirty little room?"

"I meant we accomplished something. A room wasn't there, and then after our effort there was a completed room."

"Were you paid for your effort?"

"No, I did it out of friendship."

"Have you done any construction for any other friends?"

"No."

"Who bought the two-way mirror?"

"I did."

"Did you pay for it, and were you reimbursed?"

"Roscoe paid for all of the materials. We used his Home Depot charge card to pay for everything."

"Who installed it?"

"Roscoe and me."

"That must have been some big job?"

"It took us a week."

"Mr. Carmichael didn't let people onto the second floor of his office during construction, did he?"

"I don't know."

"You know no one went up there. It was a secret room, wasn't it?"

Oz didn't answer. He knew the answer. He just didn't want to say it.

Pierce suggested they take a comfort break, but Sammie wasn't going to be sidetracked.

"We'll finish this line of questioning first. Hold it in. This was a secret room that you and Mr. Carmichael built so that there wouldn't be any workmen who could gossip about the two-way mirror and the secret room?"

"Yes."

"It was your little secret?"

Oz nodded his head yes.

"I need a verbal response."

"Yes."

"Are you married, Mr. Oz?"

"Yes, twenty-five years."

"At the time these videos were made you'd been married more than twenty years, right?"

"Yes."

"Do you think marriage is a relationship of trust?"

"Yes, absolutely."

"Do you trust your wife?"

"Definitely."

"What's her name?"

"Susan."

"What did Susan say when you broke her trusting relationship and videoed your friend Mr. Carmichael and women having sex?"

"She was devastated." Oz's voice got shaky.

"How did she learn of the claims against you?"

"I told her."

"Did you tell her before or after we sent the letter to Mr. Carmichael?"

"It was after."

Sammie paused and let the camera remain fixed on Oz.

"Did you tell her before or after the lawsuit was filed against Mr. Carmichael in November, 1996?"

"It was after."

"Did you tell her before Mr. Carmichael revealed your name as the cameraman?"

"No, it was after."

After each question, Sammie waited a full minute and simply let Oz squirm on camera.

"Did you tell her before the DA's office contacted you?"

"That's when I told her. I've scarred her for life. That's my punishment."

"I wouldn't be so sure. A jury's going to decide your fate and punishment for your intentional wrongful conduct toward my clients and others. You admit you acted intentionally?"

Pierce objected, "That calls for a legal conclusion."

Sammie insisted, "That's the same threshold question a jury will have to decide before they award punitive damages. You acted intentionally?"

"I knew what I was doing."

Again, Sammie was listening. "You knew you were videoing the sex acts, but the women, my clients, didn't know what you were doing, did they?"

Oz didn't answer right away. "Carmichael told me they knew. I never met any of them. I was in and remained in the room. It appeared to me that they knew I was there. Your client danced around the room and did a routine on the stripper pole. That was done for the camera."

Pierce shouted, "We're taking a break. I'm not going to piss myself. We'll reconvene in a half hour."

Sammie chided, "Boy, you must have to go pretty bad."

The half hour break turned into lunch. Morty and Davis made a few minor comments, but there was no constructive criticism.

"You're hitting a home run," Davis proudly told her.

When they resumed, Sammie announced, "This is a court-ordered deposition, with a seven-hour limit. I've used two hours and ten minutes. We've taken our lunch break, so I've got four hours and fifty minutes left."

Pierce inserted, "We'll take as many breaks as I may require."

"Is there something wrong with your bladder, Ms. Pierce?"

"Just ask your questions."

Sammie did for the full seven hours. Oz claimed that Carmichael told him that Bucky had advised him it was okay to do the secret videos in order to protect himself from rape charges.

"You didn't believe that, did you?"

"I sure did."

"You were just building that secret room to get your jollies off, right?"

"I did it because I enjoyed filming."

Then Sammie asked a question she didn't know the answer to, which was always dangerous. But one of the purposes of a deposition was discovery, to find out the answer to a question. The Davis team had debated whether to ask this question.

"Did you masturbate during the filming?"

"No, that would have affected the quality of the product."

Again, Sammie was listening, "So all my clients were to you

were products to which you would masturbate after the filming was completed?"

Oz hesitated and then answered, "Yes."

Sammie let the camera roll. Oz's last response would shock several members of the jury if they ever got to trial. It wouldn't play well with the mediator either. Sammie's intentional delay seemed like an eternity. Sammie eventually pulled from her briefcase the 1970 University of Tennessee yearbook. She turned to a picture of Phillip Oz.

"This is your picture in 1970?"

"Yes."

"You had brown curly hair?"

Pierce interrupted, "What's your point?"

"Let's make this yearbook the next exhibit, exhibit fourteen. Have you recently purchased a wig and a false beard?"

"No."

"Did you on July 3rd wear a brown curly haired wig and false beard?"

"No."

"Where were you on July 3rd?"

"I can't answer that question exactly. I watched TV, did some things around my house. I can't tell you anything specific. I know I was with my family on the fourth, but the 3rd was almost two months ago, I can't give you a blow by blow of what I did that day. I couldn't tell you right now."

"Were you anywhere near Hillwood Country Club's seventeenth hole?"

"No."

"I remind you, you're under oath."

Pierce jumped in. She knew exactly what Sammie was doing

but couldn't stop her. "We all know about that terrible accident at Mr. Davis's home. I resent your implying that my client had anything to do with that tragedy. My client doesn't have to prove where he was on the 3rd. He's innocent until proven guilty."

"Careful, Ms. Pierce, you're not under oath, but you are on the record. I'd be worried that your statements may be construed as aiding and abetting or an overt act in an ongoing conspiracy."

"If you have proof of my client's involvement in that matter, produce it. If not, move on."

All Sammie had was a maybe. So, she moved on, but she obviously rattled Pierce, and that wasn't easy to do. Sammie kept at Oz, and in the last hour reviewed his financials. Most of his property was held jointly with his wife, Susan. Like Carmichael, Oz had made an identical claim against American Insurance. That case was stalled in federal court. There was no way to collect a big judgment from Oz. Sammie didn't know it but Oz's limited funds would play into Morty's mediation game plan.

CHAPTER FIFTY

THE MORE THE MERRIER

Thursday, September 4, 1997

(THIRD PERSON)

Davis woke up when Liza left the bed to go to the bathroom. She returned within a few minutes, and he wanted to start the day off with a little romance. As she reached the bedside, she placed the two pugs in bed with them. That was her signal that she wasn't in the mood for any monkey business. After almost twenty years of marriage, Davis knew debate was futile, shook it off, and jumped out of bed and into the shower. He'd been outmaneuvered, and he knew it.

A quick cup of black coffee and he was out the door. He elected to drive his Wilson silver Vette on this beautiful fall morning. There wasn't a cloud in the sky. Sucking on an orange Tootsie Pop, he slid into the cherry interior and drove slower than the speed limit with the top down. The car drove smoothly on its four new tires.

He never ate breakfast other than the three pastries that were fresh from the Rosario's market, brought in every day by the ever-faithful Bella. However, this morning he'd have to skip his feast. She met him at the door with unexpected news, "Don't get too comfortable, you're off to court. Sammie's getting your briefcase. You're still going to be late, Judge Howard said eight, and not a moment later."

"What are you talking about? I don't have court this..."

She cut him off, "The court's hearing our motion to consolidate discovery. I just got a call from Martha, Judge Howard's secretary. She said that he's ready to hear you out and, then, he'll decide. From Martha's tone, my guess is that he's already decided the issue."

Davis knew that secretaries talked. Martha and Bella had known each other over ten years. He figured the judge had already prepared a draft order and Martha had typed it and was talking. Davis smiled and got excited, "This ruling could be really big. The defendants will be absolutely furious if Howard grants our motion."

Bella asked, "Who's arguing the motion?"

Davis replied, "I don't know. I thought I'd figure it out on the way over there."

The older woman insisted, "You should let Sammie do it, especially if you think the judge has already made up his mind."

"But if I'm wrong, the argument could make the difference."

"Don't sell her short. If that's the case, she can do just as good a job as you could."

Davis didn't agree. His ego wouldn't let him. She prepared the brief and was familiar with the arguments and on September 1, she recently passed the bar. He sighed and said, "I'll turn over the reins." Just then Sammie appeared in the doorway with Davis' briefcase, a graduation gift from his parents with his initials, "BAD", bloodied from the Plainview cases. She also was carrying her identical briefcase with her initials "SAD", but no blood.

On the way to the courthouse, Davis handed the baton to Sammie. She got pretty excited and she quickened the pace. Twice, Davis asked her to slow down. It was September and still pretty hot in Nashville, and he was sweating profusely because of his weight and lack of exercise. She'd recently gotten her Bar results and was now eligible to argue in court.

"Slow the hell down, please. It's our motion. They can't start without us."

They arrived at the courtroom to find it already crowded, almost to capacity. The two defendants, Carmichael and Oz, were present; Carmichael tried to attend most hearings, with court permission, it got him out of the townhouse. Carmichael's defense team of Covington & Burling sent Gray, Tate, and two associates to impress the judge that they considered the motion critical to the case. Oz's sole representative was Pierce.

There were plenty of other legal talent and clients present to support or challenge the plaintiffs' motion to consolidate discovery. John Whitefield, the American Insurance counsel, and a bald senior vice president from Carmichael and Oz's homeowner's insurance company appeared even though that case was pending in federal not state court, like the others. Davis didn't know Whitefield, or the insurance executive. They hadn't filed a brief, so their position, unlike the others, was unknown. All of the defendant cops, their lawyers, the sued district attorneys, their lawyers, the five TBI agents, and federal agents' lawyer also showed up. All of those defendants filed briefs in support of the motion. In the corner sat DA Johnson Tory, Chief Gerry Neenan, Jack Barnes, and Bucky Lee.

Judge Barry Howard entered with a stern expression on his face. Each lawyer and client were trying to read the judge, without success.

Howard cleared his throat, "Where am I, at the circus? Who are all these people, Mr. Davis? I'm going to let you make the introductions."

She'll be tested with fire and brimstone.

"If it please the court, the plaintiffs motion to consolidate will be argued by Ms. Davis, not me. She recently passed the Bar, and I'd like to introduce her to the court."

Howard was genuinely surprised that Davis would relinquish the reins for such a critical motion. Barnes and the other lawyers in the courtroom were stunned.

"Welcome to the Third Circuit, Ms. Davis. I look forward to a long and prosperous relationship."

Howard administered the oath, and Sammie was admitted to the Circuit Courts of Davidson County.

"Now can you please explain who the hell everybody is in my courtroom and what the hell they're doing here?"

Sammie stood at her full height, which in her heels was over six two, and announced, "If it please the court, I am Sammie Davis of the law firm of Steine & Davis, and on behalf of the plaintiffs, allow me to introduce to the court the following members of the Tennessee Bar and their clients."

It took her quite a few minutes to identify everyone in the courtroom, and when she got to John Whitefield, she paused, "Mr. John Whitefield represents American Insurance Company, which is a defendant in the United States District Court for the Middle District of Tennessee in an action filed by Mr. Carmichael and Oz against their homeowner's insurance carrier. I do not know the gentleman next to him. I suspect he's a representative of that company?"

John Whitefield stood and addressed the court, "Ms. Davis is correct. This is Bertrand Strange, an Executive Vice President of American Insurance. We have an interest in the taking of these depositions, but our theories are not inconsistent with those of the plaintiffs in your case. I suspect that after Ms. Davis' questioning of these law enforcement defendants, I might have one or two questions, but

Ms. Davis would have already covered the bulk of my questions. We support the concept of consolidation. There's no question we'd have massive duplication if separate depositions were taken. We hadn't filed a brief, and I thought I should make American Insurance's position known to the court and put it on the record."

Howard acknowledged all of the parties present and asked Ms. Davis to proceed with the plaintiff's motion.

"May it please the court, I submit to you that we have a room full of defendants. With the exception of Mr. Bucky Lee, all of them are public servants sworn to protect the public. The police officers and TBI agents keep our streets safe, and the DAs implement justice. They're all working for the taxpayers. Now, the defendants in our case, Carmichael and Oz, committed serious torts. We've got tapes to prove it. The allegations against Carmichael and Oz are not based on circumstantial evidence. Those tapes are direct evidence of their conduct. In contrast, the claims of Carmichael and Oz against these public servants and Mr. Lee are based solely on circumstantial evidence. They've raised these claims against these public servants and propose they should depose them as many as three, possibly four, times."

Howard interrupted, "Why would these public servants be deposed four times?"

"They'd be deposed in our consolidated case involving our three female clients, the Bucky Lee case, the law enforcement and district attorney case, and the defendants Carmichael and Oz's claims against their homeowner's insurance company. Both defendants claim that their intentional wrongful behavior is covered under their homeowner's policies."

Sammie waited a moment. No follow-up question, so she continued, "These defendants are abusing the system, and now they propose to waste taxpayer dollars. I'd suggest that we charge them a fine, but it's more important that these men provide their public service."

Pierce had enough of Sammie Davis. She objected, "Your Honor, May I be heard?"

"Wait your turn," Sammie snapped back at the only other female in the room. She knew Pierce was trying to throw her off.

Howard agreed and directed Pierce back to her seat.

Sammie's rhythm returned, "This isn't just about taxpayer dollars. It also involves our sense of justice and fairness. What Mr. Tate and Ms. Pierce are proposing is to give them four opportunities to secure inconsistent testimony. Why should these witnesses give four depositions? That's too much of a burden for them to suffer. They have one story to tell and should tell it only once by deposition. The facts are the facts. What the law enforcement defendants have to say in their depos will not change from case to case; same for the DAs. Each will testify consistently, so why have four depositions?"

Sammie paused to let her point sink in, "Hopefully these matters will never get to trial and will be resolved through settlement or mediation. Regardless, the court should be fair and not impose an unreasonable burden on these defendants."

Sammie took a deep breath and reminded the judge, "Mr. Tate and Ms. Pierce originally included these other defendants in their answer to the Swann complaint. It's hard for them to deny that their claims against these other defendants are not related to the plaintiffs' cases."

Sammie impressed everyone in the room, including her adversary counsel sitting at the defense table. Most important, she impressed Jack Barnes, DA Johnson Tory, and Judge Howard, who turned to Pierce, "Okay, it's your turn, Ms. Pierce."

Pierce began her argument, "Judge, the defendants in your court originally thought all of these parties and my claims against Mr. Lee and the law enforcement personnel should be resolved in one case. It was you who separated the claims into four lawsuits. You said it would be too complicated to address so many claims in one case. We took your decision seriously and planned our strategy based on that decision. Now the plaintiffs ask the court to reverse that decision and consolidate discovery for the defendants charged by my client and Mr. Carmichael. Such a reversal would create an appealable issue to the Court of Appeals. My client and Mr. Tate's clients have already been deposed. I can assure you that all these lawyers want a bite at my client and Mr. Carmichael. It isn't fair that they give multiple depositions, and these other parties don't have to. My clients have a due process right to confront the defendants they've sued in accordance with the Rules of Civil Procedure and under the Constitution."

Sammie realized that the judge would be sensitive to a claim that by consolidating discovery, he'd be depriving them of their constitutional right.

However, without warning, Howard interrupted, "Enough of this dog and pony show. First, I'm glad you invited these non-parties to my court. I needed to see the number of defendants who would be deposed four times for the judicial economy of consolidating discovery. The law enforcement defendant's depositions shall occur in this courtroom the week of Monday, September 8th through Friday, the 13th. There's nothing scheduled in this courtroom on those days. The case that was set for trial and the backup case both settled. None of my other cases are ready to go to trial. I will cancel motions for that Friday. You shall go from 8:00 a.m. till 6:00 p.m. I'm giving you one hour for lunch and four fifteen-minute bathroom breaks. You should be able, in that fifty hours, to depose the three Metro officers, the three assistant DAs, and the four TBI agents. That's ten depositions. That's an average of about four hours per deposition. These depositions shouldn't vary much and once a few have been taken, they should be pretty redundant. Chief Neenan shall be limited to a seven-hour deposition on Monday, September 15th in his office; General Tory shall give a seven-hour deposition on Tuesday the 16th in his office, and Bucky Lee shall be deposed for no more than ten hours at Jack Barnes' office on Wednesday the 17th. Ms. Pierce and Mr. Tate shall have a total of five hours, Mr. Davis two hours, Mr. Barnes, two hours and a one-hour rebuttal. I know that will be three long days but you'll get the discovery completed."

Pierce rose to her feet and complained, "I object. That's plain arbitrary."

"It's discretionary, it's reasonable, and that's what the Court of Appeals requires." Howard ruled and left the bench.

Davis was very proud of Sammie. She had a good day. He was also satisfied with Howard's ruling. He'd gotten most of what he wanted from the court.

CHAPTER FIFTY-ONE

THE CIRCUS

September 8-10, 15th, and 16, 1997

(THIRD PERSON)

Tate and Pierce conducted the depositions of the law enforcement defendants. Covington & Burling assigned four associates to help them prepare for the task. Their first assignment was to vet each of the officers by delving deep into their backgrounds. They were pretty disappointed by their expensive efforts. None of the three Metro police officers or the four TBI agents had any black marks on their records. Agent-in-Charge Arnold Pyle had twenty-two years with the TBI. He was a man of substance. The other three agents held up well during cross-examination. Before working for the bureau, Agents Moore and Chavez were decorated Navy Seals.

Before the deposition of Arnold Pyle began Tate gave a little speech,

"This deposition of the agent-in-charge of the TBI investigation is for discovery purposes only. Based upon the order of Judge Howard, we have been limited to one deposition. Accordingly, unlike the deposition of Roscoe Carmichael where the court specifically restricted the examination about his arrest and drug charges, Ms. Pierce and I intend to question this witness about those matters."

Tate agreed to allow Pierce to start the questioning. Pierce inquired of the man who was in charge of the federal agents the night of Carmichael's arrest, "Mr. Pyle, the search warrant issued by Judge Wyatt for the Carmichael farm relied exclusively on the sworn affidavit of Anthony Reynolds?"

"Yes."

"Mr. Estes had a previous criminal record before the warrant was issued?"

"Yes."

"He'd been held guilty for criminal contempt for failing to cooperate with a court, right?"

"Yes."

"In the past he went to jail for eighteen months to protect Mr. Carmichael rather than answer your questions?"

"Correct."

"Did Mr. Estes explain why he cooperated this time rather than stay silent again to protect Mr. Carmichael?"

"No."

"You just didn't ask or didn't care?"

Davis objected, "Compound question."

Pierce broke the question down, "Did Mr. Estes tell you why he was turning in Mr. Carmichael on this occasion rather than protecting him as he'd done in the past?"

"We'd arrested Mr. Estes for the selling of a large quantity of cocaine. He was facing, independent of Mr. Carmichael, serious criminal charges and a sentence of at least ten years, so he was motivated to help us. We convinced him it was in his personal best interest to help us."

"What was the deal you made with Mr. Estes?"

"If he helped us arrest and convict Mr. Carmichael for distribution of cocaine, the charges pending against him would be dropped."

"You made it clear to Mr. Estes that you wanted his help to get Mr. Carmichael?"

"That's fair."

"Mr. Carmichael's arrest and conviction were key to Mr. Estes securing his freedom?"

"Yes."

"The focus for the issuance of the search warrant relied upon the credibility of Anthony Estes' affidavit?"

"Mr. Estes gave accurate information upon which a valid arrest was made."

Pierce then asked, "Mr. Estes was placed in witness protection?"

"Yes."

"How's Mr. Estes doing?"

"He's dead. He died from arsenic poisoning."

"Have you arrested any suspects?"

"No, but I have my suspicions."

"Care to share those suspicions?"

"No."

"So the defense never had an opportunity to question Mr. Estes?"

"No."

"His affidavit isn't admissible at any trial?"

"Correct."

Pyle was furious at Pierce for the line of questioning. Tate took over the examination of Pyle. He attacked the farmhouse warrant as overly broad.

"Do you see the words airstrip on the warrant?"

"No."

"Do you see the word driveway on the warrant?"

"Or any reference to a jeep or vehicle?"

"No."

"Agent, you were involved in the 1989 arrest of Mr. Carmichael, weren't you?"

"Yes."

"There was a search warrant for drugs and cash issued associated with that arrest?"

"Yes."

"You found very little drugs?"

"That's not correct. A very small amount of cocaine was there, along with a naked sixteen-year-old girl."

"You didn't find what you expected to find under the search warrant?"

"That's correct. But Mr. Carmichael was convicted under that warrant of two misdemeanors as a result of the search warrant."

"So, Mr. Carmichael was found guilty for matters outside the original intent of the search warrant?"

"Yes."

Pyle was a pretty good witness. Neither Pierce nor Tate thought they'd made much headway with him. The next day, Pierce and Tate took the deposition of Chief Neenan. It lasted only an hour because he had very little personal knowledge of the facts. It was apparent from his discovery deposition that he shouldn't have been named a defendant in the case.

On the 16th, Katie Stone, court reporter, gave DA Johnson Tory the oath, and Tate began the questioning. Tory provided his educational background. He went to undergraduate and law school at the University of Tennessee in Knoxville.

"I was elected district attorney the first time in 1986, reelected in 1990 and 1994. My term ends December 31st, 1998."

Tate pulled out the search warrant.

"Do you see any reference to videotapes on that document?"

"No."

"So why did the police seize seven videotapes that were private property of Roscoe Carmichael?"

"I had a confidential informant who told me that he was distributing large quantities of cocaine from his home and his office."

"You didn't find a shipment of cocaine at the Music Row office, did you?"

"No, sir. It was a smaller amount, approximately twenty-six grams."

"The informant was wrong about the amount of drug at the office?"

"Correct, but he was right about the farmhouse."

"You got a supplemental warrant to search for videos at the Music Row office?"

"Yes."

"Did you think the cocaine was in those videotapes?"

"No. I had a second informant who told me about the tapes."

"Who was that second informant?"

"Bucky Lee."

"How did Bucky Lee come to tell you about the tapes?"

"I got a call from him asking if we could talk but not at the office."

Tate established that Tory's and Lee's relationship before the call was strictly professional in nature. They'd never eaten a meal together and didn't go to each other's home.

"Bucky tried lawsuits in Davidson County, both criminal and civil, and he always dealt with one of my assistant attorney generals. I knew him from the courthouse but nothing more. My staff thought highly of his ability and his ethics."

"Did the two of you meet?"

"Yes, we arranged to meet at Radnor Lake the Sunday before Carmichael's house and office were raided. There is a picnic table about halfway around the lake. We met at sunrise before there were many walkers or runners."

"What did he tell you?"

"Nothing at first. He was nervous, and I didn't push him. He finally asked me if I was investigating Roscoe Carmichael."

"I hesitated in answering the question. I joked and said, 'Why, are you offering a plea bargain?' I knew he'd represented Carmichael in the past. He assured me that he no longer represented Carmichael, but I was still reluctant to give him information. It was a weird conversation. I don't meet with lawyers on park benches and discuss their former clients." Tory took a drink of water.

Tate pressed him, "Did you have any substantial conversations about my client Roscoe Carmichael?"

"He started talking about confidentiality and the fact that a lawyer had an obligation to keep the confidences of his clients but that a lawyer also had ethical obligations as a member of the Bar to his profession and to the community. I just let him talk. He was working out the problem in front of me, and I didn't want to interrupt. Finally, he told me that Roscoe Carmichael had told him that he'd filmed women in his office bathroom dressing and undressing without their knowledge. He inferred that he watched them go to the bathroom. He said the thought of what Carmichael was doing disgusted him, that it was not only an invasion of their privacy, but he thought it must have been a crime, like a Peeping Tom."

Tory took another drink of water and resumed his answer. "I told him that my office suspected that Carmichael was dealing drugs and that we did have an ongoing investigation. My remarks were very general. I didn't reveal we intended to issue a search warrant that week."

"What did you do with the information?"

"At the time, nothing, but when the police informed me that there was a secret room with a professional camera and that there were a large number of videotapes at Carmichael's office, I told them that I would get a supplemental warrant to seize and inspect the tapes. There was a two-way mirror into the bedroom and exercise room and a smaller one into the bathroom."

"You admit that the original warrant didn't cover videotapes?"

"Yes."

"You admit that if you hadn't had your conversation with Bucky Lee, you wouldn't have confiscated those videotapes?"

"I can't answer that with a yes. The TBI and the Metro police found the secret room without any help from me. A camera and a large number of videotapes were in that secret room. The cops called me for further instructions. I didn't call them. The police already had reasonable suspicion that there had been videotaping without any information from Bucky Lee."

"What did you do after your conversation on the bench with Lee?"

"It was a Sunday, and I went to the office and did some research and prepared a memo to file. It wasn't a public restroom but private where the filming took place. Many of the cases I reviewed involved children. I started looking at the obscenity statutes. I was shocked. I couldn't find a crime to fit the facts. After checking state law, I checked federal law. I figured we'd go in on the drug warrant and see what we found. I never expected to find a secret room or two-way mirror. I never thought there was a cameraman. I can't speak for Mr. Lee, but I don't think he knew about those facts either, or he would have disclosed them to me at the lake."

"So, Mr. Lee didn't tell you about Mr. Oz?"

"We didn't know of Mr. Oz's involvement until Mr. Carmichael's arrest. Mr. Carmichael first admitted there was a cameraman, and he identified Mr. Oz. We could tell that from the tapes there was a cameraman. He gave up Mr. Oz during questioning. He didn't want to take the rap by himself."

"Your office hasn't charged either Mr. Carmichael or Mr. Oz with a crime for videotaping, have you?"

"No. We figured that Mr. Carmichael will be spending plenty of time in prison on the drug charges and that Mr. Oz will also have a lot to deal with the civil suits."

"Did you know that Mr. Carmichael had filed a disciplinary complaint with the Board of Professional Responsibility against Mr. Lee?"

Tory hesitated, "When?"

"At the time Lee told you about Carmichael filming women in the bathroom."

"I learned about those charges at a later date."

"Would knowledge of the disciplinary complaint change anything you did during the search of the office?"

"I can't say. It certainly would have been an additional motive for Lee to report Carmichael, but I can't answer that question."

"Did you at any time confront Mr. Lee about the disciplinary complaint?"

"Yes, about a week after the search was executed and the tapes viewed by my office, one of my assistant DA's told me about the complaint Carmichael filed against Bucky Lee, and I asked him about his dispute with Carmichael."

Tate pressed on, "What did he say?"

"He claimed the fact he told me about the women and the bathroom was separate from his dispute with Carmichael. He told me Carmichael believed he was entitled to a portion of one of his fees earned more than a year earlier."

"What did you do after that conversation?"

"I continued through the police department to try to find the women in the videos. We found only Lizzy Swann. Mary Doe called us, and Mr. Davis found Jane Doe. Carmichael settled with three of the women: Strong, Watson, and I forget the last one's name. So, Carmichael found them. There's still one unaccounted for."

Tory testified that he was present when Elizabeth Swann viewed her videotape, "She was upset, embarrassed, and angry. She said she felt violated. Lizzy Swann came alone and about two hours later, she had to be driven home."

"Other than the plaintiffs and their counsel, who else has seen the videos?"

"I don't know the names of all the TBI agents who saw the videos. You've sued four and Arnold Pyle and three others who were present when I looked at the tapes. You've sued the three DAs who I viewed tapes with, the chief and the three officers."

Tate handed Tory a piece of paper, "Is this the log that reflects who saw one or more of the tapes?"

"Yes." The log contained a list of the defendants sued by Carmichael and Oz.

"Did you ever find tapes of women changing in the bathroom or going to the bathroom?"

"No."

"So, the information Mr. Lee gave you wasn't accurate?"

"Well, we did find seven tapes of Mr. Carmichael having sex with women that Mr. Oz videoed. There was a mirror to the bathroom but not video of the bathroom."

"That wasn't what Mr. Lee told you that you would find?"

"Correct."

"Why did you show the tapes to three other DAs?"

"I wanted their input. This wasn't a run-of-the-mill case. I thought they could help me figure out what to do."

Tate had Tory describe the sex acts on the tapes. He'd already seen the tapes. He just wanted to make Tory uncomfortable, which he surely did. He testified that the discovery of the videos was shocking.

Pierce was up next. Her focus was on her client, Phillip Oz. Tory admitted that he was surprised to learn from Carmichael that Phillip Oz was the cameraman. Tory established that Carmichael was tight-lipped for the first day of questioning. He didn't know why Carmichael changed his mind and turned in Oz.

She concluded by asking, "You're not aware of anyone seeing the videos prior to the raid under your search warrant?"

"Correct."

"It was the police and your office that publicized the tapes for the first time to the women, other police officers, and DAs?"

"I don't know of earlier publications."

"So, Bucky Lee was the proximate cause of the publication?"

"I don't agree. Carmichael and Oz created the tapes and the reason for their disclosure."

The DA's lawyer, Barnes, Davis, and none of the other lawyers had further questions for the district attorney. They all figured they were on the same side.

CHAPTER FIFTY-TWO

A LAWYER'S DEPO

Friday, September 19, and Monday, September 22, 1997

(THIRD PERSON)

After Johnson Tory's deposition, Pierce and Tate filed a motion to exclude the videotapes based on the testimony of the district attorney. As a result of the defense's motion, the deposition of Bucky Lee was continued a few days so the court could hold an emergency hearing and rule on the motion. The tapes were a critical part of the plaintiff's case, and their admissibility was important to how the defense conducted the deposition of Lee. In fact, the filing of the motion was a sign of weakness by the defense. Prior to this move it was uncertain which party would challenge the tapes. The defense blinked and tried to take the tapes off the table.

The Davis team didn't have much time to pull together a response. Basically, their arguments were that the tapes spoke for themselves and that they evidenced the intentional wrongful conduct of the defendants. The brief concluded, "We live in a civilized society where men and women engage in consensual sex all the time. Sometimes people are in love, and the purpose is to procreate the species. Other times men and women agree to have a more casual relationship to satisfy a more basic human instinct. As long as both parties are of legal age, this is a private matter. But no one ever expects to be betrayed and be displayed and recorded like an animal in a zoo without his or her permission. A sex partner who does that has acted outrageously and should be punished to whatever extent a jury determines. These tapes are a critical piece of evidence that a jury must see in order to evaluate the appropriate amount to award in damages."

The defense argued that his deposition made it clear that it was the actions of Bucky Lee that precipitated the issuance of the supplemental search warrant, and the confiscation of the tapes. Pierce and Tate's argument that Bucky Lee was an intervening cause didn't fly with Judge Howard. The motion filed with the trial court preserved the issue for the appeal, where the defense felt it had a much better chance to succeed.

Bucky was a likable guy, and Carmichael wasn't, but appearance and demeanor were much more important at the trial level. On appeal, the parties would be evaluated based upon how their testimony read in a transcript. The appellate judges were all lawyers bound by the Code of Professional Responsibility. Lee, under the Code had an obligation to preserve the confidentiality of what a client told him. Tory emphasized that Lee relied on the fact that Carmichael was no longer a client when Carmichael told Lee his tale, without warning. Tory pointed out that Carmichael placed Lee in an ethical dilemma: protect his former client or protect unsuspecting women? The analysis of the circumstances was further complicated by the fact that Carmichael didn't tell Bucky the whole truth about the secret room, two-way mirror, and cameraman. Another wrinkle was the dispute between Carmichael and Lee over the fee and the fact that Carmichael had reported Bucky to the Board. Tory admitted that it clouded the issue of whether Bucky acted in revenge or for the good of the women.

These were the issues to be explored at Bucky Lee's deposition. Judge Howard decided to increase the time limit on the direct by Pierce and Tate from five hours to seven hours, as provided in the federal rules. Davis was given two hours to complete his examination. Katie Stone was designated the official timekeeper, and the deposition was set for Monday, September 22nd at Jack Barnes' office.

Over the weekend, Davis enjoyed his family. On Saturday he and Jake played a round of golf at Hillwood Country Club. At the turn, Jake was two up on his father. Davis wasn't perturbed. Their game was match play.

Jake tried to unnerve him, "You should have made that putt on the last hole. Your hands were shaking a little bit."

"You worry about your own game, and I'll worry about mine."

Davis tied it up on the fifteenth. The sixteenth, a two-hundred-yard par three over water, was a challenging hole. Davis put it four feet from the stick and made the putt going one up. Jake fell apart double bogeying the hole. One down, Jake hooked his drive into the woods, and Davis went straight down the middle. The match was over. Jake would sulk all weekend.

On Sunday the Davis family including Sammie and Morty ate lunch together around the Davis pool. Davis had a double helping of fried chicken, corn on the cob, baked beans, cole slaw and corn bread. After lunch, the Davis team had a brief meeting about the Lee deposition scheduled for the next day. It was agreed that Davis alone would attend and that Sammie and Morty would go to the office and take care of other business.

Davis arrived at Jack Barnes' office at 8:15 a.m. He had two cups of coffee before anyone showed up. Katie Stone arrived next. While she was setting up, she whispered to Davis, "How about lunch? I deserve a good meal after a marathon deposition like this one."

Davis thought of his wife, who was still mad at him for placing the family in jeopardy. "Let's see. I'll probably work through lunch."

"Who are you kidding? You're not missing a meal. I think you're a little afraid of me."

"I am, and I should be. You're a dangerous woman."

"I am, but danger can be fun."

The other lawyers and Lee arrived before 9:00 a.m., the scheduled start time. Pierce began the questioning. Bucky went to Samford University in Birmingham and law school at the University of Tennessee.

"No, I didn't know Johnson Tory at school. I graduated three or four years before him. I've been licensed to practice law in the state of Tennessee since 1968."

Pierce established that Lee never represented her client, Phillip Oz.

"I knew who Phillip was, but we didn't have a professional or social relationship. I knew he was a friend of Roscoe Carmichael."

Pierce asked, "When did you learn of Phillip Oz's involvement in this matter?"

"When I saw a television report by Alice Krieger."

"Mr. Carmichael didn't tell you at any point?"

"No."

"Did District Attorney Johnson Tory tell you at any point?"

"We did discuss Mr. Oz after it was reported by Ms. Krieger."

"What did the DA say to you?"

"Tory confirmed the news report that Oz was the cameraman. We talked about the fact that Carmichael didn't tell me about the cameraman, two-way mirror, and secret room. He told me he never found any bathroom tapes, but that the tapes were of Carmichael having sex with these women."

"Why did you tell the DA that the tapes were of Carmichael watching women going to the bathroom?'

"Because I knew that there was a Peeping Tom statute, and the DA would investigate a crime."

"Mr. Carmichael told you he'd had consensual sex with these women?"

"I didn't know whether or not it was consensual. I wasn't there. I hadn't seen the tapes. I just had Carmichael's word as to what happened."

"He never claimed he raped anyone?"

"No."

"To your knowledge, it wasn't criminal to have sex with any of these women, including the three women who have sued Mr. Carmichael and Mr. Oz?"

"That's correct."

"And you looked for a crime but couldn't find one?"

"That's correct."

"So, you lied to DA Johnson Tory so he would get an indictment for the sex crime of being a Peeping Tom?

"I wouldn't call it a lie. I wasn't there. All I had was Carmichael's description of the events. I may have placed the focus of my conversation with Roscoe on the bathroom."

Pierce asked Lee about his representation of Carmichael. Lee indicated that for more than twenty-five years he considered himself Roscoe's lawyer.

"I represented him on some juvenile matters, in his divorce, the sale of two businesses, the purchase of a business, about a dozen contract disputes, and in his 1990 statutory rape trial. He was sentenced to eleven months and twenty-nine days for contributing to the delinquency of a minor and providing cocaine to a minor."

"After he got out of prison, did you represent him?"

"I may have done something minor for him, but in 1994, we had a major falling out."

Lee described how Carmichael, as a third party, referred a substantial land deal on which Lee earned a ten percent contingency fee of $75,000.

"About a week after it closed, Carmichael called, demanding his portion of the fee. I explained that I wasn't allowed to fee split with a non-lawyer. He kept insisting that I promised him a third of the fee, or $25,000. When I denied that promise, his response was 'fair is fair.' I tried to calm him down, but it got ugly. He wouldn't back off, and I told him to find another lawyer because we were through. That made him even angrier, and he filed disciplinary charges against me. Ultimately the Board dismissed the charges. He claimed the Board sided with me because I was a lawyer. He asked me to represent him in his pending drug charges. I was his one call from jail. We had a pretty heated conversation. He threatened to get even with me for refusing to help him in his time of need. I'm surprised Gray hasn't told you about our conversation. I referred Carmichael to Covington & Burling. I called Gray to let him know to expect his call. Carmichael threatened to get even with me. I guess including me in this lawsuit is his revenge."

Pierce questioned Lee about how he billed Carmichael.

"I generally would have billed him hourly."

"Did you keep up with your time through a time sheet or tickets?"

"Yes."

"Where are those records?"

"Most have been destroyed. I had a mass shredding when I quit the practice of law and went into teaching."

Pierce went over the conversation with Carmichael when Lee learned about him taping women.

"He was pretty drunk. He was loud and obnoxious. I didn't want the information, but once I had it, I didn't know what to do with it. I wasn't sure it was truthful. Once I was confident it was true, I felt compelled to disclose it to someone who could stop that kind of behavior in the future."

"When did you decide to go to the DA?"

"I waited about two months. I called him, and we met on a Sunday morning at Radnor Lake on a bench."

"Weren't you worried that you were violating a client's confidence?"

"Absolutely. I struggled with what to do. I knew I owed him the protection of confidentiality, but then I thought of the women he videoed. I'd never met them, but I had to do something."

"Why didn't you go to the Board of Professional Responsibility rather than the DA?"

"That's a reasonable question. The Board didn't have any control over Carmichael. He wasn't a lawyer. The Board's control was over me. My first thought was to protect those women and to stop Roscoe from hurting any other persons. At the time the DA seemed like the right move. I'm not sorry I did it, despite the repercussions. What Carmichael and Oz did was outrageous, and they should compensate these women."

"You did this to them by telling the DA?"

"That's bullshit. They made the films, and Roscoe was dealing drugs. They created the situation, not me. I'm confident a jury will understand why I reported Carmichael. He needed to be stopped. I'm glad I played a small role in bringing this matter to light."

Pierce ended her examination, and Tate took over. He didn't really ask anything new, but he pushed hard. "You lied to the DA about the bathroom, didn't you?"

"I planted a seed."

"That's just a polite way of admitting you lied?"

Bucky admitted he misled the DA because he wanted the DA to confiscate the tapes.

"You betrayed my client?"

"I didn't betray him. You first need to have someone's confidence to betray them. Carmichael was drunk and bragging in the open where anyone could hear. We didn't like each other. He had no expectation of privacy."

"You don't know that. He was drunk and therefore not thinking straight. You took advantage of him?"

"Not as badly as he took advantage of those women. When it came down to it they were innocent and used bad judgment getting involved with the likes of him, and he was just an ass. I did the right thing and sided with the innocent." Tate got frustrated and asked only thirty minutes of questions.

Barnes had no questions, but Davis asked one, "You indicated that the women should be compensated by Carmichael and Oz for their intentional wrongful conduct. Are you of the opinion they should be punished?"

Pierce and Tate objected, arguing that Lee wasn't qualified to make that determination. It was a jury question. Davis directed Lee to answer.

"I think punitive damages are appropriate. The jury should follow Judge Howard's instructions. Look at the thirteen factors that the judge tells them to consider and award seven figures of punitive damages against Carmichael because of his net worth. The jury should award a lesser amount against Oz, who is definitely, based upon his actions, mentally sick and has a lesser net worth. The purpose of punitive damages is to teach the defendants a lesson, so they won't repeat their wrongful conduct and send a message to others that such conduct will not be tolerated."

The deposition ended there.

CHAPTER FIFTY-THREE

A DEFENSE REQUIRED

Wednesday, September 24th, 1997

(BENJAMIN DAVIS' VOICE)

I was still in the doghouse with my wife, and I slept in till 8:00 a.m. I thought about playing hooky, ditching the office, and trying to win back my wife, but there was too much on my plate. My to-do list was four pages long, single-spaced. There was always too much to do. That was the problem. I'd tried to convince Morty to hire another attorney and paralegal, but the old man was stubborn. He liked the idea of a small firm, "We're intimate, and the clients like it that way." The Carmichael case had taken a toll on the firm, draining its human resources. The Davis team was physically and mentally exhausted.

I drove slowly to work. I wasn't in any rush. When I got to the office, I stopped at the coffee machine and got a black cup of gourmet coffee and two apple turnovers. Once at my desk, I noticed there was a message from Jack Barnes marked urgent. I picked up the phone and dialed, "What's on fire that needs my immediate attention?"

"Judge Thomas Wise ruled in the federal case in favor of Carmichael and Oz."

"You're kidding, right?"

"No, I'll fax you the order. I guess the decision helps you if it's upheld on appeal. You can bet American Insurance will be filing an appeal in the Sixth Circuit federal Court of Appeals. This ruling is astonishing. It gives you a deeper pocket to collect any judgment, especially against Oz."

I thought about the availability of insurance proceeds to pay part of a judgment that might be awarded by a jury. I felt better, "Fax me the order."

Ten minutes later, Bella handed me the order from the United States District Court for the Middle District of Tennessee. It read;

ORDER

This came before the Honorable Thomas Wise on the declaratory judgment complaint of the plaintiffs Roscoe Carmichael and Phillip Oz. The plaintiffs have identical homeowner's policies with the defendant American Insurance Company ("Company"), which were eventually attached to the complaint. The court has been asked to determine if the Company has an obligation to provide a defense to the plaintiffs as defendants in three lawsuits pending in the Third Court of Davidson County, Judge Barry Howard presiding. These lawsuits have been consolidated for discovery by Judge Howard, which he set at least one of them for jury trial beginning February 3rd, 1998. ('Privacy Actions") These Privacy actions do not allege negligence on the part of the defendants, but only intentional torts. The Company denied the plaintiffs a defense and coverage because the Privacy actions alleged only intentional torts, which the Company claims were not covered under the policies. The court finds that:

1. The contract between the Company and the plaintiffs was written by the Company and therefore should be read against the Company, which had complete control of the language of the contract.

2. The contract does not state with specificity that the Company will only defend actions founded in negligence. The contract does not specifically exclude a defense of its insureds charged with intentional torts. The court finds that the Company is obligated to provide a defense in the Privacy Actions including attorney fees in this action.

3. The court further finds that the policy limits of the Company are available to pay compensatory damages only.

4. The court finds that any award of punitive damages in the Privacy Actions shall not be covered by the policies as such coverage would be against public policy.

5. Costs of this cause are assessed against the Company.

ENTERED THIS 24th DAY OF SEPTEMBER
HONORABLE THOMAS WISE, JUDGE
OF THE UNITED STATES DISTRICT COURT

I reread the order; I couldn't believe the court had required not only a defense but also payment of compensatory damages in the event of a judgment. I rode the elevator to the sixth floor and used his key. My old friend was up, reading the newspaper. The court's ruling hadn't had time to make it to the paper.

"To what do I owe this visit?"

Without saying a word, I handed him the order. He put down

his newspaper and read the order out loud, then said, "I'm not surprised. I thought this could happen. It's basic contract law. He who controls the terms of a contract must live and die by its terms. I bet some corporate lawyer gets fired over this one. You can also bet the Company's drafting a new contract as we speak."

He paused, "This is a good thing. It means there may be something worth getting from Oz. This gives us leverage with the insurance company. I think you should send an invitation to our friend John Whitefield to the October mediation."

I didn't quite believe my old friend. He never mentioned this possibility. "What do you mean? American Insurance hasn't been included in our mediation."

"Well, I think it needs to be invited. Call their lawyer and extend an invitation. Don't bother giving notice to Tate or Pierce. Let's surprise them. It will throw them off balance."

I went upstairs and found John Whitefield's telephone number.

"John, Ben Davis, I just read Wise's decision, I guess you plan on appealing."

"Damn right. This order's a joke. The Court of Appeals will reverse it for sure."

"Maybe. It's a question of law. What does the contract say? Wise is right that under Tennessee law, because the contract is silent and was drafted by the insurance company, it's read against the drafter. I bet this ruling places your company's costs at $500,000 between Covington & Burling, Gray, and Pierce's legal fees and costs. I know our expenses are about $100,000 and we have almost a thousand hour in the cases. I bet Pierce, Gray and Tate have been less judicious with their time and expenses."

"You're right, but we're not going down without a fight."

"File your appeal, but attend our mediation as our guest. Bring a decision maker from the Company, and maybe we can get these lawsuits settled. What do you have to lose?"

"I don't want to send Carmichael and Oz the wrong message."

"They don't know I'm inviting you. We'll put you in a separate room. Initially the defendants don't need to know you're participating. It can be our little secret. If we start making progress, we can bring you into the discussions. If the talks go nowhere, you can slip out with them none the wiser. Let's face it. The entire negotiation may just blow up, or it might settle all the lawsuits. You don't have much to lose."

I provided Whitefield with the date, time, and place of the mediation.

Whitefield wasn't convinced, "I'll think about it."

"You do that. Talk to the Company's board. They could spend another $100,000 on an appeal and be in the same place a year from now. By then I'll have my jury verdict, and you'll be on the hook for whatever compensatory damages the jury awards."

Whitefield wasn't happy about his client's situation. I wanted to give the lawyer hope, "Morty has a plan for the mediation. The mediator, Judge Sanford will take charge and I believe get these cases settled. I suggest that you come along for the ride. You don't want to be left behind."

The phone call ended, but I didn't like how the call had gone. I put a cherry Tootsie Pop in my mouth and started sucking hard. I glanced at my yellow pad. I still had fifteen tasks to complete, so I plunged right in. I made call after call, often followed by a confirming letter. Unfortunately, the Bar had grown so fast that I no longer knew every lawyer I dealt with, while others I knew couldn't be trusted. Putting agreements in writing had become standard operating procedure.

Morty popped into the office around eleven, and I took him to lunch at the Captain's Table directly behind the offices. Morty had a chef salad, while I ate a ribeye and baked sweet potatoes. Over lunch I recounted the conversation with Whitefield.

Morty insisted, "After that order, he'll come around. His presence should work in our favor with Pierce and Oz."

Back in the office after lunch, I continued to whittle down my list.

Bella broke in, "I've got a new client on line three. He specifically asked for you, or I would have shuffled him to Sammie."

The firm was trying to build up Sammie's client base. Any new client was generally assigned to her. The case turned out to be a substantial fee and Sammie was off to the races.

CHAPTER FIFTY-FOUR

CHARGES BROUGHT

Thursday, September 25, 1997

(THIRD PERSON)

Bucky Lee maintained a Tennessee law license for twenty-nine years, since 1968. During that time, he had only one complaint filed against him with the Board of Professional Responsibility. That incident was for allegedly offering to split a fee with Roscoe Carmichael. After reviewing the complaint, the investigating attorney recommended and the Board agreed to dismiss the claim.

Roscoe Carmichael's time had come, despite the fact he had both criminal charges and civil suits filed against him. He was now in the driver's seat, and he could taste revenge. Carmichael, relying upon Lee's deposition and the deposition of DA Johnson Tory, filed his second complaint against Lee with the Board alleging, rather convincingly, that Lee had violated his obligation of confidentiality when he went to the DA with information about Carmichael's alleged violation of certain women's privacy. Carmichael insisted that because of his longstanding attorney/client relationship with Lee, the communication was protected.

The charges were delivered by certified mail to the Nashville School of Law administrative offices for the entire staff to see. The return address was unmistakable. Bucky was sent for and opened the letter in front of the Dean. He saw no point in hiding the problem. The Dean had been an ally. After he read it, he handed it to the Dean for his review. The envelope contained two documents, a cover letter from the Chief Disciplinary Counsel and a three-page handwritten letter from Roscoe Carmichael to the Board, which had obviously been dictated by Tate. The cover letter read,

Address omitted

Dear Mr. Lee,

Enclosed please find a complaint filed by Roscoe Carmichael alleging violation of your obligation of the attorney/client relationship. Mr. Carmichael in support of his complaint has filed the deposition of District Attorney Johnson Tory dated 9/16/97 and your deposition of 9/23/97. Based upon a preliminary review of the facts presented to date, there is probable cause to require you to answer the complaint and for the Board to hold a hearing to determine the merits of the complaint.

Joni Smith
Chief Disciplinary Counsel

The Dean handed the documents back to Bucky and cleared his throat as he looked down, not a good sign. He said, "This is going to be a problem for me. Those assholes on permanent staff are going to be after your scalp. I'll try to hold them off, but I don't know whether I'll succeed."

Bucky looked the Dean straight in the face and told him, "If it makes any difference, I still think I did the right thing."

"So, do I, but that may not be enough."

The two men shook hands, and Lee left the office to make an important phone call. He needed good legal advice and had to break the bad news to his attorney Jack Barnes. He decided to fax Barnes the documents and wait for his call. He didn't have long to wait.

Barnes tried to calm Lee down, "I know this hurts and you're frustrated, but the charges aren't unexpected. They are the consequences for your righteous actions. We can get them dismissed. The key is putting on the right proof at the hearing."

Bucky surprisingly asked, "You think it will come to a hearing?"

"The Board has no choice. The letter indicates a hearing will be necessary. It knows a jury trial is hanging over your head. The key is for the Board hearing to happen after the Swann trial in February so the Board can at least see how one jury judges your credibility against Carmichael's."

"Great, I don't know if I can hold on to my teaching job very long. My students and the Dean could waver if it takes that long."

"The Board won't be willing to automatically give you a pass. We need to see if I can get Morty's help, and more important, the help of his clients. You acted to help those women, I'd hope that they'll return the effort and testify before the Board."

They hung up, and Barnes called Morty. "I feel responsible," Barnes began, but Morty interrupted, "How are you responsible? Bucky's a big boy. He did what he thought was the right thing to do. In fact, for what it's worth, I think he did the right thing."

Barnes argued, "If he had called me before he made the call to Tory..."

Morty interrupted him again, "What would you have done? Tell me you know for sure? Who knows what you would have said? I suspect you would have told him to go talk to the DA, and the result would have been the same. I can't say for sure what I would have told him. It was a tough question that he was obviously struggling with."

Morty didn't have an answer but tried to be upbeat, "That's the outline of Bucky's response to the charges. If you need affidavits from our clients, we'll be happy to provide them. We obviously don't look at Bucky as the proximate cause of the publication and disclosure of the videos. We think he did the right thing, and we're willing to say so. My clients will testify that they're grateful."

"That's easy for you to say. You're suing Carmichael, who's brought the charges. I'd say both you and your clients are biased."

"Nobody's perfect."

"There's another problem."

"Only one?"

"Bucky's actions were knowingly and intentional, and the language of the insurance policy is clear. The contract covers negligent acts, but not intentional ones. Unlike American Insurance Company, his malpractice policy specifically excludes intentional acts. Carmichael's and Oz's amended complaints have alleged that Bucky acted intentionally by going to the DA. If the jury finds that as the basis of liability, coverage is voided. That's a hell of a lot of legal expense, costs, and potential jury verdicts."

Morty knew that Bucky was looking at some serious exposure, possibly bankruptcy. He assumed Bucky's carrier had hired Barnes. "How's he paying you?"

"I got the carrier to cover his expenses until the amendment. They paid me $30,000, but with the amendments filed, they put Bucky on notice that their defense terminated, and if judgment was based on intentional conduct rather than negligence, coverage was voided. The company has refused to pay me any longer until his case is adjudicated. Bucky's paid me $20,000, if he can't get coverage restored that will be my final fee. I'm keeping my time just in case the court later orders an insurance company to pay my fees and expenses."

Morty didn't know the exact dollar amounts, but he estimated, "All of these cases will settle. American Insurance is looking at more than $700,000 in attorney fees and costs already in these cases. It's choking on Judge Wise's order. We've invited Whitefield and a company representative to the mediation. American will be motivated to get these cases settled."

Barnes turned serious,

"I hope you're right because I don't think Bucky can take much more of this. His job at the Nashville School of Law is in jeopardy, and if the Board finds against him, he could be on the street without a job or a law license. He loves teaching, and his law license is essential to teaching at a law school. Some faculty members have already turned against him. His students saved his job, but if his license is suspended or revoked, they won't have a leg to stand on. He'll be gone."

"You can count on Ben, Sammie, and me to do whatever we can to help Bucky. Hopefully my game plan will work at mediation."

"You wouldn't care to share your plan with me so I can lift Bucky's spirits?"

"We're still working on it. I'll let you know when we've got it finalized. Give my best to Bucky, and tell him, if he'd called me, I would have given him the same advice that you did."

Morty, who'd served eight years as president of the Disciplinary Bboard, made Barnes feel a little better, but not much.

Morty marched into Sammie's office. She had been assigned the task of preparing the mediation statement that would be given to Judge Sanford in advance of the mediation. It was due on October 1st.

"How's the statement coming?" he asked.

"I'm still polishing it, but if you'd like a copy, here it is."

She handed him a thirteen-page document with exhibits A though H.

"I'll read it and get back to you. Give your uncle a copy, and we'll all polish it together."

Later that day, the threesome met in the library and compared notes. Morty opened the meeting, "Exceptional job, Sammie. You made every point we needed to make in a clear and precise way. Judge Sanford will appreciate where we're coming from. We need to set up an appointment with all three clients and educate them about what to expect. Don't make the appointment too early, at least after ten.

He shared with Sammie and Davis his conversation with Barnes earlier in the day. "We've got to settle these cases not only for the benefit of our clients but also for Bucky. He doesn't deserve what's happening to him. He did the right thing, and he shouldn't be punished for doing that.

CHAPTER FIFTY-FIVE

DRY RUN

Friday, October 3, 1997

(SAMMIE DAVIS' VOICE)

I rounded up the clients for a pre-meeting, at 8:00a.m., despite Morty's instructions that the meeting not be scheduled before 10:00 a.m. I sensed that we had a real problem. The two male members of the firm didn't appreciate the nature and extent of our problem. I realized that our clients weren't on the same page. I'd seen the development of this rift since Carmichael's deposition. Lizzy Swann was ready to face Carmichael and Oz while the Does were petrified of him. I'd been working closely with the clients, and I recognized the difference in the attitudes between them.

I'd mailed a draft mediation statement to each woman. The final version was fifteen pages long with exhibits A through K. There was a report from both of the experts on each client. I was careful to make sure that each client got only a copy of her expert's reports, protecting the confidentiality of the others. Jane Doe's rehab counselor also provided a report.

I agreed with the decision not to share with our clients the defendants' mediation statement. Their document contained still photos made from the videos and promised to play the tapes at the mediation. We'd objected to the playing of the tapes at the mediation. The defendant Carmichael claimed in his statement that he'd be found not guilty in his criminal case. Tate pointed to the rulings by Judge Peck excluding evidence as a basis for the proposition that the TBI acted illegally. The statement failed to mention that Carmichael's paid agents were working from the inside. Peck's two clerks were working together to get Carmichael off; Carmichael hoped these young men would influence the judge.

After the clients reviewed their final package, I answered a few questions. Lizzy asked, "What impact will Judge Wise's order in the federal insurance case have on the collection of our judgment?"

There were toughs question I wasn't able to address because I didn't know the answer to, and I wasn't authorized to reveal the negotiating strategy to the clients yet. I tried to be helpful,

"All of our claims are intentional torts, so we can collect all of our judgment from either or both defendants. Judge Wise's order finds that American Insurance must provide $1,000,000 of coverage for each defendant. They both had the same homeowners policy. American also was at risk to reimburse hundreds of thousands of dollars of attorney fees and costs if it lost the appeal."

Mary Doe became alarmed, "You mean there could be a whole new lawsuit after the jury finds in our favor?"

Sammie had been right. This Doe was frightened.

"Mary, we talked about what was involved with an appeal. The defendants have an automatic right to appeal once and put up a bond during the appeal. American would make the bond for some amount more than judgment. We'd earn interest at 10%."

"How long will the appeal last?"

"Depends on the judges you draw and their dockets. Some panels work harder than others. There's a briefing schedule that takes about a hundred and twenty days. Then there's a hearing, and then we wait for a decision. That's when we wait, and sometimes we wait, and wait. Some judges should leave the bench. When they're assigned to write a decision, write the damn decision."

The firm had two cases that were stuck in the Court of Appeals, and both decisions had been assigned to Judge Jackson. I took the lengthy delay personally.

I identified several potential appealable issues, some that already existed, and others that would arise during the trial. "During the course of the trial, we will be constantly reevaluating where we think the jury stands. If we believe that we are winning the case, we will be reluctant to create appealable issues. In other words, if we are winning, we will get more conservative in what questions we might ask and what documents we might introduce into evidence."

Swann followed every word, but the Does were scared shitless. Mid–sentence I realized my mistake. Too much information at one time. The Does were overwhelmed. My pre-meeting had backfired.

The two clients' heads were spinning. No one had explained the appeal process in this much detail before, and it was a complex and lengthy course. I could see the concern on their faces. I insisted,

"Mediation is our best alternative. It's an informal process where the parties are thrown together with an experienced judge or lawyer who tries to bring the parties to settlement. The parties have agreed to Judge Sanford as our mediator. He served as a trial judge for sixteen years and served on the Court of Appeals for eight years. He retired last year, and he was selected because all of the parties believe he will be fair and reasonable."

Well, Judge Howard ordered us to mediation!

"I'm not sure mediation is the right move," said Lizzy Swann. "You gave the other side our mediation statement, we might have been better off ambushing them at trial. There's no guarantee mediation is going to work."

Jane Doe asked, "Can Sanford force a settlement, so we can avoid a trial?"

"No, he can twist arms, point out weaknesses with your case, and warn the parties about the risk of a trial, but he can't force anything."

At ten o'clock, Davis and Morty joined the group. Morty assumed control of the meeting. "Good morning, ladies. You've read our mediation statement, and Sammie has explained the process to you. Do you have any questions for me?"

Lizzy raised her hand.

Morty laughed and said, "You don't have to raise your hand, Lizzy."

"What do you put our percentage that we can settle this case at mediation?"

"Lizzy, this case will settle before trial. It may not settle at mediation. Just remember the closer we get to trial, the more nervous the defendants will get. This has been and continues to be a very expensive process. Sammie, how much has the firm advanced in expenses?"

"About $98,000."

The women were shocked by the dollar amount.

"As you can see, this firm is committed to this case. Sammie, how many hours do you think the three of us have in these cases?"

"About 1000 hours."

Morty smiled. It was a warm, inviting smile. He'd relied on it for more than fifty years with clients. Some clients trusted him with their lives, others with their fortunes, and then others with their legacies.

"We're on the same team. Steine & Davis is betting on you."

Morty explained the recent decision by Judge Wise in the insurance company case. "A good lawyer can argue either side of this appeal, and I'm a good lawyer. It seems dishonest to provide insurance coverage for intentional wrongful conduct. Some bad lawyer got fired over that one. They already have a new homeowner's policy. Carmichael and Oz will get their attorney fees and expenses reimbursed unless the Court of Appeals reverses. From our point of view, this is a really good thing, an additional deep pocket with $2,000,000 of coverage. We already knew Carmichael had assets, but Oz's financials didn't reflect much."

I reminded the women that Steine & Davis had accepted their cases on a one-third contingency basis.

"What about a trial? Why not let a jury hear our story and decide the case?" Lizzie said with conviction.

"Are you crazy? I don't want to tell my story. I want to get this over with. I want to settle. I'd settle tomorrow," Mary Doe blurted back.

Morty realized he needed to take charge of the situation.
"Hold on. You've lost sight of the purpose of the mediation. You get to tell your story to Judge Sanford. Sandy's a fair man. He'll listen to you, and that will be far less stressful than appearing before a jury in an open courtroom. He'll apply and follow the law. Until Wise's order is overturned by the Court of Appeals, he'll enforce it. The law in our state is unclear. That's the fault of the legislature and/or the Supreme Court, but we took care of that."

I handed each of them the recent legislation passed by the Tennessee legislature that would go into effect January 1, 1998.

"He'll follow Judge Wise's order and lean on American to contribute to a settlement. He knows everyone wants to settle these cases."

"Not everybody," Lizzy insisted.

Morty explained his game plan to the clients. They probably didn't understand every nuance of his strategy, but he made the effort to get them on board. When he finished, Mary Doe remarked, "We trust you to do the right thing."

Morty's simple response was, "I always try to."

CHAPTER FIFTY-SIX

LONG AWAITED MEDIATION

Monday, October 6, 1997

(THIRD PERSON)

The Davis team drove the short distance down Hillsboro Road to Judge Randolph Sanford III's home in Davis' dark blue Bentley with the top down. The judge lived in Franklin, Tennessee, a quaint suburb of Nashville, which hosted a pivotal battle of the Civil War. The residence, during the battle, was used as a Confederate hospital and the family, out of respect for those who died or injured elected not to remove the blood stains from the oak floors. The judge thought the touch gave his home character, and it did.

As they drove to Franklin, Morty complained that the mediation was called for 8:00 a.m. He insisted,

"Everybody needs to relax. I've never been to a mediation where anything productive occurred in the first four hours. Lawyers don't get serious until the afternoon session. I suspect this mediation will not get the cases settled today. We'll be driving back here tomorrow."

He pulled a Cuban from his coat breast pocket, lit it, and started puffing on the cigar. His smoke kept getting in Sammie's eyes in the back seat. She shifted her position to behind the driver and stuck her head out of the car to avoid the smoke, her long blonde hair blowing in the wind. Anything was better than that damn smoke.

Davis scolded the old man, warning him about the fine tan leather upholstery, "Dammit, Morty, be careful with your ashes. This isn't your pickup." Davis was pretty particular about both his cars, both convertibles. He impulsively bought the Bentley and got in serious trouble with his wife and the Vette was a gift from a client, Albert Wilson.

They drove up the tree-lined driveway of 124 Maple Drive they were immediately impressed with the beautiful flower garden which surrounded the front of the house. It had been an Indian summer and the trees still had their leaves and the flowers were still in bloom.

Davis, always attentive, noticed the black Cadillac and black pickup with Arkansas plates off to the side and pointed them out to Morty. Arthur, met them at the front door. He was a tall thin black man, who'd worked for the Sanford family since he was a teenager, more than sixty years. Now in his mid-seventies, he was more of a companion to the judge than a servant, especially since the Judge's wife died three years earlier.

Morty made the introductions,

"Arthur, this is the infamous Ben Davis and his niece, Sammie."

"Hello, Mr. Morty, Mr. Davis, Ms. Davis; it's a pleasure to make your acquaintance. The Judge has been looking forward to today; he misses sitting on the Court of Appeals."

Judge Sanford joined them in the foyer, "Good morning, Morty, Ben. And, who is this lovely young lady?"

Sanford, at age seventy, still had an eye for the ladies. He was immediately struck by Sammie's beauty. Like Arthur, he was taller than Davis, who was six feet two, and Sammie, who was five feet eleven, but at least two inches taller in her heels. Sanford had gray eyes and longish silver hair, well over his collar and his ears. He wore a blue blazer with some type of emblem on the breast pocket, pink dress shirt, no tie. He looked chic and casual at the same time. He spoke with a strong southern accent.

"This is my niece, Sammie, she just passed the Bar, wrote our mediation statement and has been involved with these cases from the beginning."

"Complicated cases. Law's up in the air." Then he addressed Sammie, "So you drafted the mediation statement?"

"The bulk of it. I had some help polishing the document from these two gentlemen."

"Nice job. Easy read and well organized. Troubling case, I'm not sure what a jury will do."

Sammie didn't know whether the Judge was just trying to throw her a curve ball, in his own polite way. She did what she did best with men and smiled.

Sanford was impressed that the young lawyer didn't take the bait.

Morty pointed out, "We noticed the Arkansas plates. I take it those are the boys from American. You might want to have Arthur move their car if you want their presence to remain a secret. Where do you have them stashed?"

Sanford, proud of himself, not realizing his obvious mistake, "I hid them in the pool house. They've got a TV, a fridge, and a pool table. We may never hear from them again. At the very least that should keep the three of them occupied until we're ready for their cooperation. American sent Robert Patterson, an Executive Vice

President and Burton Cox, an in-house attorney to represent the Company along with John Whitefield, its local counsel. Cox is convinced that American can get Wise's order reversed on appeal. I'm not so sure he's not right, but maybe we can change his mind. From what I've read and what Morty's told me, American should listen for economic reasons. Legal arguments may not be the best approach."

No one argued because the law was so unclear, and Wise's order went out on a limb.

"I'm putting your group on the screened-in-porch closest to the insurance people since you already know they're here. Come on and I'll get you all situated, and then I'll get their keys and have Arthur move their car."

Sammie hesitated, "I'd better wait outside for our three clients. I'm sure we can find our way to the porch."

She left the three men standing in the foyer and headed for the front door. The Judge watched her leave more closely than Davis cared for. As the men walked down the hallway Sanford pointed to two heavy oak doors and commented, "That's my study. It's the most comfortable room in the house. I thought I'd put Bucky and Jack Barnes in that room." They continued towards the porch, Davis noticed family portraits adorning both walls. The Sanfords had lived in Franklin for over one hundred-fifty years dating back before the Civil War, and the portraits reflected the length of their line.

The clients arrived, and Sammie escorted them back to the porch where Morty and Davis waiting. There was a warm October breeze with two large wooden ceiling fans cooling things down. As instructed, the clients came appropriately dressed in their Sunday best, no jewelry. The other parties were assigned their designated rooms. Pierce, her client Oz, Tate, Gray, Carmichael and two Covington & Burling associates were assigned the kitchen. There was a circular table with eight chairs. It was close quarters. Arthur placed the law enforcement defendants, a total of thirteen, in the den and brought five folding chairs in to accommodate the size of their group.

Judge Sanford invited the group from the kitchen and the porch into the dining room. Mary Doe took one look at Carmichael and started shaking uncontrollably. Sammie grabbed her hand and squeezed. Mary wanted to run, but Sammie held her even tighter and pulled her into a seat.

Judge Sanford couldn't help but notice the fear on Mary's face; he smiled in return. He began, "Good morning. This is mediation and it is a safe place for all of the parties to be heard. I can't promise we'll settle any of these cases but my expectation is that you will all keep an open mind. The Rules of Civil Procedure and Evidence are relevant but not controlling. For the purposes of this mediation we're playing by my rules, as interpreted by me. Don't worry I've got a good feel for our judicial process, I was a trial judge for twelve years and sat on the Court of Appeals, for two eight years terms. So, for the last thirty years I've watched or reviewed many jury trials. You're here to see if we can settle these cases rather than go to trial. In order to effectively do that we're going to have to talk about the pitfalls of a jury trial, and the strengths and weaknesses of each of your cases.

The Judge paused for effect, and then moved on.

"For example, these lie detector tests of the three plaintiffs performed by Billy Tanner are definitely inadmissible at trial, but for our purposes they carry some weight. Would Mr. Carmichael and Mr. Oz be willing to test their credibility?" Neither Tate nor Gray answered right away, so Carmichael did, "I thought I didn't have to prove anything."

"That's at trial, we're trying to get at the truth and settlement, our goal is different. Mr. Carmichael has filed certain ancillary cases. If I can get those settled, then so much the better, but that is not my primary goal. I'm focused on the cases filed by Ms. Swann and the two Does. If I do my job today, everybody should leave here today a little bit unhappy and not very happy."

A few people at the table laughed.

"I'm not going to waste time having the lawyers make an opening statement. I've read all of the material provided and I've watched the seven videos. Here's how we're going to proceed; the three plaintiffs are going to have up to fifteen minutes each to tell their stories. During these three presentations all of the lawyers are to remain silent. I don't want any objections or distractions. I will not tolerate interference. After the plaintiffs have their say then Mr. Carmichael and Mr. Oz, in that order will make their responses. After the parties have spoken, then each side will present proof through the persons on their witness list, to be examined and then crossed. I will not be permit playing the videos but let me assure you that Judge Howard will allow the jury to see at least six of the seven tapes. Ms. Doe you can expect your husband to have to watch your tape and endure questioning about your infidelity and its impact on your marriage."

Mary got visibly shaken again. Sanford paused again and then turned and said, "Ms. Swann, you filed the first lawsuit, why don't you start us off."

Lizzy Swann spoke with determination for ten minutes. Her description of her pain and suffering was vulnerable and personal.

"I made a mistake. I trusted Roscoe Carmichael, who conspired with Phillip Oz, took my error in judgment, and made it into the worst experience of my life. I'm hoping a trial will give me closure..."

Judge Sanford jumped in, "You want to try the cases?"

"I'm not afraid to go to trial, I've agreed to participate in this mediation out of respect for my lawyers, who think this is the best way to go. I've got confidence that a jury will find the defendants conduct outrageous and unacceptable. These men should go to jail for a long time for what they've done. Money isn't enough, they should die and rot for all I care."

"How many jury trials have you attended?"

"None."

"Ms. Swann you have no idea what a jury will do in this case. The law is unclear and I've lived the law the last thirty years. I'm sure your lawyers have explained how important jury selection will be, particularly in this case. You've got great lawyers representing you, but if the jury pool is weak, made up of old women and men, you're going to lose. Let me ask you, is your mother still alive?"

"Yes sir."

"If your mother wasn't your mother and sat on a jury and watched your video, do you think she'd award hundreds of thousands of dollars?"

"I don't know, and I haven't told her about the lawsuit. I'm too ashamed, but my mother's not going to be sitting on the jury. She lives in Seattle."

"Yes, but somebody's mother will sit on that jury."

Davis had told Lizzy the same thing, maybe coming from the judge it would take some wind out of her sails and her defiance that she wanted to go to trial. The judge persisted,

"Your mother may not get to see the video, but the lawsuit is a matter of public record. Once you go to trial all of the evidence will be a matter of public record. Seattle is still within the continental United States."

Davis thought the Judge was out of line intimating that Lizzy's mother would learn the details of the litigation. He insisted,

"We'd file a motion to seal the videos."

"And that motion may or may not be granted," the Judge remarked.

Mary Doe was so nervous that Jane Doe volunteered to go next. She had multiple intimate moments with Roscoe Carmichael. She admitted that all of her rendezvous with him were in an effort to advance her career. She admitted doing cocaine and excessively drinking during these sessions. She'd had a drinking problem in college and throughout her twenties. For her thirtieth birthday, she went to rehab and had remained clean until the disclosure of her videotape in 1996. She'd been sober for more than six months. She did a good job, despite nerves. Carmichael gave her a hard look and Sammie proudly watched as she gave one right back.

Sanford asked her a few questions ending with, "Thank you, Jane. Do you think you'll keep your real identity a secret during and after the trial?"

"I don't think so, I'm being stalked by a reporter named Krieger. She's not stopping until she gets the whole story."

"She could be a problem. She's been following the story," Davis added.

Sanford pointed out, "I suspect that any settlement would include confidentiality and non-disclosure clauses, but Ms. Krieger isn't going to be a party to that contract, and from what I've seen from her coverage, she's going to be a pain in the ass until she gets her story. You'd better plan on your true identity coming out if we go to trial."

Davis had to agree with the Judge and admitted to himself that the use of an alias was probably a mistake. The probability of disclosure shook the last plaintiff witness, Mary Doe. She wasn't ready, so Sammie asked for a ten-minute break. She dragged Mary to the bathroom. It was a small powder room, and it was crowded with just the two of them. Sammie turned on the water and grabbed a fancy hand towel, ran it under the water, and patted it on Mary's forehead.

"I need you to pull it together. The defense is evaluating how a jury will assess you. You need to be able to communicate your story to the jury. If they think you can't do that, then we're going to trial and probably appeal. That will mean years of litigation. Just do the best you can. Tell the truth, and remember how you felt the first time you watched your video. Let Judge Sanford feel your pain."

She sat her down, which was a good thing because she couldn't remain standing, her legs were so shaky and too unstable.

"When I met Roscoe Carmichael, I was going through a difficult time in my life. My husband, David, and I viewed things differently. He wanted me to be a wife and mother, and I wanted to be on stage. I thought I could do all three roles. I'd performed in community theater to rave reviews. I sang in the church choir. It wasn't enough for me, and when Carmichael invited me up to his office to sing for him and possibly sign a contract, I forgot about what was important in my life. I've apologized for my lapse in judgment to my husband. There have been serious consequences for my actions. We had to leave my husband's hometown. David lost his tenure with his employer. He's had to start over as a commissioned salesman, rather than manager of a box retailer store, with the prospect of becoming a district manager. David agreed to change our lives to let me scratch my itch. We've compromised. David gave me two years to pursue my singing. I may succeed or I may fail, but at least he gave me the opportunity to succeed."

Mary did the best of the three of Davis's clients. When describing the video's, she twice broke down. She wasn't play acting, the emotion was genuine. Sanford was softened by her story. Davis was convinced that he'd made the right decision by moving to consolidate the cases. There was strength in numbers and it helped that the judge heard three similar but distinct stories.

Sanford turned to Roscoe Carmichael, "You've got serious drug charges to address. Let me assure you it's in your best interest get all of these civil cases out of the way. Mr. Carmichael, you'll be pretty busy over the next few years defending those criminal charges and a probable appeal. From what I've read, you're eventually looking at a jail cell. The question is, for how long. You've also filed several other lawsuits which has tried to change the focus of the issue. The suing of law enforcement and DA's office was an effective delay tactic, but these suits could backfire in these privacy action. In fact, I think it's possible that a jury might award punitive damages against you."

Carmichael's neck bowed,

"You sound like you're a little biased against me. You know I moved for judge Howard to recuse himself because he was biased."

"You're a drug dealer and a sex fiend, do you really think you'll have a lot of respectable persons as friends in the courtroom?"

"Alleged drug dealer and sex fiend. The drug charges have nothing to do with these lawsuits and the sex was consensual."

Swann started laughing, but no one else joined in.

"My lawyers are going to get that farmhouse warrant thrown out. It's overly broad and won't hold up. The cash and airplane were confiscated on another parcel I owned and were outside the warrant."

The Judge pressed on, "Let's hear what you have to say about these cases, Mr. Carmichael."

Carmichael dove right into his tale. He emphasized that the sex was consensual and that the tapes proved that each woman had a good time.

"There are no regrets on those tapes. There was a camera right in the open. Who do you think that Lizzy Swann is dancing for? Who did she do that routine on the pole for? I relied on the advice of my lawyer, Bucky Lee. He said the tapes would protect me from date rape, and I was worried about that because of that lying sixteen-year-old who cost me a year of my life."

Sanford listened, but he didn't indicate he believed Carmichael. From his experience in the courtroom he could tell a liar.

"I think you've got a credibility problem, sir. No one's going to believe you. A jury is going to award a judge, the amount is uncertain."

He thought it important to point out, "If the jury awards punitive damages, Wise's order is silent on that issue. I sat on the Court of Appeals. It isn't going to find homeowners coverage for punitive damages. You might have some insurance coverage during mediation but it could be completely lost if punitive damages are awarded. I think all parties should keep that in mind. Mr. Davis you could do such a good job that you lose insurance dollars and that would hurt everybody."

Carmichael rambled on for another ten minutes and then shut up.

Oz was up last. He admitted he had a serious sexual problem because he enjoyed watching others having sex, but that he'd sought help. "I'm still seeing a therapist once a week. I'm still involved in photography but I'm using it as a positive outlet."

He admitted that it was Carmichael's idea to build the secret room, he claimed on advice of counsel, Bucky Lee. Oz admitted he never spoke directly to Lee and that all of his information's came from Carmichael. He admitted that his defense relied upon the accuracy of Carmichael's testimony.

"You must want these cases settled."

"Yes, sir."

"Your wife hasn't been deposed yet?" Sanford turned to Morty, "She'll be deposed and subpoenaed at trial, right?"

"Absolutely."

Trying to catch Oz off guard Sanford asked, "Where were you on July 3rd, 1997, at about 9:00 p.m.?"

"Home."

"Who else was there?"

"My wife, probably asleep. She goes to bed early."

The judge asked, "I guess if this mediation doesn't work out, she'll be asked about that night? Mr. Davis will you be taking Mrs. Oz's deposition if you have to go to trial?"

"Absolutely."

Oz didn't have much more to say after that comment. It was clear that he really wanted to settle.

It was about 10:30 a.m., so the judge suggested, "I think it's time for us to breakdown into our respective groups and let me visit with you. Arthur, will be bringing you a light lunch. Eat up, and then we'll begin the second stage of our mediation, where we interview of some of the critical witnesses. This is the proof you're each going to rely upon at trial. I'm in the best position to judge their credibility and demeanor. I've read the summary of their testimony in the mediation statement. Now were going to see how well each witness holds up. Somebody's lying. I can only determine who by hearing them testify in person. While you're eating, I'm serving lunch in the other rooms, and I'd better circulate and give them an update of where we are. I'm sure many of the lawyers are getting impatient."

With that said, Judge Sanford left the room and a platter of sandwiches was delivered by Arthur. The choices were turkey, roast beef, tuna, or pimento cheese on rye, wheat or white bread. There were sides of potato salad, coleslaw, the yellow vinegar type or potato chips. A similar assortment was served to every set of guests in every room, including the insurance people in the pool house. Everybody who was excluded from the dining room was bored and hungry and started eating.

CHAPTER FIFTY-SEVEN

CIRCLING THE WAGONS

Monday, October 6, 1997

Same day

(THIRD PERSON)

The judge left the parties and started off in the den with the law enforcement defendants, who were still eating. He encouraged them to continue as he said, "Carmichael's case against you has no merit. I hope to get your case dismissed as part of a global settlement. If I fail, I'm confident that your trial judge will dismiss your case and that it will never get to a jury. If for some reason it did, a reasonable jury would conclude that you boys were just doing your jobs. The fact that Carmichael sued you will work against him."

The Metro lawyer and TBI lawyer had been telling their clients basically the same thing, but it carried more weight coming from the judge. The room got more relaxed. The judge threw down two decks of cards, opened a drawer, produced a rack of chips, and suggested a friendly poker game while they waited.

"I've got a lot of work to do, and it won't involve talking to you, so sit back, play a little cards or watch television, because this is going to take a while, maybe days. I anticipate needing you at the end of this process."

His next stop was the pool house.

John Whitefield was lining up a bank shot and threw down his stick on the table when the judge walked in. "Hello Judge, where are we?"

"I've heard from the five primary parties. The three women's story vary slightly but their all believable and will be liked by most jurors. I suspect Steine & Davis will try to keep older women off the jury because of the shock value of the tapes. Your insureds; Carmichael is a liar, and Oz is a sick fool. A jury isn't going to like them. What I can't tell you is how much a jury will award Davis' clients. It could vary from client to client. It will certainly vary from jury to jury. Who's on the jury will determine the dollar amount of the verdict, and nobody can predict who's going to be in the jury pool."

Robert Patterson spoke up, directing his question to Sanford, "Do you think Judge Wise's order will hold up on appeal?"

The judge had given that question much thought.

"It's a case of first impressions. No one knows the answer. If I were on the court, I'd rule that there shouldn't be insurance coverage for intentional torts, and I certainly would hold no insurance coverage for punitive damages. I hope you guys fired the clown who drafted that homeowner's policy."

Embarrassed, Robert Patterson answered, "Best we can tell, our last four homeowners policies going back to 1983 didn't make any distinction between negligence and intentional conduct. It just never came up. Carmichael and Oz got creative, I guess."

Judge Sanford got serious, "Well, if Judge Wise is right, you'll be responsible for not only compensatory damages up to $1,000,000 for each of the defendants, but the cost of defense, including reasonable attorney fees. That's hundreds of thousands of dollars, and if you file an appeal, hundreds of thousands more for the appeal.

In a worst-case scenario, they try the case, the plaintiffs win, the plaintiffs win the appeal, and your company is still held responsible for the judgment and cost of defense. That could really happen. This case has many legitimate issues for appeal. There could even be a mistrial or a retrial and your company could be responsible not only for your own defense costs but Carmichael and Oz's as well."

Whitefield didn't like where this conversation was going, "Judge, what are you asking for?"

"I need to start building a war chest to settle these cases. I figure you really don't want to file an appeal and get an answer from the Court of Appeals as to whether your company is liable for intentional torts under those old contracts. If you lose the appeal, there'd be a six-year period of exposure of future suits under the old homeowner's policy. That could get really expensive. You might have other insured's who commit intentional torts who seek coverage under the precedent of this case."

Roberts broke the ice, "We'll contribute two fifty for Carmichael and two fifty for Oz. That's half a million. That's a lot of money for a case we should win on appeal."

Sanford sensed weakness and started pushing, "What about attorney fees and costs?"

"My company is paying Whitefield $400 an hour. We've got our own attorney fees and costs."

The judge turned to Whitefield and in a knowing voice said, "John, you know American should settle these cases. It's going to have to reimburse Carmichael and Oz for their 'reasonable attorney fees and costs,' whatever that is. I suggest it's a percentage of actual attorney fees and costs incurred. You know, generally, the hours each side has put into this case. Pierce's time is probably closer to reasonable than Covington & Burling. We can use Steine & Davis' time as a guide, but American has to reimburse the defendants some amount for attorney fees and costs."

Roberts in an unhappy voice said, "We'll reimburse them $100,000 each. That makes our total contribution $700,000. That should fill up your war chest."

Judge Sanford knew he'd be back for higher dollar amount but Robert's was right, it was a very good start. This meeting had served its purpose. American had opened its wallet and was contributing toward settlement. He was pretty pleased with himself.

The last stop was his study to talk to Bucky Lee and Jack Barnes. They'd finished their lunch and were anxious for a progress report.

"It's going well, but I don't know where you fit into the process. Are you a victim, or are you a hero? I'm worried about these Board charges. I'm pretty sure you've lost your malpractice coverage. You're exposed if Carmichael gets a judgment against you. Juries don't like lawyers, yet, a jury isn't going to like Carmichael. I need you to sit tight while I interview the witnesses who would testify at trial. I'll be back."

And with that said, he was out the door, returning to the dining room.

As he walked into the room, he announced, "Let the fun begin."

CHAPTER FIFTY-EIGHT

THE INTERVIEWS

Monday, October 6, 1997

(Same day)

(THIRD PERSON)

Sanford decided to begin the interview process with the four expert witnesses. He'd read their reports on each woman, so he knew the diagnoses and treatment plan prior to the interview. Only the Judge could ask questions, which frustrated the lawyers, especially Davis.

"Ms. Davis, what would you consider the greatest weakness of the testimony of both of the plaintiffs expert witnesses?"

Sammie didn't like being put on the spot but since she was there, she sure as hell wanted to give a good answer. She wanted to support her clients, but the question called for her to identify a weakness. Her worst nightmare. She needed to be honest, but not scare Mary Doe any more than she already was.

"Our experts maybe didn't sufficiently distinguish between the differences of our clients' trauma. We were retained by our clients in quick succession. In a perfect world they would each have independent professionals to drive home to the jury their emotional distress. We had to pull the Doe cases together so quickly, and Mary's experts only had a short time to evaluate her, but it was at least five times longer than Dr. Resnick did, and the experts who treated Lizzy Swann. It would have been better if each client had their own independent experts. Jane Doe at least will have the separate testimony of her rehab counselor. I'd also admit that their expert, Dr. Resnick is far more experienced and polished. That may or may not be a good thing, depending on the jury."

Sanford was impressed. It was a good answer. Most lawyers would have been reluctant to admit a weakness in their case particularly in front of the other side and their clients. Her answer was accurate, Resnick was far more polished.

According to Dr. Resnick, "Lizzy Swann has no permanent damage. In fact, she's a stronger person today then before the event. He reports that her only problem is anger, that will dissipate with time. He testified that "Ms. Swann has an unhealthy desire for revenge, more than money. She wishes bodily harm to both Carmichael and Oz."

Resnick painted a picture of an angry woman who the jury wasn't going to like. He opined that, "Mary Doe has saved her marriage, which had problems before she met Carmichael and has moved forward with her life. I believe that a large payment for her infidelity would cause irrevocable harm to her marriage. The money will be a constant reminder to her husband David of these traumatic events and it will ruin their relationship."

He testified that Mary Doe would be unable to face a jury in the courtroom. "She's petrified of going to trial."

The only plaintiff that Resnick believed had any serious permanent damage as a result of her contact with the defendants was Jane Doe. Resnick claimed that with psychiatric care, Jane Doe would improve and that's where funds should be directed. He admitted that "Jane's case has the greatest value before a jury because she was the most vulnerable of the three, as a recovering alcoholic. She at least has an excuse for her behavior and is working hard to correct her problem. The other two women were just greedy and a jury could find they got what they deserved."

The three plaintiffs' experts seemed out of place. None of them had testified at a trial nor had any of them been involved in a mediation. The process was strange and uncomfortable and that affected their credibility.

Sanford spent the next hour with Ingram, Watson, and Strong. He didn't need a lot of time. He'd reviewed their agreements and Ingram's perjury during her deposition.

Sanford came to the obvious conclusion, "Mr. Carmichael, those three women are liars, plain and simple. The jury's not going to believe them. Mr. or Ms. Davis are going to tear them apart before the jury and will convince the jury that you bought them off, because you did. I learned a long time ago, Mr. Carmichael, that the cover up is always worse than the wrongful act and these ladies' testimony proves your cover up. This proof is going to cost you money. I don't know how much, but it will."

Carmichael got out of his chair. "I don't know who you think you are old man..."

Sanford snapped back, "I'm the experienced judge who your lawyers hired to give his honest opinions. You just don't like what I'm saying. That might mean you'd better be prepared to get your check book out."

Tate decided he'd better intervene, "Judge, the testimony of Ingram, Watson, and Strong are consistent and a jury..."

"Mr. Tate, we don't know each other, but you need to get honest with your client. He's exposed at trial, and insurance coverage is currently available in mediation and may not be available after an appeal."

Tate snapped back, "You've yet to address our strongest argument, advice of counsel. It's our position that all of the liability should fall on Bucky Lee."

Sanford figured it was time to tone down the confrontation. "It's 5:00 p.m., let's take an early dinner break. Arthur's made his famous shrimp gumbo and corn bread. After we eat, I'll bring Mr. Lee and Mr. Barnes in and we'll hear Bucky's version of the facts."

The Davis team and clients retired to the porch where Arthur was waiting with the hot soup and corn bread. He'd already serviced the other parties and left to take care of the defendants and their counsel in the kitchen. Davis wanted to but didn't get seconds.

CHAPTER FIFTY-NINE

THE CASE GETS MORE COMPLICATED

MONDAY, OCTOBER 6, 1997

(Same Day)

(THIRD PERSON)

When they reconvened in the dining room, present were the parties and their counsel, Jack Barnes and Bucky Lee. Sanford directed Carmichael to recount when Lee gave him the legal advice to videotape women sex partners.

Lee couldn't restrain himself, "You're a lying bastard. I never told you to do any such thing. You're still mad about my refusal to fee split and my unwillingness to get you out of jail for your drug arrest. I haven't been your lawyer for years. You fired me, and I terminated you as a client."

Carmichael got out of his chair again and lunged across the table at Bucky. Barnes intercepted him and pushed him back.

Sanford screamed, "Everybody get the hell back in your seats. This isn't going to get physical. We're going to settle this with money or a trial, not with violence."

You could feel the tension in the room. It didn't seem like the cases were moving toward settlement. Sanford knew that before the parties could come together, they had to address the issues that separated them.

"Mr. Lee, tell us about your conversation with Mr. Carmichael at Sperry's and the reason you decided to go to see the DA."

Bucky spoke for twenty minutes uninterrupted. At the end, his voice was strained when he talked about how difficult his decision was to turn Carmichael in to the DA.

Carmichael blurted out, "Bullshit, a jury's going to find you violated your oath as an attorney and you're going to be held liable for all of this and there will be no insurance. You'll be holding the bag."

Bucky turned red and responded, "Shut the hell up, Roscoe. I don't have to listen to you. This is a waste of time."

Judge Randolph "Sandy" Sanford III strongly took issue with Bucky Lee, "Dammit, Bucky, act like a lawyer. This is my home and my mediation. So, sit there and shut up, and just maybe I'll get you out of this jam. Arguing with this fool isn't going to solve anything. Now, I'm going to bring General Tory and his counsel into these discussions. I want everyone to remain silent. I don't want anyone to say anything unless I ask them a question. I've been asked to try to get these three privacy cases settled. Bucky you're a witness in those cases. Mr. Carmichael you're a defendant, and it's in your best interest to get those cases off your plate in light of each of your other problems."

Johnson Tory, Detective Sanders, Agent Pyle, the other law enforcement officers and their lawyers entered the room. There weren't enough seats at the table. The judge brought in more chairs. Bucky, Barnes, and the three plaintiffs sat in opposite corners of the room. Pyle sat at the head of the table and described the drug arrest and then Sanders described the search of the Music Row office and discovery of the secret room and the tapes.

When it was Tory's turn, he said, "When they found the hidden room and reported the bookcase of tapes, I knew what they'd found."

Tory described his Sunday park bench meeting with Bucky and how reluctant he was to reveal Carmichael's identity.

"Did the tapes show what you thought they would?"

"No. Bucky told me Carmichael had videotaped women in the bathroom. I assumed either on the toilet or showering. There was a two-way mirror in the bathroom but no footage of any of the women in the bathroom. Instead the tapes showed Carmichael having consensual sex with unsuspecting females, filmed by a cameraman."

"How did you know there was a cameraman?"

"From the camera work, and Mr. Carmichael gave up Mr. Oz fairly quickly."

"How did you know the women were unsuspecting?"

"From the tapes themselves and the testimony of the plaintiffs."

"What about the tapes indicates to you that the women didn't know they were being taped?"

"You could see Carmichael making hand signals to the cameraman behind the women's backs."

"What about the testimonies of Ingram, Watson, and Strong?"

"I discount their testimony as untruthful. That's what a jury will also do; in my opinion."

"That's your opinion," blurted Carmichael.

"Quiet, sir. I didn't call on you. I'm trying to help you."

"General, how much time is Mr. Carmichael looking at for his drug charges?"

"Worst case scenario for the State is we caught the defendant with 26 grams at the townhouse, less than an ounce, a Class C felony. Under the sentencing guidelines, between ten and twenty years."

Carmichael couldn't help himself, "Peck's already held the farmhouse warrant defective, the recording has been held inadmissible, and you've lost your key witness. My lawyers will get the drug charges thrown out."

The judge clarified, "Are you willing to bet most of the rest of your life on that possibility?"

Carmichael was still counting on his inside men to come up with some scheme to get Judge Peck to dismiss the charges.
Carmichael went silent. So, Sanford spoke, "His videotaping wasn't a crime, was it?"

Sammie answered, "No, but after January 1st it will be. Morty got the legislation pushed through."

Carmichael asked, "What will be the penalty if convicted?"

"From one to five years, depending on circumstances."

"Ms. Davis, would you please escort your clients back to the porch. If you'd like to return, you may or you can remain with your clients, whichever you deem most appropriate."

Sammie knew that the team would be well represented by her uncle and Morty, and someone needed to babysit the clients.

"My place is with my clients. I'm sure my uncle and Mr. Steine will keep us well informed."

She and the clients left the room, followed by Lee, Barnes, Detective Sanders, Agent Pyle and the other law enforcement personnel. All that remained were the defendants and their lawyers, Morty, Davis Tory, his lawyer and the judge.

Sanford turned to Tory's lawyer, "You can sit here, but this has nothing to do with you or your case but, since your client has remained I'll let you sit here and listen. Your case isn't going to settle today, it's going to be decided by a judge or jury. "

Confusion fell over the room, and Sanford opened the door and Tom Miller of A-1 Amusement walked in.

"Mr. Miller, thank you for coming. Please sit down. Is your grandson Pinky waiting outside?"

"Yes, sir. He's pretty scared. I've told him there's nothing to be scared of, just tell the truth, but he's acting weird."

"Tell us what happened on July 3rd of this year."

Miller described in detail the events of that night.

"Your grandson Pinky was there that night?"

"Yes."

"So was your son?"

"Yes, Derek."

"He's Pinky's father?"

"No, I have a deceased son, Darrell. He's Pinky's father."

"When did he die?"

"About fifteen years ago when Pinky was just a baby. I raised him."

"How did Darrell die?"

Miller got agitated.

"What the hell is this about? Look, there was a mechanical problem, and some people got hurt. I'm really sorry, I have insurance..."

Sanford in a calm voice tried to get Miller to answer his question.

"Please. Mr. Miller, it's important. Answer my question. How did Darrell die?"

"He came back from Vietnam messed up, hooked on drugs. He couldn't shake the habit. and a few years later, he died of a drug overdose."

"Where'd Darrell go to high school?"

"Ashland City High School."

"Your son played football with Mr. Carmichael and Mr. Oz, didn't he?"

"Yes, they were state champions together. They were childhood friends. I never liked Roscoe Carmichael. Phillip took over his father's pharmacy in Ashland City. We live in Nashville. I left Ashland City after Darrell died, and Pinky's mother and I told him a fairy tale about his father."

"When was the last time you spoke with Mr. Carmichael?"

"At Darrell's funeral."

"What about Mr. Oz?"

"Same."

"Does Pinky know either Mr. Carmichael or Mr. Oz?"

"I don't think so, but you can ask him. He's right outside."

Pinky walked in, took one look at Carmichael and Oz and his facial expression gave it away. He sat next to his grandfather, and Sanford put the 1970 Ashland City yearbook in front of him.

"That's your daddy in high school, isn't it?"

"I didn't know my daddy, but I've been told he played football for the high school. Yes, sir."

"He played football with Mr. Carmichael and Mr. Oz?"

Sanford pointed to the pictures of Carmichael and Oz in the book. Pinky didn't answer. He stared at the book.

Sanford persisted, "You know these men. You've been communicating with them over the last year?"

No answer.

"Mr. Oz was at Hillwood Country Club on July 3rd?"

Pierce interrupted, "What's the purpose of this?"

The judge answered the question.

"Your client needs to realize that Mr. Carmichael isn't the only one facing serious criminal charges. What would you say, General?"

Tory smiled and looking at Oz answered, "There are several possibilities; attempted third degree murder, or aggravated battery, both Class C Felonies, at least ten years in prison, possibly twenty."

Pinky, who'd been silent, blurted out, "I'm taking the Fifth. I'm not answering any more questions."

Tom Miller turned on his grandson, "You idiot, what have you done?"

Nothing more had to be said. It was obvious to everyone in the room. The defendants had used their longtime childhood friendship with the boy's father to somehow convince Pinky to cooperate with them to get the boy to manipulate the mechanics. That effort caused the mayhem on the 3rd injuring Davis' guests in a twisted attempt to send a message to back off.

Liza was right. Davis would never hear the end of it.

His stubborn dedication to his clients and to the law had caused an incredible amount of pain and suffering to friends and associates. He owed them more than an apology.

Sanford thanked the Miller's and told them they'd be hearing from the DA's office. Tom Miller dragged Pinky out of the room by the scruff of his neck. Sanford accompanied General Tory and his lawyer to the den and told the other law enforcement defendants they could go home. The judge expressed confidence that they'd be dismissed as defendants before trial, not to worry and thanked them for coming.

Once back in the dining room, Judge Sanford turned to the remaining group and said, "It's time to start talking money. Mr. Carmichael, you can keep your lawsuits against the law enforcement personnel and Bucky Lee and good luck to you. They're on your dime. I've convinced American Insurance to pay five hundred thousand toward judgment of its two million of coverage and a total of two hundred thousand for attorney fees and costs to Ms. Pierce and Mr. Carmichael's lawyers."

Tate jumped in, "Five hundred thousand should settle the cases."

Davis actually laughed, "You think so! Your clients should walk away from these suits free and clear, and let insurance pick up the tab. You're out of your mind Tate. Remember, I've got your client's financials. I know his net worth. He's going to pay more than Oz because he's the one who betrayed my clients."

Tate shot back, "This is a negotiation, make a counter offer."

"A total settlement of $2,200,000 to my clients. Seven hundred thousand contributed by American, one million by Carmichael and a half million by Oz. Morty and I are going back to the porch to be with our clients. It's 7:30p.m., I'm going to recount what's happened to my clients. It's been a long day. We can come back at 9:00 a.m. tomorrow if you'd like to continue these negotiations."

At 8:00 p.m. Davis, Morty, Sammie, and their clients walked past the dining room, and out the door.

Davis remarked, "Hope to see you tomorrow."

CHAPTER SIXTY

A NEW DAY, A NEW OPPORTUNITY

Tuesday, October 7, 1997

(THIRD PERSON)

The next morning the car ride to Franklin seemed longer than the day before, probably because the plan was set in progress and there was nothing left to discuss. The ball was in the defendants' court and they needed to sit tight, Carmichael and Oz would start sweetening the pot. Morty assured his fellow travelers that the defendants would show up and would be bringing their checkbooks. His game plan was working.

The Bentley pulled up the tree-lined driveway and they were met at the front door by Arthur, who ushered them into the dining room. The American Insurance people were already drinking coffee and eating donuts. Davis joined right in. Whitefield introduced Robert Patterson and the American in-house lawyer, Burton Cox. Arthur indicated that the Judge would be down momentarily. The next to arrive were the three plaintiffs, separately.

Judge Sanford entered the room and greeted the group. He was casually dressed in a gray turtleneck and a camel's hair sports coat.

He noted that the defense team was missing, "I hope they're coming. It won't be much of a mediation without them."

As the words left his mouth, the front door opened, and the defendant parade came in. Very cool greetings were exchanged in the very awkward situation. The parties were about to talk money. Up until now, the focus had been on posturing. The Judge broke the tension.

"Let's divide up and see if we can get these cases settled. John, take the American team to the pool house. Arthur will bring your group some hot coffee and donuts. I'll come back and see you when the negotiations start rolling. Why don't the defendants remain here in the dining room, and the plaintiffs go across the hall to my study. That way I won't have to walk too far."

Everyone dispersed to their respective positions. The judge remained with the defendants, and once the others were gone, he addressed the defense counsel, "I've got each of your clients a $250,000 head start from American. That could very well disappear on appeal. I also convinced Whitefield's client to pay each defendant $100,000 for legal fees and costs. That could be used to clear up any balances owed to lawyers. That could also disappear after an appeal. Mr. Tate, how much is your client willing to add to the settlement?"

"$50,000. That's the same amount that was paid to Strong, Ingram and Watson. That's a total settlement with American payment of $450,0000, or $150,000 for each plaintiff."

Sanford didn't hide his disappointment. "I'm obliged to take all offers made, but that's a very disappointing offer. Remember, Davis has your client's financials. What about you, Ms. Pierce?"

"My client isn't going to pay more or even the same amount as Mr. Carmichael. I've seen both defendants' financials, my client will contribute $25,000 each or $75,000 total."

The judge protested, "You've got to be kidding. You're both willing to risk losing the insurance money on appeal. I thought you'd at least match American's offer. That would at least get us to a $1,000,000, halfway to Davis' demand. That would be a reasonable offer for me to take to Steine & Davis."

Carmichael decided he wasn't going to sit quietly. It was his money the Judge was spending. "This is all Bucky Lee's fault. He should be paying these plaintiffs."

Sanford was ready with his response, "You'll still have your lawsuit against Lee. If you're telling the truth, then you should be able to convince a jury to grant you a judgment in the amount of the settlement paid these women and possibly paid Watson, Ingram, and Strong, against Lee. This settlement and how much you pay your attorneys will constitute your recoverable damages. The more you pay the plaintiffs, the more you should collect from Lee."

Tate confirmed the theory of what the Judge described. Tate added, "Recovery would depend on whether the jury believed you or Lee."

"They'll believe me. I'm sure of it. In light of my payments to the other women, there is a logic to my $150,000 offer."

Oz had been quieted the entire morning. He hadn't said a word. Pinky's performance the day before had shaken him because he realized that the young man was close to giving him up. Oz was petrified of the thought of serving ten years in prison. He wasn't as tough as he looked. Susan would file for divorce. Nobody came in the pharmacy anymore. Prison might be a relief.

Oz, to date had depleted his savings by $109,675 in attorney fees and costs and owed another $138,000 to Pierce in fees and advanced costs. The American offer of $100,000 would help clean up Pierce's outstanding bill. "If you paid Davis's client $750,000. His clients together would receive a total of a million dollars."

Pierce remained quiet, but that $100,000 was on her mind too. Oz wanted these lawsuits over with, and he spoke, "I produced my financials, Davis knows my net worth. My wife is on the verge of divorcing me. She's entitled to half my net worth. I might be able to scrape together $100,000, for a total payment of $350,000."

Again, Sanford was disappointed, but he had an obligation to take these offers to the plaintiffs. Judge Sanford presented the Carmichael/American offer of $450,000 and the Oz/American offer of $350,000.

Davis spoke first and thanked him for his effort and indicated, "We'd need some time to discuss the offers and craft a counter..."

Without warning, Mary blurted out, "Let's take it and get this over with. I've had enough."

It got really quiet in the room. Sanford could tell that Mary Doe had deviated from the game plan. The clients had agreed among themselves that when approached with an offer, there would be no reaction. They'd speak with a single voice, and that voice would be Davis'. He'd been very clear, and Mary's outburst shocked some and pissed off others. The reaction was obvious. Sanford thought it best to excuse himself. As he walked down the hall, he heard Lizzy Swann's raised voice. He suspected others in the house heard it as well.

Swann shouted, "We had a plan. All you had to do was keep your big mouth shut. Our lawyers had a strategy to get us a lot more money, but the Judge needed to think we had a united front. You can't break ranks like that. It hurts us all."

Mary between tears argued, "$267,000 each is a lot of money. I'm not as greedy as you are, Lizzy."

Davis broke in. It wasn't in anyone's best interest for his clients to be at each other's throat.

"Mary, remember, Steine & Davis is entitled to a one-third fee of the gross settlement or $83,333, and you'd be responsible to reimburse the firm one- third of the advanced expenses, about $35,000 each. So, your net recovery of $267,000, after expenses and our one-third fee would only be about half that dollar amount."

Mary sat there with everyone staring at her, "That's still a lot of money."

It was Jane's turn to speak up, "I didn't go through a year of hell for $133,000. I'm entitled to more. I'd rather take my chances with a jury."

"Me too," added Lizzy.

Things were falling apart, and Morty had to take control, "First, I don't think the defendants will settle at mediation with one of you but not all of you. I could inquire, but I don't recommend we do so. Second, we don't have to settle for the same dollar amounts. You are each individual and your damages are distinct, so if Mary wants to settle for a lesser amount, she can, although I strongly discourage such a strategy. I still believe a common front is our best course of action. This mediation is the best opportunity to compensate you for your loss, yet not put you through the trauma of a trial. Please trust me and follow my lead, we've developed a game plan."

Mary Doe reluctantly returned to the fold. "Mr. Davis you're in charge. I'll let you handle our side of the mediation."

Morty released a sigh of relief. He had a real conflict of interest brewing, which he hoped would remain dormant. He told them, "We need to structure a new offer. Oz is broke and probably headed for a divorce. His pharmacy business is failing. The Miller kid can implicate him in a serious crime. The deepest individual pocket is Carmichael, who is the real bad actor anyway."

Morty paused for effect. He was about to reveal his strategy.

"I say we ask American to pony up another $150,000 in the Oz case for a total of $400,000 and have Oz individually contribute another $200,000, for an Oz gross total settlement of $600,000. That would isolate Carmichael. That would be a gross settlement of $200,000 for each of you. You'd clear roughly $100,000 each and still have an opportunity to get more from Carmichael, which would force him to counter. I'll need to talk with Whitefield and his client and make sure they're on board with separate settlements."

Morty and Davis visited the men in the pool house. At first, they objected to the idea of settling with Oz by increasing American's offer from $250,000 to $400,000 and allowing Davis to continue to negotiate with Carmichael. Davis explained that the total settlement in Oz would be for $600,000.

Patterson asked, "What if you don't settle with Carmichael and then we still have to go to trial and an appeal?"

Morty insisted, "You won't! Carmichael will settle, maybe not today, but before the February 3rd trial. I promise if you follow our game plan and it fails then your maximum exposure in the event of a Carmichael trial will be your current offer of $250,000 and $100,000 in fees, and not a penny more, no matter what the judgment or the settlement reached. You have nothing to lose as far as my clients are concerned. Your only risk is increased attorney fees to Covington & Burling which American would have whether you follow my plan or not. The attorney fees for Pierce would end today."

Patterson asked Whitefield, "What do you think, John?"

"Morty Steine and Ben Davis' reputations are spotless. They're known as truthful players. We'd hate to go to court and set a precedent that haunts us for six years. I'd follow his plan."

Davis delivered to Judge Sanford his counter offers to American and Oz.

"We're not making any counter to Carmichael's offer of $450,000. It's rejected. Please don't let Tate, Gray, and Carmichael know that we're continuing to talk with American and Oz. We plan on stonewalling them for a while."

Judge Sanford joined the defense team in the dining room and asked Pierce and Oz, "Will you join me in the den? I'd like to meet with you in private."

When the door to the den closed, sitting in one of the easy chairs was General Johnson Tory. Greetings were exchanged, and the Judge got right to the point.

"The police have been questioning Pinky Miller all night. The kid hasn't cracked. He just keeps repeating over and over his rights under the Fifth Amendment not to incriminate himself. He's like a broken record. We finally figured out he's more afraid of his grandfather than he is of the police. If we prove the two of you caused the July 3rd event, A-1 loses its $3,000,000 insurance coverage and A-1 goes bankrupt. His grandfather would literally kill him. We got the grandfather on board and he's ready to influence Pinky to tell the truth. According to Morty's plan, the cases settle and his grandson stays out of jail and he keeps his company. We told him if the boy cooperates, we will give Pinky immunity."

Oz pressed, "But the kid's taking the Fifth..."

Tory smiled back at Oz and said, "You can't take the Fifth if you have no risk of criminal prosecution. Once we grant Pinky immunity, he can't assert the Fifth Amendment. It's a catch twenty-two. The grandfather will then strong-arm this deal through. You're looking at ten years at least, once the kid comes clean. You hurt a lot of people at that party..."

Oz broke down, "I didn't mean to hurt anyone. The kid told me the munitions would clear the house and just scare the shit out of Davis's guests. I wanted to ruin his party, that's all. I had no reason to hurt anyone."

"How'd you get Pinky to help you?"

"Carmichael and I casually but intentionally ran into Pinky and told him how we knew his dad and how we were all state champs together. The kid was dying to hear about his father. His grandfather left him in the dark. He ate up anything we told him about his dad. You don't know Roscoe the way I do. He's a real sweet talker when he wants to be. He had the kid eating out of his hand. You forget Roscoe's a jewelry salesman at heart. He told him his side of this lawsuit, from his perspective. He was just following Bucky's advice, and now Bucky left him high and dry. He needed to send a message to this bulldog lawyer, to scare him, get him to back off, or at least get him to settle the cases. Pinky isn't really bright. He bought into Roscoe's narrative and assured us he could pull it off and alter the projectile slightly. We shouldn't have listened to him. "

Tory got really angry," You sure as hell shouldn't."

Pierce insisted, "I didn't know anything about this. Ask my client."

Oz confirmed that Pierce, Tate, Gray, and the grandfather were in the dark.

Tory turned to Pierce, "This is a one-time deal. I walk out the door, and your client takes his chances with a serious criminal charge."

Tory handed Pierce the new criminal privacy act that the legislature recently passed that would go into effect January 1, 1998. Neither Pierce nor Oz had read the statute before, so they took their time to read it and then reread it.

When they finished, Tory said, "Here's the deal. Your client testifies truthfully against Carmichael and then on January 3rd, pleads guilty to this statute. We agree to a sentence of four years, no parole, and he agrees to pay $200,000 to settle the three privacy actions. You then agree to testify as to Carmichael's part in the conspiracy to injure Davis' guests at the party. If necessary my office will bring charges against him for seriously injuring those people."

Tory paused and then continued, "You took advantage of Pinky Miller, who because he's sixteen, goes free. I'll let his grandfather teach him a good lesson. He's a minor, and he'd only get a juvenile record anyway, less than two years, till his eighteenth birthday. We'll let A-1's insurance company compensate the injured guests at the July 3rd party, and our friend Roscoe Carmichael goes to jail for a long time on his drug charges or I get him for nearly killing twenty people."

Pierce asked if they could give them the room. Five minutes later, Pierce informed the judge and the DA that they had a deal, except they asked that the deal not specifically deny the opportunity of parole.

Sanford went to the pool house and Tory went to the kitchen. Whitefield, Patterson, and Cox were playing pool. Sanford gave them an update on the status of the Oz negotiations.

Sanford reported to Steine & Davis that a settlement had been reached with Phillip Oz for $600,000, and Oz was pleading guilty to the new statute and a sentence of four years with the possibility of parole. Sammie used the Judge's computer and began preparing the settlement documents.

Steine & Davis accompanied Sanford to the dining room. Sanford announced, "The plaintiffs have settled with Oz."

Tate demanded, "How much?"

Davis answered, "The parties have agreed to keep that dollar amount confidential."

"We had a co-defendant agreement."

Davis again answered, "It's been terminated by Pierce and Oz."

Tate insisted, "I want to talk to Pierce.

Davis ignored Tate, "Your last offer was $150,000 in addition to American's $250,000 for a total of $400,000. Our counter is $1,000,000, with Mr. Carmichael contributing $750,000. You're an alleged drug dealer. You've got plenty of money. I've seen your financials. Your big problem is prison time, not these lawsuits."

Carmichael couldn't stay quiet.

"This is my life, not Tate's. I'm willing to cut a deal if I can improve my life. I don't give a damn about your clients. What can you do for me with the DA?"

Sanford left the room and returned with General Johnson Tory.

The DA addressed Carmichael, "You can attack our search warrants and create all the appealable issues you want, but you're going to jail for a long time. My educated guess is twenty years. You're out on bond and will spend seven figures on lawyers and will wind up in prison regardless. You'll cost the public a lot of time and money."

"What if I drop my lawsuit against..."

"Stop right there! That's not on the table. I can't make that part of these negotiations. A judge or jury will decide that lawsuit. Let's focus on these privacy cases and your drug charges."

Tory explained that Oz had copped a plea and would be testifying against him, Oz has admitted guilt to a new Class D felony for injuring Davis's guests on July 3rd. He was better off admitting guilt to that crime then admitting to a charge of aggravated assault.

"His testimony and that of Pinky Miller, will result in additional charges against you."

Tory explained that the proof would show that Carmichael was the mastermind of the July 3rd catastrophe and that he was facing serious jail time.

"So, even if you somehow beat the drug charges you still have exposure."

Davis jumped in, "How old are you, Roscoe?"

"I'm forty-six."

"With a trial, an appeal, and a twenty-five-year sentence, you'll be seventy years old by the time you get out of prison. You won't be able to get it up. You'll probably die in prison." Tory added, "If you pay Davis' clients the additional $750,000 he's demanded so his clients are paid a total of $1,000,000, I'll agree to a fifteen-year sentence, and you'll be out by sixty-one years old, in time to collect early Social Security."

Carmichael, as a drug dealer, was used to calculating numbers and dollar amounts.

"How much would it take for me to contribute to the total American and Oz contributions for your clients to clear $1,000,000 after attorney fees and costs?"

That question put Steine & Davis on the spot. Morty had no idea how much the firm had advanced in expenses. Davis knew it was about $100,000. So, they needed a total settlement of $1,600,000.

Davis answered, "We've got $100,000 in expenses and our fee is a one-third contingency. We need $750,000 from you for our clients to clear $1,000,000."

"I don't want to die in prison."

Carmichael knew his challenge of the search warrant was a long shot.

"You've got a deal if you reduce my charges to a Class C felony and agree to a sentence of ten years."

It took a day and a half but Judge Randolph "Sandy" Sanford got the job done. The three privacy cases were settled and dismissed with the thanks of Judge Barry Howard and the citizens of Davidson County. Carmichael and Oz's case against American Insurance Company was settled and dismissed. Carmichael's cases against Bucky Lee and the law enforcement personnel proceeded.

CHAPTER SIXTY-ONE

THE REST OF THE STORY

October 7, 1997- January 2, 1998

(THIRD PERSON)

Sammie and the clients had been waiting in the study for several hours, without a word, and the tension had been growing. When Steine & Davis walked through the door, Davis could tell he'd made a mistake not updating the clients and Sammie on their progress of the negotiations. Sammie scolded him with her eyes, but didn't dare reprimand him in front of the clients. It had been a tough mediation, and he'd lost track of time. It was close to four o'clock, and other than coffee and donuts at the start neither he nor Morty had eaten anything all day. The remnants of a tray of sandwiches and ice tea were on the coffee table. Davis was famished but he had to report the settlement to his clients.

The clients could tell by the lawyers faces that a deal had been made.

Davis spoke first, "Good news, ladies. Mr. Carmichael and Mr. Oz are going to prison, and the three of you will be paid a total of a million dollars after attorney fees and costs. That's $333,333.33 a piece, I hope you're pleased."

The Does were ecstatic.

Lizzy Swann didn't seem as excited. It was apparent from her body language that she wasn't satisfied, and her displeasure was confirmed by the tone of her next statement, "Steine & Davis earned a fee of half a million and will be reimbursed all of its advanced expenses?"

"Absolutely," Davis responded unapologetically.

She pressed him further, "How much prison time did Carmichael and Oz get?"

"Carmichael agreed to ten-years, and Oz got four years under the new criminal privacy statute."

Swann was very unhappy, she was out for blood.

"How much of that ten years will he actually serve?"

"If he behaves himself, he'll serve two-thirds of his sentence, about seven years."

"That's not enough. The son-of-a-bitch should be shot. Oz will be out in less than three years, you call that justice?"

Davis reminded her, "Oz's conduct toward you wouldn't be criminal until next year, and Carmichael's criminal case would have dragged out for years with a trial and appeal. He would have remained out on bond the entire time. He had the money to fund an appeal till the end."

Still not satisfied, Swann asked, "When will they go to prison?"

"General Tory gave Carmichael two weeks to raise his $750,000 and report to prison. Oz can't plead guilty until January 2nd, until the law goes into effect, and he needs the additional time to raise his $200,000. He'll go to prison right after the new year."

Morty weighed in, "Ladies, it's been a long year and a hard fought fight. We need to take a deep breath and enjoy this moment. I'd like to call Bella and have her close the office and join us, and let's all go out and celebrate together."

Davis' stomach was grumbling, and his blood sugar was low. He was agitated by Lizzy Swann's remarks and needed to eat. It was agreed that they'd drive over to Hillwood Country Club for drinks and an early dinner. Davis used his cell phone to call Bella and asked her to arrange for a private dining room and insisted that she close the office and join them. He then called Liza, who was feeding the dogs, and invited her to the party.

She declined, "I've never met these clients. This is a business celebration, not personal. Enjoy your victory with them tonight, and let's celebrate as a family tomorrow."

Davis worked hard at keeping his business and personal lives separate. Liza, as usual was right. As they drove to the country club, Davis who was upset about being cross-examined by Swann, asked his old friend, "Did we handle the mediation correctly?"

The old man didn't hesitate, "Our clients got a fair settlement. We made a great fee, we recovered our advanced expenses, the bad guys went to prison, and our clients didn't have to go through the embarrassment of a trial. Both defendants are going to jail. We got a new law passed that protects future victims. Tom Miller and A-1 kept their insurance coverage, so they didn't go bankrupt. Hopefully the grandfather will discipline Pinky, and he'll learn an important life lesson. Your wife didn't get sued, and there will be insurance proceeds to compensate your injured guests. I'd say justice was served."

Davis wasn't satisfied with the answer, "Did we act ethically?"

"We may have taken advantage of John Whitefield, his client American Insurance and A-1's carrier Aetna Insurance Company. American drafted a bad contract, some young lawyer was negligent, and his employer paid the price. I don't know how the Court of Appeals would have ruled on Judge Wise's order, but Whitefield figured he was going to spend about a million dollars to find out.

For that reason, he contributed just about the same dollar amount towards a settlement. The defendants agreed to Judge Randolph "Sandy" Sanford as our mediator. I didn't hold a gun to their heads. Pierce and Gray should have figured out that he and I were close friends. Sandy may have been a friend, but it was our skills as trial lawyers that made the difference. It would have been interesting picking a jury for this case, but dangerous too. You and I would have convinced a jury that Carmichael and Oz proximately damaged our clients, but no one knows how much would have be awarded. It all depended on jury selection. Why take that risk and why expose our clients to the humiliation of a trial? Don't let Lizzy's bravado throw you. When the time came for her ass to hit the stand she'd have been scared and hoped she'd settled. Carmichael and Oz deserve the consequences of their actions. You should have no regrets. We did the right thing."

The party lasted until midnight. Everybody had too much to drink, and Davis ordered cabs to take everyone home. The next day Steine & Davis remained closed and the Davis family and the firm went out to Morty's farm, Squeeze Bottom, did a little fishing on Dear Lake, played horseshoes, and ate fried catfish, which they'd caught. It was a perfect day, one that none of them would ever forget.

A week later, paid in full, Carmichael was off to prison, where he'd spend at least the next seven years of his life.

The day before Halloween, the Judge granted General Tory, Chief Neenan, the DA offices, the detectives and the TBI agents motion to dismiss Carmichael's lawsuit. The court held,

"The plaintiff ... Roscoe Carmichael has alleged that the search warrant issued by the Honorable Barry Howard of the Third Circuit Court of Davidson County of his Music Row townhouse for 'drugs, cash and related items' was improper and overly broad and that the supplemental search warrant as to 'camera equipment and videos' was improper. The court finds no merit to these allegations and finds as a matter of law that Judge Howard followed proper procedure. The plaintiff Carmichael further alleges that the DA's office and law enforcement personnel were the proximate cause of the publication of the tapes of seven women who the plaintiff Carmichael videoed having sex with him. The court finds, as a matter of law, that the law enforcement personnel and the DA's office as part of their responsibility and duties had to view those tapes, show those tapes to the women in question and had to conduct a reasonable criminal investigation, which included the use of those tapes. The court finds that the defendants did not exceed reasonable use of the tapes and dismiss with prejudice the plaintiff's cause of action and tax all costs against the plaintiff Roscoe Carmichael."

Carmichael received his copy of the court order by certified mail in prison. He wasn't happy at all. Prison didn't agree with Carmichael. He tried to keep to himself, but he had several forced friendships.

Phillip Oz had some difficulty raising his two hundred thousand dollars, but he did so before the end of the year. He sold the pharmacy for far less than it was worth. His wife divorced him and took more than half of the marital estate, which after the settlement payment wasn't much. By January 2nd, even after American's payment of $100,000 he still owed Amy Pierce $45,673 in fees and $12,345 in advanced costs.

Davis figured, it couldn't have happened to a nicer gal!

Steine & Davis usually held a holiday office party on December 28th. Rosario's Market catered it, and the bar was well stocked. Clients, members of the Bar, jurists, friends, and family attended. The party was an accepted expense every year.

Bella had reconciled the books the day before and announced, "It had been a better than average year because of the Carmichael/ Oz settlement and reimbursed expenses."

Six hundred thousand dollars in December has a way of saving a small firm's year. Bella and Sammie each received a Christmas bonus of $60,000. Davis' bonus was twice that, $120,000. Morty kept the rest. He funded the cases and was the senior partner.

Davis, with Morty's approval announced, "Over twenty-years ago I met and became employee of Mr. Morty Steine, a lawyer of great distinction, who has taught me my craft and helped me become the lawyer I am today."

Morty blurted out, "Don't blame me for your shortcomings."

The room broke into laughter.

"I did pick up some of your flaws, but for the most part, I'm proud of who you've helped me become. This year, my niece Sammie graduated Vanderbilt Law School and passed the Bar and began her practice with the firm. She's already excelled in her first year to such an extent that she's earned the formation of Steine, Davis & Davis."

Davis revealed the plaque he'd presented her at graduation with the new name of the firm. It would be hung at the entry to the office. All eyes turned to Sammie.

In a strong and clear voice, she asked, "Am I the first or the second Davis?"

The room went berserk with laughter.

When the evening ended and all the guests were gone, the only ones who remained were Morty, Sammie, Liza, and Davis. There was a cab waiting downstairs to take the Davises home. The others only had to commute to the sixth and ninth floors. As the Davises were leaving, Sammie asked, "When you took me in six years ago, did you think my name would be hanging next to yours?"

Davis smiled and chuckled, "Your Nana Shelly gave me no choice. In fact, I'm not sure you're not the first Davis on that plaque."

She gave her uncle a big hug. Morty and Liza were watching and listening to the exchange with tears in their eyes.

Sammie looked over at her aunt and the man who put her through law school, "You've all given me so much. I'm going to make the most of this opportunity."

Davis reminded her, "Always try to do the right thing."

EPILOGUE
(THIRD PERSON)

Steine, Davis & Davis attacked 1998 with gusto, taking on new hourly clients and contingency cases. Before the year's end, Davis had convinced Aetna, A-1's insurance company, to settle all twenty of his guests' claims, including Randy James, the student bartender. With Davis' help Randy was enrolled in the summer session and was beginning to make up for lost time.

With the Carmichael/Oz case in the rearview mirror Davis stayed on top of his to-do-list. Despite settlement and the new year, aspects of the Carmichael/Oz case lingered. Carmichael's lawsuit and board charges against Bucky Lee still remained, which prompted Jack Barnes' call to Steine, Davis & Davis. Barnes reached out to Davis for help.

"I was hoping that Morty, Sammie and you would testify at Bucky's board hearing at the end of the month."

"You don't think calling the three of us is overkill?"

"The board needs to hear from three generations of lawyers that Bucky did the right thing. Morty's a former President of the Board; despite her years, Sammie is very impressive, and you're a pretty persuasive fellow."

"We'll all do whatever we can."

"I'm glad you feel that way. I've got an even bigger favor. I need at least two of your clients to testify at the hearing. Which two would you recommend?"

Tough question.

"Jane Doe definitely. Let me talk to Sammie about who should be the other one."

He'd vote for Mary Doe. She had a better story to tell, and he still had a bad taste in his mouth from Lizzy Swann's final remarks. She took her money but she wasn't happy. She wanted revenge and she didn't feel that she'd gotten it.

"How's Bucky holding up?"

Barnes didn't answer tight away. When he did, his voice got lower, almost to a whisper.

"Not good. To say he's depressed is an understatement. He's been suspended from teaching, and he's given up his law practice. Besides, who's going to hire a lawyer who breaches the attorney/client relationship? There's nobody lining up outside his door."

Davis felt sorry for his friend. He didn't deserve this. Barnes continued, "Our trial judge is sitting on the motion for summary judgment. He's waiting to see what the Board does. If the Board dismisses the charges, my money is that the court will follow suit. I'm banking on it. I'd like to set aside two days to prepare with you and your clients. Confer with your partners and clients, and get back with me. The only bright spot is his contact with Pinky Miller."

"What are you talking about?"

"As you know, the DA elected not to bring any charges against the sixteen-year-old and left his punishment up to the grandfather. He figured the old man would be tougher than the juvenile justice system. The kid was going to be in his junior year of high school.

The grandfather was a no-nonsense guy. He shipped the kid off to one of these labor/work camps in the mountains of Colorado for twelve weeks. I understand conditions were brutal. He got back last week, and he's being tutored by Bucky, who's helping him get his GED. It's the grandfather's logic that Pinky can't directly help the persons he injured on July 3rd so at least he can get to know one of the other victims of Carmichael and Oz's wrongful conduct. He has an interesting perspective on the situation. He heard Bucky lost his teaching job, and in his mind, Pinky's at least giving Bucky the opportunity to teach, something he loves to do."

Ending the conversation, Davis, said, "I wish Bucky well. I'll get back to you on the date for the five of us to meet with you to prepare for the hearing."

On March 28th everyone appeared at the Andrew Jackson Office Building on the 5th floor. No cameras were allowed in the hearing room. The only case on the docket was Carmichael/Bucky Lee. The Board that consisted of five members would hear the proof. A majority would decide the case. There were pre-hearing motions filed by Vincent Gray, Tate had flown back to Washington never to be heard of again in Middle Tennessee. The Board ruled that the videos would not be played. Carmichael wasn't permitted to wear a suit, he appeared in an orange jumpsuit and was ushered in and guarded by three-armed prison guards.

The hearing lasted two days, and twelve witnesses testified. The star of the hearing was Sammie. Dressed in a gray suit with a midnight blue blouse, her long blonde hair was tightly pulled into a ponytail. She spoke directly to the Board, making eye contact with each of the five members. She treated them like a jury and told them the story she wanted them to believe. She started off discussing the balancing of responsibilities that an attorney owes to one's client and those obligations that one owes generally to society under our justice system. She emphasized that on certain occasions the choice was clear because the code was clear, and an attorney's obligation was spelled out.

"For example, if a client confides to you that he is about to commit a murder or a terrorist act, you'd have no choice but to go the authorities for the common good and to protect the victims. Well, Mr. Lee was faced with a similar choice. It just required a little more reflection. But in the end, he made the right decision for several reasons. First, the attorney/ client relationship with Mr. Carmichael had terminated. Second, Mr. Lee hadn't given any advice on this subject matter. Lastly, the public good, the safety of future victims outweighed remaining silent to protect a former client on an unrelated matter."

The Board didn't rule immediately, but took the matter under advisement. They knew people were waiting on their decision so a short-written opinion was released within forty-eight hours after the close of the proof. There were two decisions, a majority one and a dissenting one. The vote went down three to two.

The majority opinion read in part,

> "The attorney/client relationship is not a traditional business relationship like a salesman and his or her customer. A salesman must simply act reasonably in his or her dealings, while an attorney owes a fiduciary obligation to their client because the attorney has a greater understanding and knowledge of the law, and the client is relying upon the attorney's expertise. For these reasons, communications between an attorney and the client are considered confidential. Certain other fiduciaries, such as doctors and priests are required to maintain confidential communications.

Bucky Lee has been licensed to practice law in the state of Tennessee since 1968. During those thirty years only one other ethical complaint has been brought against him by the same complainant, which was dismissed. Mr. Carmichael also has a pending lawsuit in the Circuit Court of Davidson County arising from the same breach of confidentiality, and he asserts that he paid over a million dollars in settlement, attorney fees, and costs as a proximate result of Mr. Lee's breach of their relationship.

The obligation to preserve a client's confidence survives the termination of the attorney/client relationship. The fact that the communication is given in a public place does not destroy the confidential nature of the communication. The physical presence of third parties does not destroy the confidential nature of the communication unless they hear it and are intended to hear it. Mr. Lee does not claim anyone else at Sperry's restaurant overheard his conversation with his client. An attorney has an obligation to report to the authorities a future crime even if he or she learns of that crime in a confidential communication. Mr. Carmichael wasn't charged with any crime in connection with the making of the videos. An attorney is not obligated to report to authorities or to the victim of a future tort what he might be told during a confidential communication.

In 1996, it was not a crime for Mr. Carmichael to secretly videotape women having consensual sex with him. Mr. Lee violated the attorney/ client relationship when he communicated to the District Attorney Office that Mr. Carmichael was videotaping women in his bathroom. This was a false statement, and even if he'd accurately recounted the conversation, it would have breached his duty of confidentiality.

The Board, within its discretion, can privately censure, publicly censure, suspend, or revoke Mr. Lee's law license. A majority of the Board finds that it is important that other members of the Bar be made aware of Mr. Lee's wrongful conduct and therefore elected not to consider a private censure. The majority was torn between public censure and suspension, and compromised on a one-day suspension of Mr. Lee's law license, effective the day following entry of this ruling."

The dissent opinion was short and sweet,

"The majority correctly outlines the obligations of an attorney to one's clients and former clients. What the majority ignores is the obligations of an attorney as an officer of the court and his or her responsibility to serve justice. The ethical rules, which govern our profession, are a living and breathing thing that must be viewed based upon the totality of the circumstances presented. Mr. Lee weighed all those circumstances and decided he owed a greater obligation to unsuspecting females who Mr. Carmichael would violate in the future. We in the dissent hope we would have done the same. For that reason, we, dissent from the majority and would dismiss the charges against Mr. Lee."

Despite the encouraging words of the dissent, the ruling was a real problem for Bucky. The trial court based upon the Board's decision denied the motion for summary judgment. It specifically held that it was going to let a jury hear the facts, be instructed on the law and reach a verdict. Carmichael vs. Lee was set for June 3, 1998. If the jury found that Bucky acted either negligently or intentionally they could award a judgment in excess of a million dollars.

Bucky fell into a deep depression. He was prepared to file for bankruptcy and lose his home. Davis, Morty, Sammie, and the Does committed to testify at the trial and to meet in advance to prepare with Barnes.

On May 5th, Davis got the anticipated call from Jack Barnes.

"Hey, Jack, do you think you'll need a full two days to get us prepared to testify at trial?"

"Nope."

"Just a day?"

"Nope, I won't need your testimony after all."

"Did you settle? Where did Bucky get the money?"

"No settlement, no money. The son-of- a bitch was murdered in his bed by his cellmate. The lifer took a shive and gouged out his eyes while he slept."

"Holy shit. Was it a lover's spat?"

"Not that simple," insisted Barnes.

"They found that somebody deposited $333,333 in the lifer's ex-wife's bank account, as trustee for their kid. The guy had nothing to lose, he'll still remain in jail for the rest of his life. No harm, no foul. It was a hit, ordered by someone who wanted revenge. Chief Neenan and agent Pyle think it may have been Carmichael's ex-partners, the Cubans. The theory is that the hit was ordered because Carmichael didn't reimburse them for the confiscated plane and $500,000 back when Carmichael was arrested. Why, do you have any alternate theory and suspects?"

"He was an asshole, isn't that reason enough? I'm sure there's at least a dozen suspects. I'm sure I'm on that list."

The name Elizabeth "Lizzy" Swann flashed across Davis's mind, but he dared not say the name. She was mad enough. Davis wondered, what happened to the remaining 33 cents? Davis decided to change the subject,

"What about his estate. It could still pursue Bucky?"

"In a recent Will his high school football buddy, John Candy is named executor of the Will and he called to tell me he was dismissing the lawsuit, without Carmichael the case couldn't be won."

"That's great news, Bucky should be relieved?"

"Bucky's had enough, he's letting his law license lapse. He's throwing in the towel and just wants to fish and play golf. He says he can dig up his own worms and buy either used golf balls or better yet fish them out of the lake. He's really disappointed in the majority of the Board. They should have backed him up."

"Can he still teach?"

"What law school is going to hire a professor to teach law who doesn't have a law license?"

Davis agreed that Bucky got a raw deal. Like the dissenting board members, he believed in his heart he would have done exactly what Bucky did, but you never know until you're tested. Morty had drilled into both he and Sammie to "always try to do the right thing" even though at times it might not be the easiest route.

"Please pass along my best to Bucky, and tell him to give Morty and me a call, and we'll do a little fishing out at Squeeze Bottom."

With that the call ended. Davis felt bad for Bucky. The law had been his life, and at the very end, it turned on him. Davis shared his conversation with Barnes with the rest of the office, and they commiserated over poor Bucky's fate. There was a selfish silver lining that neither they nor their clients had to testify at the trial.

The next day a young woman appeared in reception and asked to see Mr. Davis. Bella recognized the young woman immediately.

"Whom shall I say is calling?" Asked Bella.

"My name is Pamela Leonard, I know or, I knew Roscoe Carmichael."

Davis escorted Ms. Leonard to the conference room. He knew her as woman # 7. Introductions were made, and Davis asked,

"Where have you been?"

"In hiding, but when I read about Roscoe dying, I figured it was safe to come out and collect my money. I heard those other girls got a million dollars. The police have videos of Roscoe and myself. I know I should have stayed and fought alongside the other girls, but I didn't have the stomach for it."

Davis listened for forty minutes or so, and then without warning, blurted out, "Ms. Leonard, I hate to inform you that you've waited too long to take any action. You've waived your rights. They've become stale. The statute of limitation, the time you had to file your lawsuit, has run out. I'm very sorry."

The disappointment on her face was apparent. She'd already spent the settlement monies. Davis explained the concept of statute of limitations and the obligation of a plaintiff to act and not sit on their rights and file a lawsuit. He explained that because she'd known about the Swann lawsuit for more than a year that her time to file suit had passed. Woman # 7 seemed stunned and disappointed.

Davis stood, signaling that the meeting was over. "I hope you understand the law must set parameters and deadlines which we all must follow."

She didn't really understand. The woman walked out without saying good-bye. She didn't like the advice she'd been given. Davis didn't like giving it, but he was only the messenger.

I guess always doing the right thing doesn't always have a happy ending.

GLOSSARY OF TERMS

Affidavit—a sworn written statement

Affirmative defenses—a legal excuse for a defendant's conduct, which the defendant has the burden to prove.

Answer—the first pleading filed by a defendant, in response to a complaint.

Arraignment—a hearing in which a defendant declares his guilt or not guilty plea.

Attorney/client privilege—the right of confidentiality of communications by a client based on a fiduciary with an attorney.

Attorney/client relationship—a special relationship between an attorney and their client imposing the greatest obligations upon the attorney to his or her client.

Beyond a reasonable doubt—the burden of proof in a criminal case. The state must prove all elements of the crime to the satisfaction of the judge/jury so that there is no other reasonable conclusion.

Bond—the dollar amount required by the court for a defendant to be released prior to trial. The dollar amount must be sufficient to guarantee the appearance of the defendant to appear at all required hearings and trial.

Board of Professional Responsibility—a board established by the Tennessee Supreme Court to monitor and enforce rules established concerning the ethical conduct of an attorney who practice in the state.

Challah—cake like bread traditionally used by Jews in connection with introducing the Sabbath.

Circumstantial evidence—indirect proof of a point of fact. Proof by inference.

Class B felony—the second most serious category of felony under state law. A defendant found guilty may be sentenced between 8 and 30 years.

Class C felony—the third most serious category of felony under state law. A defendant found guilty may be sentenced between 3 and 15 years.

Compensatory damages—an award by a judge or jury to compensate the plaintiff for their injuries proximately caused by the defendant.

Complaint—the document that starts a lawsuit

Contempt of court—a party that violates a court order can, in the discretion of the judge be held in contempt.

Counterclaim—a claim brought by a defendant against the plaintiff who filed the original lawsuit.

Court of Appeal—the intermediate court between the trial court and the Supreme Court. Every civil party has a right to an appeal what happens in a trial court to this court. A three-judge panel reviews the judgment in the trial court and a decision is determined by a majority of the panel.

Cross-examination—the questioning of a witness by the attorney for the party who did not call the person as a witness.

Defendant—the person sued in a lawsuit

Deposition—the sworn testimony of a witness taken as part of the discovery in anticipation of trial.

Direct evidence—evidence that is on point requiring no inference. This type of evidence can be either an admission or document that establishes a fact.

Direct—examination-the questioning of a witness by the attorney of the party that calls the witness.

Executor—a male representative appointed in a Will. A female representative is called an Executrix.

Ex-parte communication—a written or verbal communication between an attorney and the court without notice or participation of the attorney for the other party.

Fiduciary duty—a duty arising from a special relationship between parties where one of the parties has either additional knowledge or education which the other party doesn't possess.

Fifth Amendment—a constitutional right of every criminal defendant, which allows them to remain silent, not testify and self-incriminate themselves.

Interrogatories—written questions posed as part of the discovery process which must be answered under oath.

Kiddush—the blessing over the wine, said by Jews to introduce the sabbath.

Miranda warning—a legal obligation imposed by due process under the Constitution that the police during an arrest must inform the person bring arrested of their right to remain silent, that anything they say may be used against them in court and their right to an attorney and if they can not afford one, the state will provide an attorney.

Motion in limine'—a motion filed before trial asking the court to rule on a preliminary matter as to an issue of law or evidence.

Motion for summary judgment—a motion filed asserting that there are no material questions of fact and that all that remains are questions of law. The purpose of this motion is to resolve a lawsuit without the need of a jury trial.

Negligence—when a person violates a duty owed to another and they act unreasonably.

Overruled—when a judge disagrees with an objection raised.

Plaintiff—the party that files a lawsuit.

Plea bargain—an agreement reached between the state and a criminal defendant as to their guilt and recommended sentence.

Preponderance of the evidence—the burden of proof in a civil case. A plaintiff must prove their case is more likely then not. A plaintiff must tip the scales of justice in their favor by 51%.

Punitive damages—imposed by a judge or jury to punish the defendant for their intentional, fraudulent or reckless conduct. These damages are only granted after a judgment for compensatory damage have been awarded and then a separate mini-trial based upon 13 factors, the most important of which is the net worth of the defendant. The award must be sufficient to change the defendant's future conduct and to send a message that such wrongful conduct will not be tolerated.

Putz—a Yiddish word for a person who is a jerk.

Recklessness—when a person acts with disregard for the consequences of their actions.

Reversible error—a ruling by a trial court that is contrary to the law, who which an appellate court requires a new trial.

Sequester of a jury—when a trial court orders that a jury shall be confined from the rest of the world during a trial and deliberation to avoid them being influenced by outside sources other than the evidence introduced at trial.

Shiksa—the Yiddish word for a gentile girl or woman.

Sidebar—a communication between the court and attorneys that cannot heard by the rest of the persons in a courtroom during trial.

Sustained—when the trial court agrees with an objection raised.

Will—a document, usually sworn to and witnessed that sets forth how a party intends for their estate to be distributed.

ABOUT THE AUTHOR

A. Turk was born in 1954, in Brooklyn, New York, and he grew up on Long Island. He earned a BA from George Washington University, an MBA from the Vanderbilt Owen Graduate School of Business, and a JD from Vanderbilt School of Law. He was licensed to practice law in Tennessee in 1980. In 1983 he also was licensed, but never practiced, in New York because of a promise he made to his mother.

A. Turk for more than thirty years was a prominent Nashville attorney and a veteran of fighting courtroom battles. He garnered national media attention in 1994 when he won a unanimous US Supreme Court decision, which held that 2 Live Crew's parody of Roy Orbison's song "Pretty Woman" did not require a copyright license. With the support of NBC, HBO, Time Warner, *Mad Magazine*, and others, A. Turk won this landmark case preserving the right of commercial parody under the Fair Use Doctrine.

A. Turk recently retired to begin his second career as an author of courtroom dramas based upon his personal experiences. First Do No Harm is A. Turk's debut novel, where he introduces his fictitious alter ego, Benjamin Davis. The Benjamin Davis Book Series will explore and address the same legal issues and moral dilemmas that A. Turk faced during his legal career.

A. Turk has been married to his wife Lisa for 39 years and they have two adult children, Jessica and Ben, as well as three pugs. A. Turk currently splits his time between Nashville, Aspen, and Palm Beach Shores.

In Focus with A. Turk

I made my living as a trial lawyer for over thirty years; my job was to get the jury to accept my client's version of the facts and apply them to the law as instructed by the presiding judge. I didn't necessarily reveal all of the facts and every detail. Some matters were intentionally glossed over. My role was not necessarily to present every material detail, but rather to direct the jury's attention to the proof which benefited my client, or if out of necessitity to present a negative fact in the best positive light because it was going to come out anyway.

Like a trial lawyer, a novelist, tries to tell his or her readers the story trapped in their mind trying to escape and be told. In 2010, I retired from the practice of law and began my second career as an author writing legal fction and courtroom drama.

After thiry years of practicing law and completing five books in the Benjamin Davis Series I've learned that the goals of my two professions are simply not that different. I've found that the methods of completing the responsibilities of each profession are the same; persuading either the jury or the reader that your storyline is believeable.

As an attorney often the finances of one's client determines the methods and extent of prepararion for trial. Time is money, so if one is being paid hourly, financial restrictions can directly correlete to the amount of time that can be spent getting ready for trial. A plaintiff or defendant with resources has the luxury to hire a top quality law firrm such as depicted on the USA television series,

Suits, formerly starring Meghan Markle, currently the Dutchcess of Sussex. Such a firm can retain the services of all types of consultants, one's which assist in jury selection, the likes of Bull, played by Michael Weatherly in the CBS television series.Bejamin Davis in Seond Degree retained such an expert because his client was a United States Senator.

Generally the law firm of Steine & Davis, nor I, had such resources, our clients were either small businesses or injured persons. In real life, I, and as reflected in the book series Steine & Davis often had to advance tens of thousands of dollars in a case because of the clients inability to pay expenses as incurred. Often I would have more than half a million dollars outstanding in advanced total expenses at risk at varied times. I could not afford jury consultants, instead I relied on a more primitive form of jury selection.

I would post a notice "mock jury trial, $75 for 6 hours work. Lunch, snacks and drinks provided."(At the time minimum wage was less than $5) in a public place such as convenient mart/gas\ staton and/or grocery store. I would usually get a response of between 15 and 30 participants. Using other lawyers who were friends a presentation of the evidence would be admitted and what were believed to be the critical documents were intoduced into evidenced. The presentation lasted between anhour or two and was videotap. The participants were divided into two groups and then placed in separate rooms where their deliberations were videotaped. A verdict form with questions was given to each jury concerning both liaility and ssmsges. The responses to these verdict forms helped in formulating our strategy for trial.

When I approached writing First Do No harm, the first book in the Benjamin Davs Series I carried forward my experience. I gave an edited draft of the manuscript to a froup of forty friends and friends of those friend, some of who I didn't know and let them read the document. I then divided the "focus group member" into three goups with whom Dimples , my editor and I met separately. We eat, we drank and they provided constructive criticism, Identified inconsistencies andmade suggetions. Many of the corrections and ideas were included in the final product This process wsd used in all books. One Memorial Day, poolside I over-served that focus group and the discussion got a little over heated.In retrospect it was funny, but at the time each side fervently held their position. I enjoyed the debate, which resulted in somebody being pushed into the pool.I have repreated my use of the focus groups with each novel becase I strongly believe the process has improved my work. The persons identifed in the Acknowledgement should be proud of their contribution to the Benjamin Davis Series .

ACKNOWLEDGEMENTS

I first want to thank my wife Lisa, who I have cleverly disguised as Liza in the Benjamin Davis series. We've been married almost thirty-nine years and for that reason alone she deserves a medal. I'd also like to thank my children Jessica and Ben, who have had to endure being depicted as Caroline and Jake in the series. I'd also like to acknowledge my parents, Fred and Renee, both deceased, who taught me right from wrong. My family and my faith define me as a person.

I'd like to thank my editors, Dimples Kellogg and Caroline West, who hopefully have caught my grammatical and spelling errors and who's feedback and effort made this book a more enjoyable read. Dimples has been a contributor on all of the five books; this is Caroline's first involvement in my process. I'd like to thank Dan Swanson for the cover. Dan has created the cover on all of my books and I'd like to thank his wife, Darlene Swanson for the formatting of the book.

As used in all of my books, I again relied upon the Focus Group method. These individuals are friends or friends of friends, who read an early manuscript, then meet as a group, provide me with feedback, upon which I revise the manuscript to a finished product. Thank you; Brandon Bubis, Martin Bubis, Anita Dowdle, Douglas Dowdle, Tom Forsythe, Karen Goldsmith, Steve Goldsmith, Elliot Greenberg, Steve Lefkovitz, Paula Milam, Tom Milam, Suzy Perlman, Lisa Silver, Miriam Silver, Jania Tiner, David Tiner, Jessica Turk and Robert Whisenant. I'd like to thank all of my members for their input and lively debate.

I retired from the practice of law in 2010. In the last nine years I've written and published five books. I've enjoyed writing the Benjamin Davis series, and admit I miss trying jury trials, but not all the hard work of getting a case ready for trial. Although my law license is current I think I'll remain retired and continue writing the series. I guess I prefer the control that writing affords me, rather than the uncertainty and reality of the courtroom.

CPSIA information can be obtained
at www.ICGtesting.com
Printed in the USA
LVHW082329260919
632416LV00003B/3/P

9 780989 266390